LARGE
PRINT
EDITION

RANDOM
HOUSE

Judith Guest

Errands

Published by Random House Large Print
in association with Ballantine Books
New York 1997

Library of Congress Cataloging-in-Publication Data
Guest, Judith.
Errands / Judith Guest.
p.   cm.
ISBN 0-679-77419-X (large print)
1. Large type books.   I. Title.
[PS3557.U345E77   1997]
813'.54—DC20   96-41557
CIP

Random House Web Address:
http://www.randomhouse.com/
Printed in the United States of America
FIRST LARGE PRINT EDITION

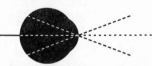

This Large Print Book carries the
Seal of Approval of N.A.V.H.

for my grandparents,
Harry and Margaret
and for my grandchildren
Priya, Jesse, Harry, Olivia, and Isabel

Acknowledgments

My four-year-old granddaughter, when asked if she knew the name of Grandma's new book, reached for the tale that has been my trademark: "It's *Jack and the Beanstalk!*" Would that it were so! And would that every writer could thank all those people she consults, pesters, argues with, and whines to, in the making of one novel. This book in particular was a long time coming, and there are those people who stand out.

My agent, Pat Karlan, whose faith and fierce loyalty saw me through tough times. And my writing buddies, Rebecca Hill and Elizabeth Anderson, both of them tireless, careful readers. My doctor, Phil Sidell, who gave of his time and medical knowledge. Tom Ware, who taught me everything I know about fishing. My nephews, Andy Teggelaar and Jamie and Nick Guest, whose brains I pick concerning all things adolescent, and Monte Montgomery of Alpena Computing Center, who calmly and good-humoredly saved my files and my sanity. Margaret Boshoven, my friend of more than fifty years, who knows all of my stories by heart and who first urged me to write this one down.

I am also grateful to my grandparents, Harry and Margaret, and my great-aunt Jean, since it is their combined experience that I meant to record. And to my husband, Larry, who has the patience to live with a writer. Finally, to my sons, Larry, John, and Rick, whose language and lives haunt these pages, and whose love and support make me grateful to be a mother. For this is what means the most to me and is the stuff of which I write.

—Judith Guest
Harrisville

It was a good journey—long, perhaps—but a good journey under a pleasant sun. Do not look for the purpose. Think of the way we came and be a little proud. Think of this hand—the utter pain of its first venture on the pebbly shore.
      —Loren Eiseley, *The Immense Journey*

From The New Shorter Oxford English Dictionary:

Errand. A journey made for a special purpose; an expedition; a mission.

I love this wider take on the word. The modern view is so limited; shallow in its definition. I read once that those founding fathers who came to explore the New World called their mission "an errand into the wilderness." I can only think that each life—the whole of life—must be simply that, and nothing less.
            J. G.
            July 1996

Part One

1

North of Bay City, past the small highway town of Au Gres, past acres of sugar beets and fields of grazing sheep, they enter the slow curve in the road that leads onto a view of Lake Huron; a surprise every time. Like listening to a piece of music, not sure in its initial sweep of theme whether you've heard it before, knowing only that you love it.

From the backseat comes Julie's cry: "I see the lake! I see it! I win!" She, quickest of eye, most competitive of the three siblings, rarely loses this game.

"So you see it, big deal."

It falls to Harry, the eldest, always to throw cold water on these triumphs. His head faces forward; he won't look. Loser's ploy: it's a dumb game, anyway.

For Keith's part, once he's seen it, he can't take his eyes away. Stretching eastward as far as the eye can see; infinitely restless, irresistible. Today it is a fierce electric blue, threaded with whitecaps. During a summer storm it can sometimes look like liquid pewter, while, under paler skies, it bleaches out to nearly white. A perfect day for the Sunfish. How did Annie and the kids manage to get it on top of the car? Harry and Jimmy must have climbed up there with the bungee cords.

"I'm not sleeping in the top bunk this year," Harry announces from the backseat.

"Can I, Mom?" Julie asks.

"Honey, you're on the studio couch."

"Mom, I'm nine years old! When do I get to sleep in a real bed?"

"I'll sleep on top," Jimmy says.

"No, you won't."

"Why not?" Harry asks. "Why can't he, Mom?"

"You know why. Because he walks in his sleep. We'll figure something out," Annie says. "Maybe move the beds over by the window—"

"That won't work," Harry says gloomily. "It's so friggin' hot on top. You just lay there and fry."

"I hate that studio couch," Julie moans. "It sags! I'm gonna be restless the whole time!"

Rebellion and discontent seep into the car as swiftly as the air is sucked in through the vents. In the rearview mirror he can see Harry making a face to match Julie's whine, while Annie's hands tighten on the wheel. He imagines her thoughts moving ahead to meet the coming tasks: raise the blinds and open the windows, unpack the car, fix lunch. She's pushing it. Through Tawas City, East Tawas, Oscoda . . . slow to forty-five, then to thirty, back up to seventy just past the "City Limits" sign. Hoping to get there without a major confrontation. Get to the beach, that's the ticket; spread out. Everybody to a neutral corner.

"Take Sominex," Jimmy offers in his TV-announcer voice, and the car erupts into laughter. In the cargo area, Lucky leaps to his feet, barking hysterically; he can't take all of this emotion.

Neither can I, Keith thinks, glancing again at his wife of some seventeen years. Seventeen years exactly, as of the eighth of this month. In khaki shorts and a red T-shirt, her hair pulled back from her face. She likes to fasten it with a ribbon or a barrette, nothing that hangs on her neck to get in the way. Julie is looking more like her every day. Except for her blond hair, which came from him, of course.

All of them have his hair and eyes, her skin and delicate features; her intensity, too. This is a good thing. He's always been too easygoing. Not ambitious enough. Lazy is another word for it.

"Mom! Butterfly weed!" Julie cries. "You said we could stop!"

With a sigh Annie brakes and slows, pulling off onto the shoulder of the road. "Let Harry get them, Jule. I don't want you crossing the highway. . . ."

But Jimmy is already out of the car and into the ditch, picking swiftly as sunlight pours over his shoulders. Only mid-June and his hair is as pale as straw. His T-shirt hangs to the bottoms of his shorts. Eleven years old, this middle child of his, the peacemaker of the family. *Please God don't let anything bad happen to him.* The thought slides through his mind, as it does about each one of them a dozen times a day. He didn't expect that. Is it normal? This is all so new to him. He's never had any dealings with the "dread factor," as Annie calls it; that is her territory. Jimmy used to tell her, "Mom, don't worry about what might happen, just worry about what does."

Now he checks for traffic, lopes back to the car, and hands the bouquet to his sister.

"They'll all be dead by the time we get there," Harry predicts.

In a moment they are back on the road. Traffic is thinning as they head farther north, the highway sinking between the walls of hardwood and pine, brilliant white, shimmering black at its end point.

"Dad, look at those trees . . . see how the bark looks like fish scales?" Harry points out the window and his eyes leave the road to take in the thick, ramrod trunks, strung together like telephone poles.

"Norway pines," he says.

"Want to take a quick tour through town?" Annie asks him.

"Sure."

Groans from the backseat.

"Mom, it's too hot! Let's just get there. . . ."

"It'll be fast," she promises. She turns right at the light, in front of the redbrick building with the ice machine out front. The sign announces:

HOMEMADE PASTIES
NOW SERVING PIZZA

"There's the Top-Stop!" says Julie.
"There's the stoplight!"
"There's the teenager!"
Old family joke—a town so small it serves up only

one of everything. Not true anymore. It's fast becoming a hot spot.

They drive down the steeply sloped hill to the marina, with its rock breakwater. The summer he and William camped out in the state park they came here every morning to hang out with the town kids. That was the summer he had the crush on Helen Ferguson. Watching waves smash against the wall of rock, sending spray high into the air, waiting for Helen to show up.

They circle back to the highway, passing the Mill Pond with its new waterwheel. For years there was nothing here but an old wooden bridge across the dam. Now there's a plaque and a modern pump and all the amenities to attract the tourists. Last year at the Fourth of July fireworks, there were over two thousand people on the hill. He knows he should be happy for the merchants of the town, yet he hates to see this happen. Harrisville was supposed to stay the way it was when he was a kid.

As they cross the railroad tracks they can see the green shingled roof of the cottage. Like a lonely sentinel, leaning into the side of the hill. The roof sags more than ever; rust stains spill down the white siding. They drive down the road, and beach grass brushes the underbelly of the car.

"What a dump," Harry says softly.

"You'd think they'd paint it once in a while."

"Mom, what if there's bats again?"

"There won't be," she assures them.

They have rented this same cottage every summer for the past six years; since Julie was three. Annie parks beside the toolshed and rolls down the window. He can smell sweetfern mixed with the pleasant, fishy odor of the lake. Harry has the key, and all three kids jump out and run to the side porch.

"Want to take a walk?" he asks her.

"Just let me empty the cooler. . . ."

From inside the house comes the cry: "Mom, it's hotter than hell in here!"

"I can't find a vase for these flowers!" says Julie.

Annie puts down the window of the tailgate and Lucky is out in a flash, chasing a squirrel up one of the tall pines in the front yard. She gets out, goes to the back, and lifts the lid of the cooler.

"I knew it . . . dammit, I forgot the tuna fish!"

He stretches his arms along the back of the seat, puts his head back, closing his eyes. A moment later she's beside him.

"You okay?"

"I'm fine. Let's just walk."

They head south along the beach. North is the more domestic route; flattened hills strewn with motel cottages. South is like virgin territory, its high banks overgrown with cedar and pine, rising at a sharp angle from the lake.

Ninety miles straight across is Canada—Kincardine, Allenford, Owen Sound. Places he has looked up on the map, planning to visit them by sailboat someday.

All the things he will not do. Never sail across Lake Huron, never go horseback riding in Montana, never see his kids graduate. Never finish the three-season porch he started last year. Never see snow again. Odd that here, in this place where he feels safest and most at home, these thoughts lie in wait, washing in with the waves. Somehow he expected the lake to be neutral in all of this.

Sand squeaks under their feet and he swings his arms lightly, fixing his eyes on the black rock, twenty minutes away in the distance. When he studied geology in college he learned about these rocks— that they were part of the Canadian Shield. This one, shiny and smooth, hollowed out on top, allows for a tight group to sit with their legs dangling over the sides. They've had family picnics on it, but more often he and Annie would walk to it alone, usually after dinner, to talk over the business of the day. He remembers, too, from that same course, that the Great Lakes, ancient river valleys scoured out in the Wisconsin advance, are the only glacial features visible from the moon.

Beside him, Annie pushes her toes through the sand, fists doubled in the pockets of her shorts. Lucky trots happily along behind them.

"Mom wanted me to put him in a kennel," she says. " 'At least leave the dog behind, Anne Marie, you don't need that hassle.' I didn't hear her offering to take him, though." She grins. "Maybe we should've left the kids instead."

"Yeah."

He squints at a triangle of sail barely visible on the horizon, moving it along the line with his eyes. *She'll be fine. I know she will.* Nineteen years ago they met, at the start of his sophomore year. At a fraternity mixer that he and Rich nearly skipped. She was standing in the hallway taking off her coat, and he stopped on impulse to introduce himself. And changed his life forever.

She was so intense; she dazzled him with it. Somebody with plans, ideals, opinions. She would get a four-point, join Wyvern and Phi Beta Kappa, win a Hopwood in her junior year. She adored jazz and astronomy and toasted pecan rolls and no, she didn't believe in God—good grief, hadn't he ever read Bertrand Russell?

"Why are you smiling?" she asks.

"Just thinking about the olden days. Do you remember that farmer in Black River where we used to pick raspberries? He called his place Dear-deer Acres. . . ."

"Right. He had all those rude signs saying, 'Customer back!' "

"What was his name?"

"Howard Barlow."

His memory is going. He knows it; so does she. The headaches, tremors, blurred vision, weakness—all of it getting worse. These are things they should be talking about. Except that there is no forum. Whenever he thinks about it, fear floods through him and he's back in that tiny, overheated office with the rust-colored wallpaper embossed with silver maple leaves, silver mini-blinds drawn against a watery November sun. Holding her hand, trapped there, caught by the series of letters—MRI, EEG, CAT scan—while heat ticks away in the radiators beneath the window. Hearing the words *tumor, aggressive cancer, inoperable*. And he, ever the high-school English teacher, ready with his critical evaluation: No. Not like this, too corny, too melodramatic.

No room for memory anymore with the tumor growing, threading its way despite the drugs designed to slow it down. The fact that someday there will be a cure for what is wrong with him, that it will happen in someone's lifetime, just not in his— gee, what a bad break that is. What more is there to say?

Better stick with the stuff that makes sense. That, in a mere few hundred thousand years, this lake will again be a river valley slowly filling up with vegetation and sediment, the water drained away; on a geologic timescale, lakes are fragile and short-lived. Last night he read an article about a huge source of gamma rays in the Milky Way, a gravitational pull so strong that it sucks entire stars, even light itself, into its core. This, at least, he can understand.

He is faintly aware of the hum of traffic; here the highway swings closer to the shore. There are no houses on the bank above; no room for them between the highway and the railroad track. The breeze has shifted to the northeast, bringing the cooler air, but the sun still feels warm on his shoulders. He pushes the sleeves of his sweatshirt above the elbows as Annie takes his hand.

"We should go back. The kids'll want to swim."

"Right."

They turn around and head back. Far down the shore they can see Harry, fists on hips, standing beside the cedar swing that belongs to the people next door. Hixon is their name. It comes to him easily; he's grateful for that.

Harry is taller, more wiry than Jimmy, his body not yet developed except for his arms, which are strong, powerful, from years of swinging a hockey stick. He's wearing trunks several sizes too large for him—it is the fad these days. Harry, the worrier. Evidently they've been gone longer than they thought. Past the period of kid comfort. Like a sentry, he will stand watch. Too big of a job for a thirteen-year-old; no wonder he's been such a pain in the ass lately.

He can barely see that it's him; beyond a certain distance, everything blurs. He's getting used to it now. What's clear is only what's close. Raising an arm above his head, he makes a signal in the air to let him know that all is well.

2

Jess climbs the short flight of steps to her sister's kitchen. The house is silent and strangely peaceful;

no noisy nephews charging down the stairs to claim her attention. The tuna fish is on the counter, right where Annie said it would be. She stops to read what's on the refrigerator: a cartoon of a gorilla combo under a banana tree, singing, *"Peelings . . . nothing more than peelings . . . "*

The room is spotless. The wood floor shines; the blue chairs that she and Annie painted last summer, pushed against the oak table in perfect symmetry. Through the window she can see the bird feeder, with its supply of sunflower seeds. Just like Annie, to fill it before they left.

She drops her keys on the table and pulls out one of the chairs. It still feels odd, this freedom from work. Two weeks since she left Patterson Agency, Inc. She should never have taken the job, she knew it from the beginning. Nothing but filling out forms, endless forms, and filing. Insurance was a tedious business. How had she stood it for eight months? She hated the place, hated the feeling of helpless boredom she fought each day as she drove to work.

Now she has her parents worrying about her, calling to ask if she's found something yet. Well, better that than her losing her mind. And it gives them something to think about besides Ryan's divorce.

The truth is, she hasn't had a job she liked since Bluestocking Builders. That was by far the happiest working experience of her life. *Bluestocking Builders—we came, we sawed, we conquered!* Their slogan for the TV ad that was never produced. The first all-woman construction company in the city. They didn't make it past the first year, the same year the housing industry took a dive. Still, it was a great job. She'd love to do something like that again.

She glances out the window, sees Ryan's car pulling into the driveway. She takes this small miracle for granted—that he will always show up; that he will be exactly on time. Watching him now as he comes up the walk, she notes the crisp look of his gray suit, the pin-striped shirt and dark tie. Handsome and serious looking, getting ready to pay a call on an important client. She gets up to open the back door.

"Hi." The businessman's smile. "I'm looking for the lady of the house."

"She's not here."

"Okay. Then I'll have you instead."

He takes her in his arms and she slips hers under his suit coat, loving the solid feel of muscle beneath his shirt. His hand at the small of her back is soothing, makes her aware of the tension there.

"What's up?" he asks.

"Annie called. She forgot the tuna fish. So I told her we'd come over and eat it up for her."

"Sounds good. I've got a two o'clock appointment out on Telegraph. I tried to move it back, but no luck."

"Then we'd better have lunch first."

He grins down at her. "Oh, I don't think so."

Taking her hand, he walks with her toward the stairs. "Does this mean I don't get to see you tomorrow?"

"No, this is extra."

"Good."

The mirror on Keith and Annie's bedroom dresser gives back a dark blur as they enter. The shades are drawn against the sun. He takes off her shirt, kisses her open mouth, gently pulling at her tongue with his teeth. His hands on her bare skin feel warm.

"I've been missing you since Tuesday."

"Me, too."

He loosens his tie and she lies down on the bed to watch him undress: first the tie on the dresser, then the coat over the back of Annie's old rocker. He unbuttons his shirt—front, then sleeves—folds it on top of the coat. Then his trousers lined up by the creases, placed on the window seat. His watch and the heavy gold ring on the table beside the bed.

She loves the ritual of it, the exactness that somehow speaks of innocence, making her suddenly think of Harry in his kindergarten days—all of his crayons lined up in a row with the points facing the same direction.

Not an ounce of fat on him, no extra flesh. She loves his long legs with their bony kneecaps, one with a scar—a baseball injury, from college. The shaved back of his neck and his thin, graceful wrists—all are sexy to her, all perfect. She slips out of her shorts, pushes the comforter to the foot of the bed.

The last time they made love in this room was a year ago February—Presidents' Day weekend—when Keith and Annie were skiing at Boyne with the kids. She baby-sat Lucky and took care of the plants, and the two of them played house—grocery shopping and cooking, shoveling the driveway, taking long walks in the snow, watching movies. *Sunset Boulevard, Body Heat, Mrs. Soffel.* Diane Keaton, the wife of a stuffy prison warden who leaves her husband for a convict she helps break out of jail.

On Sunday morning they drank tea and ate English muffins, read *The New York Times* sitting at opposite ends of the brown leather couch, like an old married couple.

The way he absolutely knows her body; there is never a moment of wishing for more, or less. That quiet sigh that is his own exhalation of surrender. All the things that she has taken to her heart—bike riding, carpentry, crossword puzzles, furniture auctions, jazz, thunderstorms, old movies, Irish breakfast tea—are things that he has loved before she got there. What they have is affinity. She looked this up once in the dictionary: *from the Latin affinis: related by marriage.*

He glances at the clock on the nightstand. "One-twenty—Jesus. I gotta get moving." He rolls away from her, standing up.

"Oh, right," she says, yawning. "Do me and then go sell a warehouse."

He grins down at her. " 'Do you'? That's a nice expression. Could you make me a sandwich? I'm going to be late."

He leaves the room, and in a moment she hears the shower running. She pulls on her shorts and shirt, quickly makes up the bed.

Downstairs in the kitchen she takes the tuna fish from the refrigerator, opens the freezer to search for some bread. None there, but there are some crackers left in the cupboard; Annie must have forgotten them. The plan is to stay up north until September, when the kids go back to school and Keith starts chemotherapy. A long time for them to be away.

Outside, a squirrel is at the feeder. Gray and doughy looking, stuffing seeds in his mouth as fast as he can. Greedy little bugger, keeping the birds at bay. He doesn't need this meal, but it's there, so why not? Jess raps at the window, shooing him away. Let him work for his food, like everybody else; let him eat acorns.

Ryan comes downstairs, tying his tie.

"I've got to take Cheryl to swimming lessons tomorrow. It'll be close to seven. Want to go out for dinner?"

"Sure."

She can sense when he's already gone, back to business, thinking about the rest of his life. This, too, she takes for granted: that empty feeling that begins even before his car is out of the driveway. Did his wife used to feel this way, too? She doesn't like to think about that. It's been over for Ryan and Lucia a long time now, nothing but the parental part remaining; two people working out responsibilities and logistics. The divorce will be final in six months. See? No one got hurt. It all worked out. She explained this to Annie on the day that he filed. But Annie is the practical sister, questioning everything, always mindful of how things can go wrong.

"It's not that I don't like him, Jess. But there are people who think they're in a Russian novel. People in love with loss . . ."

"And you think that's Ryan?"

"I don't know. He's been married to her for ten years. He's got a seven-year-old daughter. . . ."

"Look, I love him. And he happens to be married. There's nothing I can do about that right this minute."

"That sounds more like paralysis than love."

Later Annie apologized, but they don't discuss it anymore.

Now his arm comes around her from behind. "Love you," he says against her ear.

"There's no bread," she says. "You have to eat the tuna fish on crackers."

"Drat." He takes a drink of ice water that she poured for him. "How's the job hunt going?"

She smiles sweetly. "Knock it off."

"I'm just asking," he says, "because there's something on your mind."

"No, there isn't."

"Yes, there is." He looks up at her. "Is it Keith?"

She lets go a sigh. "I keep thinking they're so far away. And it's thirty miles to the nearest hospital. What if something happens?"

"Nothing's going to happen, Jess."

"How do you know?"

"I just do."

How is it that all of the men in her life tend toward knowing everything? Her father is one who can't tolerate being caught without an answer—which car to buy, whom to vote for, what to think about the world situation. Now that he's retired, it's extended to the best way to scrub a floor and arrange one's kitchen cupboards. And Keith—ever since he and Annie were married, he has taken on the role of Jess's big brother, mostly on the issue of her love life.

"Just don't marry him, Jess," he begged her, the summer she was dating the roofer who looked like a gypsy.

"I'm not even thinking about it," she assured him. "I just graduated from college, I'm not like you guys, I'm in no hurry."

"You don't like him because he's a roofer," Annie said. "You're a snob, Keith Browner."

"Hey, I'm a high-school English teacher, people look down on me all the time. Don't I ever get to look down on anybody?"

She's glad at least that he likes Ryan, has liked him from the first; it helps to balance Annie's view. For herself, she loves everything about this careful man, his gentleness with his daughter, and the respectful distance he keeps with Annie. And the way his suit coat lies flat and smooth across his shoulders, a half inch of shirt cuff showing below the sleeve. She wonders if, when they are married, they will have wild, sweaty sex in the afternoon. Probably not. Probably they'll be too busy arguing over who left the sprinkler in the driveway or whose turn it is to do the grocery shopping.

She pulls out a chair to sit next to him, and there on the seat is a black wallet and a fielder's glove with H. BROWNER scratched into the side. Soon she'll be getting another call. Her nephew can't be without these for long. She'll mail them with some peanut-butter kisses. They love getting presents from her while they're on vacation.

3

On Monday morning it rains. Annie first hears the rumble of thunder, like a truck coming down the highway; minutes later the storm is upon them— huge drops pelting the sand, washing out all of the ground heat. Water is pouring from the eaves. The lake is invisible, but she can hear it crashing out there, beyond the sand hills. What time is it? A momentary surge of panic that she forces down. Keith must be in the bathroom. Or else downstairs making breakfast. Or with Julie on the porch. They like watching the rain together.

Then she remembers. The rain is drenching the beach towels and bathing suits, the blankets she was airing on the line. She meant to bring them in last night, forgot all about it. Pulling the covers up over her shoulders, she buries her head beneath the pillow.

A moment later Julie's breath is in her face, smelling of toast and raspberry jam.

"Move over, Mom."

She lifts the sheet and pulls her daughter in. The move lets in a shaft of cooler air.

"Thunder is like a dog growling. G-g-g-r-r-r-r-m-m-m."

"Um-hmm."

"Is it going to rain all day, d'you think? If it does, I'm gonna be bored."

"Are you? Then we'll have to do something."

"I know—we could have game day! Let's play Monopoly and have prizes . . . can we, Mom?"

"We'll see."

"Don't say 'we'll see.' That always means no. Just say 'okay.'"

Half-awake, she sees the trap, ready to spring shut on a word. "Let's talk about it at breakfast. Where's Dad?"

"Haven't seen him."

She throws off the covers, reaching for her robe as Harry appears in the doorway.

"What's for breakfast?"

"Did Dad go out for a walk? Harry, did you see where he went?"

"He's right outside, Mom."

She wraps the robe tightly around her, hurries downstairs in her bare feet. Through the screen door she sees him leaning against the railing on the side porch.

"Cardinal just landed on that branch," he says, pointing toward the shed. He mimics the bird's call— a series of ascending whistles, then one descending. An answering call comes from the tree. He peers through the mist while Annie looks at him, at the side of his head where the upside-down question mark is starting to fade, his hair finally growing in. A pointless wound; they hadn't been able to do what was needed.

Under the white T-shirt his shoulders look bony and thin, the khaki pants riding too low on his hips. He's losing weight. He should be putting it back on after the hospital, should be eating more. Well, she knows what to do about that—go into town to the hardware store and buy a scale, make him get on it every day, prove to her he's getting better. He owes her this. She's good at getting him to do what she wants. She will stuff milk shakes, cheeseburgers, lemon Bismarcks down him until he chokes.

"We're having game day," Julie announces.

"No way," says Harry.

He is not for anything where you have to sit still; always twitching, touching things, taking them apart. He can't rest even while he's watching TV or eating; it is why nobody likes to sit next to him at mealtimes.

"Jim found a kitten underneath the porch," Keith says. "He's been trying to give it some milk."

Jimmy rounds the corner, carrying a ball of gray fluff. The kitten's legs thrash wildly in the air, and she gets a sudden whiff of wet fur and urine.

"Oh Jimmy, put it down, it smells awful!"

The kitten squirms free and bolts across the yard, disappearing under the low-hanging cedars. Julie looks accusingly at her mother.

"Mom, she can't help the way she smells."

"Here, kitty, here, kitty!" Jimmy is down the steps with Julie at his heels.

"They'll get soaked out there," she murmurs.

"That's what you do in Harrisville on rainy days."

"Hey, Mom!" Harry calls from the kitchen. "I found a waffle iron! Let's have waffles!"

"Waffles!" Julie echoes. "Goody, can I have the first one?"

"If you come in and set the table."

Annie makes some batter while Keith cleans up the waffle iron. It looks as ancient as the cottage itself.

"Well, she's gone," Julie says, coming inside. "Poor thing, she looked like she was starving."

"How do you know it's a 'she'?" Harry asks.

"Dad, I need some sunglasses," she says, ignoring him. "Can we go into town this morning?"

"You won't need 'em. It's gonna rain all day," says Harry, the prophet of doom.

She makes a face at him. "You don't know everything."

"Yeah, I do."

"I'm gonna see if that old Monopoly game is still around." She rummages in the closet beneath the stairway, where the games and puzzles are kept.

"No way," Harry says again. "I didn't come up north to play stupid games, I can do that at home."

"Jimmy, go wash your hands," Annie says.

"I wish we had a cat."

"That kitten belongs to somebody, Jule," Annie says. "I'll bet its mother is out there looking for it right now."

"Anyway, we don't like cats in this family," says Harry. "We like dogs, don't we, Lucky?"

"Lucky belongs to you. I want something that just belongs to me."

"Lucky belongs to the family," Jimmy says.

Tail wagging hopefully, Lucky rises and comes to the table.

"Lucky, go lie down," says Keith.

"Anyway, dogs are different than cats."

Harry makes a goofy face at her. "Duhhhh!"

"Dad, tell him not to do that. He's always doing that to me!"

"Don't do that to your sister," Keith says.

"Everybody come and sit down," says Annie.

The waffles are passed around, and for a few minutes there is peace while, outside, rain drums against the roof accompanied by the rhythmic slurring of the waves.

Jimmy is the first to finish. He gets up from the table to poke around inside the closet.

"Hey, look! Brand-new puzzle, fifteen hundred pieces. 'Sailing on the High Seas.' "

"We're not gonna do a puzzle," Julie says. "We're gonna have game day."

Harry starts to set up the card table. "You guys can play Monop if you want. I'm gonna do this puzzle instead."

"See? Every time I try to make a plan—"

"Every time I try to make people do what I want, they decide to do what they want!"

He has caught her tone exactly; even she can't miss it. Abruptly she rises from the table and stomps up the stairs, the angry cadence ending in the slam of the bedroom door.

"The fairest thing," Jimmy says after a moment, "would be to vote."

Annie gets up to clear the table. She's lost all taste for these power struggles, doesn't care anymore about fairness, doesn't want to spend an ounce of energy sorting it out. Julie is a controller and Harry is—who knows what Harry is? He's been impossible since Christmas. Of course she knows why, but she doesn't want to think about it; thinking only makes her feel more helpless, reminds her of her own need to be in control. Turning her back, she loads the dishes into the sink.

Meanwhile Harry the Victor is humming quietly as he sets out the puzzle pieces around the rim of the table. All of the edge pieces first, that's the way she taught them. Jimmy moves over to help.

Behind her she hears Keith get up from his chair. He'll go upstairs and talk to her, get her to see it's not the end of the world. Then he'll take her into town for sunglasses.

She hears his steps on the stairway; too slow, too slow. But she doesn't want to think about that, either. Resolutely she turns on the hot water, running it over the dishes.

Into the afternoon she sits in the rocker, knees drawn up, feet tucked under her. She's reading a book she found on the shelf, about the conquest of Annapurna. The man who wrote it, Maurice Herzog, was the leader of the French Himalayan Expedition. She reads of his bravery during the climb; he lost fingers and toes from frostbite and nearly died on the trip down.

She remembers reading another book about this same mountain; a much later conquest. Herzog's was the first, more than forty years ago. He looks so young in these pictures; she wonders if he's still alive.

What moves her most about mountain climbing is

the quiet expertise of the Sherpas, carrying equipment and messages from camp to camp, interpreting,
transporting injured explorers on their backs over
impossible terrain. They are the real heroes, and they
do it all without credit, without ever being awarded
the mountain as a prize.

Across the room, the boys are engrossed in their
puzzle; Lucky lies asleep beneath the card table.
Anyone looking through the window would see only
peace and harmony.

Keith and Julie are playing cribbage. He has taught
them all to play cards. He's a good teacher—patient
and enthusiastic; his students love him. After the
operation there were so many letters sent in to the
school newspaper that they had to publish a special
issue. One girl wrote that she couldn't see any point
to Shakespeare, but at least Mr. Browner had made
her wonder about it. It was his favorite one. He
brought them all home in a manila envelope on the
last day of school, and they went into the current
cardboard box, along with the kids' papers from this
year, assorted sailing catalogs, pamphlets, postcards,
theater programs, ticket stubs, erasers, thumbtacks,
small change, pieces of chalk. Stored under the
bed, next to last year's box. The box from the year
before was moved to the hall closet, to make room.

She never meant to marry a saver; she who is terrified of clutter, having grown up in a house where
clutter was King. Her mother said everything you
threw away would hang on the end of your nose

when you died. She was a junk junkie, saving everything from scraps of leftovers to socks without mates
to empty jars to cardboard boxes. Their basement
piled high with them. Around every doorknob, a
thick collar of rubber bands.

She vowed she would never let this happen to her;
yet now her own closets overflow with junk, and the
stuff piles up year after year; broken furniture con-
signed to the garage for repair, storage space given
over to no-longer-working-items-but-with-useful-
parts. In the basement are cans of paint, varnish,
turpentine, caulking compound, patching plaster,
roofing cement, wood stain, shellac. A warehouse of
spare curtain rods.

"Let's take a little break, huh, Jule?"

Keith stretches his arms over his head, getting up
to stand by the screen door. She turns the page, real-
izes she can't remember what she just read. Her mind
jumps from the sodden blankets on the line to the red
Sunfish, next to the porch. She didn't want to bring it,
but that would have been too symbolic. He has taught
all of the kids to sail with it, taking each out in turn.
They'd paddle beyond the sandbar on a windy day;
skimming, they'd hang out over the edge in their
orange life jackets, calling, "Look, Mom, look over
here!"—while she lay on the beach, pretending to
read. She couldn't watch. The idea of it seemed safe
enough, but when they were out there, so far from
shore, on that blue-green blanket of water . . . but
they love the water; they are so much his children, in

build and mannerisms, in the way they acquire physical skills. There's little verbal instruction; learning bypasses the brain, goes straight to muscles and nerves.

She can't learn anything that way. Hers is the more painstaking, less efficient process; things must be analyzed, worked through, picked apart. He had tried teaching her to play golf; dutifully she studied each step—grip, stance, backswing, downswing, follow-through—but they refused association, stayed separate and distinct. Her body paused and jerked its way through them, one at a time.

Keith stands, looking out at the rain. Hands in his pockets, he hums: "My mom gave me a nickel . . . to buy a pickle . . . I didn't buy a pickle . . . I bought some . . . CHEWING GUM. . . ."

"Dad, don't sing that," Harry says, looking up from his puzzle. "You been singing it all day."

"Hey," Keith says. "Look who's here."

Julie runs to the door. "Oh, no . . . she's so wet she must be freezing to death!"

"Phew! Smells worse than a skunk," Harry says.

"We need to give her a bath! I'll get some soap."

Julie goes to the kitchen, runs water in the sink. In a moment she returns with a plastic dishpan.

"How about it, Mom?" Keith drawls. "Want to get in on this one?"

With a sigh she gets up, looking for the old beach towel that used to hang at the back of the broom closet. She finds it and goes to the screen door, where already a battle is in progress. The kitten, sprawled across Keith's neck, is mewing and clawing at his T-shirt while Julie swipes at its head with a sponge.

"Forget that," Keith says. "Just slop the water on."

"It'll get all over you!"

"Here, like this." Harry soaps his hands, dips them in the water, and rubs them over the kitten's back while Jimmy holds him still.

"Ow! Those claws are like needles! Hurry up!"

Annie tosses the beach towel to Julie.

"Wrap him in it nice and tight, Jule."

She lifts the squirming kitten into her arms, bundles it like she does her dolls. The struggling stops and the kitten looks around, testing the air with its pink tongue.

"Doesn't even act like he's mad," Jimmy says.

"Short memory," Keith says. "Hey, I'm mad, you little bugger, you wrecked my good T-shirt!"

"I'm gonna call her Mrs. Bennett," Julie says. "Can we keep her, Mom?"

"Hey, Mom, look at Lucky," Jimmy says. "She hissed at him and he went and stood in the corner. What a wimp!"

"Can we, Mom?"

"We'll see."

The rain stops and they sit in lawn chairs to watch the sunset. Keith drinks a glass of grapefruit juice. Annie has a beer. She sips it slowly, watching the waves unroll a white ruffle against the shore. The sun is setting behind them, across a national forest and a military reservation, but there's beauty here on the east side, the sunrise side, as it's called. The west side of the state, the Lake Michigan side, is where the money goes: clothing and furniture shops with branches in Palm Beach, Sanibel, and Saint-Tropez. But lately people have begun pushing over the top of the mitten, spilling down the shoreline toward Sheboygan and Alpena.

The horizon is stacked with rose and lavender clouds. The water is rough, some unseen storm feeding it from its core.

"This naming bit," Annie says, "is not a good idea."

"It's all right."

"I wish she wouldn't get so set on things. . . ."

"She's just honest. You always know where her heart is." He takes her hand, swinging it in the space between their chairs. "Maybe we should rent a movie tonight. The natives are getting restless."

For the last hour trouble has been brewing; now it reaches a level that's hard to ignore.

"Hey! What're you doing?" Jimmy's voice scales upward. "You're wreckin' it!"

"Puzzles are boring," Harry says.

There's an ominous silence, followed by sounds of a scuffle. Annie gets up and goes inside. A full-scale wrestling match is in progress.

"Knock it off," she says, stepping around them to get to the sink. She pulls out carrots, celery, and cauliflower from the refrigerator, begins to cut them up. They've had enough sugar for one day.

"Mom, I've been doing this puzzle and Harry just went and wrecked it!"

"Oh, who cares?" she says.

"Nice," Jimmy says glumly. "That's nice, Mom. 'Who cares?' "

She refuses the bait. "Your dad and I thought we'd go get a movie."

"Get *The Little Princess*!" Julie yells from the living room.

"No fembod movies!" Jimmy yells back.

"How about if we decide when we get there?" she says. "Julie, put your shoes on."

"Are we walking?"

"No."

"Why do I need shoes?"

"Because, Dumbo, they won't let you in the store without 'em."

Annie turns from the sink. "Harry, stop it right now. Don't use that tone with her."

A look of surprise comes over his face, as if he's been caught impersonating someone older and less protected than himself. Sometimes it frightens her, all the power she has over them. When they stop allowing her to decide what it is that makes them who they are, will that be a good or a bad thing? Will it mean that she has lost them? They're not bad kids. She knows this. And patience is what she needs; more patience, more humor.

"Get the empties from the closet, will you, Harry?"

"Mom," Julie asks, coming out to the kitchen, "can we buy more 7UP?"

The movie rentals are in an alcove in the corner of the store, the categories labeled: *Drama. Comedy. Horror. Musical. Classic.* They argue over the merits of *Top Gun* versus *Heidi's Song* until she suggests a compromise: *Blazing Saddles.* There's no such thing as agreement among the three. Only another mother would understand how this has become her life: making judgments over which kind of pop to buy, what restaurant to eat in, whose turn it is to choose the movie. She no longer has opinions on these subjects; it's too complicated.

After dinner they set up the video. Keith lies on the couch, ankles crossed, a pillow behind his head. Julie is on the floor; next to her is a shoe box lined with Kleenex, where Mrs. Bennett is sleeping.

Annie pulls the rocker around to face the TV. She strokes the pale comforter with its pattern of green-and-white flowers, the one Julie used to call her "flowah covah." They bundled her in it the night she had her earache, taking turns holding and rocking her until it was light and they could call the doctor. How odd, thinking it was wrong to bother him in the middle of the night! No matter how bad things got; it was as if their own anxiety didn't count. At all costs, you don't disturb the doctor's sleep. Things have changed a lot for her on that score. Today she wouldn't think twice.

The movie seems long to her tonight, not as funny as she remembers it. She's tempted to pick up her book and read about Maurice Herzog battling his way up the ice wall above the Miristi Khola Valley, but Julie wouldn't permit it. She expects one hundred percent participation in these family events.

Outside, the wind is blowing hard, rattling the windows on the east side of the cottage. The crashing waves make her think of socks and shoes left out, of inner tubes, books, and towels strewn on the sand. But there's none of that to worry about tonight; they haven't even been down to the beach today. So what is it that's nagging at her?

Something from the early-morning hours. Probably something left over from a dream. She has too many of them these days: violent scenes of fathomless, unfixable misery, causing her to wake to a trumpet blast of fear, a certainty that all is lost. The one about the bird singing in darkness and her hunting it down, lured by the seduction of its soaring melody. Climbing over odd, lumplike hills and underbrush to find it trapped in a thornbush with a vine twisted cruelly about its neck. She sees this picture in her mind, over and over—the bird's struggle; his terror at her approach. He doesn't sense rescue, merely added danger. And her fingers, awkward and fumbling, making things worse. Every move she makes tightening the vine around its throat. Through it all, the terrible lyrical singing, until at last the bird is freed, lying dead in her hand. All her fault—the wrong hills climbed, listening all the while with such pleasure to a cry for help, thinking it was only music.

The movie is over and Jimmy goes to the machine. "Be kind," he says. "Rewind."

"Let's play Monopoly," Julie says.

"Too late. It's after ten. Time for bed."

"We're on vacation!"

"Mom's right," Keith says with a yawn. "Long day."

"Is there an extra blanket?" Julie gives Annie a look. "I froze last night out on the porch."

"Can we take the Sunfish out tomorrow, Dad?" Harry asks.

"Maybe. If it's not too rough."

Their bedroom is next door to the boys' room, with a bathroom in between. Connecting doors on either side. The bathroom is long and narrow, with a toilet at one end, a sink at the other.

The roof of the bedroom slopes to the floorboards, the area under the eaves walled off. Keith is already in bed, and she undresses in the dark and slips the cotton nightgown over her head. Opening the dormer and swinging it inward, she hears the pounding of the waves. She knows that he is awake and watching her. She goes to the connecting door, latches it from the bedroom side.

She goes to him and he raises up on his elbows.

How long has it been since they've done this? Not that she's missed it; fear has created a kind of stupor in her. She's on hold, listening, waiting to feel safe. Taking his head between her hands, she leans over him, her fingers playing a tune on his bare back. He pulls her across his stomach, while outside the waves roll in, sizzle against the sand. For a joke, he matches his movements to every roll and crash of the waves. And then he is inside her, still rocking in that same rhythm; within seconds she has matched it, going, going; then in a rush, gone over the edge.

"Geez, how did that happen?"

She laughs, turning her head to free her hair. Then, sliding beneath him, she slips a hand in between, feeling his heart beat steadily under flesh and bone. Sexy man, with long legs, a narrow back, ankles that crack when he walks. Without warning he gives a soft gasp in the back of his throat: "Anne . . . Annie . . . !" The sound muffled against her hair.

A quick, rhythmic pulsing between her thighs and then he rolls to his side. His breath is warm against her cheek. Holding him, she turns her gaze toward the open window.

"That had to be the world's speed record," he murmurs, reaching down to pull the covers up over them. "We need more practice, I think."

They kiss for a while in the darkness, then he settles himself on his side; minutes later he's asleep. He used to be awake long after her, but now he sinks instantly down, as if to disappear inside himself.

She'd like to be able to do that, too. Instead she lies alone in the dark, listening to the pounding of the waves.

When they discharged him from the hospital they talked with the doctors about the tri-weekly cobalt treatments he'd be taking, and the symptoms they needed to watch for that signaled a progression of the disease. That same day he stood at the bedroom window while she unpacked his suitcase. It was February, below zero outside; too cold to play, but the kids were out there, chasing each other around the yard, looking for distraction, desperate to be in their bodies.

"Don't," he spoke sharply to her. "I'll do that."

She stopped at once. But then what was she to do with her hands, with her mind that needed a duty to fasten on, to hold the panic at bay? Putting the car away, hanging up coats, carrying the suitcase up to the bedroom—she needed her own distractions.

"I have to tell you," he said, "that I don't know if I can hang around for this all the way to the end."

She heard the words, let them go by. Her mother said she never knew when to stop asking questions, making it clear that this was no small personal flaw. That day she never asked a thing. He's never said it again.

This morning, looking at him through the screen door, she suddenly saw someone whose hand trembled on the railing, whose step was slow and careful, like an old man's. There are times when he is someone else, capable of making other alliances, of moving away from her.

Sometimes she protects herself by thinking the worst, by looking into the pit and then drawing back to a safe distance behind the barricades. Nothing bad will happen if she can only imagine it first. But then she turns away. He loves her. He will never leave her. And there is a way out of this. She only has to think of it.

4

The kids are waiting by the toolshed when they arrive. A banner decorated with seagulls, the loops colored in with red felt-tipped pen, reads:

WELCOME JESS AND RYAN

"Where've you been?" Julie accuses them as they get out. "We've been waiting for hours!" She holds up a tiny kitten for their inspection. "Her name is Mrs. Bennett."

She's wearing the neon-pink bathing suit Jess gave her for her birthday; her brothers are in khaki shorts, naked to the waist.

"Where is everybody?" Jess asks them.

"Mom's at the grocery store. Dad's in the house."

The door opens then, and Keith comes out. At once she's caught off guard; she can't believe he's lost that much weight in only a month! His hair is dry, wispy looking; dark circles under his eyes. She can't look at Ryan.

"Hey, travelers."

Ryan moves to take Keith's hand. The kids stand beside the car; they know her well—that she'd never show up without gifts. Glad of the distraction, she reaches into the backseat for the three paperbacks.

"You have to share," she says. "Pool your knowledge."

Harry takes the one on mammals, Jimmy the eastern birds.

"Reptiles and Amphibians," Julie reads. "This looks good!"

"You spoil 'em rotten, Aunt Jess," Keith teases.

"Hey, I'm rich. I got a job. With a builder in Troy."

"Who?"

"Chase Construction. Just a small outfit. Typing and general office work, but I'm hoping they'll let me on one of the crews, if I play my cards right." Now she can move, her limbs no longer rooted to the spot, her hands reaching out to grasp his. They feel warm in hers; she takes comfort from that.

When Annie returns they are in the living room, having a beer.

"Homemade hot-dog buns from the bakery," she announces. "For our beach roast tonight. How was the drive up?" She busies herself in the kitchen. "You haven't had lunch, have you? I've got some chicken

salad . . . oh, did you bring this nice bread?" Relent-
less cheerfulness—that's the mood being pushed
here; they are to sign up, no questions asked.

"Are we having that chicken stuff again?" Harry
asks.

"Yes we are."

Jimmy comes in from the porch. "Dad, I need a
pole for my raft." He is the inventor and family
handyman; it's how he gets his privacy needs met;
always off working on some new project.

"I took these old boards and tied 'em with clothesline," he tells Ryan. "You gotta fasten each one sepa-
rately, weave the rope in and out. We floated it
yesterday. It works great."

"No rafting," Annie says. "Not until your dad
checks it out."

"We'll pick up a pole tomorrow," Keith says.

"Tomorrow's Sunday."

"Yeah, I know."

"The hardware store won't be open."

"Sure it will."

Julie is showing Ryan her kitten. "We found her
outside in the rain. Mom almost didn't let me keep
her."

"Mom, the abuser," Annie says. "Here, put these
chips on the table, Jim."

"I think it's Mr. Bennett," says Ryan. "Feel right
up under here. See? They're tiny, but they're there."

The boys are at once hysterical, feinting and

punching at each other. Jess intercepts the look Ryan sends Annie's way; checking to see if somehow he has given offense. But Annie laughs.

"At least we won't be having any babies."

Jimmy looks at the table. "Oh, no, not moldy chicken salad . . ."

"There's nothing wrong with the chicken salad!" Annie sets the bowl down hard. "It's two days old, it's perfectly safe!"

"Safe." Keith gets up from the couch. "Interesting adjective."

He goes to the kitchen, puts his arms around her. "Just teasing," he says. "Just kidding." They stand for a moment in private communion. An awkward pause, then Julie says:

"Maybe we should go to the Lumberman's Monument after lunch."

Groans from Harry and Jimmy. "We've seen it—"

"Yeah, about a million times!"

"I've never seen it," Ryan says.

"All right, then," Annie says, pulling free. "The Lumberman's it is."

They climb into the Wagoneer after lunch. Annie is driving. It feels strange to Jess, with Keith in the passenger seat; he is the one who knows these roads, who finds his way to Iargo Springs or any of the river dams in the dark. She can't remember a time when he hasn't driven on the adventures.

"Let's play Weird Phenomena," Julie says. "You get points for seeing weird things on the road," she explains to Ryan.

"What are the rules?"

"No rules," Harry says. "You pick the phenomena, you give yourself points. It's a stupid game."

"Fine, don't play, then."

"Lions! Ten points!" Jimmy indicates two carved wooden lions beside a driveway. "Gigantic fake morel mushroom!" He points out a two-foot-high greenware mushroom mounted on a tree stump. "Fifteen!"

"Stand of dead jackpine," Jess says. "Twenty-five."

"Get real, Aunt Jess," Harry says.

They take Poor Farm Road, passing the old auction hall where Jess and Annie found the antique farm implements that hang over the family-room fireplace. This part is blacktop, the farmhouses large and well cared for, the gently rolling hills planted in wheat and corn.

"Why do they call it Poor Farm Road?"

"It's the road that the poor farm was on. Where poor people used to live. In the old days, when people lost their money the county would take care of them."

"How did they lose it?" Julie asks.

"Bad luck. The Depression. Maybe the animals got sick, or the crops didn't do well."

"Couldn't they just stay on their own place?"

"They probably couldn't afford to, Jule."

They pass a stand of poplars, stripped of their leaves by gypsy moths. Light streams through bare branches, giving it the look of early spring. The road changes to gravel, then to a dirt track, sinking lower and lower through a forest of oak and swamp cedars. The boys lie on their backs on the floor of the cargo area, heads toward the tailgate, staring out of the window.

"Holy shit!" Harry says, sitting up. "What's that over there?"

They crane their necks. Crouched in a stand of tall oaks are the biggest, blackest birds Jess has ever seen. They take off at the sound of the car, circling and drifting in and out of sight behind the trees.

"Vultures," says Keith.

"They must live around here," Julie says.

"They're feeding on something."

Annie steps on the gas, and the car leaps forward around a curve.

"Fifty points," Harry says.

Julie is outraged. "For a bunch of vultures? Anyway, since when are you playing?"

"Since now."

They arrive at the monument, walk under the row of pines to the stone apron fronting it. The trio of bronze figures rises into the air, poised on a pink granite base. Hefting a compass in one hand, the bearded timber cruiser stands in front of a huge log;

the river driver is behind and the sawyer straddles it, his curved saw balanced casually over one shoulder. For Jess, the beauty of it lies in the details: the sawyer's hat with the flaps pulled over his ears, the jauntily tied neck scarf of the river driver, the timber cruiser's ribbed socks and laced boots. He is the leader; it's in his stance, the sensible tilt of his hat.

On the base of the statue is a brass plaque:

ERECTED TO PERPETUATE THE MEMORY OF THE
PIONEER LUMBERMEN OF MICHIGAN
THROUGH WHOSE LABORS WAS MADE POSSIBLE
THE DEVELOPMENT OF THE PRAIRIE STATES

" 'Russell A. Alger, Jesse B. Atwood, William A. Atwood, Newell Avery . . .' " Julie recites the names carved into the base.

"Dad, tell her not to read all of them, will you?"

" '. . . Delos Blodgett'—isn't that a great name?— 'Temple E. Dorr—' "

"Temple Door?" Ryan takes a look. "Amazing but true."

"When I was a kid," Keith says, "this was just a statue in the woods. Now they've got the whole bit— nature walks, information center, even the fancy wooden stairway down to the river."

Below them is the scene of the postcard available at any drugstore in town: Highbanks of the Au Sable.

They follow the concrete path to a showcase depicting lumberjack life in the 1800s. Next to it is a sand pit containing a peavey hook, chained to a large log. TRY YOUR HAND, the sign says.

The boys take turns wrestling with the hook.

"It was named after a guy named Peavey," Keith says. "He was a river driver. Then he went into the flour business, where he's now rolling in dough."

"Oh, ha, ha," Julie says.

"Dad, we've already heard this," Harry says.

"Let's go," Jimmy says. "I'm hot. It's too hot of a day for the monument."

"Mom, can we go back on Poor Farm Road? I want to pick black-eyed Susans."

"The highway's faster, Jule," Annie says. "People will want to swim."

The car is quiet on the way home. Jess, in the back-seat next to Ryan, looks out the window at the wooden fence posts speeding by, barbed wire stretched between them, posted with "No Tres-passing" signs.

"Dad," Julie says, "what did you tell me about the Loud family?"

"They were lumber barons. That's how they got a dam named after them."

"Now I remember. I used to think they called it Loud Dam because it made so much noise." She turns to Ryan. "Did you know there are five dams on the Au Sable? Foote, Cooke, Loud, Alcona, and Five Channels. Really six, if you count Mio."

"Blah, blah, blah," Harry chirps from the cargo area.

"Hey!" says Ryan. "Over on the right! Deer!"

Annie stops the car. Standing, motionless, by the side of the road are a doe and two fawns; the doe is poised with ears pointed forward, tail twitching. Her babies, a reddish- brown color, their white spots still visible, watch her every move.

"Mom, put down the back window. I want to see how close I can get."

Annie puts it down and Jimmy gathers himself to climb over the tailgate. Just then the doe turns and plunges off into the woods, the fawns at her back. In seconds, the green sea of foliage closes impenetrably behind them.

"Gorgeous," Ryan breathes.

"She had a big scar on her shoulder," Harry says. "Like she'd been nicked."

"You mean shot at?" Julie asks.

"Probably not," Jimmy says. "Probably it was from a tree limb."

It is how Jimmy is choosing to view things these days, she notices. Another, subtler difference she has found: a level of preoccupation in Keith's manner, as though he has moved off to the side in the way of an observer, putting himself on the edge of things, rather than at their center.

"A doe and two fawns," Ryan says. "What do I get for that?"

"Ten points," Jimmy says.

"C'mon, give me a break. I'm holding out for fifty at least."

"These scores are gonna be way out of line," Harry grumbles.

Julie is first out of the car when they arrive home.
"Dad, can we take the raft out?" Harry asks.
"Not without a pole," Annie says. "It's too rough."
Lucky is barking frantically as Jimmy opens the door to the cottage. At once he's about his dog business of licking hands and sniffing at crotches.
"Wait for somebody to watch you," Annie calls after Julie, who is already heading for the beach. "Harry, go down and watch your sister."
"Oh, crap, why do I have to?"
It seems to Jess that it is in that same shocking instant that Annie's hand cracks against his cheek. Not loud, but it carries—to Julie, whose mouth is a round O of surprise; to Ryan and Jess, near the tailgate. Jimmy at once disappears inside the house.
"I've just had it with you," Annie mutters. She gets out, slamming the car door behind her.
Harry's back is straight; he sits like a statue on the seat. Keith opens the door on the passenger side, gets in beside him in the back. Jess sees his arm go around the sturdy shoulders. She closes her eyes, seeing a world in negative—black porch railings, white tree trunks, amber leaves.
Ryan touches her arm. "Time to go for a walk."
She rubs her forehead, realizing suddenly that she has a headache. Turning, she follows him down the sandy slope toward the lake.

5

"If you're not too sick of driving," Annie says, "we could take a ride over to the marsh. I need to pick some blueberries."

"Sure, I'll go with you," Jess says.

They gather up coffee cans and plastic pails. The rest of the group is at the beach, Keith and Ryan watching the kids swim.

Away from the lake the air is hot and still, heavy with the smell of meadow grass and sweetfern. Annie drives north of town, then onto a wooded trail thick with velvet dust. Jess hears the cry of an ovenbird: ". . . teacher, teacher, teacher . . . !"

"Before I forget," she says, "Mom and Dad want to stop by on their way to Mackinac. If that's all right."

"When are they coming?"

"Next weekend. With the Curtises."

Annie frowns. "I wouldn't care if it was just Mom and Dad. . . ." Then, briskly: "Never mind, that's fine. They can have dinner here and still make the last ferry to the island."

"You don't have to feed them," she says. "They don't expect it. They just want to see you." Is this the wrong thing to say? She doesn't want it to sound as though it's been discussed. But Annie doesn't seem to notice.

"Dinner's no problem. I have to cook anyway."

She pulls up under a large oak tree, shuts off the motor.

"It's so hot. Let's make this fast."

They take their pails and separate, moving through the low-growing brush. Jess goes across the road, her eyes searching ahead of her for the telltale milky-blue haze.

Her fingers move quickly, dragging the berries from their branches. She isn't a clean picker. Her father always used to grade them as they brought their pails for inspection; hers would be brimming, but with maroon and green ones, stray stems and leaves. Annie's pail would be less full, but her berries were always ripe and immaculate.

She used to think it was because of her inferior eyesight; now she knows it's a more serious flaw, and much less fixable—a lack of attention to detail. It is the same with her life. Because she isn't fussy enough about the small stuff, it has a way of suddenly turning into something much larger. This is not Annie's way; she is a careful person, a stickler for the details.

But they are more alike than they are different, and they have always understood one another; born six years apart, they know each other's reasonings and moods, have been friends as far back as Jess can remember.

Odd to think of one's skin containing nerves and muscles, veins, tendons, organs, and blood; all that keeps one's body separate and apart from others. No matter how near, there will always be that defining micron of skin. As far as what's happening to each of them here and now, they may as well be on different planets.

Annie is already back at the car when she arrives with her two full pails.

"That's plenty, don't you think? We have enough for a pie for tonight, and blueberry pancakes tomorrow."

They start back along the wooded trail, and Annie turns to her: "Do you remember when Aunt Adele and Aunt Glenna used to come and stay with us in the summer?"

She laughs. "Whatever made you think of them?"

"I was actually thinking about Aunt Glenna's husband—you know, the one without a name? They always just called him 'husband.' We never met him. I remember telling Mom I didn't think he existed. She didn't even carry a picture of him in her wallet."

"I remember they used to take over our bedroom and we'd have to sleep in the basement. Then they'd fill up the dresser with perfumes and nail polish and all kinds of makeup. And they were always asking, 'Is this as far as these windows open, Rosie?' or 'How soon before we'll have more hot water?' I never figured out why, when they lived in New York City, they'd want to spend their summer vacations in Detroit. . . ."

"Well, you could say they wanted to be near their little sister," Annie mused, "or maybe it was just that nobody else invited them and they were too cheap to pay."

"They always liked you better than me," Jess says. "They sent you pink roses when you graduated from high school, and all I got was a card saying, 'Good luck.' "

Annie looks over at her. "Anyway, I'm glad my kids have you for an aunt. They're lucky."

Moved by this, she reaches out to pat Annie's arm.

"I'm sorry about what happened today," Annie says. "I'm not usually such a lousy mother."

"Oh, Annie . . ."

"He gets on my nerves something fierce. He's lazy and he talks back, and he treats his brother and sister like shit. . . . I've been so hard on him lately, though, it scares me."

"There's a lot of stress. . . ." Jess murmurs.

"It wasn't even him today," she says. "I was just upset. It was something I saw back in the woods, when we stopped to look at the vultures. A dead deer, lying back from the road. You were all looking up at the birds. That's why I pulled away. It was all bloated. . . . I didn't want the kids to see it."

Jess is surprised. In the past they would have stopped and gotten out, gone as close as they dared. Annie has always been curious. They would have filled their eyes and noses, filled their heads with the sight, as they attempted to comprehend. But death is not something about which she has any curiosity these days.

"I've never slapped him before," Annie says. "You know me, Jess, I'm a screamer, not a hitter." She rubs her forehead. "Sometimes I feel as though I'm just losing it. . . ."

"What did Keith say?"

"He . . . we all talked about it together . . . he wants us to . . . I guess he just wants everyone to get along." She gives an impatient flick of her hand. "Did Ryan . . . was he shocked?"

"No, of course not," she lies, wondering why her tendency is always to cover up for each of them with the other.

Annie glances over. "Does Lucia know he's up here with you this weekend?"

"He never leaves town without telling her where he's going."

Sensing this, too, as an evasion, Annie steps firmly on the gas. Jess knows she doesn't approve of the way things are being handled, doesn't think Jess asks enough questions.

What more does she need to know? Ryan and Lucia live apart. They have weekly contact, because of Cheryl. She doesn't feel any urge to be involved in those specifics. Even after they are married, she senses this will be true. You have to live your life according to what comforts you, not what the rest of your family thinks you ought to be doing.

"We'd better get back," Annie says. "Those two are determined to float that raft today. They think if they do it out of my sight, it won't count."

• • •

"I'm so hot. I'm sweating."

"Lie on your back. You'll get more breeze," Annie says.

Jess is on her stomach on the beach towel, eyes closed, her straps pulled down off her shoulders. She has on her black bathing suit—the one she hopes makes her look thin. She likes her body—sturdy and big-boned, like her father's; a serviceable unit, is how she thinks of it.

Years ago she and Annie used to do this together, on mattresses in the backyard. Catching the tan-a-rays, they called it.

She sighs. "I don't want to believe this is bad for us."

"I know. Pass the peanut M&M's, please."

The water is a rippling blue quilt, the breeze pushing out from the trees. Annie sits up to rub oil on her arms, reaches under her towel to redistribute the sand more to her liking, as Ryan and Julie come down from the cottage.

"How about a beach walk?" he calls.

Annie shakes her head. "You two go ahead."

"Can I come?" Julie asks.

They walk side by side along the shore, pushing a flock of gulls ahead of them. Julie points out their tracks in the wet sand.

"See the center and those two long marks—they look like flower petals, don't they?"

Jess bends to examine a ridge of debris washing up onshore; it is millions of tiny carcasses, topped with dark red antennae. She holds one out on the end of her finger.

"Look at this. Like a little mini-shrimp, isn't it? Maybe that's why the lake smells fishy today."

Julie shakes her head. "The lake smells fishy from fish."

The sand along here is rough, with small pebbles the size of pea gravel; Jess's feet are already starting to hurt. The drop-off is sharp, inclining at a steep angle for ten inches or more. Julie wades in and she starts to follow, but the cold water makes her ankles ache.

"Once when I was at the beach at Pine Lake with Emily, a June bug flew down her suit," Julie says. "She screamed and everyone thought she was drowning. The lifeguard said she almost gave him a heart attack. He said you're only supposed to scream if it's something bad. I bet if he had a June bug fly down his suit, he'd think it was pretty bad."

"What happened?" Ryan asks.

"She jumped up and down and it flew out. But then it started thundering and lightning, so we had to grab all our stuff and run to the car."

Jess laughs. All of her stories have these apocalyptic endings, like the nursery rhymes she used to love as a toddler.

"I'm gonna go in now," Julie announces, plunging in headfirst.

Ryan shakes his head. "Timid little soul."

She splashes in joyous circles, heaving armfuls of

water into the air. Both she and Annie have those slim legs and straight back, the graceful, fluid movements. Julie is beautiful in the way that causes people to look to the future: *She'll be a heartbreaker. You'll have your hands full with her.* Jess has heard these threats-disguised-as-compliments more than once. As though beauty breeds a danger that others would avoid, even as they envy it.

Now she splashes along the edge of the shore, shaking her hair down in front of her face and arching each foot as she steps off, pointing her toes straight out.

"I know two people with really weird noses," she says. "One lives right down the beach in that house with the orange shutters. I see him running almost every day."

"What's his nose like?" Ryan asks.

"Long. Like a string bean. He's got white hair in a ponytail and a big dog named Brownie. Isn't that a boring name? It's a brown dog, so he names it Brownie."

"You've got some nerve." Jess laughs. "You and your dog named Lucky."

"I didn't name our dog. I wasn't even born when we got him. What if he was our dog?" she muses. "Then he'd be Brownie Browner."

The gulls go soaring off in wide circles over the water, leaving the beach strewn with fluff and feathers. Along here the water is less clear; filmy green moss floats below the surface. Halfway between horizon and shore the silhouette of a boat skims the surface of the water.

"There's Mr. Hixon," Julie says. "He goes fishing every day at the jetty."

Ryan stoops to pick up a stone. "Hey, I think I found a Petoskey." He holds out his hand. A flat grayish stone, marked with raised designs, like miniature wheels with spokes.

Julie nods. "You should keep 'em in a glass of water so the colors always look bright. They're fossils, you know."

She loves being the expert, never gets much of a chance around her brothers, who cut her no slack; around her they wear their imaginary beanies, baloney detectors, with an alarm that goes off— *birrripp! birrripp! birrripp!*—whenever she tries to speak with authority.

"Dad has a rule," she says. "Only four stones per walk. Then you pay better attention to each one."

"Is that a family rule?" Ryan asks.

"No. He doesn't care how many we pick up." She walks with her head down, her hair still in front of her face. "My dad's really sick. Do you guys know about that?"

Jess feels her stomach contract; it comes so swiftly, with such matter-of-factness. Over Julie's head she and Ryan exchange a look.

"Yeah," he says. "We know."

"Good. I don't like talking about it. But everybody

ought to know." She scuffs along beside them through the sand.

Jess takes her hand, squeezing it. "Do Harry and Jim want to talk about it, do you think?"

A small, dismissive shrug; seconds later she lets go of Jess's hand to run on ahead, twisting her hair up behind her, into a knot.

Jess turns around. Far down the beach she can just make out her nephews, digging a trench to the water, tossing sand up between their legs. Her hands tingle, as if from an electric shock.

Beside her Ryan stands, thighs apart, blond hair whorled against his skin. Thighs that her hands were caressing just last night. I'll give it all up, she prays, I'll stop, if it will change what's happening here. A lie, of course. She sees the arrogance of it at once: *Spin me this flax into gold and you can have my firstborn child.* A futile wish, in any case. It doesn't happen that way.

That night they light a fire on the beach; Harry, on his knees, arranges a cone of dried grass and twigs over crumpled newspaper, touches a match to it. Jimmy brings out blankets for people to sit on. Both wear jeans and white T-shirts with ROYAL OAK LITTLE LEAGUE stamped in blue across the back.

"Big astrological event tonight," Ryan says. "Interplanetary caucus. Mars, Jupiter, and Venus. I read about it in the paper."

"What's a caucus?" Julie asks.

"See those three bright dots all in a line, low in the sky? That's it."

"Dad, what's a caucus?" she asks Keith.

"Caucus," Keith says. "Assembly . . . meeting . . . council . . . conference . . . powwow . . ."

"Okay," says Harry. "We get the picture."

". . . congress . . . gathering . . . discussion . . . get-together."

"Mars is supposed to be the red planet," Jimmy says. "None of 'em look very red to me."

"All I know is, the brightest one is Venus," Ryan says. "And between Jupiter and Mars, there's an asteroid called Pallas. The second largest in the galaxy. The name means 'solitary one.' "

" 'Pallas,' " Keith says. "I like that."

"How do you know all this stuff?" Harry demands.

"Dunno. There's a bunch of tiny facts rattling around in my head. Like popcorn kernels."

One by one, stars prick through the blue canopy overhead; Jess stares up at them until her eyes start to blink.

"Remember that picnic we went to at Metropolitan Beach?" Keith asks her. "What was it that woman said to her kid that got us laughing so hard?"

"She was trying to get him to eat," she says. "Something like, 'Stuff that down your devilish gullet and be done with it!' "

"That's it!" They all laugh.

"That poor woman," Annie says. "We were so

shocked at her. How could anybody talk like that to such a darling little boy?"

"Yeah, were we smug. With our year-old baby and another one on the way."

Annie sits next to Keith. His arm is behind her, resting on her back. The moon rises up out of the lake, drawing a silver path across the dark water.

"Doesn't that look like you could almost walk on it?" Jimmy says.

"Let's try!"

The kids get up to run across the sand. In the light from the moon their bodies look elongated, like stick men come to life, their voices echoing faintly. No other sound except for the crackling of the fire and a muted splashing along the shore.

Suddenly there's a slow, steady roar that Jess can feel through the ground. From over the dark contour of trees come three planes, their lights brighter than any star; moving arrows against the backdrop of night sky. They break out across the lake and the roar overcomes all sound, enters her body like water. Down at the shore the kids stand with their faces tipped toward the heavens.

"I thought the air base was closed," Ryan says.

"It is. But sometimes they come back. For maneuvers, I guess."

The kids come running.

"Time for S'mores," Julie calls.

"Oh, golly, we ate 'em all," Ryan says. "Did you guys want some?"

"Weird Phenomena Alert," Julie says. "Look at this insect nest."

She shows them a weblike affair wound around the end of the stick, like a nylon stocking stuffed with peppercorns.

"Just don't bring it into the house," Annie says.

"Why not?"

"Because. It's a nest. Those things are going to hatch."

"Mom, they're just live things," Jimmy says. "What can they hurt?"

"Leave it on the porch," Keith says, with a yawn.

They thread marshmallows on the sticks Keith and Ryan have sharpened. Jess serves up the graham crackers and Hershey's bars.

"Why is it some people like 'em burned to a crisp?" Ryan asks. "Now, my way is clearly superior—brown on the outside and melted in the center."

"Yeah, but then you end up cooking them for everybody," Harry says.

"I'm not gonna be able to sleep tonight, Mom," Julie says. "I keep hearing those June bugs bumping up against the screen. *Bzzt. Bzzt. Bzzzzzzt.* What if they get in?"

"They won't get in," Annie says.

"How do you know?"

"Because I'm psychic."

"What does that mean?"

"They don't want to get in," Keith says. "They just want to stay outside and bug you. Get it?"

"Can I sleep with Jess and Ryan on the foldout couch?"

"No!" the sisters say at once.

"I'm sorry," Annie says. "What can I say? I'm sorry sorry sorry you have to sleep on that lumpy studio bed."

Julie laughs her tinkly laugh. "You are not, Mom. You're just faking it."

The sisters look at each other; Annie rolls her eyes.

Keith yawns. "Let's head up, guys. This was a long day."

"Dad, you always say that," Jimmy says. "They're all the same length!"

"Smart guy."

They fold blankets and pick up pop cans while the boys kick sand into the fire.

"Mom, I forgot to show you," Julie says. "A piece of rose quartz I found on our walk today. Here." She hands it over.

"Thank you, sweetie."

Thinking about this, Jess wonders at the gentleness of her niece, her fragility in the face of what is coming; wonders also at the gift, saved out from the walk and not shared with the rest; a secret kept only for her mother.

6

They walk south, toward the rock that looks like a whale. A bird cry echoes from the line of cedar trees,

keening and repetitive: *cheeburger, cheeburger . . .*
Keith looks out at a lone gull wheeling over the
water, zeroing in for a kill. The bird dives, coming up
with a flash of silver in his beak.

"This is nothing like where I grew up," Ryan says.
"Good old Canton, Ohio. Only inland lakes and flat
flat flat. My family's still there—parents and grandparents on both sides. My sister married her childhood sweetheart. He went away to med school, but
he came right home again. Now he's in practice with
his dad."

"So when are you moving back?"

Ryan laughs. "About when hell freezes over."

"Funny how things work out," Keith says. "I
always saw myself as the great adventurer. So here I
am in Michigan, blocks from where I grew up. And
my brother, who I thought was nailed to the floor,
ends up in Seattle."

"I never knew you had a brother."

"William. Two years older. He and I used to walk
this beach every summer. Walk it, look for treasure,
cart the stuff home. I felt like Captain Kidd. I had this
feeling the lake was mine, that I owned it." He
laughs. "I still do."

They pass a thicket of yellow flowering bushes,
scored at intervals by fallen trees. The sand along
here is darkened by underground springs, pumping
currents of water onto the beach; skinny fingers in
search of the lake. Hitting these ice-cold strips
reminds him of the time at camp when he and

William took the canoe out in the middle of the night, tipped over in the river, and had to swim to shore. The coldest water he'd ever been in, in his life! They wanted to ship them home after that, but William threatened to tell about the counselors paddling over to the girls' camp across the river every night after the boys were in bed. William, the dealmaker. For agreeing to keep their mouths shut and not do anything life threatening, they got to stay out their two weeks.

He bends to pick up a stone, turning it over in his hand.

"I heard about your rule," Ryan says. "Only four per walk."

"I haven't found the perfect one yet," he says. "Been looking for a long time. When I do, I can quit. One day Julie and I went out for a walk and she found a crayfish claw. Then a little further on she found another. She got the idea she'd pick up every one she saw and by the end of the summer she'd have a nice little collection. All of a sudden that day, there were crayfish claws everywhere. A crayfish bonanza. Her hands were full, mine were full, all of our pockets. It was a collector's nightmare. The challenge was gone."

"You need to find those things one at a time, or it's no fun," Ryan says.

"Right. Now they're in a box, out behind the shed. She never looks at them."

Along here the topography is different—the bank

closer to the lake, climbing at a steeper angle. The undergrowth is all bracken, thick and curling, some of the fronds already starting to turn. The birch and cedar trees lean out over the water. They watch a flock of Canada geese circle overhead. From the air the birds are sleek and graceful, but on the ground they look to him like drab, lardish lumps waddling along the shore. Not very friendly, either; they'd peck your eyes out over a crust of bread.

"So you've been coming up here since you were a kid?"

He nods. "My mother never liked it. Maybe because my dad liked it too much. He was pretty obsessive about it. All he ever wanted to do was fish and sit on the beach. Or tramp around in the woods. My mom's more of a city girl. But we came up anyway, almost every weekend."

They reach the rock, stop to examine the names carved into its surface—David 1959; Effie '67; Whiskers '68. On the other side: Brandon '89; Anita and Larry, 1977; Rob USAF scratched inside a crooked heart. The names of the nineties are sloppily done, spray-painted in garish colors.

"Where's your initials?" Ryan asks.

"Never did carve 'em. I always forgot to bring my knife with me."

They sit on the rock, facing the lake with their buttocks resting in the hollow. The air is warm and windy. They watch as a trio of sailboats makes its way southward.

"I'm hoping things work out for you and Jess," he says.

"They will. They have to." Ryan squints his eyes, looking out at the horizon. "My divorce will be final in January. I'd like to buy a house, get out of that apartment, get settled."

"I'm glad you two came up here," Keith says. "Makes things seem normal. I guess that's what I hate about it the most—the stupid abnormality of it all." He smooths his hand along the surface of the rock. "My kids are going to need somebody soon. To keep an eye on them. Give them advice when they need it. I'd like it to be you."

Ryan looks over at him. "You mean while you're in the hospital. During the chemo treatments . . ."

"I mean when I'm gone." He looks away. "Is that an unfair thing to ask? I see the advantage people have in this situation. You can ask someone the most outrageous favors. Nobody wants to be caught denying a last request."

A short silence. Then Ryan says, "Well, but that's way down the road. I mean after the chemo and everything . . ."

"I'm not having the chemo."

Another silence. He rests his elbows on his knees, looks down at his wrists, at the flesh pulled taut across the bones. "I sometimes wonder how something can take so long and, at the same time, things feel as if they're moving pretty fast. . . ." He stares out at the carpet of diamonds, taking a measure of comfort from its immensity. "It helps just knowing the lake is out there. That, no matter what else is happening, it'll always be a great day at the beach. I hope my kids feel that way about it. And my kids' kids. Now, there's a concept. My kids' kids." He looks into the glare of the sun, using his open hand as a shield. "Don't get upset about this, okay? It's just stuff that I'm thinking about."

"I guess I don't believe it's really happening," Ryan says at last.

"I'm past 'I don't believe it.' Comes right before 'I'm pissed' and 'What a shitty world this is.' Followed eventually by *'C'est la vie.'*" He turns the cuffs of his pants down, brushing sand out of them. *"C'est la mort."* He looks over. "You haven't answered my question."

"Of course. Sure. I'll look after them. I'll do anything you want. But you do feel safe up here, don't you? I mean, in case anything were to happen . . ."

"Oh, it won't be here. I won't be that lucky. There's no place I'd rather be, though. It's where I belong."

"What does Annie think?" Ryan asks. "About the chemo?"

"I haven't told her yet." He turns to look down the shoreline. The beach is nearly empty; towels scattered on the sand, tennis shoes and comic books, a deflated inner tube. The hour before dinner, before the sun drops below the trees.

"Everybody's dealing with this in their own way.

Annie thinks she has control if she gets mad, if she worries like crazy over dumb stuff. Sometimes I have to remind myself her problems are different from mine." He climbs slowly down from the rock, brushing off the seat of his pants.

"My parents got married when they were eighteen," he says, "and my dad took a job cutting pulpwood. Then he bought some land and started a farm. Grew corn and tomatoes and muskmelons—honey rocks, they call them here—the best you ever tasted. He was forty-eight when he died. Had a heart attack in his truck. Pulled off onto the side of the road, and by the time they found him, he was gone. I was a sophomore in high school. I remember one of his friends coming up to me at the funeral saying, 'Don't feel bad, son. He lived a full life. He did everything he ever wanted to do.' " He looks over at Ryan. "D'you believe that? He was forty-eight years old. I mean, what was the guy thinking?"

7

"D'you guys have to go?" Julie asks.

"Yep. Got to get up tomorrow and go sit behind a desk and type boring letters and answer the phone."

The kids, slouched on the sofa bed watching a *Star Trek* rerun, seem wilted, depleted of energy. Even the kitten's yellow eyes are wide with languor. Jess packs up her gray duffel, gets her wet suit off the line. Annie hands her a plastic bag of blueberries.

"Don't let them get crushed."

They say their good-byes on the porch, then again as they drive away. Jess waves to them out the window. As they turn onto the highway Ryan reaches for her hand.

"I'm glad I have a job," she says. "But I don't want to go to work tomorrow."

"Me either. Real estate's a dumb profession." He sighs. "One guy out to make a killing, the other looking for a steal, and me in the middle trying to convince both of them they got what they wanted."

They cross the railroad tracks, where, next to the Bobcat Bar and Grill, a foursome is teeing off for twilight golf.

"Should we chuck them, then?" she asks. "Turn around and go back?"

A short silence. "I don't think so. There's harder stuff going on there."

He has touched the source of her pain; she doesn't want to think about that now. "What did you and Keith talk about on your walk?"

"Not much. He told me a little about his brother. Do you know him?"

"William? Not very well."

She can only recall William's rambling toast at the wedding, a hymn to his baby brother, who was always thought "a tad backward" by the rest of the family (several embarrassing examples followed), but who somehow managed to land himself this prize of a girl. Through it all Keith wore a tight-lipped grin, while Annie, in the midst of bride euphoria, beamed fatuous love out at everyone. Jess assumed she wasn't even listening, until she noticed her sister's left hand with its new ring, the diamond winking in the candlelight—graceful small hand, with its wicked middle finger aimed straight for the ceiling. She smothered her laughter in a fit of coughing as Annie's eyes met hers; Annie doesn't like William, she knows that much.

The air in the car feels cold; she reaches behind her for her sweatshirt. "Your binoculars . . ."

"I left them for Julie."

"That was nice of you."

"Yeah, I'm nice." He smiles at her.

"Did you have fun? I thought he was pretty good, didn't you? Except for the Lumberman's Monument. He seemed tired when we were there."

Another silence. "I think he's feeling worse than he lets on."

And again her heart begins a rhythmic thudding against her ribs. She will listen, sit still against the seat, take in the information without doing damage to nerves or viscera, fit it into some context for evaluation. She doesn't have to get upset.

"Once they're home," she says, "things will be better. As soon as he starts the chemotherapy."

"He told me he isn't going to do it."

"But he's got to! What did Annie say?"

"He hasn't told her."

She is swept with a sudden feeling of helplessness,

born out of the dark recesses of the night, out of a world full of danger. She wants to blame her sister for this; the way she worries about every little thing—the kids talking back or refusing to take turns, her putting too much olive oil in the salad—it's all so she won't have to think about the rest. She won't talk about it, so he's made this decision without her.

Again Ryan reaches for her hand. "This is hard, Jess, no matter what. But it's his call, don't you think? I mean, I've read about chemo, that it can be worse than the disease. . . ."

"It's all we have!"

No, it's out of the question. He has to do this; it will slow the thing down, maybe even halt its progression. Her own craziness takes the form of fantasies: overnight they will find a cure; or it will suddenly turn out to be nothing—one day he will wake up feeling better, and they will go in for tests, only to discover the tumor mysteriously shrinking; a year from now they will look back on it all as a bad joke.

And what is her role in all of this? She should have paid better attention, should have asked Annie some hard questions. She should have taken her hand when they were together in the car . . . except that she knows the gesture wouldn't have been welcome. Annie draws strength from her aloneness, from her refusal to look. And where is she to get hers from? Her heart contracts in grief and she crosses her arms over her chest, as if to shield herself from the question.

The telephone is ringing as she lets herself into the apartment. It is their mother, of course, wanting a full report.

"Jessie? You're so late. I was worried."

"We stayed for dinner, Mom."

"How is everything? How are the children? I told her not to stay up there if it was too much. . . ."

"Everything's fine. The kids are fine. Swimming and having a good time. Julie adopted a kitten."

Rose Lewis sighs. "Lord, not another pet. What's she thinking? She lets those kids argue her into anything. She needs to start laying down the law."

Hard to steer a neutral course; her mother will find something to criticize in the most innocent of revelations.

"Did she say if she wants us to come next weekend?"

"Yes. But I wouldn't go for dinner."

"No, of course not. But, Jess, she used to have people for dinner all the time. Is it that bad? How is he doing? Is he eating? He wasn't eating a couple of weeks ago."

"I never heard that. He ate everything this weekend. Listen, things are all right. It's just that the Curtises . . ."

"The Curtises are friends of the family."

"I know. But I think it's hard for her to"—she hesitates, looking for the right phrase— "put up a social front right now."

"Well, we certainly don't expect that," her mother says stiffly. "The Curtises understand the situation. For heaven's sake, we've known them forever."

Now her mother's feelings are hurt, as if their visit were an occasion for phoniness.

"She's distracted, Mom. That's all I'm saying. And you know how she likes to be the perfect hostess."

Now what is she doing? Getting in deeper; if Annie were listening, she'd be furious. Casting a longing eye at the cupboard over the refrigerator, she thinks about the bottle of Irish whiskey up there. She wants to take a shower, wash her hair, get a nice buzz on, read a chapter from the new mystery beside her bed. Slide off into dreamless sleep. But her mother isn't ready to let her go.

"I don't see how we're going to get through this," she whispers. "What's going to happen to them? She never finished college, and now with those three children. I've tried to talk to her—"

"Mom, I gotta go," she interrupts. "I've got to get up early. I'm working tomorrow." Her mother will have Harry in jail and Jimmy in a car wreck, Julie pregnant and on the streets, all because Annie didn't get her B.A. in English studies. Yet, what would it be like to watch your child suffer, to know there is nothing you can do? She can't imagine how people learn to bear these things.

8

Quietly the day begins; quiet beside the lake. He sits on the shore, against a bank where the sand was pulled away by the hungry water when the lake was high; all that's left is a great hollowed-out curve, grass growing from its top, like a thick mop of hair in the wind.

PREDICTION FOR AUGUST: STEAMY. The headline in today's paper. Yet here it's cool: a breeze blowing in off the lake, the sky a glorious blue without a cloud in sight.

Annie brings letters down to him on her return from the store. He weighs them in his hand. The first is from his brother:

Keith,

Buddy Lasko is the guy you're thinking of. The one they caught up on Billie McCallum's roof. But the cops never came, I'm sure. As for the episode of the canoe, I must have blanked it out. I don't have any memory of it.

Mother keeps me posted as to your status. I'm coming for a visit soon; time and work pressures have intervened, but I'll be there early this fall when things are less hectic.

WB

He returns the single sheet to its envelope as Annie comes back with glasses of orange juice for them both.

"What does he have to say?"

"Not much. You can read it."

She takes up the letter, scanning it while she sips her juice. "Did you invite him here?"

"Left-handedly, I think. In the way of all us guilty people."

Her tongue clicks sharply against her teeth. "What is it exactly that you have to feel guilty about?"

Hard to explain, even to himself. And the day is too beautiful; he's feeling calm and detached, freed up for more important things. He shrugs off her question.

"I can't believe he forgot about the canoe, though. We had such a great time out there in the middle of the river, laughing like hell, knowing our ass'd be grass. . . ."

"Weren't you afraid you'd drown?"

"I've never been scared swimming," he says. And it's true; it always feels right, like what he ought to be doing.

The other letter is from his mother. She writes every week, her spidery handwriting tensely upright, carefully spaced across the page. Annie leans over his shoulder as he reads:

July 26th

Dear Ones,

Feeling sad today, thinking of you up there and me so far away. Then the telephone rang and William was on the other end! He said he'd be here in September. He says Boeing is laying off, but he's not worried.

I wanted him to come sooner so that he could drive me up to see you. What I really want is for you to come home. But maybe I worry too much. And Annie is such a capable person. I'm sure she will be amply repaid for her devotion to you. By the way, did the children get my package? I never know if I should notify the post office or not.

Always thinking of you and wishing you well,

Mother

"Maybe you could write her," he says. "So she knows they got the stuff."

"I had the kids do it. They probably crossed in the mail."

He looks at her. "Do you think we ought to go home?"

"Do you want to?"

"No."

"Then we won't," she says, getting up to stand behind his chair. She rubs the place on his neck where the headache usually begins, and he leans his back against her.

How will it help if they are at home? Seeing people, listening to well-meaning lies about how great he looks, how terrific he's doing. The pressure to report every change—weighing and wondering, thinking about it all the time. Up here he doesn't have to do that.

"I don't know why," he says, "but her letters always depress the hell out of me."

"Don't read them," she says. "I can read them. And answer them, too. They're addressed to both of us."

"Yeah. Maybe so." He grins, reaching up to put both hands on her arms. "You're a good kid. You'll be amply repaid for your devotion."

No worries; not today. The only real one is the glitches. To wake up in the middle of a day with no idea how you've gotten there, no memory of time having passed. Dressed, watching TV, eating a meal or resting on the couch, aware that it's your first conscious moment. Followed by a rush of pure panic. It happened yesterday: lying on the couch, a pillow under his head, the ice water sweating in a glass on the table. Julie beside him in the rocker, reading Nancy Drew—*The Clue in the Crumbling Wall*. Her hair damp, falling about her shoulders in ringlets. She'd been swimming already. But wasn't it early morning?

Lifting his arm to look at his watch, finding the face of it blurred. His head heavy on the pillow, eyes burning in their sockets; such effort, just to raise an arm! And something was wrong with the light, too intense for early morning. Asking the time. Four o'clock in the afternoon. That was the longest gap yet; nearly a whole day gone by. Julie was fussing with the blanket, arranging it over his chest. Her skin pale as honey, her fingernails perfect half-moons. He wanted to hug her, but feared that it would send her a signal of his terror. Thank God that only hours were lost. But it's what makes him afraid to go to sleep at night; if time is stolen from him, this is how it will happen.

Harry tiptoes into the bedroom to stand at the edge of the braided rug; bare feet, the bottoms of his shorts dripping. He's holding up a stringer, with a fish on the end of it: pale white belly and black fins. He raises up to get a better view.

"Where'd you catch it?"

"Mill Pond. There's a bunch of 'em, two- and three-pounders. Jumpin' right out of the water."

"What'd you use?"

"Little Cleo. He just grabbed it from me!" The proud angler, grinning in triumph.

"He's a beauty, Harry."

"Jimmy got one, too. Only, he slipped the hook when we were netting him."

"Come here. Let me see."

Harry holds the fish so he can touch it. Dark green, almost black, the skin slightly sticky; an earthy, fresh smell. He sees himself, the proud angler, showing off his catch to his own father—a fat, yellow perch. Out on the jetty with a group of other men in the early morning; the web of fishing lines crossing dark water at the mouth of the Au Sable.

In that same double mirror stands his grandfather,

and then Harry with his own son, and on and on. Dizzy with the impact of it, he runs his forefinger down the fish's slippery flank.

"You know how to clean him?"

"Sure. Like you showed me."

"I'd like a bite of that nice fat fillet."

"You can have it all, Dad."

That night they play liars' poker. Harry and Annie sit on the floor while Julie curls up in the wicker rocker and Jimmy sits with Keith on the couch. They pass the hand of five cards facedown around the circle.

"Three jacks, a king, and a nine," says Harry, handing them to Julie.

"Think of the odds, Jule. . . ." Jimmy says.

"I think they're there," Julie says. "What d'you think, Dad?"

"No fair asking Dad!"

"I'm leaving you room, Jule," Harry says.

"What a con!" Jimmy says.

Julie hesitates; takes the cards. "They're here!" she says. She passes the hand to her mother. "Three jacks, a king, and a ten."

With each pass, the value of the hand must go up. Jimmy is being set up by his brother; they all know it. He claps a hand to his forehead. "Don't take 'em, Mom," he pleads.

"Sorry, sonny." Annie's hand reaches out for the cards.

He feels a mild quiver begin in his eyelid; a muscle movement only, a tic. He leans to adjust the pillow at his back.

"Three jacks, king, queen," Annie says, handing the cards to Jimmy. He sees her arm in front of him, stretching forward; then a great hollow space like a yawn enters his mind and the room tips onto its side. He can hear Jimmy's voice, thin and faint, as he stiffens, feels the spasm rip through his face. A sudden crash of thunder, then darkness. Listening inside himself to the small motor grinding and grinding away. Mind and body not in sync; having been assaulted, his body is in panic, his heart racing. Yet he feels oddly relaxed, emptied of tension, his mind clearer than it has been in days.

Then, as swiftly as it began, it is over; he lies, flat on his back, staring up at the ceiling. Annie is bending over him, a bottle of pills clutched in her hand. Above her head, brown water stains curl into a corner of the ceiling.

"I'm okay," he wheezes. "I'm fine."

The sound is hollow in his ears. There is a sensation, languorous, as of warm oil running through his veins. She puts the pills down, presses both hands to her face, and he sees her knuckles, hard knobs of rose and white, before him.

"Where are the kids?"

"Right here. Harry's calling the doctor."

"You look scared," he says.

"So do you!"

"Mom, Harry's got him on the phone." Jimmy stands in the doorway. "I brought the water."

"Bring it here." Annie gets up. "Stay with your dad."

His body is suddenly his own again; the trembling has stopped. He feels his heart slip into the slow, regular beat. He smiles up at his son.

"How you doin'?"

"Kinda shaky," Jimmy says. "How about you?"

"I'm okay."

Jimmy holds the glass of water up to his lips and he drinks; the taste of it is pure and sweet in his mouth.

"Your hand was really wiggling." Jimmy demonstrates. "Were you doing it on purpose? You weren't, were you?"

"No."

"Was it a seizure, d'you think?"

He nods. They have talked about this as a possibility. "Did it scare you?"

Jimmy thinks for a minute. "No."

"Good." He takes a deep breath, closing his eyes. He feels very tired, as if he could sleep for a long time. "Maybe you'll be a doctor," he says. "You'd make a good one, I'll bet."

Annie is back. "He wants to know if you can move your arms and legs."

"Yeah."

"Do you have any weakness? Does your head ache?"

In fact, the headache that he's had all day is gone. He tells her this, and she goes to report it to the doctor. He's so tired, he needs to rest, just for a moment. The next thing he knows, the kids are gone and the room is dark, except for the glow from one small lamp. Annie sits watching him from the rocker, her elbow crooked, a hand resting against her cheek.

"Time's it?"

She looks at her watch. "A little after eleven. How do you feel?"

"Good. Fine. Where are the kids?"

"In bed. They're asleep."

"What did the doctor say?"

"He said to take twice the amount of medication from now on. He said call back in an hour and give him a report. I told him you were sleeping."

He raises up on his elbows. "How long did it last?"

"A minute. Maybe less."

She gets up, comes to the couch. Taking her hand, he puts his other arm around her. They have been waiting for this. Focal seizures are to be expected, they were told. It will lead to other problems; the signal system will begin to malfunction. The pattern is random, but its elements are predictable and certain. When and how often, how much damage—these are the only unknowns.

"He wants to see you," she says. "He told me we should come home." She clears her throat, looks down, as if ashamed. She is rocking gently, back and forth, and he holds her tight, to steady her. *All right, all right*. Then he swings his legs over the side of the couch.

"Got to take a leak."

A momentary dizziness when he stands up, that's all. He moves toward the bathroom on his own, balance perfect, all of his limbs working. Annie follows, watches while he stands in front of the toilet, one hand resting against the wall. He feels slightly cold, shaky; on the outside edge of illness.

Such an eating away, day by day; such a slow process, this dying. The same as being born.

When I was four years old, I played with a stray cat under the front porch. After a while I felt dizzy, my chest so tight there was no way to get a deep breath. They took me to the hospital—tan room with tan shades pulled against the sun; a high, narrow bed; a man with a silver eye in the middle of his forehead. The needle in my arm, the knot in my chest slowly dissolving, the air moving in and out.

"You have asthma," they said, and it became for me the meaning of the word illness; *after that, when someone didn't come to school because they were sick, I knew what was wrong.*

I had allergies: to cats, horses, dogs, ragweed, hay, goldenrod, grasses, dust, pollens, molds. After the first attack, I always knew when one was coming—an aura, a warning tickle in the back of my throat; a try for a full breath; when you can't make it, you know.

In college, the hobo party at the Phi Delt house, walking into a room knee-deep in hay, knowing I'd be leaving soon. Having to explain to a girl I hardly knew that I needed to go to bed, while somebody else danced with her and took her home. Thank God it wasn't Annie. Before Annie. "B.A.," Rich always said. I never had an attack after I met her; I grew out of it, the year I turned twenty.

Now I am obsessed with this new disease inside me—what causes it? How does it happen? Was it something that I did to myself? The tumor is above and behind my left ear. As if it matters. As if it makes a difference where, or how a disease goes about the task of multiplying cells, of destroying, changing, diluting until the job is done. It isn't necessary to understand it in order for it to do its work.

I watch a small green worm, suspended from a beech tree by an invisible thread, swaying some twenty feet in the air. Like a trapeze artist, curling and climbing in space. A delicate, precarious dance. I feel afraid—smothering fear of the undertow, of Death, with a capital D—that I will become helpless, dependent, lose control. That it could all be taken out of my hands, in the next seizure, or the one after that. That I will somehow fail at this, won't do it right. I cannot think of a time when I have ever felt so lonely.

At the breakfast table he watches Jimmy slice an apple with a red-handled paring knife (bought from Riebow's, where they're stored in plastic buckets, blades in cardboard scabbards, thirty-nine cents, throw them away when they get dull). He carves with care—first in halves, then quarters, then a V-cut to get rid of the core. He arranges the slices in a perfect circle on the pottery plate. Next to it is a jar of peanut butter, a table knife sticking out of it; next to that, a waxed paper sleeve of crackers and a half-eaten Sara Lee pecan coffee cake, still in its aluminum tin. Bacon draining on a paper towel.

"Can I have some of that apple?" Julie asks.

Jimmy reaches behind him on the counter for another one to cut for her. Harry comes down in his skivvies, scratching his head and blinking like Stan Laurel, a gash from shoulder to navel across his torso, where he fell jumping over a log.

"Mom says nobody at the table in their underwear," Julie says.

" 'Mom says, Mom says,' " he mimics her. "Get a life."

"Then *I* say," she says. "Who wants to look at your dumb old Louie?"

"It's not a Louie." He spreads a slice of apple with peanut butter. "It's a penis. Call it by its real name. Right, Dad?"

"If it needs calling."

"Don't call it a hogan," Harry says. "Or a weenie. Or a tallywhacker."

Jimmy snickers.

"Don't call it a Johnson—"

"Knock it off, Harry."

"Knock what off, Dad?"

Now they all snicker, teaming up against him.

He grins. "You guys think you're pretty funny."

Annie has been talking all morning on the telephone in the hall, her voice muffled. He hears the click, clack of the receiver being replaced; then, moments later, the sound of it being lifted again. He doesn't ask whom she's calling. There's a need for him to be always touching her these days; it is how they best communicate; gestures rather than words.

"Jess is coming tomorrow," she tells him. "She'll take the kids back with her. . . ."

He nods. Anything will be fine.

"I've got it," Harry says. "Why don't we make up a bed in the back of the Wagoneer? Dad can ride back there with Lucky."

"And Mrs. Bennett," Julie reminds him. "That'll be fun."

Annie laughs. "Always with a plan. He's just like my dad. He can make any scheme look like the best idea in the world for at least five minutes."

"Remember that summer we went to Maine?" he asks her later. "They were the kids from hell on that trip. I really didn't care if they fell off the mountain."

"Yeah. Until you found out they actually could do it."

They'd been horsing around, chasing each other through groups of tourists—" 'Scuse me! 'Scuse me!"—those imperious, child voices, pretending apology while ordering people out of the way. He can still remember the brutal drop-off on the back side of the mountain, the frantic search that followed—combing the crowds for a glimpse of a black cowboy hat, an orange-and-white plaid shirt, Julie's pink ruffled shorts. That rush of relief when they were found.

Another memory, of those Sundays spent at Grandpa Browner's, the shades drawn against the blistering sun, listening to the play-by-play of a Tiger game. He used to love those afternoons; lemonade stirred from fresh-squeezed lemons, the thick pile of rug underneath his cheek, smelling of camphor and pine needles. How old was he then? Ten, maybe. When did Grandpa Browner die? He can't think for sure; a number of years before his father. He remembers Grandma Browner living with them for a while; then suddenly she, too, was gone. All these people who've disappeared from his life.

He's remembering so much now, at the same time that he's forgetting things he thought were carved in stone upon his memory. What keeps him from them feels like something alive—a black snake whipping around inside his head, cutting off current wherever it lands.

The names of certain household items—*toothbrush, folding chair, window shade*. Sitting there in front of him, and he can't retrieve the labels; they mock him. Sometimes a word will return—in seconds or minutes, but the search is painful. It feels like a pit in there, a mine shaft of jumbled symbols that don't make sense. The memories he can do without, but words are the tools he lives by; they are how he gets around. It terrifies him when one of them vanishes, the loss crippling him by inches.

I am remembering a day in June; the lake like a rippling blanket. The last swim of a Sunday. Knowing it was time to leave. Swim out, kick hard, lift water with your arms. Go as far as you dare, toward that promise. Then Dad would call and wave me in; I'd start back, eyes open underwater, watching the light flash below, playing over ridges of sand made by the massive press of moving water, water that holds me up, floating as if without weight.

I live on a sea of feeling, shutting down thought. It never leaves, this sense of loss; I need to reconquer it each day. All around me, like a veil; people floating by on the outside, waving, smiling; sometimes they talk, but I can't always hear them. They don't see the veil, don't know it's there. Or maybe they do.

The way to do it is to harden your heart. You begin to die the minute you enter the world; it's over the day you're born. Life is a gift, and what we call ourselves in this world is that giving point; all other lives since the beginning are merely unconscious parts of me.

When I was little and I used to stay with Grandpa and Grandma Browner, I felt safe in their affections, yet endangered by that old stone house with all of its mysteries—the closets and crannies, perfect hiding places except if you tucked yourself too carefully away until you felt you had disappeared, even from yourself. Rooms full of ancient possessions: a dark oil painting of poppies in the alcove; that angular staircase with its cuckoo clock issuing a series of squawks and creaks every quarter hour. Behind a closed door, a second set of stairs that led to an attic; the dry, earthy odor mixed with the smell of mothballs, the flower-printed garment bags, folded clothes in cardboard boxes. Innocent in daylight, but all those things sitting up there in the dark were terrifying; thrilling, too.

The boxy garage with its windowless side door, white on the outside, but through the doorway, nothing but blackness as big as the world. Next to it, the garden—a riot of orange, pink, and blue flowers, the rows marked by wooden tongue depressors labeled in Latin: Nicotiana. Sanvitallia. Impatiens. Linum. Rudbeckia. *Standing in the sunlight next to that dark envelope, peering into nothingness; looking inside your own soul.*

The truth is, most of the time I feel as if I'm already dead. But that is freeing, too; for if I am, then I can be present, here and now, without judgment or plan, without fear.

Sound of jets streaking overhead: *wallow-wallow-wallow.* Tonight he sleeps on the couch. He's restless at night, needing to walk around sometimes; Annie worries if she hears him, so he has stayed downstairs. He sits up, listening hard for a moment, his mouth dry, head pounding. In the morning she will come down and make coffee; they will sit and watch the sun come up. He'll tell her about his dreams. He imagines his conversation with her: "I had another celebrity dream. This time it was Jesus. I met him on the street corner, and he hit me up for a loan. Only, I was wearing pants without pockets. I told him I was sorry. If I'd known I'd be seeing him, I'd've worn a different outfit."

One about Jess, too; she was having a baby, in labor at the dog races, but Ryan wouldn't leave because he'd bet a hundred dollars on the last race. He kept saying, "I gotta stay till the end, I gotta stay till the end!" He takes that as a good sign about them.

The night air is moist, heavy with the promise of rain; a sliver of moon out over the water. There's a reason he's awake; it's something that he must do. Out on the jetty in the darkness the lake is howling, smashing against the rocks, flinging water high in the air. *I can do this.*

He pushes himself up gently. Not here. Not yet. Breathing deep, breathing below the pit of his stomach; no need to think about it. On and off, on and off; a warning light flashing at the edge of his eye. Strange lights, streaks of blinding white, like a flash-bulb, a curtain snapping open. It could mean the onset of another seizure. Or he could be going blind. Just in case, he looks hard at everything now—at his shadow along the railing, his reflection in the hall mirror. The flashing stops.

Standing at the bottom of the stairs, he looks up,

sensing a black door amid the flowers; that slit in the white-painted wall. Perfect surrender.

Proceed from the point of doubt. What's stopping you? Let go of this stage, trust in the next to appear; the eternal, the part that just goes on.

Annie. He should be with her. Some nights he has been too afraid, too lost even to hold her. Not tonight. But he must climb slowly. Up the steps, one by one; then left, to the bedroom. Dark in there, too, but all will be well. Don't wake the kids. Careful steps. One after the other. She's in there, waiting for him.

What works is honesty. He wants to talk to her about graduations and engagements, weddings and grandchildren, how it is to imagine himself not being here for it, not being here for his own old age. Maybe it means that he will be here somehow, just not in this form.

There is no better moment to begin preparing for this death, to stop judging it, just accept it. He always thought it would be like swimming, hoped it would be as easy as swimming. Something has happened here, something has approached. *Ready? Ready to swim out?* Has he answered already, without knowing it?

The air feels thick; it's hard walking. Yet he feels relaxed; no need to push, to try for anything. He's focused now, his vision inward; seeing to the core. The last swim of a Sunday; going in the opposite direction, out with the waves toward silence. *Do it now.* The best time, the last Sunday, no going back.

Part Two

9

August 7, 1995

Dear Mrs. Browner,

It is with sorrow that I write this letter on behalf of myself and the faculty. Those of us who will miss Keith most can share your pain, even as we know there is no way to lessen your grief. Our heartfelt sympathy goes out to you and your family.

> Sincerely,
> Ray Blount, Principal
> Redding Senior High

August 10, 1995

Dear Anne Marie,

Adele and I hoped to attend the funeral but weren't able to get time off on such short notice. And the airlines don't consider it an emergency when you are only an aunt.

I hope the flowers were fresh. At the last funeral they were so tacky and wilted I swore I'd never go with a florist I didn't know.

If there's ever anything we can do, be sure to call us. Maybe you could come for a visit when things calm down. I'm sure your mother would take the children.

> As ever,
> Aunt Glenna

August 12, 1995
Dear Mrs. Browner,

I am a sophomore at MSU. When I read about Mr. Browner in the paper I just felt so bad. He was always cracking jokes and in a good mood. I remember when he ran the projector in the horserace booth on Senior Night. He was the best English teacher I ever had. I just wanted you to know.

Yours Truly,
John Minster

August 14, 1995
Dear Anne,

I've wanted to write, but it's only since the funeral that I've been able to organize my thoughts. I'm so sorry about Keith. Ever since college, I've always thought of you as one of the lucky ones—your wonderful marriage and those beautiful, healthy children. But I guess no one's life turns out exactly as planned, and we must each play the hand we are dealt.

I've missed seeing you over the years. Maybe now we'll keep in better touch.

Fondly,
Mary Louise Whelan

August 15, 1995
Dear Anne,

I wish I knew what to say. My best teaching years were the ones I had with him. School will never be the same.

We'd like to take your boys camping with us this fall. Our kids would love it, and it would make us feel we were doing some small thing to help out. Let us know if this would work for you. Meanwhile we'll be thinking of you and your family. Wishing you all the best,

Jennifer and Alex Frame

August 17, 1995

Dear Annie,

No need to thank me. As you know, the neighborhood organizes itself. Peter and Emily returned all the dishes, but if there are loose casseroles lying around, let me know and I'll find their owners. Recipe for rotini salad enclosed; your kids seemed to like it. We're off to Nebraska, back the day before school starts.

Love,
Paula

August 20, 1995

Dear Anne Marie,

Since last November we have been praying for you. None of us can know why these things happen, only that they happen for the best. Jesus said, "Come unto me all ye that are heavy laden." He is the only one who can help, for He is the only one who can see all the way. Try to think about those dear children who are also a part of God's plan for you, and a source of your comfort. Also the fact that Keith has gone to a larger life where he is free from pain.

I'm sorry there are money problems on top of everything else; it does seem a shame that you have to suffer this, too. But I know that you will come through this with flying colors.

Affectionately,
Roger and Amelia Curtis

August 30, 1995
Annie,

This is the hardest letter I've ever had to write. What the hell can I say? He was a great guy and my best friend. I keep remembering how happy he was the day you said you'd marry him. It isn't fair; you both deserved better.

It's a fucking mystery to me why the best people get taken and those who never do a damn thing for anybody live on and on. Let me know if I can help in any way. I'd do anything for you, I hope you know that.

Your friend always,
Rich Campbell

"Annie!"

She awakes with a start, jerked to an upright position, listening intently in the darkness. The sound came from the wall at her back; she knows that voice, has known it forever—explaining a complicated set of directions to the boys; reading aloud to Julie; in darkness, in sex. It's him. He's here, somewhere, calling to her, urging her to pay attention.

Moonlight spilling a harsh, blue-white glow over everything, bright enough to illuminate shape and detail. She stares at the pile of odd items bunched on top of her dresser, willing the assemblage to translate into the familiar, while a wave of anxiety washes over her. Surely he'll summon her again. Or is he waiting for her to come to him? But why in some other room at this hour of the night?

Panicky, she climbs out of bed; hurrying, tripping over something; the pointed tip of the rocker bangs against her ankle, and the answering pain is excruciating. Sinking to the floor, she searches for it, her breath audible in her throat. He would bark his shins regularly on that chair, used to threaten to cut the rockers back—*Too bad if they're Shaker, they're too damn long!* On her knees now, rubbing at the pain with her hand. Can't be, can't be, hurts too much, unending don't want to be here let me change places. I want to change places.

As if that could save her. It won't help. Nothing will save her, nothing in this house, none of the things she loves most—all of them painstakingly searched for, refinished, scrubbed to the grain, smoothed and oiled until the wood glows. Who cares? They are useless as sticks; dead things. Staring eerily back at her in the half-light, reflecting her own emptiness.

She stands in the kitchen, talking on the telephone to Jess as they perform one of their rituals:

complaining about their mother. Behind her, the kids squabble around the table.

"I'm not upset, I'm furious. What's she doing anyway, running around, talking to people about our finances?"

"She tells Amelia everything, you know that."

"Well, I don't like how it comes around and smacks me in the face. And that religious business— was she talking to her about my emotional state?"

"That's Amelia's emotional state you're looking at."

"The next thing you know there'll be people at my door, telling me I need a more personal relationship with Jesus. Listen, today she came over with a whole pile of corduroy pants she bought for a dollar at a garage sale, every pair ratty as hell."

Jess giggles. "Don't feel bad. She brought over a bathing suit for me that looks as if it's been hanging on the back of somebody's door for five years. She can't help it, it's her ticket into heaven."

Annie shifts the receiver, anchoring it between shoulder and neck as she strips silk from the corn— one hand holding the ear firmly, the other twisting back and forth down the length of the cob. All in the wrist. Another ritual, as is this freedom to gossip and complain, knowing that it will go no further. Behind her the noise level increases.

"Pig! Leave some for dinner!"

"You're the one taking it all, hog!"

"What's going on over there?" Jess asks.

She glances over her shoulder. "I don't know. They seem to be fighting over butter."

"Harry's spreading it on his bread an inch thick!" Julie says.

Harry makes a face. "It's not your butter, boss lady, so don't sweat it."

"I wish you were in some other family," Julie says. "I wish you lived in Pakistan."

"I'd better go. They're homicidal. It's that time of day."

The air is heavy, thick; sweat is running down her sides; her shirt sticks to her back. Bending to pull the chicken from the oven, she winces as a blast of heat pours out at her. Why is she roasting a chicken on this, of all days? The kids would be happy with BLTs. She has shopped and dug weeds from the garden, changed the beds, and cleaned the entire downstairs, all on the hottest day of the year.

Six o'clock, and the evenings should be cooling off; instead they get hotter. Last weekend they closed the municipal pool. It always closes on Labor Day, they said when she called. Stupid, idiotic policy.

"Somebody set the table, please."

"It's Jim's turn. I did it yesterday."

She piles the corn onto a platter, and immediately they argue over who gets the biggest ear, the one with the most rows, the whitest kernels; it's a habit. She wishes they'd bite their nails or pick their noses instead.

"Would you boys like to go camping this weekend?"

"Who with?" Harry asks.

"Mr. and Mrs. Frame and their boys. Brett and Stu."

"Fret and Stew," Harry says scornfully.

"Mom, we hardly even know 'em." Jimmy's tone is full of reproach.

"You could get to know them, couldn't you?"

"I'll go," Julie says. "Can I, Mom?"

"Go for me," Harry says. "You like to hang by your knees and eat Nutter Butters. So do they."

She puts place mats, silver, napkins, and glassware next to the plate of chicken. A compromise; she hasn't actually set the table.

"Besides, I don't need any new friends," Harry says.

"Yeah, you got at least two," says Jimmy.

Julie snickers as Harry leans back in his chair, tipping the legs up.

"Harry, don't do that, please."

The legs come down with a bang. "I need six bucks," he says. "Materials fee for biology."

"I thought I already gave you that."

He shakes his head. "That was for something else."

"Why can't I go?" Julie asks. "Didn't they invite me?"

"No."

"Oh, yeah, that's right," said with a sneer. "I'm a *girl.*"

"What's for dessert?" Jimmy asks.

"What's your hurry? We haven't finished dinner yet."

Annie sits down at her place, wiping sweat from her forehead. She helps herself to some chicken, feeling the hard knot return to her throat. She has trouble eating these days; nothing seems to taste right.

"I gotta get goin'," Jimmy says. "I've got stuff to do."

Always in a hurry, never stopping to relax; it's always on to the next activity. He gets up to peer into the freezer.

"There's no ice cream. Nothing but a loaf of bread in here, and two cans of lemonade."

"That can't be right. I had a whole half gallon. . . ."

"Maybe a robber came in," Jimmy suggests.

She goes to look for herself, turns an accusing eye to the table.

"I didn't do it," Julie says.

Harry continues to eat, looking down at his plate.

"Was it you, Harry?"

Instantly he's out of his chair. "Why is it always me? Nobody else in this house ever does a damn thing!"

"Harry, don't leave this table. . . ."

But he stomps out the door; moments later his bike rattles by the side window. Is it her imagination, or does every meal seem to end like this? Lord, I am tired of being the family cop!

Julie's voice is smug: "Harry's such a pain."

She sits alone at the table, picking at the chicken breast. The telephone rings, and Julie rushes to answer it.

"Mom, it's for you. Paula." She hands the receiver over.

"Hi, Annie, are you eating?"

"I guess we're finished."

"Have you an extra can of tomato sauce?"

"Let me check." She rummages through the cupboard. "Sorry, no."

"How about nutmeg?"

"That I have," she says, grateful to be of some use.

"Good. I'll send Peter. Oh, wait. Aren't I lucky? Here's Harry. Hon, would you mind zipping back home to pick up some nutmeg for me?" Cheerily into the phone: "Thanks. Gotta run. Talk to you soon."

She wipes off the table, sets the nutmeg out on the counter, then turns toward the door. She doesn't want to be around for Harry's return. Julie and Jimmy have disappeared upstairs. Behind her Lucky senses that she's off for a walk, stands, wagging his tail in a hopeful way. She doesn't want his company either, or the task of curbing his friendliness. She heads up the street, away from Paula's house.

She will walk to the park, try to cool off. No

thinking. She's tired of thinking and rethinking everything that happens: Paula, who lives half a block away, who used to come over every other day, and who now sends recipes for rotini salad in the mail, chirps gaily in her ear over the phone. That's right, don't get too close, it might be catching.

The school board, with their fancy floral arrangement at the funeral, fighting to save themselves money by having his layoff termed "long-term disability," rather than "retirement."

And these kids; they'll be the death of her. Harry's temper, his silence that presses against doors and windows like a suffocating tent; Julie stuffing food in her mouth every time she turns around. She probably ate the ice cream and lied about it, but it's Harry who gets on her nerves. And Jimmy, with that dreamy uplift to the end of his sentences; the minute she hears that, she knows something's wrong, or about to go wrong.

She leans against the fence, her fingers hooked into the chain link, while, above her head, a helicoptor drones its way across the sky.

He would never put up with this if he were here. Mary Louise Whelan, daring to set up a disaster competition over this . . . thought you were one of the lucky ones . . . *Fondly, my ass*. The prospect of seeing her makes Annie want to cross her fingers in front of her, warding off a hex. And Aunt Glenna. Wondering what she could possibly do to help. *How about coming to the funeral, for starters?* The airlines don't consider it an emergency if you are only an aunt. And she has the nerve to talk about tacky. These blunders she will never forgive, no matter how long she lives.

Across the field a baseball game is in progress; the voices come crisply at her:

"Get a hit, Mark!"

"That's it, Jerry, work the batter!"

Two fathers, willing their sons to perform.

"Attaboy, Mark. Protect the plate, now!"

"Okay, Jerry, that's puttin' it in there!"

The way of the world; someone's going to be disappointed.

Behind the bleachers, a young mother stands with her daughter. The girl whines, pulling on her mother's hand.

"All right. You can go on the merry-go-round, just *don't* take off your socks and shoes!"

Wild hibiscus grows along here—giant pink-and-coral-colored trumpets with deep-yellow centers. She tried to grow it herself in the backyard, but it didn't survive the winter. Yet here, next to the ball diamond, in this driest and dustiest of corners, it flourishes year after year.

The chain link feels hot to her touch. She moves away, walking down the path, clasping her elbows with her hands. Nothing feels right anymore—cleaning house, cooking, washing clothes, paying bills—meaningless tasks put there to drive her to exhaustion, making her feel like a ghost in her own life. To walk away from all of this, following the highway as it curves out of town—what a relief! The evening would grow dark, covering her . . . and why not? What's to stop her? It makes as much sense as this life she's living. Slogging through mud, rolling a stupid boulder up a hill, dragging three kids behind her. Barely paying attention, except to chauffeur and settle arguments and say no to them. They'd do as well, maybe better, without her.

10

"These first three chapters are more or less review," says Mr. Boxer. "We'll be discussing them in class on Monday."

Harry shuffles his feet, pushing his backpack under the desk. He hates math, has hated it since third grade when they were learning multiplication tables and he would hide in the bathroom until the lesson was over. After that he hated short division, followed by long division, fractions, and percentages. Most of all he hated stupid story problems. Who cares if the two trains travel toward each other at different speeds? Who cares if they crash head-on and everybody on board dies of a heart attack?

"If anyone needs help, there'll be work sessions before first hour every Friday. All are welcome. No need to phone ahead."

Mr. Boxer grins, looking straight at him. What the hell does that mean? Glancing to his right, he sees

Rex Beers with his head down on the desk. Mr. Boxer seats them alphabetically —another weird thing. In the front row: Beers, Browner, Cindy Brubaker, Alan Coombs, Marty Cress. Nobody's done that since grade school.

Rex Beers is a transfer student from someplace in Iowa; he came into school three days late wearing a gold hoop earring in his left ear, black jeans, black high-tops without socks. His jeans are *old* old, not the fake torn stuff that everyone else buys at Ragstock.

"After we finish this, we'll be moving on to the theorems you'll need to know. . . ."

Need to know. What a joke. It's all a waste. Why learn the stuff in the first place, when you're never going to use it again? Eighth-grade math, the most useless class in your life, just like seventh. If he was the principal, he'd make sure people at least got the straight dope on that.

He looks up at the clock: eleven-ten. "A" lunch starts in five minutes. That means peeling down two flights of stairs to the end of the hall to stow his math book in his locker, getting out his lunch and social-studies book; then back to the second-floor lunch-room. A ten-minute trip, leaving fifteen to eat lunch. No food allowed in the hall, no bringing your lunch to fourth hour, no buying Cokes from the machine ahead of time. Nothing but stupid rules. School ought to be run like an office, with people going to their jobs, doing what they want the way they want to do it. They should have classes that would help in your real life, like fly-fishing or beekeeping or moviemaking. But, no. Civics. Math. Science. Social studies. Same old shit they had in grade school, except the teachers are older and the classes are longer.

"By November we'll be working up to some of the more complex algebraic formulas. . . ."

Rex Beers is sleeping now, a thread of drool trickling from the corner of his mouth. Mr. Boxer doesn't seem to notice. Or else he doesn't care. He wears the same yellow-striped tie to class every day, and has Coke-bottle glasses and a geeky little mustache. He looks exactly like what he is: Math Wizard. Somebody said he lives with his mother in a trailer park in Romeo. He seems like a nice enough guy, though, other than making you sign your life away in exchange for a math book.

He'd like to be sleeping through this class, too. Last night he was up half the night, out of bed about ten times—first for water and then to pee; checking on where he'd left his baseball mitt and his wallet; finally chasing down a lightning bug that flew into his backpack and lay on the floor of the closet, blinking on and off, until he thought he'd go nuts. He got up to carry it downstairs and put it out on the front porch and there it sat, not moving for five minutes. He thought he might have killed it. Finally it flew away, but not before his mother showed up in the doorway.

"What are you doing out here? Don't you know it's three o'clock in the morning?"

She has only two moods these days—*No Comment* or *Off the Wall*. You never know which to expect.

He shifts his body in the chair and his arms skid across the damp surface of the desk. The room is boiling. The least they could do is not let the damn building get any hotter than it is outside. Bad enough to have to be here, without sweating to death.

Meanwhile Mr. Boxer drones on while he imagines himself riding his bike across the fields and down to the river; swimming or fishing. Snitching apples from McInerney's orchard—the best apples around; hard and juicy, with purple skins. Arkansas blacks, they're called.

The bell rings and twenty-six pairs of arms push up from the desks and twenty-six bodies shuffle down the aisles, funneling toward the door. Harry grabs his backpack, getting to his feet.

A pretty blonde is tapping the teacher on the arm. "Mr. Boxer, I missed the assignment for tomorrow. . . ."

Kara Roberts. Harry remembers her from art class last year.

Rex Beers lifts his head, groaning aloud and stretching his legs. "Is that a butt-ugly mustache or what?" he says to Harry. "This class bites the big one, huh? The whole school sucks. Reminds me of the place I came from."

"Where's that?"

"Davenport. Good old Hide-A-Bed, Iowa." He snickers.

A crowd of people is trying to jam itself through the narrow doorway; Kara is suddenly at his elbow. Her lavender sweater has tiny flowers knitted into it, fastening at the neck with a heart button.

"Harry," she says. "I'm sorry about your dad. Danny Schust told me last hour."

He stares at the pink stone dangling from a gold chain around her neck. Why is she saying this to him when she barely knows him? And Danielle Schust is someone he went to grade school with, he hasn't spoken to her for three years. He gives her a curt nod, turning away, but the crowd ahead blocks his escape. He looks over his shoulder, through the wide sealed windows, at the green expanse of lawn in front of the school. Then suddenly a hole opens up and he is through the doorway, hurrying down the hall, not looking back.

Rex catches up with him. "You got 'A' lunch? I'll eat with you."

He steels himself, dreading what's coming. Why can't everybody just forget about this, ignore it, mind their own business?

"What are the lunches like here, anyway? Are they as bad as they look?"

"Worse," he says, relief coursing like warm water through his limbs. "The only thing they got worth eating is pizza. That's about once a month."

"Figures. My other school was like a junior jail," Rex says. "At least here you can wear what you want. We had a riot over that last year, just like at Attica."

"No running!" Susie Eggleston calls out from her station near the wall. She's been hall monitor at this same spot for the last two years.

"Get a life," Harry mutters, and Rex laughs.

Their lockers are in the same wing. They deposit their books, take out their lunches. On the way back they pass the library, where two ninth graders stand kissing and oblivious (Yeah, sure, let us know how it is, will you?), their fingers laced together at their sides.

A group of boys are whooping it up outside the john. One of them waves.

"Hey! Harry Browner! How's it going?"

His hand cuts a swift signal down by his side.

"Who's that dweeb?" Rex asks.

"My brother."

Rex glances back. "Looks like a farmer. He gonna have a party on his shoes and invite his pants down?"

They are outside the lunchroom now. The lockers in this wing have been freshly painted. The same puke color as last year.

"Attic-a! Attic-a!" Rex chants. "D'you know that movie? *Dog Day Afternoon?* Al Pacino?"

"Yeah, I know it."

"Great movie," Rex says. "We should rent it. *Attic-a! Attic-a!*" Marching ahead of him into the crowd, waving his brown paper bag, like a flag.

11

He stands in the bedroom doorway, watching her as she lies on her side, her head propped with a pillow, staring at the TV. The sound is turned down to a low murmur. She's watching *Oprah*.

"Mom, are you busy? I wanted to ask you something."

Her gaze shifts to his face.

"I'm going over to Rudimans' to mow the lawn. Nordstroms live next door and they asked me to do some stuff for them, too. Okay?"

"What stuff?"

"Mowing, taking in their mail, feeding their cats. They're going to Europe."

"Are you sure you'll have time, with school and hockey?"

"Yeah, I can do it."

"I don't want you spending all your time working, Jimmy."

"I gotta go to Rudimans' anyway. It's not that far."

"Well, it's your decision." Her eyes drift back to the screen.

"They're gonna pay me twenty-five a week."

"Oh, I think that's too much. Don't you?"

He shrugs. "They said it'd cost more than that to board the cats."

She smiles at him. "Okay. Rich man."

"I thought you could use it for whatever you want."

Her brows knit together. "Use what?"

"I'll just give you my passbook and you can take money out whenever you want it."

"Jimmy, that's your bike money. Anyway, I don't need it."

He hesitates. "I heard you talking the other day to Aunt Jess. . . ."

"Well, forget that." She draws him in, takes both of his hands in hers. "Listen, I say lots of things when I'm talking to Aunt Jess. Don't worry, we're not that hard up." She reaches for her sweater on the back of the chair. "What time is it?"

There's a clock sitting right next to her on the nightstand. Plus, *Oprah* comes on each day at four o'clock, she knows that. Sometimes she seems so out of it; it makes him feel he's riding an elevator going from the top to the bottom very fast.

"Four-thirty."

"Feed the dog, will you, before you go? And stop listening in on my phone conversations."

She's smiling again; a smile that used to make him feel a flush of well-being, of seeing the world as a safe place where things work out for the best. Only now he knows better: things have already worked out for the worst; there's no way for them to be fixed.

Oprah hurries up the aisle, waving her microphone, looking for somebody to talk to. Glancing toward the window, he sees the round table his father

worked on for three weeks, refinishing it in the basement; stripping, bleaching, mixing the stain himself
to get the exact color he wanted—golden oak, he
called it. The top looks just like butterscotch; he used
to sneak in here to lick the varnish sometimes, it
looked so real.

Abruptly he turns away. The house is still, except
for the TV; Julie in her room with the door closed,
probably writing in her dumb notebook that she hides
under her mattress and thinks nobody knows where it
is. Harry is never home; he spends all of his time with
Rex, either at Burger King or the mall. Not that he
gives a rat's ass.

Once after school he trailed Harry to Rex's house.
Riding on the opposite side of the street, keeping
back so they wouldn't see him. But at the corner
Harry turned and rode back at top speed, grim-faced,
hissing: "Get outta here, would you? Get your damn
nose outta my butt! Go get some friends of your
own!" What a jerk. He doesn't even want to fish anymore. Too busy hanging out with horseface Rex,
smoking cigarettes and copping hood ornaments off
cars.

He scoops dog food from the bag into a white
plastic dish—three quarters of a cup mixed with
warm water to make gravy. Lucky comes running,
almost falling over himself; his whole back end
wags. Dogs have it so easy; cats, too. Nothing but
eating and going for walks, or else curling up to sleep
in the sun. Creatures of habit, his dad would say. The

thought makes his stomach dive; an arrow of pain enters his body, and he moves his arms and legs in a scissoring motion, looking to distract himself.

He studies a blackish-green beetle on Lucky's tawny coat. Tiny, metallic looking, with a V of antennae. He watches it crawl through the fur, then lift off with stiff wings in a graceful arc, flying off.

He opens the screen and Lucky shoots out the door. Jimmy waits for him on the top step, watching him do his business at the back of the yard. Crouched on all fours, as far away from the house as possible. Every night it's the same. Then a little sideways skip and hop, tail flying, and he's back.

"I took you for a walk yesterday."

Lucky whines and dances around his feet, making a pest of himself until he yells: "No! We're not goin' anywhere, so cut it out!"

He pulls his passbook out of his back pocket. For two years he's been saving. Christmas and birthday money from both grandmas, plus work. Two hundred fifty dollars. Now with this new job he'll have enough to buy the bike by next month—a purple-and-black Trek with grip shift and hub release. He'll go to Glaspie's and put down a deposit, in case the price goes up.

A relief when she refused his money; yet he feels a stab of guilt. He wishes she wouldn't do stuff that makes him have to worry about her. Last week he woke up in the middle of the night, positive that she wasn't in the house. He had to get up to check; she was asleep, but at first he couldn't believe it, he'd been so sure. Something had waked him, had made his chest freeze up so tight that he could barely breathe.

Across the yard from him Lucky sinks to the grass, forelegs extended in a running posture, chest rising in regular rhythm. His muzzle is turning gray, gray hairs on his underbelly and all through his coat. Getting old. He'll be eleven this spring. He read somewhere that ten is old for a big dog. He'd better not go and do something stupid, like die on them.

Looking at his watch, he stands up. Five o'clock. Time to pick up the key from Mrs. Nordstrom. She heard from the Rudimans that he was very reliable, she said. If he's lucky they might even pay him part of the money in advance.

12

Thursday, 3:00 P.M.
The last day of August. I'm in my room and Mrs. Bennett is with me. The pigeons are outside my window. At first I liked them, but now I don't. They have mean red eyes like devils and when I look out all I see is pigeon poop. It is toxic to humans. Plus they never stop saying *woo-aah woo-aah* all day long. I yell at them but they just keep doing it.

This is a list of all the things I've done that I can't tell anybody about. I am putting in one a day and when I fill up this book I will buy another one.

The first thing happened a long time ago at grandma Lewis when I went over to the stone house with all the pink flowers. The lady came out and said little girl you better not touch those flowers in a very mean voice. I acted like I didn't hear her and then she started yelling who do you think you are? Whose your mother? She had on dirty tennis shoes with holes and no laces. I tried to go around her but she was blocking the sidewalk and yelling never never take things that don't belong to you. I said your not the boss of me. Then I ran into grandmas yard.

The second thing was over at grandma Browners when Delores Leonard and I were eating grapes in the alley and a lady said she was calling the police. We only ate about three but she called once before when a baseball went in her yard so I knew she would. We hid in the garage and after while I heard Dad looking for us but then a police car went by so we didn't come out. When he finely found us he hugged me so hard I couldn't breath and then he balled us out for hiding and said never do that again.

These are the first bad things I ever did when I was five. I was only going to tell one but they go together because I didn't want to visit either grandma for a long time. Now I am 9 and I don't care. It is Thursday. School starts in five days.

Friday, 11:00 A.M.
This happened when we first moved here. Emily Milne and I made frosting out of milk and XXXX

sugar and ate the whole thing. We washed out the pans and put things away so nobody would know but boy were we sick! We can never do that at Emily's because everybody gets up too early. Mom and Dad always used to sleep late on Saturdays and Sundays. Sometimes Mom would say let's go to church but Dad would say he was going to church, to Saint Mattress.

School starts in four days. I will be in fourth grade at Jefferson elementary. My teacher is Mrs. Posen. She is old but nice. At least I hope she is better than who I had in third grade. Miss Held was so lazy she used to say class let's all put our heads down about twelve times a day. She was the worst. Everyone called her Miss Hell.

Last night I dreamed about a house we lived in but it wasn't ours and Mom had a baby that was so ugly! She kept calling it her darling girl but it had a face just like a gorilla. It cried and kicked but Mom didn't see anything wrong with it. She even asked me if I wanted to hold it. Sometimes dreams are so real I wake up and feel bad for a whole day.

Saturday, 8:00 A.M.

Sometimes I get sick of school because there's too much boring stuff. I hope this year won't be so bad. Last year I faked a stomach ake so I wouldn't have to go.

I have a cat named Mrs. Bennett. Shes gray with white whiskers and a white star on her chest. Her eyes glow in the dark. At night when she runs across the yard they are like tiny flashlights coming at you. I call her B because Mrs. Bennett takes too long. Shes a good hunter. She already caught 5 mice. She eats everything, even their insides. She catches birds too but nothing good, no cardinals.

Thursday, 3:15 P.M.

School started two days ago and it is worse than I thought. Mrs. Posen talks so soft you can't hear her and before everything she says now boys and girls. Now boys and girls take out your green notebooks. Now boys and girls time for music. She says it a hundred times a day. The only good thing is Pinky Corelli sits next to me. She is fun. We drew pictures of everybody and made up names for them like BIPSY FOOF and DWEEB CLEPPENHEIMER and MR MUD X MAD. I asked her if she wanted to sleep over Friday night and she said yes. She never even had to ask her mother. I remember her from Brownies last year when she taught herself to knit with two pencils and a piece of string.

Sunday, 1:30 P.M.

I said I was going to do homework but I'm writing in here first. Pinky came over Friday and we watched a movie and Mom let us make popcorn. The movie was about a guy who is a plumber and can't read. Nobody knows it not even his girlfriend. It was good but sort of boring. Pinky wanted to make carmel corn so we did but it hardened in the pan and I stuck it out by the garage so Mom wouldn't see it. Big mouth Harry had to tell!

Pinky has pierced ears. I am going to ask for them for Christmas. She thinks Harry is cute. I told her he never says anything nice and is always blabing on people, but she doesn't care.

I forgot to write about when we were over at grandma Browners once on fourth of July. It was a big party with lots of people and I opened the bathroom door and a lady was in there going. She said oops and I laughed so hard I had to run into the bedroom and shut the door. After that every time I saw her I started laughing. Now I feel sorry. I hate it when Im in the john and somebody pushes the door open and then acts like your the one whose dumb.

Monday, 5:15 P.M.

We are starting a unit about earth and how things are not as good anymore. I know its true because I used to get the best candy at Colemans but now it all tastes the same and comes in ugly red and brown wrappers. The good humor truck came down our street every day and it had really good popsicles and creamsicles but now there's only an ugly blue bus that plays music from horror movies and all the stuff is full of air and melts before you eat it.

I was late getting home from school because I am library captain for the week and Mrs. Posen asked me to help carry books. Harry said Mom was ready to call 911. She was walking up and down in front of the house. I don't know why because it was only 20 minutes and anyway he is late almost every day.

Wednesday, 6:30 P.M.

Today after school Harry brought someone home named Rex Beers. He has black hair and blue eyes and wears an ear ring and is sooooo skinny. He told me a friend of his was rollerblading one day and hit his head and it split open like a watermelon and all his brains fell out. What a liar.

One day Mom and Dad were at the hospital and I took $1 off dad's dresser and went to Colemans and bought all penny candy. I ate some of it but there was still a lot left. I didn't want to bring it home so I put it in the mailbox. Last summer when we were up north I took 2 packs of Kit Kats from the IGA. The same day I peeked in the cabin down by the state park and saw a lady with no clothes on. These are about the worst things I can think of.

Friday, 4:08 P.M.

I found a wet spot on the carpet where Mrs. Bennett took a pee. I said come here you bad girl but she wouldn't and then she yawned and stretched out on the floor for me to scratch her stomak. I tried to clean it up but I could still smell it so I sprayed some of Mom's Chloé on it.

On TV they were talking about some homeless

people. They don't know what will happen to them when winter comes or their children. I wish they had poor farms around here where people could go and get taken care of. But I don't ever want to go there and leave my own house and all my things. For instance I'm sure you can't take pets.

Yesterday Pinky got on my bed and pulled her pants down and told me to tickle her butt so I did. She said she would do it to me, but I said no. I wrote this down but I'm going to scratch it out pretty soon. I said I was going to put down everything and this is one of the things.

Monday, 5:30 P.M.

Jimmy gets his new bike Saturday. He says I can have his old one. I like boys bikes better than girls because of the bar. You just swing your leg over it.

Today when I got home the phone was ringing so I answered it and somebody wanted Dad. I said he wasn't home right now and to call back later. I don't know why. Then I went upstairs and put a pillow over my head.

I've been keeping this book under my mattress but I know Harry is spying on it so I am going to move it. There are plenty of good places. For instance behind the bookcase or in my robe. I saw this in a movie once. No one ever looked in the womans closet and that is where the missing broch was. Some people think they have to know everything just because they are the oldest. It doesn't mean they are smarter. Your an idiot if you read this Harry but you won't because you will never find it. Ha ha!

13

"At least the house is paid for. The life insurance took care of that. We had it on a land contract. I've always felt nervous about it—that they could take it back if we missed a payment."

Annie sits holding the half-empty beer glass in one hand. Ryan, beside her on the couch, has his arm across the back of it, listening intently, as if it's the first time he's heard it.

Not like Annie to go on like this, telling the same stories over and over. It's hard to know how to react. A different Annie than Jess has known, shrugging off all attempts at consolation, then taking offense at some remark and lashing out at the guilty party.

"But he was careful. He paid every bill on time, even early. I'm not that organized. I could see myself screwing up and forgetting." She winces into her beer, as if it's medicine she's been ordered to take. "Maybe I should have invested the money. But I don't know anything about investments."

"Nothing wrong with paying off the mortgage," Ryan assures her.

Sitting across from them, Jess strokes the arm of the old flowered chair, the one that sat in the front window of her parents' house. Her mother let her have it when she moved into the apartment; it was always her favorite comfort spot.

"Besides death benefits and pension, what is there?" Ryan asks. "The health insurance transfers over, right?"

Annie shakes her head. "You have to be in the system at least eight years. He was only there six. We knew it was a risk, but the district was expanding and it was where he wanted to be." She frowns. "They gave us a ninety-day grace period on the benefits."

Jess gets up. "Why don't I go make us some coffee?"

These surprise visits of her sister's are happening more often now; she might stay twenty minutes, or two hours. She has always been good at reading Annie's moods before they surface: *Annie's worried. Annie's unhappy.* Or, *Annie's pissed.* She's reading something now, she isn't sure what.

In the kitchen she sets out sugar, milk, spoons, and cups, rummages in the cupboard for the stale scones left from the weekend. Wrapping them in a damp cloth, she sticks them in the oven.

Annie comes to the doorway. "I ran into Maggie Moran at the grocery store. She talked to me for twenty minutes about their Andersen windows and central air and their new cellular car phone. And those wonderful kids who never do anything wrong."

"The older Maggie gets, the more she looks like a cardinal," Jess says. "That little topknot and her nose like a beak."

Annie laughs. "I guess I'm jealous. All my kids do is ask me for money and fight about whose turn it is to do stuff." She opens the oven door. "Did you make scones, Jessie? I love your scones."

"Mom's recipe," she says, carrying the tray into the living room. Annie pours coffee for them.

"The money's going to be tight. I'll need to get a job fast. The union was trying to help him get long-term disability. Retirement is only three hundred a month, it won't even pay the insurance premiums. If he'd been able to get disability—even for a year—it would've made a big difference. Of course, that was before the doctors screwed up."

An awkward moment. They've heard this before, also.

"They said two years. But they knew that wasn't true. They just didn't tell us. We might have been able to do something." Her voice takes on the familiar edge. "We shouldn't have been wasting the summer. The treatment should have been more aggressive. Why wait for September to do the chemo? Why not start right away?"

"I don't think it was wasted. . . ."

"They said the chemo might not take on the first round. Dr. Evans spent an hour explaining this to me—how to tell the difference between side effects and an advance of the disease. What was the point of all that, when he already knew?"

Jess looks away, holding her coffee cup to her lips, blowing across it, watching the liquid ripple against the rim. The point, to her, is that doctors are human, fallible; but Annie won't hear of this.

"I need to use your bathroom," she says, jumping suddenly to her feet and disappearing down the hall.

Jess and Ryan look at each other. Keith should have been at home, close to the hospital, in case of an emergency. The doctors screwed up; they lied; the medications made him worse, they were the wrong medications. He was taking too much, too little—a litany of misdiagnosis, deceit, and neglect.

Eight weeks he's been gone, yet she can see it as clearly as the night it happened: the telephone call at three in the morning, the drive up north to pick up the kids. The sun coming up as they arrived; the red Sunfish propped against the porch, and a clothesline full of beach towels. Annie's stoic efficiency. Is she crying now, in the bathroom? She's only seen her cry once and that was after the funeral, when she was worn out from talking, from giving people her attention.

She comes back, and her mood has changed again. Glancing at her watch, she says, "I'd better get back. Those kids who are supposed to be such a comfort to me won't think to put themselves to bed." She gives them each a swift hug, fairly diving through the doorway. Jess follows her to the door.

"Call me tomorrow," she says as Annie hurries across the lawn to the car. She closes the door, leans against it, breathing in the colorless, benign air of her apartment.

"I didn't know the health benefits ran out after ninety days," Ryan says. "That's not good. Has she started to look for work?"

She nods. "There's not much out there. . . ." Especially for someone out of the job market some fourteen years. She tries to put the thought out of her mind. She's not used to worrying about Annie; it was always the other way around. In fact it scares her to death to be the one concerned, trying to think of solutions.

"I'm wondering if there might be a vacancy in our office," Ryan says. "It'd just be clerical, but it could work into something. I'll ask." He pulls her down beside him, slipping an arm around her shoulders. His other hand rests on her thigh.

"I've been thinking," he says. "I'd like us to look for a house instead of an apartment. Somewhere over near Lucia and Cheryl. So that she can come straight from school on the days that I have her, instead of me picking her up on the way from work. How does that sound?"

"Fine with me."

"And I think maybe we ought to start spending some time with your sister's kids. So she gets used to the idea of being part of this other family, too. D'you think Annie will go for that?"

"Sure. Of course."

She has some apprehension about these two groups coming together. From what she's seen of Cheryl, she seems a sad, sullen little girl, very different from her niece; she wonders what her tough, boisterous nephews will make of her. On several impromptu stops at her apartment, Cheryl has been distant, anxious about being late for dancing class. Then there was the trip to the zoo where she ate something that upset her stomach soon after they arrived and they had to take her home.

"She's nine, going on thirty-five," Ryan always says. "She needs to learn how to have fun."

From her experience, this is something you're born with, or you're not. But, then, what does she know? She's never been a mother before.

". . . so that, on or about December first," he is saying, "we'll be ready to make the move."

"On account of . . . ?"

"On account of the divorce being final November thirtieth."

"You got a court date?" She sits up to look at him. "And you sat there the whole night without saying a word?"

"Well, if you recall, we opened a beer and then your sister showed up." He folds her into his arms, gives her a long kiss. "Love you," he says at last against her hair. "On second thought, let's just leave everybody here and run away to Key Largo or Bimini, what say?"

The Chase brothers are out checking job sites when she arrives the next morning; Harriet, the office manager, has turned the job of opening up the office over to Jess. She fields calls from suppliers and subcontractors and enters the estimates and contracts into the computer. At ten-thirty Harriet arrives, her arms full of groceries.

"I never saw so many pregnant women in my life as there were at Farmer Jack's. Something's up. How're you, Jessie?" She unloads a bird feeder and a bag of birdseed onto her desk. "I'm going to hang this on that scrawny little tree out front. Every day I watch those poor things scratching around for food. They're starving!"

A handsome woman in her sixties, Harriet Chase has square shoulders; her white hair is cut severely short. In addition to being the brothers' aunt, she is the comptroller and chief investor of Chase Construction. Her one nephew is an architect; the other, a carpenter. When her husband died, she took over the business and now the brothers work for her.

Steve, the eldest, is brisk and intense, and when he's going over paperwork his brows knit together like an angry five-year-old's. He carries his lunch in a paper sack, eats the same food every day—tuna fish on whole wheat with a dill pickle—exactly what his kids are having. His wife takes the same lunch to her volunteer job at the junior high.

Jess and Tom, the bachelor brother, are closer in age and have more in common; he has the sharper sense of humor, and she likes the easy way he accepts his brother's opinions and advice; it reminds her of her relationship with Annie.

At noon Ryan calls from the office. "There's a clerical position opening up at the Southfield branch. Tell Annie to call Ed Poole and use my name."

"I'll call her right now. You're a sweetheart."

"Right, I'm your sweetheart. How about going out to dinner with me tonight?"

"I thought Cheryl had a swimming lesson."

"Canceled. Too much chlorine in the pool or something. Let's go to that fish place."

"Pick me up at seven. I need to wash my hair." She hangs up and dials Annie's number. No answer, and the message machine isn't on. She tries her several times, but no luck.

Tom comes in through the back door, hanging his coat on the hook. "Jessie, Al's going to call about those cedar shakes that got lost in transit. Tell him they're at the lumberyard and he can pick them up."

"Thank God," Harriet says. "Where were they?"

"Jessie found them. She made about a hundred phone calls and suddenly they showed up."

Taking up her lunch bag, Jess crumples it, tossing it toward the wastebasket. She shoots, she scores! Miming at Tom as the missile goes in.

"Peace, poise, and patience," Harriet says. "What did I tell you? Old Quaker directive. My mother used to say it all the time."

"I like the one about somebody in trouble," Tom says with a grin, "and somebody else coming along to save his ass."

14

When she comes in from her interview she finds the letter, hidden under a pile of bills; somehow she must have overlooked it when she brought in the mail. She recognizes the handwriting: it's from her mother-in-law.

Glancing up at the clock, she sees that it's nearly four; the kids aren't home from school yet. Julie is probably down at Paula's, although she and Emily seem to be on the outs these days. She should talk to Paula about this. Jimmy, off somewhere trying to make money, no doubt. Harry roaming the streets with Rex; Rex, of the strange, wild-eyed look and the earring. Anyway, wherever they are, they haven't raked the leaves. She's asked them to do it every day this week.

Opening the freezer, she searches for an idea for dinner. She should have stopped at the store on the way home, but she was too dispirited. The second interview this week. The first, with Ryan's company, had gone well, but later they called to say they had decided to go with someone with extensive computer background. And this one—she knew she wouldn't get the job the minute she walked in. It had lasted all of seven minutes, after which the man informed her he could afford to be very choosy (for a clerk/typist position at an insurance agency!) as he had two hundred applicants for the job. He planned to interview them all. It reminded her of Rich Campbell on his return from Christmas vacation at college, telling everyone he'd kissed a hundred girls on New Year's Eve.

She would have hated it there, anyway—the cramped, shabby look of the office and the ugly green draperies; an odd smell hanging over everything, like the odor of burned toast. Yet the man's obvious lack of interest had hurt. That was what was so hard about interviewing—feeling rejected over a job that you wouldn't want if you got it.

At least she's making her phone calls and getting a few appointments; most people don't even want to talk to her when they find out how long she's been out of the job market. Her volunteer service—years of running pancake suppers and school carnivals, designing fliers, chairing meetings, hiring guest speakers for PTA—seems to count for little. The interviews are all alike, conducted by people who barely look old enough to be college graduates. *Where do you hope to be in ten years? Lying on a beach somewhere in the Bahamas,* she'd like to say. *What are your special skills? I can cluck the National Anthem.* She can, having perfomed many times at family talent shows, where each was called upon to contribute a particular feat: Jimmy and his double belly-button trick; Harry balancing seven peas on the blade of a knife; Keith wiggling his ears and eating a paper napkin. The thought of it makes her smile.

She opens the letter from Nell. Why would her

mother-in-law be writing to her when she lives only a mile away? At their last dinner she held them captive with stories of William's triumphs at Boeing and his latest dealings with the Department of Defense. William, who showed up at the funeral with his girlfriend, Reba, the stage actress. What did he think it was, some kind of social event?

Nell's monogram is at the top: EJB. Eleanor Julia Browner.

October 15, 1995
My dear Anne,

I hope you are feeling better than when I saw you last. You seemed so full of sorrow that night. I trust as time goes on that you will reconcile yourself to what has happened. Seeing you brought so low is bound to be hard on the children; not to mention those dear friends and family who have been so good to you and who deserve some return for their kindness.

Our church teaches that grieving too much holds our loved ones back from the spiritual journey they must take. They need to be unencumbered in order to make their way. I hope this will help you to be strong, as it did me when I lost my Edwin. This is part of your task as the one who is to stay behind.

I will be leaving for Florida soon, as William has offered me a much-needed vacation. I will be at the Sanibel Moorings address through the holidays and will send a check in the mail for you and the children as it gets closer to Christmas.

With all best wishes,
Nell

She puts the letter down on the table. *I would like to kill her. I would like to take her neck and just wring it.*

The back door opens and Harry comes in, his dark hair combed into a cocky wave, wearing pants at least four sizes too large—all the rage now in junior high. He goes to the refrigerator, taking out a Coke.

"Mom, I decided I'm gonna quit hockey."

"Fine with me."

"Fine?"

She shrugs. "One less driving pool."

He looks at her for a long minute. Then: "Okay. Great. That's it. I quit." He goes to the cupboard. "We're out of peanut butter."

"I'm going to the store right now. And while I'm gone I'd like you to rake the leaves."

"M-o-o-o-m!" Pain and exasperation in his voice. "I'm not going out there by myself!"

"Do a third of it. Do from Andrews' over to the maple tree."

"That's almost half! Where are they anyway? They're never home when it's time to do work. Can't we do it after dinner? I'm fagged, I gotta lie down."

"When they get here, tell them to help. Tell them I said I want it done now. No excuses."

He makes another halfhearted attempt at resistance, then gives up and slams out the door. She hears him getting the rakes out of the garage. He'll be on the others the second they arrive. She shouldn't offer him that job; he gets too much pleasure out of it.

When she returns, there are three skimpy piles of leaves scattered across the lawn; the rakes lie, abandoned, in the driveway. An empty trash bag is draped over the porch steps. Harry is at the kitchen table, reading the sports page.

"Harry, I thought I said . . ."

"I'm not doing it alone. They worked about two minutes. Plus, the stupid rake's busted."

"Where are they?"

He gestures with his head, and she calls up the stairs: "Jim! Julie!"

"Mom, Harry's acting like he's the big boss, telling us where to rake and everything—"

"I don't care about that. I want you to get out there. And don't come in until I tell you to."

"He takes the best rake," Jimmy says. "Then when it breaks he comes over and grabs mine. How are we supposed to do it with only two rakes?"

"Figure it out!"

For a while they take turns coming to the door, trying to bait her: "Mom, it looks like it's gonna rain. . . . Mom, this bag's got a rip in it. . . ." But at last they leave her alone. She quickly puts together a sausage-and-potato casserole and makes a bowl of coleslaw.

Watching them through the window, she senses her separation from them as a physical force. She has less and less energy available to them, to anyone, for that matter; to all those dear friends and family expecting a return on their kindness investment, she would issue this statement: reconcile yourself; don't tell me about it.

There are two kinds of people in the world: those who tell you what you should be doing to straighten out the mess of your life, and those who want nothing to do with you. She wishes Nell were one of the latter. All those years of putting up with her pointed questions, coupled with the wide-eyed look: "You use regular bleach on the boys' shirts? Have you ever tried just plain lemon juice?" or, "I thought peach skins were poisonous, because of the spraying," or, "You always skip breakfast? Isn't it supposed to be the most important meal of the day . . . ?"

That same technique applied to every important decision they have made: the move to Royal Oak, buying the house, having too many babies too close together, sending them to the wrong Sunday schools, the wrong summer camps, the wrong pediatricians. She has been avoiding contact with her since the funeral, not wanting to say something she'd be sorry for later. Why bother? Here is a woman with whom she has absolutely nothing in common; certainly not grief.

She stands at the window, watching Mrs. Bennett play hide-and-seek, burying herself under a pile of leaves, streaking out as Julie scoops them up. She stares out at the bird feeder, empty of seeds; empty all fall. Now and then a lone chickadee stops to check.

"Something stinks over here." Harry sniffs in the far corner of the family room.

"I don't smell anything," Julie says.

Annie sets the casserole on the table as Jimmy comes in through the sliding glass door.

"Better put your bike away. It's gonna rain."

"It won't melt. Besides I wouldn't want it catching something up next to yours. Why'd you buy that femmy color anyway? *Magenta*."

"What's wrong with it?"

"Looks putrid."

"To you, maybe." Julie takes a huge portion of salad. "But then you're color-blind, so who cares what you think?"

"Pass the casserole, Harry."

He hands the dish across the table as rain pecks at the windows. Thunderstorms predicted for the next forty-eight hours.

"Rex called," Julie says, her mouth twisting around the word, making it come out "rakes." "I think he's the weirdest friend you ever had."

"You'd better change that litter once in a while, Jule," Harry says. "Cats stop using it if you don't."

"She uses the litter box!"

"Then how come it stinks so bad over in the corner?"

"Somebody talk about something pleasant, please," Annie says.

"How about hummingbirds?" Jimmy says. "We saw a movie today in biology. They feed eight times an hour. They fly forward and backward and upside down."

"Mom, this won't work," Julie says. "What if somebody's talking about something really boring?"

"Like hummingbirds," says Harry.

"Like sports," Julie says. "If they start talking about sports, I'm gonna throw up."

"May I suggest that we devote part of the conversation to positive remarks about the meal? 'Nice potatoes, nice sausage, nice broccoli, et cetera.' "

"How about if we say positive things about what we wish we were eating?" Harry asks.

"Yeah, like nice milkshakes."

"Nice brownies," says Julie.

"Nice apple pie . . ."

"Nice moo shoo pork with extra pancakes . . ."

The telephone rings, and she gets up to answer it.

"Annie? It's Rich."

"Rich . . ."

"Campbell. I've been thinking about you and I just wanted to hear your voice. See how you're doing."

She turns her back to the table. "I'm fine, Rich."

"Kids okay and everything?"

"Fine."

"Good. You got my letter?"

"Yes. Thanks."

"I'm sorry I didn't make it to the funeral. I was in the Philippines. I was so damn shocked when I heard. Dick Potter said it was a brain tumor. When did they discover it?"

"Last November."

Behind her, Harry gets up to open the sliding glass door; rain billows into the room.

"Mom, Harry's got the door wide open!"

"Trying to get rid of that pissy smell . . ."

"God. So fast. I'm sorry, I wish I'd . . . I would've liked to have talked to him—"

"Rich," Annie interrupts him. "We're just in the middle of dinner here. Maybe another time . . ."

"I'm sorry. I forgot about the time difference. Listen, I called to tell you I'll be coming to Detroit on business next month. I'd like to see you. I could drive out to your place, or we could meet somewhere, whichever's better. . . ."

She turns toward the window, where rain is streaming down the glass. She doesn't want to see Rich Campbell of the rumpled silk suits, doesn't want to see anyone from her former life. If people have a need to talk about this, let them find someone else; let them talk to each other.

"Either way is fine," she lies. "Just give me a call."

"I don't know the exact date, but we've got a case coming up for trial. I'll be doing some preliminary work there."

The kids are finished eating; they clear the table, and Harry turns on the TV.

"I'll let you know next week," Rich says. "You sound good. Are you?"

"I'm fine." *Please don't make me say it again.*

"Okay, then. Look forward to seeing you."

She hangs up, picks up her plate from the table, carries it to the sink. If her meal is interrupted, she has no desire to go back to it; the look of congealed food on the plate makes her stomach feel queasy.

She loads the dishwasher, wipes off the counters. Then, pouring herself a cup of coffee, she sits down to watch TV with the kids. It's a show she's never seen before, full of vulgar, dark humor. The characters are grotesque; she doesn't get half of the jokes. Leaning back, she watches through half-closed eyes, laughing when they laugh.

Harry goes for Cokes while Jimmy switches channels, calling out options: "Hey! *Best of Saturday Night Live.* Want to watch that, Mom?"

She shakes her head. "I guess I've seen enough."

She gets up from her chair, retrieves Nell's letter from where she has hidden it behind the flour canister. Upstairs in her bedroom, she turns on the overhead light—the hardest moment of each evening.

The room jumps into view; the bed made, everything in order. No ghosts anymore, just emptiness. She sits down at the desk and opens the letter, reads it through carefully once more, just to make sure. At last she takes pen and paper from the middle desk drawer.

Dear Nell,

I'm sorry you are worried about me. I am trying to hold things together the best way I can. As for the kids

She breaks off. This is not what she means to say at all. She tears the letter up and sits, staring down at the smooth oak desktop. She traces the grain of the wood, the dark circular stain of a glass. She read somewhere of a simple home method for taking out these stains—was it olive oil? She can't remember.

At last she begins again:

October 18
Nell,

I'm full of sorrow because I've decided I don't believe in spiritual journeys. I believe he's dead. And dead is dead. Maybe this is why I'm "grieving too much," as you say.

What I need around me are people who aren't sure they have all the answers and who don't think others lazy or ungrateful because they're not doing things just right. Those people are the hardest to find.

You mentioned your Edwin, gone some sixteen years, and William, of course. But not one word of your son who has been dead less than three months. What I am wondering is, where is your sorrow?

Anne Marie

15

"D'you know where Mom's eye stuff is?" Julie comes into his room. "I can't find it."

"What eye stuff?"

Jimmy looks up from the book he is reading: *Secrets of the Druids*. He found it on the religion shelf in the school library. It is full of unfamiliar words, passages packed with mystery, and he loves it. He is sitting at his desk in front of the window, watching the afternoon sun as it slips behind the rooftops. He will have to stop soon; the little kids will be coming out of their houses to trick-or-treat before it gets dark.

"I'm supposed to be a gypsy." Julie twirls her black skirt. "I need some red lipstick, too." Wrapped tightly around her head is a black cloth that covers her hair. Huge gold hoop earrings dangle from it. A blouse of some shiny material is tied in a knot at her waist. Her red high-heeled boots clomp over the bare floor.

"What's that you're reading?"

He closes the book. "Nothin'. Did you look in the bathroom?"

"Yeah, it's not there. What're you wearing? Not that shark outfit again, I hope."

"I'm not going out."

"How come? D'you have hockey tonight?"

He shakes his head. Friday, but the schedule is

blank. Maybe because it's Halloween, but he doubts it; they don't change the game calendar for anything.

"I'm gonna hang around here and give out the stuff."

"Sounds boring. I wish Mom would let me go over on Vinsetta with Pinky. This street's full of little kids. All you get are baby suckers and Juicy Juice boxes." She sits down on his bed and slips off her boots, rubbing the top of one bare foot with the other. "I just saw Kimberly Rosen. She's a Pilgrim again."

Jimmy snickers. Kimberly Rosen is in his class at school. She's been a Pilgrim on Halloween for the last three years. How can she still fit into that costume? Or do her parents keep buying her new ones?

"Harry went with Rex over to Huntington Woods, where the good candy is," Julie says. "She lets him do everything and she won't even let me go six blocks over to Pinky's."

Their mother calls up the stairway: "Kids, come down and have something to eat before you go."

Jimmy shoves his book into the bottom drawer of his desk, under a pile of papers. Outside the window he can see a crowd of kids moving slowly up the street.

"Honey, where's your costume?"

"I'm not going."

"Why not? Go as a hobo. Get some old pants and a T-shirt and tie a bandanna around your head—"

"I don't want to, Mom."

The doorbell rings and he grabs up a bag of Tootsie Pops, tearing it open. On the front porch are a witch, a ghost, and Little Bo-Peep. The witch's black pointed hat is tipped over her eyes and Bo-Peep's cheeks have red circles in the center. None of them has a clue, hanging back by the railing while their fathers wait for them behind the bushes.

"Say 'Trick or treat.' . . ."

"Trick or treat," they echo as he drops suckers into their bags. They scramble off the porch, the ghost tripping over his sheet. All up and down the street the porch lights are on. Mysterious figures gliding between the houses. "Trick or treat! Trick or treat!" floats through the air as if on invisible wings. The air is smoky and unsettled, full of augury. A word from the Druid book that he looked up in the dictionary. *Omen; prescience; divination.*

He goes to get the wooden salad bowl, opening bags of candy into it. He had to remind her that today was Halloween. More and more bad moments, more times ending up going wrong. Like forgetting to buy Halloween candy. Or not answering the telephone when it rings. He doesn't know what this means, but he knows it's not good.

"Don't let Mrs. Bennett out tonight." Julie comes to the door, pillowcase in hand. He has already shut the little kitten in the basement. This morning there was an article in the paper about bad things that have happened to people's cats on Halloween; he knows nobody in their neighborhood would do such cruelty; still, no sense taking chances. His new bike is locked in the garage; it's not a night to be careless.

"Are you sure you don't want to go out for a while?" she asks. "Not even up and down our street?"

"Nah."

"All right, then. I'll be upstairs, in case you change your mind."

The doorbell rings again; the porch is empty. Then, behind a tree in Andrews' yard, he catches a glimpse of Emily Milne in a pink net skirt and ballet slippers.

"I'm a ballerina! Don't I look geeky?"

He feels sorry for Peter, having such a weird sister. Lately she's been acting even more weird than usual. If she hates being a ballerina so much, why be one?

Pebbles and Sylvia are with her, Pebbles in a cowboy shirt and puffy breeches and carrying a long-handled whip. Sylvia has on a blue sleeveless T-shirt and long blue skirt, trimmed in gold. Gold bracelets on both arms. They are carrying pillowcases, too; they make the best candy bags.

Julie swaggers out onto the porch, hands on hips, her eyes looking bruised, her mouth a bright red smear.

"Emily! Sylvie! Pebs!"

Why do they always have to squeal at each other like pigs?

Julie turns to him. "Tell Mom I went. I'll be back by seven-thirty."

For another hour he is busy at the door, handing

out treats to devils, ghosts, cowboys, gorillas, nurses, princesses, Batmen, Barneys, Presidents and Mrs. Clintons. A boy rides by on a green Trek, the same model as his own. Altogether his cost two hundred and eighty-nine dollars, which left him still with $54.68 in the bank. Mr. Glaspie gave him the sale price and threw in the kickstand besides.

At seven-thirty Julie returns, looking for Pinky.

"Isn't she here yet? I came back early on purpose!"

The doorbell rings and she jumps to answer; it is a crowd of boys dressed in regular clothes.

"No costumes, no candy!" she says sternly.

They jeer at her, but she doesn't give in. It amazes him, how tough she can be. These guys look rowdy, like ninth graders; he's never seen them before.

"Cheapster!" They finally give up and start down the walk. Shutting the door, she looks into the bowl.

"Is this all that's left? Mo-o-o-o-om! We're almost out of candy and there's still kids coming!"

"We can't be." In a moment she's down the stairs, looking squarely at him. "How much did you give each one?"

"Not that much," he lies, knowing what's coming. Out of the corner of his eye he sees Julie fingering the front of her blouse. He looks down at the floor.

"What did you think you were doing? Do you have any idea how much money I spent? Thirty dollars! We haven't got that kind of money! I worry myself sick, wondering how in hell we're going to manage here," she says, "and then you throw it all away!"

Abruptly she turns and runs up the stairs, and he stands there, barely breathing, feeling his heart pounding in his chest.

The doorbell rings. *Dit-dit-da-dit-dit—da-ditt!* "Trick or treat, smell my feet, give me something good to eat, none of that crap you're passing out to everybody else!"

It is Harry, with Rex, each of them hauling a bulging pillowcase. "Hey, Jimbo! We're gonna divvy up. Wanna get in on it?"

"He doesn't like to divvy," Harry says. "Anyway, he didn't go out. Nobody to go with."

"I had plenty of people," he says. "That's not why."

"Yeah, I bet." Rex catches sight of Julie behind the door. "What's with her? She crying?"

Julie stamps her foot. "I'm not crying! There's a bunch of kids coming and we don't have any candy!"

"How come?"

"He gave it all away!"

She points her finger at him: *Jack the Ripper.*

"Why'dja do that, pimply boy?"

"Never mind," says Harry. "Here, bring that bowl over."

Together they sit on the floor and empty their sacks.

"Don't give 'em any licorice," Harry says.

"Here, you can take those butterscotch things, I hate 'em."

Quickly they sort and trade, tossing discards into the bowl. Pinky comes in, wearing a long dress with a red velvet cape; on her head is a tinfoil crown.

"I'm Princess Di," she says.

"I'm a schizocarp," says Harry.

"What's that?"

Harry and Rex laugh. Pinky moves over next to them. "I saw you up at the drugstore yesterday. I was with somebody you know."

"Yeah? Who?"

Pinky giggles. "She told me not to tell."

"Let's go." Julie is pushing Pinky toward the door, but she's in no hurry. Her eyes are puddles of metallic blue, her lipstick smeared up over her lips.

"She says she thinks you're cute." With that, she runs out the door. Harry and Rex look at each other.

"Is she squirrelly or what?"

"Hamster."

Rex crosses his eyes. They lie on the floor, tossing candies into the air, aiming for each other's mouth.

That night in bed Jimmy dreams of giving out bees, ants, wasps, worms at the door, tearing open cellophane packets and dropping the creatures into the bags. No one seems to mind; it's what they expected.

He wakes to the sound of someone crying, the wailing magnified in the darkness of the house.

"Sweetheart . . . don't be so upset. . . ."

". . . don't want us to go to the poor farm!"

Leaving his bed, he makes his way toward the voices. He stops outside the door to Julie's room.

"I don't want to move away from here . . . !"

"Hush, now, we're not moving anywhere. . . ."

Why won't she ever listen? She never listens to anything you tell her, just keeps on crying, like a big baby. He'd like to smack her when she does this, wants to say, Pay attention for once, will you? But she can't let go of a thought once it's in her head, can't get across it, either; it's like a bridge that's out.

Crouched by the door, he pulls his T-shirt down over his knees. Cold out here in the hallway. He closes his eyes, leans his head against the wall, listening to his mother's voice, gently soothing: "Honey, please don't worry . . . everything's all right."

Something different out here; usually an oblong of light cuts the floor from the window in Harry's room; tonight his door is closed. Can he hear her crying? He shivers, pulling himself into a tighter ball, stretching the T-shirt to cover his ankles.

Julie's voice is muffled, now. Probably crying into her *bankee*. She would stay in there all night if Julie wants her, but she wouldn't walk across the hall to say those same things to him.

His legs feel stiff, his ankles aching with cold. Tiptoeing back to his room he closes the door, crawls into bed. He pulls the blankets up, puts his pillow over his head, to make a cave. Lying on his side, he fingers the hard ridge of flesh under his chin where a skate blade creased it the year he started hockey. He was six. He can still remember the blurring pain, the snap of his jaws coming together. He had bitten his tongue, and it seemed much the worse injury, the pain with him every second, eating or talking.

The cut on his chin had needed seven stitches; the scar will never go away. It feels the way it always has—firm and familiar; like the pillow over his head, it provides its own kind of comfort.

16

On her way out, Annie leaves the back door unlocked. Harry has forgotten his key; she saw it in his room when she dropped off the folded laundry. She could be back from the interview before they get home, but she's never sure. Luckily it's her week off for the driving pool. When Harry was playing hockey, there weren't any "off" weeks.

Beckmann's, a chain of lumberyards recently renamed "home-improvement centers," is looking for someone for the branch store near their house. Handyman Haven, Keith used to call it; every Saturday morning was spent there when he was working on the deck. Her mind veers from this; she hates thinking about the deck with its graceful, curved floor plan (he spent hours plotting the contours on paper, trimming boards to meet the specifications), ending up as a pile of lumber outside the family-room door. She's going to get rid of it soon.

Catching a glimpse of herself in the rearview mirror, she sees her lips pressed together in a nervous frown. The trick is to try for a feeling of ease and self-confidence. But it doesn't always work; too many turndowns in a row, too many people telling her she's not needed. Thanks, anyway. Without saying it, they let her know she's over the hill. At thirty-six! Terrifying.

She turns into the parking lot, where the huge red *B* of the Beckmann logo looms over the gold cement-block building. Walking past the checkout counters, she approaches the back of the store, to what looks like a huge playpen on stilts. She climbs the stairway to the receptionist's desk.

"Mrs. Cole's office is back there."

The girl points to a room at the back. With a sinking feeling Annie sees that all of the women on the floor are teenagers. It doesn't bode well.

There are two offices along the back wall; in the first one, a man sits talking on the phone. The door to the second is open and the woman at the desk waves her inside. Annie gives a sigh of relief; at least this person is over twenty.

She sits in the chair while the woman goes through the stack of letters in front of her, marking each one with a red pencil. At last she looks up, says briskly, "I'm Denise Cole. I haven't had much time to go through your application, so refresh my memory. You do have accounting experience?"

"Yes," Annie says. "I worked in the administration

office at the University of Michigan. When I was in college."

"Nothing more recent than that?"

"At Plymouth Church, in Royal Oak. I did all of their bookkeeping and accounts payable. . . ."

"And I assume you've had computer training? Excel? Claris Works?"

She nods. The telephone rings and the woman picks it up. She listens a moment, then says stiffly, "So I guess I'm the complaint department today." A long pause. Then she laughs—a fake, tinkling chuckle that grates on Annie's nerves. She tries not to listen as she studies the neat, unadorned office; no pictures, no personal items on display.

Denise Cole, a trim, pretty woman in her late thirties, has thin lips and a tiny rosebud mouth. Her gray tweed suit looks expensive; her makeup is perfectly applied—pale pink lipstick, lilac eye shadow and liner. She hangs up the phone, quickly scans Annie's application, then looks up to give her a cool smile.

"It says here that you went to U of M, but you don't mention what degree you earned."

"I left in my junior year to get married."

" 'Single parent,' it says here. So you're divorced?"

"I'm a widow." The first time she's had to say this word. The first time she's used it about herself. All of those terms—"widow's weeds," "widowhood," "black widow"—ugly and harsh sounding to her ears.

"And who takes care of your children, then?"

"I do. That is, when they aren't in school." Aren't these illegal questions? She doesn't think any of them is allowed, but she isn't sure enough of her ground, doesn't want to appear antagonistic. The word has thrown her. She squeezes the sides of her purse together, trying for a smile; it feels pasted on her face.

Denise Cole looks up from the application. "I'm afraid we're looking for someone who's had more experience than this," she says. "We're the branch that sets employment standards for the other offices, you know. It's important that we hire only qualified people."

Annie leans forward. "But the job doesn't sound all that difficult. At least, not from your ad. And I've done exactly this kind of work. I managed the entire financial department of the church. It's a very large church—"

"I'm talking about experience in a real office."

"This *was* a real office."

She tries to say it gently so as not to sound as if she's talking down to someone, but Denise Cole's eyes narrow, and she picks up the application, moves it aside.

"Listen, I don't know how serious you are about getting back into the job market, but I suggest that if you are, you think about going back to school and taking some courses."

"Mrs. Cole, I'm very serious. I'd like to show you what I can do. . . ."

But the interview is over. "The problem is, you're just not what we're looking for. And I need someone to whom I can delegate responsibility." She gestures with an arm to include the outer reaches of the office. "With these high-school girls, that's just how it is. But I appreciate your coming in." Again, the dismissive smile.

Annie gets to her feet. Her knees are trembling. She feels the color pulsing in her cheeks. She will not thank this woman. For what? For making her say "widow" out loud? Turning, she walks out of the office. *You are a bitch,* she thinks. *And I wouldn't work here to save my soul.*

Her fury carries her to the bottom of the steps. Business has picked up since she arrived—mothers and kids piling into cars to do some after-school shopping. She walks briskly, but without direction. *It doesn't matter. Nobody knows where you've been. It's just an interview. Be glad they're not all this bad. Chalk it up to an evil day.*

Finding herself in the toy department, she stares blindly at a shelf of board games and puzzles. She spots the card game Jimmy wanted for his birthday: Rook. Picking it up, she carries it to the checkout. So the trip won't be a total loss.

•   •   •

Stopping at the bakery, she orders Jimmy's birthday cake: yellow, with caramel icing. She always bakes their cakes, but today she decides to splurge; she picks up bread sticks, too, and a half-dozen jelly doughnuts for dessert.

Julie is waiting for her when she gets home. Annie puts a pot of water on to boil, takes the leftover spaghetti sauce from the refrigerator.

"Where are the boys?"

Jimmy's at hockey practice and Harry's upstairs. "Where were you? I needed a ride home 'cause I missed the bus."

"I was at an interview."

"Where?"

"At Beckmann's."

"Did you get the job?"

"No, I didn't. How did you get home?"

"I walked." She gives a long sigh. "It was raining and my new suede shoes got all wet."

"Dry them out by the heater," Annie says. "I'll see if I can fix them later."

"You can't. They're just wrecked."

The telephone rings. Perfect timing. A dinnertime call to solicit money, asking if she'll join Friends of the Library or buy a ticket to the Shrine Circus. She picks it up.

"Mrs. Browner? This is George Rice. The manager of the Home Center on Telegraph Road. I understand you had an interview with us this afternoon. I'd like you to come in for a follow-up. Could you make it in tomorrow morning?"

Harry clatters down the stairs, takes a bread stick from the bag. Julie hisses: "Mom, tell him he has to wait!"

"But I don't understand," she says into the receiver. "Mrs. Cole said . . ."

"Mrs. Cole does the preliminary screening," Rice says. "Tomorrow you'll be interviewing with me. Would nine o'clock be convenient?"

"Yes. Fine."

"Good. I'll see you then."

She hangs up the phone and turns around. They are standing there, looking at her.

"Who was that?" Harry asks.

"The manager of the Beckmann's store," she says. "He asked me to come in for a second interview."

Julie gives her a smile. "You'll get it this time, Mom," she says.

She doesn't know what to answer. She had no idea they were even keeping track.

17

"C'mon, pimply boy. We'll only be gone an hour."

"Where you going, anyway?"

Rex grins. "Off to beat up a couple of old ladies to get their money and then go to Burger King. Pretty scary, huh?"

"I can't. I gotta do my book report."

"Do it when you get back." He turns to Harry, sprawled on the couch, watching *The Brady Bunch*. "Hey, what's with your brother? He antisocial or what?"

Harry's eyes are on the TV. He's seen every *Brady Bunch* rerun ten times, laughs at the same things each day—Greg Brady's bell-bottoms and the fact that none of the guys knows how to throw a football.

Rex strums on his leg like it's a guitar, hopping around in time to the music: ". . . that's the way we all beca-a-ame the Brady Bunch . . . !" swinging his arm in a big finish. Jimmy winces as he barely misses the lamp. He's such a jerk. Why go anywhere with these guys? Every day he watches them as they hunker around the tables at "A" lunch, acting like king shit on Turd Island.

"Okay, I'll go," he says.

"Don't do us any favors," says Harry.

Outside, the afternoon air smells damp; a rainstorm on the way. He takes off on his new bike, pedaling easily. The first day he got it he rode around, trying it out, making sure everything worked right. Then he rode over to Rex's house, a wreck of a place with peeling paint and a saggy front porch, old tires and shingles lying around the front yard. In the driveway a man was bent over a pickup truck; for a minute he thought it was Mr. Petrovich, his hockey coach, but on second glance he saw the man was younger and heavier, with a blond mustache and tattoos all over his arms. Rex's sister Geneva's boyfriend. Another jerk-off.

"You know that house where the kid got killed last year?" Rex says. "We went by at three in the morning and there was his mom sittin' on the front porch, wrapped up in a fur coat, waitin' for him to come home."

"Bull-dukey," Harry says. "She's got asthma, that's why she's out there."

"You ever hear of anybody doin' that? Just check out the cars that drive down her street at night."

"Yeah, like they drive down the street where the little kid got dragged by a truck and you hear her arm knockin' on your car door."

"Hey, that was in the paper!"

"Golly gee whiz, then it must be true!" Harry bucks his teeth in a goofy grin, but Rex refuses to be insulted.

"We better get goin'. They're not gonna wait all day for us."

They meet Mike Cousineau and Andy Cassidy at Lakeside and Rebecca Street. Cousineau's nose has a ragged scar from bridge to tip; his hair looks like a bundle of copper wires. Andy's front teeth stick straight out, like some guy out of *Weekly World News*.

They take off for the bridge; Rex is the first one across, shouting: "*The Yellow River,* by I. P. Daily!"

Harry follows, crying, "*Cat's Revenge,* by Claude Balls!"

"*Loose Stools,* by Diarrhea Brown!"

"*Lick My Dick,* by Hugh Jorgan!"

They collapse, laughing, on the other side. Jimmy drops in the grass beside a sign reading NO SWIMMING DANGEROUS CURRENT. They have gone in swimming here every summer, and nobody's ever bothered them or told them not to.

Steve Laidlaw comes down the path. "Where you guys been, anyway? I'm starving."

"Nice bike," Cassidy says as they mount up. "How many speeds?"

"Twenty-one."

"You use 'em all?"

"Nah."

As a matter of fact he does, has read the owner's manual three times and memorized the gearshift positions, but he'd never tell anybody that, it sounds lame.

"I'm gettin' a bike," Cassidy says. "Fuji. They cost six hundred, new."

They ride to the frontage road, where a community parking lot stretches in front of a row of fast-food places. Harry props his bike next to Burger King.

The bike rack is nearly full; there's room for only two more, down at the end. Jimmy parks his in the last slot, next to Cassidy's beat-up ten-speed.

"What're you doin'? Nobody locks their bikes."

"Yeah, who'd take yours, Cassidy?" Rex jeers. "The old tankmobile."

"Those locks are no good anyway," Cassidy tells him. "They cut right through 'em with bolt cutters."

Jimmy slips the key into his pocket. No need to lock it; he can see his bike from the window. Standing in line, he can just make out the purple top tube and seat post, black saddle, silver handlebars, rising slightly above the rest.

Behind him, Rex tells a story of the teacher who caught him smoking in the john. ". . . I'm infringing on other people's rights, he says. So I gotta recite the Bill of Rights in class! I go, 'All ten amendments?' 'All ten and the thirteenth, fourteenth, fifteenth, and nineteenth, about civil liberties,' he says. You got any idea how much memorizing that is?"

"Bummer . . ." Laidlaw croons to the tune of "Feelings," ". . . what a fuckin' bummer . . ."

"You gonna do it?"

Rex laughs. "In the guy's dreams."

"I need a buck," Cassidy says.

"You always need a buck," says Laidlaw. "Pay me back the ten you already borrowed."

"How about you, Jimbo? Got a buck I can borrow?"

Now they are looking at him. He hesitates; then, reaching into his back pocket for his wallet, he hands over a dollar bill.

"Thanks."

He glances again toward the windows, as if to reassure himself. Lending money isn't his idea of fun; it makes him nervous. Next to him Cassidy drums on his thighs, making the sound of galloping horses. His voice is loud, and people keep looking over.

"My dog got into a porcupine down by the creek. She got a face full. My dad had to pull 'em out with tweezers. Then she opened up her mouth and there was about a thousand of 'em, so we took her to the vet and he put her to sleep."

"For good?" Cousineau asks.

"No, pigeon wit, for the operation. She was fine as soon as she woke up. Jumpin' all around like nothin' happened."

"That dog is the dumbest mutt I ever saw," says Laidlaw.

"Dumber'n yours? A moron Saint Bernard?"

He looks around. No one at any of the other tables that he knows. They must all be from St. Ignatius, the Catholic school downtown. Beyond the windows, gray stripes of sky bubble and reshape themselves as he watches; above them, a patch of brilliant white, shot with sunlight; the darker, ominous layer closes quickly in from the right.

He should go to Nordstroms', make sure the windows are closed. He knows they are, but what if one should blow open? He'd be responsible. The trees are whipping themselves into a frenzy as Cassidy looks over at him. "Hey, lend me another buck, will ya? I'm gonna get a burger."

"I don't have any," he mumbles, knowing exactly

what he has—nine bills and some change—knowing that Cassidy knows, too; he saw him looking. Is this why he was invited, then? Some joke. He stares accusingly across the table at Harry, who won't meet his eyes. *Okay, then, fuck you.*

"I gotta get goin'," he says, getting up. "Tell Mom I went over to Nordstroms'."

The sky has changed shape again by the time he gets outside; it looks like a huge upside-down egg carton lying above the trees. It will be raining hard soon. He sees his purple bike, parked over near the door. But, no, that can't be his; it's down at the end, next to Cassidy's. He looks; looks again at the vacant slot beside the ten-speed.

A glancing blow to the heart. It was there a second ago; he just looked. Staring again at the section of rack nearest the door. Maybe this is his bike, after all; somebody moved it to make room for theirs. A Mitsubishi, with thin, gold stripes on the fenders; it's older, scuffed up, the reflector light broken. He looks again at the slot near the end, where his Trek was parked; if he focuses his eyes right, it will be there. Only it isn't. It's gone.

A roll of panic starting at the pit of his stomach; he fights it. Somebody must have borrowed it, to take it for a trial spin. They'll be back with it in a minute. He looks to the side, where Harry's bike still leans against the building.

"What're you doin'?" Laidlaw comes out the door. "Thought you had to go somewhere."

He can't answer. Waves of heat rush up into his face. He turns his head, looking around, his throat dry.

" 'S matter?"

They are all gathered about him now; Harry is at his side. "Where's your bike?"

"Somebody borrowed it. They'll be back."

"Who? Who borrowed it? Somebody you know?"

He shakes his head, barely hearing the questions as Cousineau laughs his nervous laugh.

"Shoulda locked it up."

"Call the police," says Rex, inclining his head toward the window of the restaurant. "You can call from in there."

Again he shakes his head. "He'll come back. We just gotta wait."

The circle widens then. Rex kicks at the curb, and Cassidy grabs his bike, wheeling off.

"I gotta go. See you guys later."

After a moment Cousineau and Laidlaw take off, too; Harry and Rex stand at the curb, looking down the road. The sky is dull now; an even gray. No more egg cartons. It looks as if the storm has passed over. He scans the horizon, stares down the frontage road, waiting.

"Somebody broke into our house once," Rex says. "In the middle of the night, guy comes charging in, yelling, 'Some guys are after me! Don't you see 'em? See the guns? They're tryin' to kill me.' "

"Where'd he come from?" Harry asks.

Rex shrugs. "Dunno. We just woke up and there he was, stomping around. Cops came and took him away. Geez, was he a nut."

They fall silent again, and Harry reaches down to pull up a handful of grass. At last he says, "Jim. We gotta go. Mom's gonna be worried."

"I'm gonna wait awhile," he says. "You guys can go. He won't know where I live. . . ."

"Nobody's comin', man. C'mon, I'll ride you."

A blast of pure, fathomless grief overwhelms him, not about anything he can name. He staggers under its weight, turns blindly toward it, staring into a darkness empty of mercy. He can feel the blood rushing to his face.

He stumbles to Harry's bike, gets on, scraping his shin against the chain guard. Focusing on that pain, he tries to make himself hard and white, like the bone beneath the skin.

His mother turns from the stove, knowing before they tell her that something is wrong. She looks from him to Harry, her eyes dark with anger.

"How could that happen? Did you lock it?"

He shakes his head, going to sit at the kitchen table. His knees feel suddenly weak.

"We went up to Burger King. . . ."

Tears well up in his throat. It is too big for it to matter now that she is angry at him. Gone. His beautiful bike, bought with two years of work. Gone for good. All because he was careless, prideful. Wanting to show it off, to show off his unconcern. Then, what does he do but stand there by the curb and wait for it to come back to him? Stupid!

"We should call and report it," Harry is saying. "They can trace the serial number—"

"That's brilliant, now it's too late!" His mother's voice is high and angry as she turns on him. "This is your fault! You and your smart friends who think they know it all! Jim isn't like that! You know he would have locked it if he hadn't been with you!"

To his amazement, Harry bows before this attack, ducking his head as from a blow. Without a word he leaves to go up the stairs. Their mother slams the spoon down.

"I knew something like this was going to happen!"

He stands up. "So what? It's just a stupid bike. I bought it with my own money. So I'll earn some more and buy another one, big fuckin' deal!" He refuses to look at her. At last she turns away, toward the stove.

"All right," she says softly. "Let's not talk about it."

He leaves the kitchen. At the top of the stairs he pauses, looking toward Harry's door, and for the second time this week it is closed to him.

18

"This is stupid," Harry says as he opens the door. "As if we need a baby-sitter."

"Nice to see you, too." Ryan takes a fake slap at his head.

"We're not here to baby-sit," says Jess. "We're here to beat the pants off you at Scrabble. Where's your mother?"

"Upstairs. Getting dressed. What're we having for dinner?"

"Hamburgers, baked beans, and Ripple chips. Back by popular demand." She makes her way out to the kitchen.

"Aunt Jess, d'you have any books about training cats?" Julie lifts her head over the back of the family-room couch. "Mrs. Bennett's been doing weird things lately."

"Weird like what?"

"Like chewing on socks. And peeing in corners."

"Peeing in corners sounds like a bad one."

"Plus she won't come when I call her."

"I don't think they do that, Jule. Get me an onion, will you? And empty the beans into the blue casserole dish."

Julie gets up from the couch and comes out to the kitchen. "I wish I had your color hair," she says. "D'you think I ever could?"

"Probably. But why? Your hair's gorgeous."

"I'm sick of it. It's boring. I want to dye it. Or else cut it all off."

Jess searches the silverware drawer for her favorite knife while Ryan sits down at the table to make the ground beef into patties. He has a routine of precisely calibrated hand motions that he claims makes for tastier, tender burgers.

"Pinky's cat comes when she calls," Julie says. "He's a Siamese. And I know Mrs. Bennett is as smart as Nigel."

"Pinky, the screamer?" Jess asks.

Julie giggles. "I forgot I told you that. Anyway, she doesn't do that so much anymore."

"She *would* name her cat something stupid like Nigel," says Harry, who has taken her place on the couch.

Julie opens the jar of baked beans. "Are we having game night tonight? Let's!"

"I hate game night," he grumbles.

"Oh, come on," Julie says. "We'll play whatever you want, O Boss Man of Our Lives."

"All right, then. Anything but Scrabble."

"Put a little mayonnaise in a dish," Jess says to Harry. "In case somebody might want a California burger."

"Can't we just set the jar on the table?"

"No, we can't."

The sliding door opens and Jimmy comes in, blowing on his fingers.

"Whew! Getting cold out there!"

Such a handsome kid, with his fair skin and blond hair, falling into ringlets when he sweats. The prettiest baby of them all. Jess remembers holding him as a baby, thinking if she could have something that perfect, she'd never ask for another thing in this world.

Mrs. Bennett sidles in behind him and Julie grabs her up, nuzzling her. "Bad kitty cat, you've been gone all day!" She looks up. "Aunt Jess, what do you think of Rex?"

"What do I think? I think he's the nicest Rex I know, except for a German shepherd that lives in my building."

Harry laughs.

"I think his shoes stink," Julie says.

Harry and Jim are tossing the Nerf basketball back and forth, leaping and twisting, slam-dunking into a hoop over the door frame. Such physical kids they are, with arms and legs always going.

"Will you talk to Mom about me getting my ears pierced?" Julie asks. "She always says okay, but every time she has some excuse."

She finishes slicing onions and tomatoes as Julie leans over the back of the chair, practicing her ballet positions.

"Everybody's got pierced ears. Pinky even has two in each ear. She wears little rubies in the top one."

The front doorbell rings, and Julie rushes to answer it. Jess arranges the onions and tomatoes on a plate, sets it on the table. She watches Jimmy and Harry wrestle underneath the hoop. Harry calls the baskets before they happen, raising a triumphant fist whenever he scores.

Julie returns with a tall, dark-haired man wearing beige slacks and a brown cashmere pullover. His brown loafers are meticulously shined, and his leather jacket breaks neatly at his waist.

"Here's a familiar face. Jess, am I right?"

"Nice to see you again, Rich."

Ryan wipes his hands on a dish towel and they introduce themselves. Then, turning to the taller of the boys, Rich says, "And this must be Harry, the famous hockey player."

"Harry the dropout," her nephew answers. It's one of the things she loves about him; he's not a liar and he won't fake it. Why did he quit hockey? Annie's answer was vague and unsatisfying: "He's as stubborn as Dad. You can't tell him anything." Did she try to tell him something? If so, what? She doesn't see them communicating much at all these days.

Jess offers Rich her best smile. "Annie tells me you're in town on something special."

"Not all that special. Just a tax court case. It'll drag on, I'm afraid." He indicates the basketball hoop. "I used to play B-ball with your dad," he says to the boys. "Back in college. Not on the big team, of course. Intramural. But it was lots of fun."

Dead silence. She feels a rush of sympathy for this man, who, after all, is here to do a kindness. It can't be that easy for him, either. She looks out the window into the darkness; winter is coming, Thanksgiving only two weeks away. Snow is predicted for tonight.

"I'll just run upstairs," she says, "and see how things are going."

She leans her head inside the bathroom, where Annie stands in her slip; she's staring at her reflection in the glass. Her face is pale, eyes dark with fatigue. Ever since she started work she's been wearing this same tight, strained expression.

"Rich is here."

Her sister's eyes catch hers in the mirror. "I'm too tired to go out for dinner."

"It's a beautiful night. . . ."

"I'll just ask him to stay and have a drink with us." She knows that look, has seen it before on bad days; a stubbornness that will tolerate no pushing.

"Harry could ride to the store for more ground beef. . . ."

"Harry's about to drive me nuts," Annie says. "He's prowling around the house at all hours. Then, when I ask him about it, it's like I'm sticking needles under his fingernails." She takes a step away from the mirror, picks up her brush, and begins pulling it vigorously through her hair. "Julie told Mother about him smoking out on the roof, so of course she has to call me up and give me hell about that."

"Mom's just being a grandma. . . ."

"She's driving me nuts, too," Annie says. "Bringing six-month-old bread over here from her basement freezer. I don't want her stale bread, I'd rather go out and buy a fresh loaf every day, because it *tastes* better and *looks* better and makes me *feel* better. . . ." Her voice grim, each word accented by fierce strokes of the hairbrush: "I wish she'd realize that newspaper coupons and stale bread aren't going to save us."

"You don't need saving," Jess says. "You're doing great. You just got a job, remember?"

"As a bookkeeper. Making eight dollars an hour. We can't live on eight dollars an hour, we can't even pay the bills." Her voice drops to a whisper. "Oh, shit, what am I going to do? I don't know what to do. . . ."

Standing in dumb silence, Jess feels her own heart open into pain. Annie puts down the brush, presses her hands together in front of her face. This is what she has seen coming, hasn't wanted to see. Three months. Thirteen weeks, to be exact. How could she have thought things were getting better? They are worse, much worse than anyone knows.

When Annie comes down she's wearing her long gray sweater over a gray tweed skirt; her hair falls to her shoulders, framing her face. Calm and clear-eyed. She has seen this look, too; Annie toughing it out. She'll pull it off, without a doubt. She once beat up a kid who tried to pull down her underpants on the way home from school. "He was bugging me, so I socked him," was what she told the boy's mother when she called their house to complain.

Rich crosses the room to give her a hug.

"So. You met my kids?"

He nods. "They're wonderful, just like you said."

In spite of herself, Jess winces. What will the "wonderful" kids say about this? She wouldn't put anything past them. But Annie is slipping into her coat now, ignoring the remark. "You guys behave and be sure and help with the dishes." And to Jess and Ryan: "Don't let them run over you."

As soon as they leave, Harry turns to Jim: "Where's my three bucks?"

"What three bucks?"

"Come on. You said you'd pay me back."

"I don't have it yet." Jimmy heads for the stairway.

"You probably put it in that dumb bank account of yours!" Harry calls to his retreating back, then turns his scowl on her. "You don't need to think he's so perfect, Aunt Jess."

"Did I say I think he's perfect?"

"Ha! You never want to hear anything bad about him!"

He stomps into the family room, picks up the remote, and turns the volume up on *Star Trek: The Next Generation.*

"Why couldn't they stay here for dinner?" Julie asks. "There's plenty of food."

"Be glad they didn't," Harry says darkly. "He's not gonna stick around and play dumb games with you."

So that's what all this temper is about. And the insecurity goes both ways: they haven't needed a baby-sitter for two years, yet suddenly Annie can't leave them alone to go anywhere.

"What did you think of him?" Julie asks. "He reminded me of a collie. All dressed in brown. Long hair. Pointy ears."

"I didn't notice. Were they pointed?"

For answer, Julie smiles, extending two fingers to form the apex of a triangle.

"I thought his eyes looked real piggy," Jimmy says.

"Pointy ears, piggy eyes," Ryan says. "How come we're being so hard on him?"

"We're not. We're just talking about what he looks like. Anyway, Aunt Jess didn't like him either. I saw her when he said that about Mom's wonderful children."

Jess laughs. "Oh, well, you *are* wonderful. There's just something sort of weird about saying it to your faces."

"Yeah, phony," says Harry.

"I saw a movie on TV," Julie says. "About fighter pilots. It was over the English Channel, only it was really Lake Huron. They said so in the credits. Can I have a snack, Aunt Jess?"

"Honey, we're going to have dinner."

"I miss Lake Huron," Julie says. "Mom says we're never going there again."

"Oh, no, I'm sure she didn't mean . . ."

"Yes, she did. She was looking straight at me."

"So, we'll go somewhere else," Harry says. "Big

deal." He looks up from the couch. "Will you light somewhere? You're making me dizzy."

"I know what we could do tonight," Jimmy says, after dinner. "We could put up the outside Christmas lights. Mom said she didn't want to because it was too much work."

"That's a great idea," Julie says, and the two of them disappear into the basement, returning in a few minutes lugging a large, cardboard carton. Together they lift out strings of lights and spread them across the floor. Julie takes one to an outlet and plugs it in.

"This one works!"

"Good. Hang it over the back of the chair."

"We'll need a stepladder," Harry says. "It's out in the garage. I'll go get it."

Ryan looks at Jess. "What d'you think about this?"

She shrugs. "Okay by me."

Ryan takes them up to the drugstore for replacement bulbs while Jess hunts up the heavy-duty extension cord that hangs on a hook in the basement.

"We always do those evergreens with the big lights," Julie says. "And the twinklers go on the maple tree. . . ."

"What about the 'Noel' sign?"

"On the porch . . ."

"Get your coats on, you guys. You don't want to catch colds," says Jess.

"You catch colds from people," Jimmy says. "Not from the outside temperature."

"Oh, right. I forgot."

Harry stretches the extension cord across the lawn to the maple tree. While Ryan holds the ladder for them the boys take turns stringing the lights. Jess and Julie stand on the porch, giving orders.

"Squint your eyes," says Jimmy. "That's how you can tell if they're even."

They go inside to view their handiwork, and Jess makes cocoa, getting down the Christmas mugs from the back of the cupboard while Mrs. Bennett watches from the counter. She knows she's not supposed to be there, keeps looking warily over her shoulder.

"I've been hearing bad things about you," Jess says. The cat stares back at her in haughty disdain. *I'm not afraid of you, missy.*

They sit in the living room with the lights out, watching the spots of color—red, blue, green, and white—winking in the falling snow.

"It looks like fairyland," Julie says. "I love it when everybody's house on the street is all lit up."

"I love being first," Harry says. Ever the competitor.

"D'you guys want to know a trick about Trivial Pursuit?" Julie muses dreamily. "Whenever you have the answer to somebody's question, but you don't want them to guess it, you just think, 'Sta-Puf marshmallows.' "

"What?"

"Then they can't get in your head and read your mind."

Hoots and jeers from the boys.

"Have people been doing that lately?" Ryan asks.

"Emily Milne told me about it, and it works. That's how I won last time."

"You didn't win," Jimmy says mildly. "I did. I creamed you."

"When was that?" Ryan asks.

"Last summer. When we played with Dad."

Silence again; a tidal wave of it, the endless import of his not being alive. Is this the way it will always be? Too painful, too hard. How are they all to deal with it? No wonder people take refuge in denial.

"Sta-Puf marshmallows," Julie says at last.

"It's gorgeous! How did you get it done so fast?" Annie returns at ten, her face flushed, eyes luminous. Jess is relieved; she wasn't sure what her response would be. Annie had said once she wasn't having Christmas this year, but that was weeks ago, just after the funeral.

"We should go out and make a snowman on the lawn," Annie says. "It's great packing. . . ."

"Tomorrow's a working day for me," Rich says. "Gotta be in court bright and early Monday." He gets up from the couch, and Annie walks him to the door, stands outside with him for several minutes. When she returns, the kids are watching her.

"Mom, you know we don't make snowmen," Jimmy says.

"Oh? Since when?"

"Since about five years ago."

Jess laughs. "They're jaded. What can I tell you? Did you have a good time?"

"Yes. But I'm tired." She yawns, ruffling her hair, relaxed, almost happy. It's a first. "He hasn't changed, though. Same old Rich, kind of dopey and full of himself. Only now I guess it's part of his charm."

Help comes in unlikely ways. One of their mother's famous sayings. She and Jess have spent many hours talking about How to Help Annie. Making suggestions and rejecting them. "She should take a trip," her mother says. "To some new place with new scenery, no memories attached." To which Jess counters, "Alone with nothing familiar to anchor yourself to? No, what she should do is join a grief counseling group, start talking about this, making some headway." At which point, Rose Lewis throws up her hands. "Grief group! Sounds like an invitation to suffer!"

On the way to her place, Ryan puts his arm around her.

"He didn't seem exactly Keith's type. It surprises me they were best friends."

"The kids were nervous," she says. "As if they already knew someday there could be a guy stepping into the picture."

Ryan shakes his head. "Not for Annie."

"Why do you say that?"

"Just a feeling I have. I can't explain it."

Jess opens the window slightly, feeling clean cold air against her skin. She takes his hand, squeezes it tightly.

"I hope you're wrong about that."

"Me, too. But I don't think so."

19

A gloomy Monday morning and already things are going badly. They've been fighting since the alarm went off, keeping her posted on events as they happen: "Mom, I turned on the water and he got in the shower ahead of me!" "Mom, he took the last of the shampoo!" "Mom, now all the hot water's gone!"

At the breakfast table they argue over whose Pop-Tart is in the toaster, whose book bag is in whose way under the table.

"Where's your sister?" she asks.

They look at each other and shrug.

"I think I heard her go out the back door," Jimmy says.

The last three school days Julie has dressed, packed her lunch, and gone off without a word; what's going on with her? She should pay better attention, ask some questions, maybe call Paula to see if she knows anything. Paula with the perfect daughter—Emily, who never does anything wrong. Maybe she'll call Pinky Corelli's mother instead. A nutcase, but at least she doesn't make her feel like the old woman who lived in a shoe.

She stops to take stock of herself in the mirror: circles under her eyes, her brow furrowed, mouth tense. Harder and harder to make sense of this person looking back at her. *It's this job.* Thinking back to that second interview in George Rice's office—the pleasant-faced man in the corduroy jacket, his shirt open at the neck, sipping coffee while he talked to her— "I'm anxious to fill this position . . . the work's piling up"—and herself on the edge of her seat, concentrating, wanting to give a good impression. He barely glanced at her résumé, spent most of the time telling her about company policy, outlining the various benefit packages. Then he suddenly leaned forward: "I've read over your qualifications. You've got the computer background and whatever else you need you can pick up as you go. Can you start tomorrow?" Her shock, then; not knowing what to say, finally managing a "thank you" that he waved away. She was so happy to get it, so relieved. Now she wonders if she's made a mistake.

A mad scramble going on below over a missing boot. Then Harry is upstairs in his room, rummaging through dresser drawers, swearing under his breath.

"You're not going to find it in there," she calls.

"Why not? That's where I left it." He comes into her room with a piece of paper, waving it in her face. "My homework."

"I thought you were looking for a boot—"

"That was me, Mom," Jimmy calls up the stairs. "Hey, we just missed the bus."

It is the note of exultation in his voice that enrages her.

"Dammit! That bus is there every day at the same time and everybody else manages to make it! I am not your personal driver!" Seven-forty by the clock, and already she's feeling abused, pushed around. On top of it, she'll be late for work, a fact that Denise Cole will not fail to notice.

In the car they fight over who's taking up whose share of the backseat. They despise each other, yet they can't leave each other alone. She turns in time to see Harry give Jimmy's arm a vicious punch.

"Harry, dammit, stop that!"

"Mom, you always tell me not to swear and then you go and do it."

She ignores this, steps on the gas, and the car leaps forward, ramming into the snowblower. *Reverse, reverse, idiot!* She backs the car up to peer over the hood. No damage done, Thank God. Still checking forward, she backs out of the garage. A wrenching sound, followed by a metallic thump.

"Geez, Mom! Watch where you're goin'!"

The door has grazed the side of the garage, shearing the side mirror off the car. Harry jumps out and picks it up from the garage floor.

"It looks okay. Just the mirror part got broken. Maybe we can glue it back."

Annie puts her face in her hands. She has thirty seconds to think about this.

"Put it in the backseat," she says tersely.

Now they are angels; not a peep out of them the rest of the way, waving good-bye to her from the school steps. "See ya, Mom. Have a good day!"

The employees' parking lot is nearly full when she arrives; she pulls in at the far end. Rain turning to sleet this morning; the air feels clammy as it slides down the neck of her coat. She steps in a puddle filmed with ice.

Inside, all is warm and bright; she waves to the red-haired cashier at the first station, who seems like a nice person, although they haven't met. In the lounge she takes off her coat, hangs it in her locker. The one next to hers is open, and Denise Cole's black cashmere coat is there. She can hear running water in the lavatory. Too early for an encounter. If she can get to her desk, look busy, she can avoid it for a while.

She riffles through piles of papers, looking for the work schedules she left unfinished on Friday. They must be here; they were the last thing she worked on. A thrill of nervous energy goes through her and she presses her palms against the desktop, willing herself to relax.

Searching through the piles again, she looks at each separate sheet, thinking back to that afternoon; a telephone call from Julie, asking her to pick up her sweater at the cleaners. A number of errands that she had to run on her way home—Jimmy's skates to be sharpened, a package to be mailed at the post office, a stop at Farmer Jack's. Maybe she'd gotten distracted, put the papers away somewhere. She checks her desk drawers: nothing.

A sinking feeling in the pit of her stomach. Somehow she has lost the work schedules for the next two weeks. Everyone's written requests for time off and specific extra hours. What to do now? If they are truly gone, then she must send the sign-up sheet around again. Not a costly error; just her own time and energy, but it will take the better part of the morning to reassemble and cross-reference. They're supposed to be ready by Monday noon. And everyone who's on the schedule isn't here today. Well, no help for it. Admit her carelessness and explain the delay.

She heads for the office, where she can see Denise's head bent over her desk. She looks up with the patient, longsuffering smile firmly in place.

"Something wrong?"

"I seem to have misplaced the work schedules," Annie says. "I was sure I'd left them on my desk—"

A wave of her hand. "Oh, I finished them up and gave them to Mr. Rice. He likes to see them first thing in the morning on Mondays. I find it works best if you do them before you leave on Friday." Denise's smile is forgiving. "I know how easy it is to let the work slide. But in retail, you've got to stay on top of things."

She can't let this one go by. "From now on, I'll make sure I finish them by Friday," she says. "Now that I know. So you won't have to cover for me."

"Oh, I didn't cover. I told him exactly what happened."

Torn between anger and humiliation, she has a wild urge to rush into George Rice's office and defend herself: she is not disorganized; nor is she lazy. But it is the way things are explained to her. Or else, not explained. Denise's instructions are a blur of miscues and countermands; sometimes they make her feel as if she really is stupid. And, it seems, the more she questions a procedure the less clear it becomes.

Thinking back to Friday afternoon, she remembers now that she was anxious to get out of here. She could have finished up the schedules with just a half hour of overtime. Why didn't she? This all could have been avoided if only she hadn't been in such a rush. She mustn't let Denise get to her like this.

The morning speeds by as things pile up on her desk—rush orders, orders for special Christmas items, lost orders, misdirected orders, items to be traced. When at last she looks up, it is twelve-thirty, and the office is deserted. She heads for the employees' lounge with her lunch.

The room is warm, and there are cigarette butts in the ashtrays, discarded cups on the counters. She sits at the small table and pours herself a cup of coffee. Leaning back, she stretches her arms above her head. She's starting to get a headache.

"All alone in here?" The red-haired cashier smiles

at her from the doorway. "I'll join you. Only got a couple minutes. I spent my lunch break in toys." She comes to the table, holds her hand out. "I'm Terry Whalen."

"Anne Browner."

"There's a sled I wanted to get for my four-year-old, and I've been waiting for it to go on sale, but then I got worried we'd sell out." She sets a bag down beside her, settles comfortably on the couch. "I waited on you a few weeks ago, the day you came in for the interview. I was hoping you'd get the job. I thought you had such a nice face."

Annie laughs, pleased at this kindness, feeling her spirits lift. She'd like to return the favor.

"How many children do you have?" she asks.

"Two. Adrian—he's four. And Vanessa, my little girl. She's eight months."

"How long have you worked here?"

"Since last June. I think my feet are finally getting used to it. These cement floors—they just don't give!" She indicates her package. "Twenty-nine dollars for a toddler sled, d'you believe it? Oh, well, it's a Flexible Flyer. I guess it's worth it."

Since June; six months, and with an eight-month-old baby. How does someone manage this? Annie remembers when she was a young mother; the job had seemed all-consuming.

"My husband got laid off last April," Terry says, "and it was easier for me to find something, so he takes care of the kids. He's a design engineer. They're a dime a dozen these days." She sighs. "How many kids do you have?"

"Three. A girl and two boys. Thirteen, twelve, and nine."

"You don't look old enough to have a thirteen-year-old. What does your husband do?"

"He . . . he was a teacher," Annie says. "He died. Last August."

It seems to come from a great distance; she marvels at the matter-of-factness of tone. They are words, after all, with no power to hurt her, being no longer connected to her feelings, which tumble along at some subterranean level.

"Gosh, I'm sorry." Terry's voice is hushed. "That's got to be so hard."

But this is a threshold she won't cross. Standing up, she looks at her watch. "Well. Back to work. It was nice to talk with you."

"Nice talking to you, too," says Terry.

She leaves the lounge as several of the office girls return from lunch, deep in conversation, smoking and laughing. There's no one here anywhere near her age, no one with whom she has anything in common.

She spends the afternoon composing letters, using her judgment on literary style. She goes to the files for examples, letting the recent correspondence guide her. This is the kind of work she loves: delivering the facts. A defective storm door has to be replaced; vertical blinds are on sale; slow-moving closet shelving being returned to a manufacturer. She finishes up the last of them at four-thirty.

Denise stops by her desk, selecting a letter from the "out" basket. Standing there, she reads it, brow furrowed, then holds it at arm's length.

"I don't know, I think the tone is off," she says.

"I'll redo it," Annie says. "How do you think it should read?"

"I was hoping you'd have some ideas of your own. I just would have worded it differently." She shrugs. "Never mind, it'll have to do. It's got to go out tonight."

"I'd be glad to do it over. Really, I don't mind."

Denise looks at her. "Mind? Why should you? It's your job, isn't it?" She shoves the letter back into the box, starts to turn away, but Annie stands up.

"Denise. I'm trying to do a good job here," she says. "But it's not always easy to know what you expect of me. . . ."

"I expect you to be professional." Denise turns on her. "And I expect you to make my job easier to do, not harder. So, if you're going to be taking offense every time I correct you, I can see we're going to have a very unpleasant time of it."

With that she stalks off, leaving Annie to stare at her back in confusion. The floor below is busy with customers: the checkout bays full, carts straggling into the main aisle. She can see George Rice talking to one of the aisle clerks. The office staff has left for the day.

She turns off her computer, placing the key inside her desk drawer, puts the finished letters into George Rice's box to be signed. Opening the bottom drawer of her desk, she carefully restacks the pink, green, and yellow forms into neat piles. She doesn't want to have to walk by Denise's office while she is still in there.

At last, when it's safe to leave, she goes to the employees' lounge to get her coat. It's raining again; the parking lot is slick with melting ice. She walks around a puddle that looks like a black hole. Unlocking the car, she gets in. The broken mirror on the backseat gleams at her; another sign of defeat.

The world is suddenly a place of great danger, threats coming from all sides. She sits in the driver's seat, gazing out of the window, seeing nothing but blackness; a punishment. Only one thought persists: that she needs this job. No matter what else happens, she must not lose it.

20

As if in anticipation of her arrival, Mrs. Bennett sits on the back porch; yet at her approach she darts away into the darkness. Crazy, neurotic cat, acting as though every gesture toward her is fraught with peril. She probably would have been happier left to fend for herself.

The lights in the kitchen are on; something is baking in the oven. Gingerbread. All coziness and domesticity. The family room is empty, the TV set off; an ominous silence.

"Hi, I'm home," she calls.

"Hi, Mom," Julie answers from upstairs. "How was work?"

"Like work. How was school?"

"It was fun." She clatters down the stairs. "There was an all-school assembly. Then we had art."

"How did the spelling test go?"

"I got ninety-five. I missed 'separate.' " She reaches for the hot pad to open the oven. "I made us some gingerbread."

"Good."

Jimmy is behind her on the stairway. "Grandma called."

"Grandma Rose?" Of course it would have to be; Nell has left for Florida. She didn't call to say good-bye. She'll have to make contact with her soon, hasn't heard a word since the letter. What exactly had she replied? She can't remember.

"She wants to have a sledding party at her house on Christmas Eve and have us sleep over. Can we do that?"

"We can do whatever we want," she says. "Go and wash your hands, will you?"

"Where'm I goin'?"

"Out for dinner. To a vegetarian place I heard about. Where's Harry?"

The living room is dark, and she steps inside to switch on the lights, finds the reason for the silence, and probably for the gingerbread: a broken lamp, lying on the floor.

"Kids!"

In an instant they stand before her in the doorway, faces blank. It is up to her to set the tone. A chance to be the good mom, the one she envisions herself to be on better days. Truthfully, it was an ugly lamp—Danish Modern, with a white ceramic base; it looked like a huge bowling pin. A wedding gift from some friends of her parents that they didn't have the nerve to return.

"What was the point of leaving it here for me to find? Or were you hoping I wouldn't notice?"

"We knew you'd notice," Jimmy says, and she laughs suddenly, the whole thing striking her as ridiculous. They look at each other, not believing their luck.

"Does that mean you're not mad?" Jimmy asks.

"No, I'm not mad. I've hated it for years. But how did it happen?"

They can't wait to tell her; the words *wrestling, gymnastics,* and *karate* feature prominently in the story.

"You were wrestling in the living room?"

"Yeah, because there's more room for the mattresses."

"What mattresses?"

"We took 'em off the beds."

"Look. This sort of stuff just doesn't go. Somebody could get hurt—"

"Somebody did," Julie says. "Harry missed the mat and fell on his butt." She can tell when a piece of information is getting ready to weigh in; a change in air pressure, almost a shiver of relief. "And Rex was here."

Harry groans. "God, you blabbermouth."

"Look, I told you I don't want hordes of people over here when you're alone in the house, for just this reason."

"Rex isn't hordes of people, Mom."

"He's a moron," Julie says. "He tries to act like he knows everything, but he's really dumb, Mom. I asked him how many stars there were in the Milky Way and he said fifty."

"Yeah, you following him around and reading out of your science book, you're the moron."

"Let's keep to the subject," Annie says. "Harry, get rid of the lamp, put it in the garbage. And don't do karate in the living room, don't bring the mattresses down, don't have Rex over in the afternoon—did I miss anything?"

They troop out to the car, and Julie gets in beside her; Harry and Jimmy, their remorse short-lived, wrestle in the backseat.

"Poor corpus callosum," Harry moans, "all shot to hell. I've got Alien Hand Syndrome, can't make my arm stop—!" Muffled laughter, punctuated by slaps.

Julie twists around. "What's a corpus callosum?"

"Connects the two sides of your brain," says Harry. "Makes it so you can do stuff with both hands—!" More slaps, then a yelp from Jimmy.

"You guys," Annie warns, "cut it out."

She pulls into the parking lot of a small strip mall. The restaurant, called Spinach Pie, occupies one of the storefronts.

"This is it?" Harry asks. "Looks more like a church."

They stare through the plate-glass window. "There's salt and pepper on the tables," Jimmy says hopefully.

Inside, the waiter beckons them to a table. It's still early; they are the first customers. Please, not the only ones, Annie prays. A narrow opening at the back is covered by a red velvet curtain. On the wall hangs a painting of a bearded and robed Middle Eastern figure. The face is gaunt; the eyes, deep set and angry.

They study the menu in silence. BILL OF FARE hand-lettered across the top, and at the bottom, another handwritten line advises: FOR HEALTH, HAR-MONY, AND PEACE.

Annie scans the items, looking for something familiar. It's full of unpronounceable words— Arame, Hiziki, Daikon, Seitan, Mochi. Under *House Specialties* are listed pumpkin soup and couscous. She read about this place in the paper and thought it sounded interesting; now she's sure it won't fly.

On cue Harry says under his breath, "There's nothin' here I ever heard of. . . ."

A young couple enters the restaurant, the woman with an infant in her arms. The baby's head wobbles inside the red fur-lined wrapper, its tiny face above the woman's shoulder. Annie's heart is pulled by the familiar rhythmic movement.

"Any decisions yet?" The waiter has returned to their table. "The chili's very good. It's got corn in it."

"What's couscous?" Harry's voice is stern.

"Sort of a cross between rice and pasta. It's tasty."

The boys order the chili. "And a Coke," says Harry.

"No Coke. Fruit juice, springwater, or tea."

"I'll have this," Julie says, pointing to the falafel sandwich.

Annie orders the couscous and spiced Indian tea.

"Big fight outside the auditorium today," Jimmy says. "Two ninth graders, girls. Lots of screaming and hair pulling."

"What about?" Julie asks.

He scrunches up his shoulders, grinning. "One of 'em said the other one f——d her boyfriend." He spits out the word, leaving a hollow space in the middle.

"Oh, Lord," Annie says.

"When?" Harry says. "What hour?"

"Third. Principal took 'em down to the office."

Their fruit juice arrives, and Jimmy takes a long drink, slapping the glass smartly against the table.

"What's in this?" Julie demands. "It tastes weird. Here, Mom, try it." She pushes the glass toward her.

"It tastes fine to me."

"The boyfriend's a guy who drives around school in a pickup truck and sells drugs," Jimmy says.

"Yeah, sure," Harry says. "There's always some guy drivin' around school in a pickup selling drugs."

"What?" says Annie.

"Like the lady with the asthma. I've been hearing about it for two years, but I've never seen it."

"He's a real guy," Jimmy insists.

"Oh, right." His voice drips scorn for seventh graders, who will believe anything. "That's not how you buy drugs anyway. Off the back of a truck. 'Hey, gimme that box of drugs, the one over there by the spare tire.' "

Annie looks from one to the other, wishing the talk had not taken this turn, trying to figure out what, if anything, these two know about drugs in junior high. She hopes it is all talk, that they know nothing, or at least, as little as she does. Yet shouldn't she ask? A good mother wouldn't close her eyes and expect it all to go away.

"Are people buying drugs at school, Harry?"

He looks her straight in the eye. "Dunno."

"I'll bet Rex is," Julie says. "Good old Problem Boy."

"Shut up, Jule."

"Is he?"

"Mom, don't be dumb."

The waiter arrives with their order, setting bowls of chili topped with sour cream in front of the boys.

"Holy Mary Mother of God," says Harry. "Blessed be the Fruit of the Loom, Jesus."

Laughing, Jimmy swallows a mouthful of juice the wrong way. Annie looks at Julie, who is staring with alarm at her falafel sandwich.

"Mom," she whispers. "I don't think I'm gonna like this."

"Here. Try mine." She passes the couscous, which looks and smells wonderful, across the table. Julie takes a forkful, pronounces it edible. Falafel is not what she had in mind tonight, but she will have peace at any price. The angry face stares down at her from the wall: *Foolish woman, what did you expect?*

Julie pushes her juice to the center of the table. "I gotta go to the bathroom." She's up and out of her chair, disappearing through the red-curtained doorway.

Harry puts down his spoon. "This stuff isn't that great."

She sighs. "I thought it might be fun to try something new. I should have known it was too late. We needed to do this years ago, before you guys got set in your ways."

Harry points to the infant, still asleep on his mother's shoulder. "Mom, if you brought us here when I was that kid's age, I'd've still hated the chili."

In a moment Julie returns. "What does 'no loitering' mean?"

"Means no peeing," Harry says.

"No peeing in the john?"

Harry glances over his shoulder. "Uh-oh, here comes the cop. Yep, Officer, she did it. Took a leak right where it says not to."

The brothers break into braying laughter.

"All *right*!" Annie says, and the young couple turn toward them; it is her own voice that has caught their attention. More softly she says, "Kids, *please*."

Jimmy pushes his bowl aside; it is half-full.

"You don't like the chili either?"

"It doesn't really taste like chili, Mom."

On the way home, Harry says, "I asked Grandma for Rollerblade Lightnings for Christmas."

"I saw some used, at Rolling Soles," Jimmy says.

"I don't want 'em used. They're bogus."

"How much are they?" Annie asks.

"Two-fifty."

"Two hundred and fifty dollars?" He is baiting her, but she will not be pulled in tonight; no lectures about money. She drives past the post office and the bus station, then the gray stone Catholic church, turning on Sixth Street, heading toward home. In the backseat, trouble is brewing. Hard breathing; the sound of skin hitting skin. Someone kicks the back of her seat. She presses her foot on the gas, gliding through a yellow light at Crooks Road. If she can get them home, where they can spread out, they all might make it. Suddenly she's exhausted; it's the way energy leaves her body these days, without warning.

"Julie, sit back. Is your seat belt on?"

"Mom, can't you see it is?"

Behind her comes Harry's stage whisper: "Quit looking at me, I mean it!"

"I'm not lookin' at you!"

She keeps her eyes on the road, her voice steady. "I want you two to stop this."

"Mom, I'm not doin' anything," Jimmy says.

"You are! You keep lookin' at me!"

Julie says smugly, "You wouldn't know it if you weren't looking back."

Amazing, the many ways these three know how to drive her crazy: teasing, whining, sneakiness; the long-suffering looks, the outraged innocence; the laziness and smugness and the scheming. A slow churning begins in her stomach, boiling its way upward into her heart.

"Cut it out, you dumb freak from Battle Creek!"

With a fierce, sideways jerk, she spins the car into the curb. Turning around, she fixes them with a look. They stare back at her, smirking.

"All right," she says to Harry. "Get out. You can walk the rest of the way."

"Mom . . ." Jimmy says.

She turns on him. "Shut up! The rest of you keep quiet!"

Julie looks stricken. Only Harry seems unmoved, sitting calmly on the seat, staring back at her.

"Out," she says. "I'm not fooling."

Without a word he opens the door. Closing it behind him, he stands on the curb.

"Mom, it was partly my fault. . . ." Jimmy says.

"You should have thought of that before!"

She puts the car in gear, drives off without a backward glance. Her anger propels her the rest of the way, and she parks the car in the driveway with a jerk. They climb the porch steps in silence. Again, Mrs. Bennett is waiting, and Julie scoops her up in her arms.

Once inside, the weight of what she's done crashes through, and abruptly she sits down at the table, struggles out of her coat. She hasn't felt this tired in months.

"I'm gonna frost the cake now, Mom," Julie says, and she nods, pressing her hands to her face.

Nothing to worry about; it is less than a mile to their corner. In a few minutes he'll walk in, chastened, but without an apology; that's his style. She looks toward the window; it is starting to rain. Her heart gives a painful thump, and she gets up, staring out into the streaked darkness. Reflected in the glass is the tall cupboard next to the sink, where a set of soup bowls with an embossed crest of the Olympia Hotel sits on the middle shelf. They bought them in an antique store in Greenbush. The Cedar Closet. The kitchen table came from the same store.

Nothing in this house without his stamp on it. The pottery butter dish, the pink glass salt-and-pepper shakers. Nothing matches. Nothing in this life of hers. Nothing gets done; jobs are never finished. The leaves, sodden, moldering under their blanket of snow. A leak in the laundry-room ceiling. All the mail that needs answering. Everything falling apart. Suddenly it all feels chaotic, unmanageable. Even the way the kids treat each other. None of this would be happening if he were here.

Julie is stirring confectioners' sugar into the cream cheese. "It's really stiff, Mom. Should I add some orange juice to it?"

She nods as Jimmy comes down the stairs. "He back yet?"

"Not yet," says Julie.

She looks at her watch. Eight-thirty. He's walked longer distances than this. He should be coming in the door now. Going to the stove, she puts on some water for tea, takes down the dark blue teapot. By the time it's brewed, he'll be home.

Only, he isn't. Eight forty-five, nine o'clock comes, and she stands by the window trying to stay calm, trying not to stare too hard into that well of nothingness, from which all cruelty flows.

"Maybe he went to Rex's," Julie says. "Why don't you call over there?"

She dials the number, and a woman answers.

"This is Anne Browner," she explains. "I'm looking for Harry. . . ."

"Nobody's here," the voice says. A second later the receiver bangs in her ear.

For a moment she can't make sense of this. Does it mean that he has been there, and they've left? No, that can't be right. Her mind races; she knows she's not thinking straight. Picking up the receiver, she dials the number again.

"I'm sorry to bother you, but Harry is missing and I thought he might be somewhere with Rex. . . ." Missing! Terrible word! But the voice softens at once.

"I haven't seen 'em, but I just got home. What's your number? I'll have Rex call when he comes in."

She can't tell if it's his mother or sister; the voice doesn't have an age. She gives her number, although there's no point; she's certain now that he didn't go there.

When she puts the phone down, she feels the house straining with a tension too powerful to be contained, a balloon about to burst. She puts on her coat.

"I'm going out to look for him."

"Should I come?" Julie asks.

"No. I'm sure he's just around the corner. You stay by the phone." She hears the contradiction in this. "I'll be back in a few minutes."

Rain turns to sleet on the windshield as she drives. She should have tried calling his other friends— Dave Beard and Roger Tyler, from hockey days. Except they haven't been around; she can't remember the last time she's seen them; not since school started. He wouldn't do this, wouldn't run away, hasn't done it since he was five—packing his green duffel and heading for Kenny Green's house. She had phoned ahead to tell Connie that he was coming; they had hot chocolate waiting, played Go Fish, then said if he was going to live there he'd have to get his hair cut short, like Kenny's. He called to tell her he was on his way home. *Come home, Harry.*

In minutes she reaches downtown, where she dropped him off. The blue neon pharmacy sign glows through the rain. The older, quieter part of town; not the downtown section, with its restaurants and clubs. No one on the street; no one out in this weather if they don't have to be. Sleet slides down the glass, collecting along its edge.

She parks and gets out of the car. The drugstore looks deserted; ten minutes of ten, by the wall clock inside. She pulls open the door.

"I'm looking for my son. He's thirteen years old, wearing a blue-and-green hooded jacket. . . ."

The pharmacist looks up with bland disinterest. "Haven't seen him, ma'am."

Lying to her. But why would he? No. It's she that's crazy. She stands there in the doorway, abruptly turns and exits. Why? Why did she do it? Trying to follow the thread of anger back to its turn on the spool. *You are thirty-six years old, a grown woman. And he is thirteen.*

If she is crazy, then Harry is the one making her suffer, hiding out in some store or doorway or garage, letting time go by, knowing that she will be frantic over this. No. He's never vengeful, wouldn't run away, he's a good boy. *Oh, God, if anything happens to him . . . !*

She looks frantically up and down the street. Too

many directions, too many paths. Hopeless. And he's not hiding, it's something much darker than that. He's been kidnapped, beaten up; or he's lying out there, having been hit by a car.

God, she wishes that she were crazy; crazy would be easy, compared with this. Just as a funeral is easy, compared with the pointless aftermath; the living out of an interminable life.

Something was said about coming into contact with God, being scarred by it. That's what has happened; the madness of grief. Only nothing could be further from the truth. She isn't crazy. Rather, she's enlightened. Scarred by it all, burned up inside, rendered liquid—skin and eyes, teeth and bones melting away in this white heat of enlightenment.

She needs to get to a phone, call the police right away. She turns on the radio. "... *ozone hole over Antarctica . . . from Nimbus-7 satellite over the south polar territory . . . fifteen percent larger than it was two years ago, three times as large as the United States . . .*" So. We're doomed anyway. Rip open the hole; let us fall through. Don't think for a second that it's not personal. "Man crushed by semi on freeway . . ." "Brothers die in basement freezer . . ." "Policeman shot to death in all-night pizza joint . . ." Why read this stuff every day? To know she's not the only one suffering? It doesn't help. Reading it only makes her angrier at God, makes her want to go out and take a gun to the heavens. *Why have you done this? Why?*

She parks in the driveway, and the front door opens.

"Aunt Jess called," Julie says. "Harry's at her house."

Weak with relief, she climbs out of the car. Four miles to Jess's apartment. Did he walk the whole way? *Please, God, don't let him have hitchhiked, he knows better. . . .*

They are both in the doorway, watching her.

"I suppose now he expects me to come and get him."

Jess answers on the first ring, her voice a shade too calm; too carefully neutral.

"He got here about nine-thirty. He's fine. In fact, he just fell asleep on the couch."

"I'll be right over."

"Why don't I keep him here and drop him off in the morning?"

"Because I want him to come home."

Jess says nothing, waits at the other end. Dear old Jess. A sudden rush of feeling for her sister, loyal and patient, not wanting to make any mistakes. *Be generous. This has turned out as well as it could.*

"Okay," she says, changing her mind. "His bus leaves at seven-forty. Can you have him here by then?"

"I will."

She hangs up, turning to the other two. "Your brother's spending the night at Aunt Jess's."

"Can we have some dessert now?" Julie asks.

A silent feast; they eat quickly and go upstairs. Minutes later, when Annie comes up, they are in bed and asleep.

That night, a dream of having nothing for Harry for Christmas, of wrapping the presents, not finding a single item for him in any of her secret hiding places. Finally, coming upon a pair of gloves—dark green, made of the cheapest yarn—shoved into the back of a closet; remembering she'd picked them up at the supermarket. *This will be enough.*

She wakes in darkness, saying these words aloud. For a long while after this she's awake, staring at the ceiling, crying hot, muffled tears.

21

"That was your mom. She said you could stay the night."

He pushes himself to a sitting position, scratching the side of his head, like Stan Laurel.

"She was glad to know you were okay."

He waves this away; his face darkens. Scowling down at the blanket, biting the edge of his thumbnail. "Yeah, right. I'm gonna go live in a hollow tree. Like the one in that state park in California. I'd build a floor up about ten feet, get an air mattress, some bags of food. . . ."

"A microwave," she says.

He smiles faintly, still working on the cuticle.

"What then?"

"Just live there. Come down at night when the park's closed. Go into town, get some pop, batteries for my radio, whatever I need. Go back, climb the ladder, pull it up after me. Nobody'd know I was there."

"Wouldn't you get lonely? Never seeing anybody?"

"I can see people. I'd walk around at night, look in people's windows. At least I'd be doing what I wanted." He lowers his head, picking at a scab on the back on his hand. "Mom's always wailing on me. She doesn't like anything I do."

She sits down next to him. His hair is still wet from the shower she made him take when he walked in. Shivering in his jacket, his eyes pinched into slits, he had shown up at her door, the look on his face reminding her of the time he was not yet two and had fallen out of his wagon. It had happened on her watch; Annie was taking six-month-old Jimmy to the doctor while she baby-sat. She had taken him for a walk in the wagon, had run up the steps to unlock the apartment, and turned to find him sprawled on the driveway with the wagon on top of him. Blood on his forehead. She nearly fainted from fright, thought she had killed him. Later that day, when he couldn't lift his arm without yelping in pain, they'd taken him to Emergency and discovered the broken collarbone. Guilty, guilty, guilty! Even the wagon had been a gift from her.

"She never hassles anybody else," he says. "She

doesn't say shit about what they're doing." Again he looks away. "She never even asked me why I quit hockey."

"Why did you?"

He shrugs. "I knew I wasn't good enough to make the travel team, and I didn't want to play regular. You go to a million practices and who cares, you're just playing a bunch of other guys who aren't any good. The coach said I could always try out, but I was sick of it, anyway."

"Sounds like a good decision, then." She puts her arm about his shoulders. "Well, I for one would be a very sad aunt if you went away to live in a hollow tree. I'd miss you a ton."

But he isn't listening; his eyes are fixed on the floor.

"This thing tonight wasn't even my fault. We used to do stuff like that all the time. Dad never got mad at us. He'd tell us just to look out the window at the beautiful scenery."

He pulls the blanket around him, the one they gave her last Christmas—blue, pink, and lavender stripes dividing rows of cats: TABBY CAT. TOMCAT. FAT CAT. ALLEY CAT. He's wrapped in her terry-cloth robe while she dries his clothes in the dryer.

"Julie's skipping school, you know. She's supposed to get out after me, but lots of times I get home and she's watching TV."

"Lots of times?"

He picks at the threads in the blanket. "Once in a while. And Jimmy's stealing money."

"From who?"

He will not answer this, turns away. "Everything's just all fucked up," he mumbles.

"I know. I love you, neph. You're my tough, smart nephew." Again she puts her arm around his shoulders. "We're all going to get through this."

"D'you think?" The look he gives her triggers a flash of memory: him telling her of his first day at kindergarten—where they kept the crayons, the proper way to hold scissors, why you have to wash your hands after you go to the bathroom. Then his matter-of-fact voice saying: "But I don't think I'll go anymore, because I didn't really like it that much." Poor guy, she didn't have the heart to tell him.

She gathers sheets and a pillow, another blanket from the hall closet. "Are your feet cold? You could wear a pair of my socks to bed."

He shakes his head. "Too femmy."

"Wearing socks is femmy?"

"Wearing your socks, yeah."

He lets her cover him, then turns on his side, closes his eyes as she bends to give him a kiss.

"Love you," she says.

"Love you, too." She turns out the light. "It's not so great being smart, you know," he says. "It only makes you see how many dumb people there are in the world."

"That's true."

She walks down the hallway to her bedroom, wishing that Ryan were here. She wants to talk this over with someone. She doesn't want to make too much of it. All mothers lose it at times; all boys run away from home. Still, the idea of him walking the length of Rochester Road at night terrifies her; not in this sick world. What could Annie have been thinking?

The scariest thing is that she trusts his instincts. He's not a big talker; this is the most she's heard about what's going on over there. It must be scaring him to death, if he's telling her.

When they discovered the broken collarbone, he cried tears of both pain and rage—that he could hurt this much, that this should be happening to him. But he doesn't cry anymore. She remembers then, the doctor saying he had a high tolerance for pain. The same with Annie. No wonder they are so at odds.

When she drives up in front of the house, both Annie and Jimmy are waiting for them. Harry gets out of the car, and Jimmy hands him his books.

"Thanks." He walks to the front steps, where his mother stands. "Sorry," he mumbles, looking down at the ground.

She reaches out to ruffle his hair. "Me, too." Then she looks over, gives Jess a wave and a smile.

"See you later," Jess says, driving away. *And that's*

all there is to that. A strip of papery light holding the sky aloft; it looks like it might rain again. On her car radio, Stan Getz rolls over a lazy melodic line, goosing it slightly out of tune. She is not her sister's keeper, and this is not her problem. Nothing she can do about it; no sense worrying.

"Dave Zinneman came in with a floor-sanding bid for the house on Brooklawn," Tom Chase says. "A third less than The Sandmen."

"Go for it," says Steve, looking up. "They're good. They did Perry's place over on Southfield."

"Jess, I need these invoices," Harriet says, handing her a list. "Pull them for me, will you?"

"Hey," Tom says. "Last night I had the weirdest dream. I'm working late and a guy walks into the office, sets this box on my desk. 'Here are the new work boots,' he says. I say, 'What work boots? We didn't order any work boots.' 'Government issue,' he says. 'Everybody's got to wear 'em. They cost a thousand bucks.' Then he starts unpacking 'em. . . ."

"Pretty bizarre," Steve says. "Hand me Zinneman's bid."

"Wait. You haven't heard the weird part yet. I finally recognize the guy. Who d'you think it is but Mr. Bonvino! Remember? Our old soccer coach from junior high . . ."

"Amazing."

Steve gets up, starts to walk over to Tom's desk,

and the rest of it seems like another dream to Jess: the front door opening with a metallic double click; the woman in black silk slacks and a fox-fur jacket standing in the doorway. Her dark hair sleeked back, very chic, very European. Her ears pierced with diamond studs. Fingernails glowing with iridescent polish. Dark red lipstick on a tense, pretty mouth.

"I'm looking for Jessica Lewis." The voice husky, slightly hostile. And in that instant she knows: here is life coming around to slap her into wakefulness, making sure she gets the whole picture. Heart pounding, she stands up.

The woman stares at her. "You're fat. Cheryl said you were blond, she didn't say fat. She's a very polite little girl. Isn't she?"

Harriet moves in, her voice stern: "What do you want here? This is a place of business. . . ."

"I'm Lucia Dougherty," the woman says. "The neurotic, hysterical wife. I came to see what the adulteress looks like."

A shaft of sunlight falling through the doorway, outlining the woman's head, making her skin seem milky, translucent, like that of a porcelain doll. And another odd detail: her coffee mug half-tipped, leaning against the stack of file folders on her desk. To cover her confusion, Jess moves out from behind her desk, counting squares of tile between them— fourteen in all. She feels the blood pulsing in her cheeks.

"I'm curious. What do you think it'll be like? When you're married to him and he starts cheating on you?"

Lucia moves toward her; just twelve squares separating them now. The air in the room is close, supercharged. Pressing her hands together in front of her, Jess murmurs, "I don't know what you want me to say. . . ."

"I don't want anything from you," Lucia says. "I just want you to know that I may be pregnant. And if you keep on with this—wrecking my life and my daughter's life—you will be very sorry for it!"

With that she is out the door, closing it behind her with a bang. Jess moves to sit down at her desk. She can feel both Tom and Steve's eyes on her, can't bear to look at them.

"You okay?" Tom asks.

She doesn't know what to say. "Sorry about this . . ."

And then Harriet is beside her, an arm around her shoulders. "Peace, poise, and patience, girl . . ."

She gives a faint laugh, lowers her head to look down at her desktop. *Am I crazy? Did I really think I'd never have to meet her face-to-face? What was I thinking? Going along, acting as though our lives weren't connected at any of these points . . . so now, what do I do?*

After a moment Harriet moves off; the men go back to whatever it was they were doing before the dream. At last she forces herself to look up. Finish out the day. Keep the office running, the work in order. Remember to smile.

Ryan paces the floor, eyes narrowed, mouth set. "Jesus, why am I always so surprised? Why, after eleven years, do I still not get it? This is the life she's chosen. She doesn't want to stop drinking, doesn't want therapy. Everybody's nuts except her. Everybody's evil, crazy, out to do her in."

"She said she could be pregnant."

"I haven't had sex with her, I told you that. We haven't had sex in three years."

"What did she mean, then? That she has a lover?"

"I can't imagine. Jess, I will not . . . I'm not going to let her do this to us. Just because she decides to make a fool of herself . . ."

"Not herself," she says. "Me."

"No! Listen, twice a week and every other weekend I pick up Cheryl at the house. Occasionally she'll stop me in the hallway to make some new outrageous demand. That is the extent of our contact, I swear to you! The other day she said she's changed her mind again, she's decided she wants full custody. I didn't even stop to argue, just went straight to my lawyer." He runs his hands through his hair. "You say something over and over, and finally you think she gets it. There are times when she can be as rational as any normal person. And then she does something so nuts, you know she hasn't even been listening, hasn't heard one fucking word. . . ."

"It's not all that nuts," Jess says. "It took a certain amount of courage. . . ."

"Not courage. Narcissism. Ask anyone who knows her. Ask her parents! Why do you think they're so goddamn nice to me? They're scared to death they'll end up responsible for her again. They have no defenses against her!"

And you do? She wants to ask this. Instead, standing at the window of her apartment, she stares out into the night. She has already given notice; she will be leaving at the end of the month, moving in with Ryan until they find a place. There is a house near Lucia's that they have been looking at. Old and in need of some major repairs. But it's in the right neighborhood, the right school district. All these sweet days of house hunting, of planning their new life together. How can she think of letting this go?

He comes to put his hands on her shoulders, traces the line of her collarbones. "Listen to me. I love you so much. . . . I cannot imagine my life without you. I never want to hurt you. . . ."

"Nor I you," she says lightly. "So that makes us even." But she frees herself from his hands. ————

He stands there, looking at her. "What else can I say to you? She's neurotic. She doesn't know what she's doing. . . ."

"You think so? I think she knew exactly what she was doing."

22

"Darryl, come help me put these cards up. They fell down when the kids came in."

It is one of their mother's traditions: propping Christmas cards on every square inch of woodwork in the house. They are always falling down and having to be replaced. A mark of her parents' generation that there is already a flood of them, and it's only the twenty-second of November.

Annie isn't sending cards this year, wishes she wouldn't get any, either. ". . . Evan's job continues to delight and challenge . . ." ". . . this year we'll spend three weeks in Jamaica . . ." ". . . Bill, Jr., graduated with honors . . ." Everything's great, couldn't be better. Or else they are full of bad stuff. She doesn't want to write about her bad stuff. And what else is there to say? Nothing.

With a sigh her father gets to his feet; as usual her mother ignores the action for its accompanying sound.

"You're the one who says it's nothing to put on a party. Let's see you help out for once."

"For once? Who put up every damn foot of cedar roping around that porch railing, I ask you?"

"It's not my fault you picked the coldest day of the year." Rose's tongue clicks against her teeth. "Sneezing and coughing and spreading germs all around, better hope and pray the kids don't get it."

"Snip, snip, snip," says Jess, coming in the front door. "When are you guys going to quit fighting?" Ryan is behind her, carrying a pie plate. Her mother eyes it with phony delight masking her alarm.

"We're not fighting, for heaven's sake. Now, what's that you've got, Ryan Dougherty? You're a guest here. I hope you didn't think you had to bring your own food to Thanksgiving dinner!"

"Small contribution," he says with a smile. "Made it myself. Chocolate pecan pie. My mother's recipe."

"Why, how lovely!"

Jess takes the pan from Ryan, carrying it out to the kitchen, while Annie follows her.

"Oh, you are a devil, sister."

"What?" Jess gives her an innocent look, but they both know: holiday menus never vary—it's turkey on Thanksgiving, shepherd's pie at Christmas, ham for Easter. Likewise, with the side dishes and desserts. They've never thought to challenge it.

"Did he really make it himself?"

"He did. He's a great cook."

Annie pours herself another glass of wine. "Want some?"

"Sure. I ran into your neighbor, Paula, the other day."

"Did she tell you they're not giving each other a family gift this year? Instead, they're buying a wood-burning stove for a poor family in their church."

"Good old Paula." Jess grins. "Trust her to make the rest of us feel materialistic and chintzy."

"I'm sure that's not why she's doing it."

"Oh, yes it is."

Annie laughs. "She's good-hearted. She can't help that."

"I'll bet she could if she tried."

"Dad called the kids this morning," Annie says, "doing his Happy Hank number. Remember that? 'Smile when you wake up, be happy and gay, and laugh all your troubles away. . . .' "

"I liked the cleanup song the best," Jess says. " 'Pick it up, pick it up, bumpty bumpty bum. . . .' " She hums the tune happily, and they both laugh.

"Did I tell you Harry and Jim are buying their own presents this year and sending each other the bill? That way they're sure of getting exactly what they want."

"Couldn't they just go out together? That's what we used to do."

"That reminds me. I haven't bought yours yet."

"Want to go shopping next week?"

"Sure," Annie says. "Well, I hope Ma can handle two desserts on the menu."

"Anyway, the kids'll like it."

They go back to the living room, where Ryan is seated at one end of the couch, their father at the other. The two of them are reading the *Free Press*. The kids have gone upstairs.

Their mother is at the mantel, rearranging the cards. "Annie, did you see this? Jimmy sent it." She takes one down. ". . . 'Looking forward to seeing you at the holidays . . .' Darryl and I laughed and laughed. It was so sweet!"

"He'll make somebody a great husband," Jess says, sitting between her father and Ryan and taking the newspaper from his hand.

Her mother sighs. "They're growing up so fast. I can still remember the day Jimmy was born. We took Harry to Greenfield Village and walked him up and down in his little stroller. He knew something was up. We were calling the hospital every hour, and he'd have a fit every time Darryl went to use the phone!"

"You took him to Greenfield Village, Ma?" Jess says. "At fourteen months? How'd he like it?"

"He loved it," Rose says stoutly. "You wait until you have kids of your own, Jessie. They're smarter than you give them credit for."

"I think they're plenty smart, it's you I worry about. Greenfield Village in the middle of winter with a baby in a stroller . . ." She shakes her head, grinning.

"It was fun, wasn't it, Darryl?"

Her father drops the paper. "Rosie, it was twelve years ago, how would I remember?"

Rose brings the turkey to the table, and Annie and Jess carry out bowls of potatoes, squash, peas and carrots, gravy, dressing scooped from the bird. Next come the olives, butter, rolls, and cranberry sauce.

"One Thanksgiving," Julie confides to Ryan, "Harry came to the table with black olives stuck on all of his fingers."

"You always tell that story," says Harry, "and you weren't even born when I did it. Pass the dressing, please."

"I like this meal," Julie says, "but what I really like is a turkey samwish with all dark meat and cranberry sauce."

"Samwish," Harry says. "You're such a lame-o."

"You're the lame-o," Julie returns, "with all those olives on your fingers." She crosses her eyes, wiggles her hands in front of her face.

"Nothing like a big meal," her father says, changing the subject, "followed by an afternoon of football."

"Not that you can ever stay awake for it," says her mother.

It occurs to Annie that her children have had ample instruction in how to bait one another.

"Turkey has tryptophan," Jimmy says. "Natural sedative. That's why everybody falls asleep."

"Where'd you hear that?"

"We read about it in school."

"Grandma Rose," says Julie, "did I tell you I want a dark blue Champion sweatshirt for Christmas, size large?"

"Yes, but why so big, honey? You'll swim in it."

"I like stuff big, so it fits you for a long time."

Ryan gets up from the table, comes back almost immediately. Jess smiles up at him.

"Nobody home?"

He shakes his head. "They must be out for a walk."

"What about you, Jim?" says her father.

"A skateboard," Jim says. "John Cardiel Slick with gullwing trucks and jelly ball wheels . . ."

"What is that?" Jess laughs.

"And I also want a Mystic Ball," says Julie. "You know, one of those things that you ask questions and it answers you?"

"Geez, do they still have those? Your mom and I used to do that all the time," Jess says. " 'It is certain.' 'Ask again later.' 'My sources tell me no.' "

Those lazy afternoons, tossing the ball back and forth, watching the triangle bob up from within the ink-filled sphere: *When will Jess quit borrowing my Chloé perfume without asking? Will Annie's boyfriend try to French me? Will Jess ever get a boyfriend of her own, so she can stop bothering mine?*

After dinner, while they help clean up and their father turns on the TV, Ryan makes another phone call.

"Still no answer," he says, coming out to the kitchen. "I'm sure they're home, though. I'm going over there. See you later, Mr. and Mrs. Lewis. Thank you, the meal was great, as always. Good company."

"Nice to have you," her father says.

Jess walks him to the door while Annie checks on the kids, watching a Disney special on the bedroom TV. When she comes back, her mother says, "Before you leave, I want to talk about Christmas. I thought we'd take the kids sledding Christmas Eve day, have soup and bread when we come home, and you can spend the night here. . . ."

"The kids want to go skiing, Ma. I'm thinking of taking them up to Pine Ridge."

"You mean over Christmas weekend? Oh, Anne Marie, no! We always have Christmas here. . . . I thought we'd get up in the morning and open our presents and then Roger and Amelia would come over. You know they love to see you and the kids. . . ."

Her resolve hardens; the last thing she wants is to spend Christmas morning with the Curtises. "I really haven't decided yet what we're going to do." Hoping it sounds straightforward, and not argumentative. It's a matter of survival; she doesn't want to be here, can't be here. Something else better happen between now and then.

"Just think about it," her mother urges. "I wanted to give you enough warning. . . ."

"Warning!" her father echoes. "What are we talking about, some sort of missile launch?"

He never misses a thing, keeps track of every nuance of conversation, no matter how trivial. Of course they all know that nothing their mother says is trivial, or accidental.

Jess returns, stretching her arms over her head. "Well, the old tryptophan's working. Gotta go home, take a nap before my company comes. Ryan's bringing Cheryl to spend the weekend."

"Oh." A pointed look from her mother. "Does he do that often?"

"Nope. First time ever."

That's right, that's the way to handle her, Annie thinks. Bold. Ready to stand and fight. Their mother is one who likes to choose the battleground; she lets this go by. "The meadow is a dangerous place." A line from *Bambi* that Keith used whenever he would get into it with their mother. She winces. Last year at this time, when he was here with her. Only weeks after the diagnosis. When they still had hope—for treatment, remission, who knew?

"Thanks, Ma; thanks, Dad." Jess bends to kiss them both.

"Call me," she says to Annie as she goes out the door.

They move to the family room, and Annie sits in the rocker before the fireplace. Her father is in the wing chair. Her mother goes to put the dining room in order, spreading the lace cloth and arranging the candles on the table, making sure they are ramrod straight in their holders.

"Last night a bunch of kids were outside on the

corner," Annie says, "throwing snowballs at cars. I had to go out and be Old Lady Browner, yell at them for five minutes. Why is it kids never think about consequences? Life is so damn easy for them." She takes a sip of her coffee. The ensuing silence feels awkward.

At last her father says, "So, how is work coming?"

She shrugs. "All right."

"Too bad you couldn't have found something you liked better."

"There wasn't a lot to choose from. And my résumé's pretty lean."

Her father nods. "It's a bad time to be looking. Man across the street lost his job. Fifty-two years old. Company merged with another one, all of a sudden he's the expendable man." He snaps his fingers.

"Who's that?" Annie asks. "Not Mr. Hoffman?"

"No, no. They moved away. Long time ago—"

"Not that long," says her mother, returning to the room. "Just a couple of years."

"Oh, Rose, it's five if it's a day. . . ."

"You don't know what you're talking about, Darryl. They were still here when Jess moved back from California."

"Well, she's been back five years at least," says her father, turning to Annie for corroboration.

She nods. She would bring them back to the subject, if it were one in which she had any interest. She rocks in the rocker, holding her coffee in her lap.

"That chocolate pie," her mother says, "was just

delicious. And to think he made it himself. . . . Of course, after a big meal like that, it's always nice to have something not quite so sweet. . . ."

Don't pursue this; let it go by. Only, she can't.

"The kids liked the chocolate, Ma. They don't like pumpkin."

"What do you mean? Jimmy had two pieces!" For a moment her mother stands before the hearth, thinking whatever thoughts she will think. At last, a shade too firmly, as if looking for an argument: "Ryan Dougherty is a very nice man . . ."

This bait she does refuse. He *is* a nice man. He is her friend; patient, helpful, generous. It's what she needs most from people these days.

". . . but he's a little . . . odd, wouldn't you say? Those narrow lips . . . and his eyes . . . you can barely see them when he smiles."

Her father snorts. "You make him sound like some kind of mutant, Rose."

"Narrow his lips and crinkle his eyes all you want," Annie says. "It's not going to change the facts."

"Yes, well . . . maybe if he was divorced . . ."

"The divorce will be final as of next week. So you can relax and stop worrying about her, Ma."

"Is that true?"

"November thirtieth." Why does Jess refuse to do her own work around these two? And why does she let herself be drawn into it? *Nothing ever changes.* Still, she babbles on: "She didn't go looking for this, you know. Sometimes things just happen."

Gazing into the fire, her mother nods, her lips in a firm line. "You can't always keep trouble away. That doesn't mean you have to offer it a chair to sit on."

23

A little after eight, by the clock. She expected him here by the time she got home. Maybe he stopped by his apartment to pick up something.

She turns on the kitchen light, sees the bakery bags on the counter. So he's been here. She checks through them: jelly doughnuts, oatmeal-raisin cookies (Cheryl's favorite), a box of lemon tarts. He wanted to spend the weekend here, instead of at his apartment. "I want her to see that you have a life. That you're not just somebody we happen to see whenever she's at my place. That's my fault. A mistake. I don't want her to be surprised when we move in together."

Tomorrow they will take her and Julie to the movies, followed by dinner at Annie's. What will Cheryl think of that? Another girl exactly her age, and two tough, rowdy, almost-teenagers. A lot for a nine-year-old to absorb all at once.

"She knows how to work hard and be polite—all those grown-up things," he says. "Now she needs to learn how to have fun."

She understands this in theory; still, she's not sure this is the place to start. Cheryl still seems afraid of her; she probably knows more than Ryan thinks she does. Her timid-but-firm refusal of every friendly gesture, and those big dark reproachful eyes—what has Lucia told her? She stares out the window at black, bare trunks of catalpa trees, feeling a sudden wrenching sadness.

"She's talking about suing for full custody again. She does it periodically. It's a ploy, a way to push things back."

"Will it?"

He shook his head. "This issue was settled months ago. I don't believe she even wants it, it's just something more to argue about."

A door slams in the parking lot; it must be them. She glances out of the window, seeing her elderly neighbor's Buick with the lights still on; Bootsie, her black-and-white dog, yipping in hostile frenzy in the front seat. Head bobbing at the window. Ditzy, ill-natured dog—he hates everybody in the complex, regards them all as his enemies. Why do people own pets they must always apologize for? As if life doesn't hold enough hazards in the field of human relations.

"I wish we could have found a house by now. But it'll happen. And this'll work out temporarily, won't it? You don't mind being crowded into my place for a month or so?"

She assured him it would be fine. Last night while she packed up the kitchen there was a knock at the door. When she answered, it was her neighbors from across the hall. They brought her a bouquet of flowers. They wanted her to know she would be missed! She invited them in for coffee.

They were doctors, both of them gay. They worked together at the AIDS hospice in Hazel Park. Witty and gentle-spirited, great gossipers, they stayed for an hour while they filled her in on the latest happenings in the rest of the building.

"We're going to miss you," they said. "You and your boyfriend in the gray Plymouth." And here she'd thought of herself as the Mystery Woman of the complex!

Ever since grade school she's had a passion for secrecy, giving herself points for sneaking through alleys and making it all the way home without anyone seeing her. She had no idea where she'd gotten this bent, often thought about being invisible and sneaking into places, making off with treasure.

Several summers ago she took the boys to the grocery store with her, and then to run some errands. Driving home, she turned her head to the backseat, caught them stealing strawberries from the grocery bag; stealthily, so as not to draw attention to themselves. Living for the sheer joy of things, not aware of any consequences. Or was that part of the thrill?

She'll take a shower while she's waiting. She goes to the bedroom, strips quickly, turning on the water in the bathroom. While she waits for it to heat up she counts the tiles over the sink. She has a lifelong habit of counting things—pieces of laundry going into the washer, Life Savers in a roll, her steps on the way to anywhere. Now, looking up, she measures the distance from the top of the wall: three, six, nine, twelve, fifteen tiles. "Selfish bitch." What Lucia had meant that day. "You're not selfish," he assured her. "You know how to take care of yourself. They're two different things."

In the beginning, at their first meeting, he had taken out his wallet to show her the picture. "I have an eight-year-old daughter. My wife and I are separated. We got married because we were pregnant. It seemed like the sensible thing to do. Maybe it was just the Catholic thing to do, I don't know." His hands around the coffee cup were slender and capable; his brown eyes held hers. "We've both wasted a lot of time thinking any minute it would start being fun."

"Is that what marriage is?" Her tone had been flippant. "I'm just asking, I wouldn't know." But he took it seriously.

"Yes. I think so. At least that's what I'm looking for this time."

They talked that night for hours. He even told her about the day his daughter was born. "I kept thinking, 'Hey, she's alive!' And all of a sudden it dawned on me: 'Hey, she could die.' " Shaking his head. "Hell of a responsibility, this parenthood stuff."

And then, that first time he took her to bed, he told her how much he admired her. "You're a happy person. That too seems like a crucial thing to me."

She had laughed. "Aren't you impressed that I'm a carpenter's apprentice? That I was the sixth-grade jacks champion at Pattengill School?"

"That, too. I especially admire these red underpants, they remind me of Christmas."

"There you go, talking religion again."

He had kissed her stomach, her bare breasts. "I think you are my religion."

The telephone is ringing when she steps out of the shower. She grabs a towel from the rack, on her way to it.

"Hello?"

"Jess, there's been an accident. . . ."

"Ryan? Where are you?"

"I'm at Beaumont, at the hospital. . . . It's Lucia . . . she . . . they were on their way home—" His voice breaks.

In the silence her heart thumps wildly. "Ryan, what is it, what happened . . . ?"

"They were . . . it was on I-seventy-five . . . they hit an abutment. . . . Cheryl was thrown out of the car."

"Oh, God!"

"They're calling in a neurosurgeon."

"Do you want me to come?"

"No. Jessie . . . my baby, my little girl!" He is crying. She holds the receiver tight to her ear, feeling a dull opening inside her chest. She presses a fist, hard, into the hollow space.

"She didn't have on her seat belt. She always wore it. She would remind me to put mine on. . . ." He is crying again. "She told me to pick her up, but then they weren't at the house, so I went to the store and dropped the stuff off . . . and then I went home. And I got the call. . . ."

She closes her eyes, leans against the wall.

"The neurosurgeon is going to see . . . if there's brain damage. Her head hit the windshield."

"You mean, Cheryl . . ."

"No. Lucia. Her parents . . . I put a call into them in Texas. . . . Jess, the doctor's here," he says. "I have to go. I'll call you back."

And then he is gone. She hangs up, stands very still in the half-light of the bedroom, the towel wrapped around her. She's shivering with cold. What has she done? Is this going to be her fault? *Keep on with this. Just see how sorry you'll be.*

Remembering what she told Annie, when this all started. "Lucia doesn't want this marriage." Easy to be glib with someone else's life. *All illusions must go.* A sudden, fierce longing for safety, for someone to understand. She has to talk, can't bear to sit here alone, waiting. She picks up the telephone, dials Annie's number.

Part Three

24

New Year's Day, 8:00 P.M.

Its a long time since I wrote in here because too much happened. I couldn't write it all down. First the accident. It was on Thanksgiving night. Ryans little girl and her mother got in a car wreck and they are still in the hospital. They are both sick but especialy Ryans little girl.

Then my Aunt Jess moved in with us. She lost her apartment and she's looking for another one so Mom told her to come here. Jimmy and Harry are in the same room and she has Harry's old room. She and Ryan are going to get married but just not right away.

After that came Christmas. I got everything I wanted—a blue Champion sweatshirt, a necklace and $25 from grandma and grandpa, a book about the stars from Aunt Jess. Finally Mom let me get my ears pierced and I got perfume and 3 pr. of ear rings from her. It was still the worst Christmas. The week before I skipped school and was watching All My Children. And there was a guy who use to be on Young and the Restless! He use to be a bad guy who was in prison but now he's somebody's brother and everyone likes him. I wish it could be like that in real life. I wish when people died it would turn out they were just on some other channel for a while.

NEW YEAR'S RESOLUTIONS:

1 keep room clean
2 don't bite nails
3 clean litter box
4 do dishes without fighting
5 don't skip school anymore
6 don't brag
7 don't lie
8 don't look in mirrors so much

Tuesday, 7:30 P.M.

School started today. It is as boring as ever. I went to Pinky's and didn't get home until 5:30 and Harry called Mom at work. Now I have to tell her every time I go anywhere but Harry can still be late whenever he wants. It's not fair. I don't know about Mom these days. Sometimes she is nice but mostly she is not. Yesterday she said I had to clean up my room because it was an EYESORE and I couldn't go anywhere till it was done. She never use to be that way. She always acts like she's mad at me.

Pinky got a new playhouse for Christmas. It has a table and chairs and sink and refrigerator. It even has carpet on the floor and curtains in the windows. Her dad made it for her. I don't like him though. He's always hanging around when we play. He says how you doing little girls? Having fun? What a geek. My Dad would never do that.

Wednesday, 6:00 P.M.

I can't wait till I can wear my new ear rings. I have to wear gold posts for two months, and Harry keeps saying I have to wear GOALPOSTS! He is so LUDI-CRUST. Also I have a new hiding place for this book. It is inside a box of colorforms. I never play with them anymore so nobody would look there if they were so nosy, Mr. Harry Smartass!

Today Emily came over and we made chocolate chip cookies. I can't decide if she is my best friend or Pinky. They are both cathlick but Emily worries all the time if she's a good cathlick. Pinky says it doesn't matter. She says you can't be a cathlick unless you were born that way. Then they both asked me what I was and I said I was nothing. Emily says there's no such thing. She thinks she knows everything. After-ward she told me her Mom doesn't like her to play with Pinky because Pinky is boy crazy.

Right before Christmas some kids were singing carols outside our house. They only sang half of Away in a Manger and then they pounded on the door so Mom gave them some money. They just looked like BUMS! I hate those carols anyway, they all sound so sad and then people sing them in front of your house and ask you for money. That is not the Christmas spirit.

Friday, 5:30 P.M.

Tonight we are having pizza. Aunt Jess puts onions, mushrooms, garlic and motsarela on it and it's very good. Its called white pizza. She said Ryan was coming over too but then at the last minute he couldn't because he had to go to the hospital.

Rex Beers is a jerk. Today he wouldn't stop flipping the channels so I took away the remote and he punched me in the stomak. He is always loitering around our house! He doesn't know decimals, doesn't know about plant cells or microbes or bacterium. And when they were playing Miami Vice he said to Harry got another dead corpse sherif. He is dumb!

Today I had to call Mrs. Bennett for an hour before she finally came. Just when I start worrying there she is dainty-footing around. Aunt Jess says that is what cats do but I wish she wouldn't do it to me.

Sunday, 5:30 P.M.

Today we went to grandma and grandpa's for dinner and Mom and grandpa got in a fight at the dinner table. He called her a goddamn liveral and after that nobody said anything but pass the meat pass the potatoes pass the peas. It made me think of the night when Mom and Harry got in a fight and Mom went haywire and made him get out of the car and walk home. I hate to go in cars anymore because something bad always happens. Now Ryans little girl has something wrong with her blood and Aunt Jess says they are very worried about her. I heard them say she might even die.

All day long Grandma kept saying bless your heart

to me. I am the only one she ever says it to. Every time she does it Harry and Jimmy make a mark in the air like they're keeping track. Once she said bless your little heart and they counted that too. We stayed until nine o'clock and after dinner we watched a show on TV where a guy balanced a typewriter on his chin. All this time Mom and grandpa still weren't speaking.

Monday, 4:45 P.M.

I haven't skipped school or bitten my nails or lied or looked in the mirror except to comb my hair and brush my teeth. Sometimes if you do everything right bad things won't happen. I don't want Ryans little girl to die, that would be a very bad thing. Even if I don't know her.

I wish I had a sister instead of 2 brothers. We could trade clothes and sleep in the same room in bunk beds and go to the mall and it would only take a minute to do dishes because we would work together. Boys have to argue over everything and when you play games with them they only cheer for themselves. They make up cheers like you got to FIGHT to win, but when they lose they wine or get mad and throw the game on the floor. I said it should be you got to WINE to win, but they didn't think it was funny.

We are starting a unit about astronomy. Aldeberon twinkles and Mars shines evenly. I already know a lot of this, about the big dipper little dipper orion and the seven sisters and casseopeea, the big W in the sky, because Dad taught me. He knew everything about them. At night on the beach we always would lay on our backs and talk about them. He taught me lots more, but I can't remember. I just wish he was here.

25

"Mom, go up and look at my bedroom. I got up at six this morning and cleaned it."

"Good for you," she says.

"No. Go and *look*."

Julie's tone is emphatic, and she puts the newspaper aside; no sense trying to read it now. "As soon as I finish my coffee."

Harry comes down with his book bag, slinging it on the counter and heading for the refrigerator. Then Jimmy's boots clatter on the bare wood. How can they create such noise in simply descending a flight of stairs?

"Mom, I need three dollars to buy a ticket for *Romeo and Juliet*," Jimmy says. "Our English class is going."

She reaches for her purse.

"And I need a new box of colored pencils," Julie says.

"I thought we just—"

"I know, but they were the wrong colors. Yellow ocher and midnight blue . . . I need them for this map I'm making. It's only two dollars at the school store." That telltale wheedling, meaning it is a nonessential.

She hands Jimmy the three dollars. "Not this week," she says to Julie.

Meanwhile Harry rummages in the refrigerator. "Where's the leftover pancake batter?"

"Julie used it yesterday. No Coke for breakfast, Harry, put that back."

He heaves an enormous sigh as Jess comes down the stairs, tying a bright yellow scarf over the neck of her gray sweater.

"Mom, are you going to my school conference today?" Julie asks. "Tell Mrs. Posen about my room. She says I don't have good work habits."

"Since when?" she asks, knowing she's being primed, wondering what else there is in store for her.

Harry gives a snort, and Julie looks over. "You have the fattest lips," she says. "I just noticed. They're way fatter than anyone else in this family."

"What d'you think, Aunt Jess?" Harry asks. "Are my lips fat?"

"Of course not."

"Look before you say."

She makes a point of looking. "They're fine."

"On girls, maybe," Julie murmurs under her breath.

"Enough," Annie says firmly. "Jule, you're going to miss the bus. And don't forget your hat. You don't want to catch cold."

Her daughter's look is scornful. "You catch colds from people, Mom, not from temperature."

After they're out the door, she turns to her sister: "How is Cheryl?"

Jess shakes her head. "Not good. Yesterday her white count shot up again. She was vomiting all day." She goes to the refrigerator, takes out the pitcher of orange juice. "At least they think they know what it is now. They're giving her massive doses of penicillin. Ryan spent the night last night."

"What about Lucia?"

"She'll be going home Friday."

"Well, that's good. . . ."

"Yes. He's lined up a housekeeper and someone to come in and fix the meals. It'll be a while before things are back to normal, though. At least a couple of months."

"Can she manage alone, then?"

No answer. Jess's back is to her, taking a glass from the cupboard, pouring juice, drinking it down quickly. Then she says, "He's moving back there for a while. To give her a hand." Said too carefully; her voice absolutely neutral.

She can't keep the concern out of her own. "Oh, Jess. You mean he's giving up the apartment?"

She's nodding her head. "Gotta go. I'm late again. For the third day in a row." At the door now putting on her coat, she smiles, her hands searching her pockets. "I seem to be having trouble getting organized these days. Now I've lost my gloves."

"But what does this mean?"

"What? The apartment thing? Nothing." She turns away. "Am I on dinner detail tonight?"

"No, I am. I'll stop at the store on my way home."

She takes off her coat, listening while Terry tells of Vanessa's latest bout with croup.

"We were up with her all night . . . so scary."

"Did you turn on the shower?" Evelyn asks. "That's the best thing. . . ."

Betty says, "When my grandson had it they took him straight to the hospital. A thousand bucks for one night, can you imagine that?"

Terry nods. "That's just what we were afraid of. . . ."

Denise sighs. "I'm glad I decided not to have children. We lead such a hectic life, my husband and I. He's a stockbroker, you know." She shrugs out of her black cashmere coat. "We're out nearly every night, what with parties and dinners, all the rest . . ."

Annie turns away, embarrassed. She pours herself a cup of coffee. Out of what obscure grievance comes the urge to say this?

". . . and our friends are all doctors and lawyers . . . professional people. . . ."

Yet in some weird way, it makes her look vulnerable, for the first time. As if there is a need to impress these underlings—lowly cashiers and office help—with the worldly importance of her life.

"When my kids were little," Evelyn is saying, "I

used to hate winter. Every week it was something different—croup, fever, earaches, sore throats . . ."

"Pinkeye . . ."

"Nosebleeds . . ."

"Head lice!"

They are all laughing now, even Annie; she's looked upon as a part of the group now, ever since Terry befriended her. Yet the fact that no one feels insulted by Denise's remarks puts her on the outside.

"Mrs. Cole is the nicest person I've ever worked for," Evelyn said just the other day. That they would hold this opinion, so contrary to hers, is disturbing. Is it her, then? Why does she feel so harassed? Why, when she asks a simple question about the reason things are done a certain way, does Denise treat it as if she's being a nuisance? "Now, why would you need to ask that?" is the standard answer. That she is the target of Denise's hostility is apparent to her; yet it doesn't register on anyone else. Is she imagining it, then? Is she being paranoid? Every encounter with her superior seems to call it into question.

"I'll be needing you to come in early next week," Denise informs her as they leave the lounge. "We'll be working on inventory."

"How early?" she asks, and Denise turns abruptly to study her.

"Would you mind answering a question for me, Anne? Just exactly what are your ambitions here?"

For a moment she's stunned.

". . . Because it's important for me to understand just how you see yourself. I mean, in the overall scheme of things."

"I'm not sure what . . ."

"Are you at all interested in moving up, or is this simply a paycheck to you?"

Moving up? Where is there to go? Other than your job? She wants to say this, wants to stand here calmly, ignoring the tone of false concern. *Forget it. Just do your work.* The skin on her back is on fire, itching maddeningly.

"What time would you like me on Monday, then?"

Denise is looking at her. "I'm curious. You've never really had to work before, have you?"

Her shoulder is killing her now; her hands tingle, as if from an electric shock. She refuses to stand here like a servant, answering rude questions and then waiting to be dismissed, she doesn't care what happens. To hell with this woman, with everyone else as well. She is in her mother's kitchen and it is Sunday, after the explosion: "You are so rageful these days, Annie. I'm afraid for you. . . ." What had that even been about? She can't remember. Some statement by her father about feminism or homosexuality or Jews in Israel.

"Stop badgering me, Denise," she says, surprised at the menacing tone. *Who is this person?* "I'll come in whenever you want. But I won't put up with this shit from you for another minute." With that she turns away, walks back to her desk.

• • •

Mrs. Posen is ready for her in the colorful, brightly lit schoolroom.

"In general, her grades are good. Of course she's very bright, but she's having some trouble with her spelling. . . ."

Mrs. Posen has freckles; her voice, soft and breathy, reminds Annie of her own fourth-grade teacher, Mrs. Crattie, who used to wear her hair in a bun, fastened in back with metal skewers that looked like knitting needles. They called her "Mrs. Crappie."

She places the file folder on the table. On the cover Julie's name is written in red felt pen—red for girls, blue for boys, she notices.

"I feel it's important for the parents to identify with their children's problems . . ."

That must be the reason for squeezing into these god-awful, uncomfortable child-size desks.

". . . and of course, with Julie the important issue is continuity. So it's been difficult. Because of all the absences . . ."

"What absences?"

Mrs. Posen turns the attendance book around. She points out the red circles—one for each day that's been missed. Annie counts them: ten, since November!

"I don't know a thing about them," she murmurs.

Mrs. Posen is nonplussed. "Oh, dear . . . well, I sent the notes home . . . she always has a good reason . . . I guess I should have called. I never suspected . . . look, if you'd like, we can have a special conference."

From there she goes to Clara Barton, parking in the back lot, hurrying down the hall to discover that James Andrew is morose, a loner, easily discouraged, a "follower type."

"I've tried to interest him in some of our projects," says Mr. Haynes. "Somehow he manages to avoid any of the ones involving student interaction. . . ."

"But he loves science," she protests. "He loves to invent things. . . ."

"He's good at following directions, I'll give him that. But he won't ever experiment. He's a pretty timid little soul. . . ."

Still smarting, she moves on to Harry's math class, where Mr. Boxer informs her that Harry is five weeks behind, that he hasn't turned in any assignments since Christmas.

"It's not that he doesn't get it. But he doesn't apply himself. Not an unusual problem in eighth grade." He smiles at her. "The hormones are raging, as we know. . . ."

She looks away, toward the windows. Dark now, nearing six o'clock. "His father was . . . he used to help him with his math. I'm terrible . . . I don't understand half the stuff myself."

She hears him closing the grade book. "I hold special help sessions Friday mornings at seven-thirty. Listen, I'm sorry . . . I heard about his father. If there's anything you think I could do . . ."

At that, she reaches for her purse. She doesn't want this, either; stands up. "Thank you for telling me. I'll take care of it."

She allows him to walk her to the door.

At Farmer Jack's she scans the meat department, rejecting pot roast (not enough time), pork chops (too expensive), chicken (they had it last night), ignoring the lamb and beefsteak (not in her budget). She picks up a shallow brick of frozen ocean perch. Cheap enough, and it'll feed the five of them. Hefting it, she is aware what a perfect club it is, should she have the urge to bash someone with it. No shortage of candidates today.

Rehearsing her lecture on the drive home, she has her foot to the floor when the whir of a siren cuts through her conversation. Glancing up to see the patrol car in her rearview mirror, lights flashing. *Damn!*

"That caution light turned red, ma'am, before you went through it, you realize that?"

Silently she shakes her head.

"You were going fifty in a twenty-five-mile-an-hour zone. It's a busy street, ma'am. Lots of children on it."

"I'm sorry. . . ."

He nods politely. "All the same I'm afraid I'm going to have to issue you a ticket."

He takes forever to write it up while she sits, with cars gliding by in the darkness, furiously humiliated.

People staring, relieved it isn't them. She knows because she's done it herself. *Idiot!*

"I can't believe you did this to me," she storms in Julie's face the moment she arrives in the door. "Whatever in the world were you thinking?"

"Mom, school is boring!"

"I don't care if it's boring! It's your job!"

"Well, but I don't get paid for it, do I?"

"No more days off, do you understand?"

"What if I get sick?"

"If you're well enough to crawl, you're going."

Jimmy is devastated, his pale little face looking up at her in utter misery.

"What should I do, Mom?"

She doesn't know what to say. "You might try being a little more ..." What ... popular? Happy? Leaderly? How does one go about that? "Maybe you could try being nicer to Mr. Haynes," she suggests.

"Haynes is a massive dink," Harry pronounces from the couch. He, of course, is the toughest nut; no remorse, no attempt at an excuse. He refuses to accord it any significance.

"I'm not gonna flunk math," he says. "I'll probably get a D in it. D is passing."

"Does the idea of being grounded for the rest of the year mean anything to you?"

He shrugs. "I don't have anyplace to go."

"What I want to see from you, Harry, is at least a B in there."

He looks up at her, blue eyes like ice. "Or what?"

Or you can start looking for a new place to live, she wants to scream. "Believe me, I'll think of something," she finishes lamely.

"I don't get it," Jess says. "How can somebody be both a loner and a follower? Who is he supposed to be following?"

"Don't start picking on the teachers. It's not their fault." Her back is killing her, and she shifts position on the couch, trying to get some relief. "My question is, Why do they all decide to be jerks at the same time?"

"Annie, they're not jerks. And anyway, statistics are all on your side."

"Meaning what?"

"Meaning they're smart, white, and middle class. So the deck is stacked in their favor."

Silence. "In other words, quit complaining."

"I didn't say that." Jess sighs. "Maybe you just shouldn't have tried to tackle all three conferences the same day."

"And then I have to go and get a stupid traffic ticket."

They are in the family room, at opposite ends of the couch. "I need to start cleaning up my life," she says. "Squirt some of these buggy people off my windshield. I can't figure out what I've ever done to Denise Cole to make her dislike me so. Everything she says makes me want to scratch her eyes out."

Jess puts down her magazine. "Does she have any kids?"

"No." Annie sits up. "God, I wish I didn't."

"Oh, Annie . . ."

She forces a grin. "Just kidding. Forget it." But of course she won't, can tell it by the way her shoulders hunch. A careless remark, considering this morning's conversation.

Later on, in bed, she buries her head beneath the pillow, pretending to sleep. Long ago, in the attic room at her grandparents' house, she lay with every nerve alive, awaiting the dawn and word that her mother had given birth to a baby, whose big sister she would be. Impatient, just as she always was at Christmas, plundering the closetful of presents under the stairs, loosening paper, untying ribbons to get at the secrets inside. Always having to know things ahead of time.

Now there's nothing left to know. More to the point, what's left is just more bad news. Still, there are things expected of you; questions, commands, decisions to be made, with the minutes ticking by so slowly it makes you frantic. The kids are wrong, her whole life feels wrong. Something wrong, too, with Jess. But she can't summon up enough energy even to ask.

Maybe things aren't as bad as they seem. But she doesn't believe that, doesn't believe in things being better than they appear. No shortage of people telling

you how to behave—heed the caution lights, love
your kids, be there to help those in need, come to
work early. All the while you're out there sitting on
someone's goddamn grave. Five months. Is the same
as five minutes. Lord, I miss him, I miss him, this is
too hard, I can't do it, don't even know, anymore,
how to try.

26

Harry unlocks the door, brushing snow away with
his boot. Lucky bounds down the stairs to greet them.
Rex is behind him, sticking his hand through the hole
in the storm door.

"What happened?"

"Jimmy locked the door on me."

Racing to be first out this morning, he'd gotten
halfway to the bus stop before he saw he'd forgotten
his backpack. By the time he got back, the door was
locked against him and Jimmy was laughing on the
other side. He'd given it a vicious kick, and to their
mutual horror the glass exploded into the room. Julie,
at the kitchen table, shrieked as if she'd been stabbed.
They cleaned it up, dumping the glass into the
garbage can out back, but there was nothing they
could do about her; she was collapsed in a huddle on
the floor, not to be comforted. Finally in desperation
he yelled: "It's only a stupid door!" and she sat up,
wiping her eyes, turning it off like a faucet. He could
kill her when she does stuff like that.

"Hey, Lucky, want to go for a walk?" Rex asks.

Lucky jumps and whines, pawing the air in joyful frenzy as Rex leads him to the door, opens it, closes it again.

"Not right now. Maybe later."

Harry opens the refrigerator.

"Got anything to eat in here? What's that?"

"Pea soup."

"Sea poop? Arrggh, no thanks. How about some of that cheese?" He leans down into Lucky's face. "Walk, Lucky? Huh? Want to go for a walk?" Lucky dances frantically on his back paws.

"Don't tease the dog, okay?" He finds the paper bag with two Cokes that he has hidden in the meatkeeper.

"You could tell your mom it was a prowler," Rex says. "Tell her what the guy looked like, you know—dirty jeans, baseball cap, scraggy beard. . . ."

"She wouldn't buy it."

Julie comes down the stairs, a blanket trailing from her shoulders. "Where'd you get that Coke?" She flounces over to the TV, turns it on.

"How come you're home?" he counters.

"Dentist appointment. Mom gave me a ride."

"So she saw the door."

"Uh-uh. She dropped me off out front." A little smile. "But I told her about it." She looks at Rex. "You have the weirdest haircut I ever saw on a human being."

"That so?"

"Look how far you have to go to get to your head!"

Rex grabs the blanket from her. "Little peahead tattler, let's teach her a lesson!"

She gives him a look, plops down on her knees in front of the TV. "Now, she is a bitch." She points at the screen. "She is evil, we want her dead." She bounces up and down on her knees. Her pink ballet slippers peek out from beneath her butt.

Rex inclines his head toward the stairway, putting fingers to his lips, miming a swift intake of breath. They take their Cokes and go upstairs.

Once inside the bedroom, Harry shuts the door, takes a pack of Camels from his jacket pocket. They light up, and he crosses the room to open the window.

"That Melanie Raymond is kinda cute," Rex says. "Big hair, nice knockers. She live around here?"

"Not really."

"Maybe we should go see her. Or else maybe go to Piccadilly Circus."

He shakes his head. "I dropped six bucks over there yesterday."

"Cousineau and Pappas are gonna be there."

Rex wanders about, picking up things and putting them down. Jimmy's book bag is open on the floor. Baseball cards, comic books, smelly socks, pajamas, underwear—all strewn about. Why can't he keep his crap on his own side of the room?

"Where's the puley puker, anyway?"

"Hockey practice."

"I thought we were going to talk to him today. About being the lookout."

"We haven't even picked a store yet."

"Best Buy." Rex burps. "Arrgg. Weird taste. You think Pop-Tarts go bad?"

"Probably that moldy hot dish we had at lunch. Listen. I think we oughta work on this plan awhile. . . ."

Rex shrugs. "Work on it all you want, sooner or later you gotta do it. Anyway, I've lifted bigger stuff than a camcorder." He inhales, blowing blue smoke into the room. "But we definitely need a lookout. So, how about it? Raymond's or Piccadilly? No sense hanging around here."

There's a knock on the door.

"Go away," he says.

"I need to talk to you."

Crossing to the door, he opens it, sticks his head out. She's standing there, twisting a rope of her hair in her fingers.

"What d'you want?"

"Mrs. Bennett's gone. I haven't seen her since this morning."

"She's around somewhere. Just go watch TV."

"She's not. She's always waiting for me on the back steps." Trying to peer around him into the room. "I just called Mom at work."

"Why'd you do that? You're not supposed to call unless it's something important."

"This *is* important!"

"It's a cat," says Rex, coming to stand next to the door. He has deposited his cigarette butt on the windowsill.

Julie stares coldly at him. "You're an infant. You don't know anything." Turning away, she clatters down the stairs.

Harry shuts the door, bends to pick up a wet towel from the floor. He tosses it onto Jimmy's bed.

"Let's go," Rex says.

He shakes his head. "I got a couple things to do around here."

"Like what?"

"Just things."

He has no intention of taking Rex over to Melanie's. He barely has the nerve to go himself. Her parents are both lawyers, and they live in Huntington Woods on a wide, curving street of mammoth houses. He pictures her—brown eyes with long lashes, that funny little half-grin, the way she cradles her books in her arms, with her fingers tucked inside the sleeves of her sweater. She is the prettiest girl he's ever seen, and she told him that she's wanted to meet him for a year, ever since she saw him at a football game in seventh grade. As for him, he might be in love, but he's not stupid. He's not about to introduce her to any of the weird people he hangs out with, at least not right away.

• • •

Julie stands beside the sliding door. Her forehead is pressed against the glass. Her hand wipes away the steam from her breath.

"I know you guys were smoking up there," she says.

He doesn't answer. It's raining lightly; the rainiest winter that he can remember. What snow there is out there will soon turn to slush.

Screep, screep. Her hand wipes across the glass. He goes to get a glass of milk from the refrigerator, and she turns away from the window, leaves the room. He sits down in front of the TV. In a few minutes he'll call Melanie; she said she'd be home this afternoon.

Julie comes back, shrugging into her parka. She has her boots on.

"Where you goin'?"

"Out to look for her."

"Oh, cripes. Wait a minute, then."

"You don't have to come."

But he gets up from the couch, grabbing his coat from the back of the chair. "I don't want Mom getting all pissed at me over this. . . ."

"Hurry up," she says. "It's starting to get dark."

They walk quickly, looking left and right. The rain is a heavy mist, and they have already covered several blocks. He knows it is pointless. Too small of a target, too much space. She could be anywhere. She could be on the block they just finished searching.

"Sometimes she goes down to Conroys'," Julie says. "Mrs. Bennett . . . Beeeee . . . !" She calls into the gloom. Like Mrs. Letovsky across the street, who used to call to her dead cat in the middle of the night. It gave him the creeps. "I hope nobody decided to steal her."

"Nobody's gonna steal her." Why would they? he wants to ask. Instead he says, "She's too fast, anyway."

"She is, isn't she? And she doesn't like strangers very much." She's walking ahead of him. "I'm gonna go up Brookview and then circle back around."

"Jule. It's too dark. She might even be home by now."

"D'you think?"

"Maybe." But he's not sure anymore; her anxiety is contagious. And the blackness is yielding up strange shadows, ominous shapes in the road. Near the corner is a bluish mound settled into a shadow of darker blue at the street. He walks behind her, keeping his eyes on it. It could be a squirrel. No; too large for a squirrel. Maybe a chunk of ice that has fallen off somebody's car.

Julie stops, her hands clasped in front of her. "What's that?" she asks. "D'you see it?"

He does. He's known in his heart for the last few minutes. But she whispers, "It's not her. It's too small, I think. She's bigger than that."

A mound of wet, gray fur. Still, he doesn't want to

be right. The closer they get, the more he is sure of it. Thin little body lying at the curbside; tiny ears, tight to her head; pink nose, pink tongue.

"Is it her, d'you think?"

He bends to look; reaches out to touch the body. Not stiff; not warm, either. He turns it on its back, sees the white star on the chest. Julie has seen it, too. He hears the swift intake of breath behind him.

"But she's all right, isn't she? Is she okay?"

A car pulls to the curb beside them. "You know, this is what happens when you let animals run loose. Why don't you kids take care of your pets? You shouldn't have them if you're not going to look after them!"

Harry looks up. He doesn't recognize the voice; it is no one that he knows. Beside him, Julie's hands clutch at her coat. Tears are starting to spill down her cheeks.

"There's a leash law, you know. . . ." The man leans to the passenger door. "You kids need a ride somewhere?"

He stands up, glaring into the car's dark interior. "We live there." He points to the house across the street. The car starts up, then stops. As if he can't decide whether to move on or continue the scolding. Harry waves it away brusquely. Then he bends to lift the cat in his arms.

She's weightless, her body limp, her sightless eyes

staring up at him. There's no blood, no sign of a wound. Beside him, Julie is crying hard now. Snot running from her nose.

"Shh, it's okay. Mom'll take her to the vet."

"She's moving, isn't she? I can see her paw moving. Is she sleeping, maybe?"

He doesn't answer, feels a rush of guilt—for what he cannot imagine, for everything he doesn't understand in this life, every way he's messed up.

They put her on a towel in the kitchen. Her mouth is open, eyes not quite closed; behind the lids are pale greenish slits. Julie sits, stroking the limp body.

"All the way home her paw was moving. She'll be all right. We just have to get her to the vet." She pushes gently at the legs, willing them to move on their own.

"She must've got hit by a car. . . ." Jimmy murmurs.

Julie shakes her head firmly. "Nothing's broken. See? There's no blood anywhere." More tears. Lucky comes into the kitchen, sniffing curiously at the gray bundle.

"We need to take her now," she says. "Maybe we should call a taxi."

Harry kneels beside her. "Jule. I think she's gone."

"If we take her up there," Jimmy says, "they'll just keep her."

At this she sits upright, wipes her eyes. "Okay, then. What should we do?"

They wrap the kitten in the towel, and Julie puts the small bundle inside a shoe box. Harry fills the teakettle at the sink.

"The hole doesn't have to be real deep, does it?"

"You don't want some animal coming along and digging her up."

They put on their coats, get shovels from the garage. Harry pours the boiling water on the ground beside the unfinished deck, where the snow has melted and the dirt is not so packed down. The three of them take turns digging. At last Harry brings out the yardstick: nearly two feet deep.

They place the box at the bottom of the hole, shovel the dirt on top of it. Julie tamps it down with her bare hands.

Afterward they go back inside, watch a rerun of *The Cosby Show*. The Huxtable kids trying to air out the bedroom so their parents won't find out they were smoking.

"She was probably on her way home when it happened," Jimmy says.

Beside him, Julie starts to cry again. He doesn't look at her, reaches down to pick a piece of lint from the sweater Grandma Lewis gave him. She bought it at a garage sale for fifty cents, along with a cookie jar shaped like a chicken. Dark brown striped with tan and green at the chest. Hand-knit, she told him. That's something these days.

"Harry," Jimmy says. "What are we gonna do about the door?"

He shrugs his shoulders, doesn't feel like talking about it now.

"I bet we can fix it. Put a piece of plastic in there instead of glass. Then it'll never break."

He doesn't answer. Julie keeps crying, sliding her hands over red, raw cheeks. Only a cat, he thinks. Think of them like blue stars. Hot, blue stars have the shortest lives with high internal temperatures, consuming fuel at a faster rate than the sun. Stars like Vega, which have only a few hundred million years left. Only a cat. Not like it's a person.

"We didn't have her very long, did we?" Julie says at last.

"Anyway," says Jimmy, "now she's with Dad."

At this Harry turns on him. "Don't say stupid things like that!"

A shocked silence. "Jimmy's right," Julie says. "They're in heaven together. There's anything up there you want—pets and horses, beaches, hockey rinks—"

"Fine. There's telephones, too. Call him on the WATS line, why don't you?"

They both look at him. Wearily he closes his eyes. He can't help it, can't help saying what's on his mind. "He's dead, you guys. He's in the ground. Just like the guy who got biffed at the air show when the plane blew up in midair and all his guts came down on everybody. It's over, you know?"

"Why you acting so mad about it?"

"I'm not mad!"

"You saying you don't believe in God?"

"I believe in Him," he says. "I just think He's a jerk."

27

A message for her on the machine: "Jess, I'm working late. Be home around nine. Get Julie to help you with dinner. There's pizza in the freezer."

She takes off her coat, sits down at the kitchen table. No other messages. These days she lives from meeting to meeting, pushing time. Five days. Three days. Only two more days. *Lord, I love him. I am lovesick. It is a sickness, I swear.*

Last week, when Cheryl was released from the hospital, she felt relieved; her leg was mending nicely, the blood disease under control. Good news, wonderful news. So why does she now feel as if she's fallen into some great dark hole?

Valentine's Day. Just three days ago. He appeared at the door, a box of Sanders chocolates for Annie and the kids, a purple silk blouse for her. He made her try it on then and there. It fit perfectly, felt wonderful, so soothing against her skin. He wore a blue oxford-cloth shirt. Fresh from the laundry, she could tell. Looking so thin, his face almost gaunt. She saw the spattering of freckles on his hands, the clean slash of hair across his brow, felt warmth flooding downward.

Sex can become an obsession, a drug; you don't care about anything else. Afterward you are sated, full, as lazy as a cow. What else matters? After sex she is full of him, smelling his aftershave, his sweet body scent on herself.

She once took a psychology course in college, and the term *obsessive-compulsive* fell about her shoulders like a mantle. She felt vindicated, understood at last. No need to agonize anymore. "Obsessive-compulsive," she says whenever she catches herself. But it's harder now, much harder; they are never completely alone. They have to sneak up to her room after everyone else is in bed. Or else, do it on the downstairs couch, like a couple of high-schoolers. Abstention breeds obsession. Marathon nights, four-hour stints, after which he then has to get up, stagger into his clothes, and go home to his other family.

"Ryan, we need to talk about this," she told him the other night. "About how things are going."

"They're going as well as they can go. It won't be much longer, I promise."

But this no longer reassures her. For some reason it makes her think of last summer, when they were sailing on Lake St. Clair. The wind had come up out of the north as they were coming about, wrinkling the smooth silk water, and suddenly they veered off, nearly capsizing. She wasn't afraid then; they were both good swimmers. And in a moment the yawl had righted itself, and they were laughing at their close call. She doesn't feel like laughing anymore. The damage here feels somehow permanent, predicted. She did it on purpose, I know she did. And hasn't she gotten exactly what she wanted? He's living just four miles away, a phone call away. But she wouldn't dream of calling him, cannot imagine a scenario in which she could bring herself to do that.

The phone rings and she grabs up the receiver. "Hello?"

"Jessie, what's going on? Dad and I haven't heard from you two for ages!"

She sighs. "Nothing much, Mom. Everything's fine."

"I heard about the conferences. Annie's got to get a handle on this. It doesn't get any easier, I know from experience."

It makes her want to laugh. From where did her mother glean this experience? Surely not from Annie, of the high marks and sterling character, who never caused them a moment's worry.

"Mom, don't panic, they're not going to turn out like me."

"Well. I'm sure she doesn't want Harry becoming a juvenile delinquent. . . ."

On cue, Harry, the JD, hollers down the stairs: "Aunt Jess, I need a ride to Blockbuster Video!"

She covers the receiver. "Can't you go on your bike?"

"It's raining!"

"Believe me," her mother says, "those grades will make a difference when he tries to get into college. . . ."

"Mom, hang on a minute." She calls to him: "I'll take you after dinner!"

He comes down, hangs over the railing, the better to nag at her. "It'll only take a second, I know what I want."

"Why don't you come over here for dinner this week?" her mother says. "Bring Ryan, if you like."

"I'll talk to Annie about it."

"What's to talk about? Come next Saturday. Oh, and tell her Amelia's daughter is having another baby. That makes six."

A reproving cluck, and her mother is gone, but Harry is now at her elbow. To divert him, she asks, "Did you guys remember to bring the garbage cans in?"

He rolls his eyes. "We never took 'em out. We were late for the bus."

"They always forget to do it," Julie says. "Aunt Jess, you should've seen this house I passed on the way home from school. Crummy old swing in the front yard, a baby bed out in the snow, about a hundred other broken-down things! A piece of dock, an old trailer with the door off . . . there was so much junk it was just ludicrous."

"Ludicrous. Where do you get those words?"

"What're we having for dinner?"

"Pizza. Unless you want to help me make maca-
roni and cheese."

She sighs. "I think I'm too tired to cook."

"C'mon," Harry begs. "Run me up to Blockbuster,
it'll only take two minutes."

"Is there some reason we can't go later?"

"Yes!"

"Why?"

"Because I don't have anything to do right now!"

In spite of herself she laughs, reaching over to rub
his head with her knuckles, feeling the hard knob at
the base of his skull—a Lewis trait, inherited from
his grandmother.

"Where was Rex today?" Julie asks. Drawling it.
Rakes.

"Dunno," he says.

"I thought you two were glued together." Said
sweetly. Eyebrows arched. Trying to start something.
These two are the magnetic poles around which the
house arranges itself; when they are in harmony, all
is well.

To distract her niece, she says, "Set the table, will
you?"

"Why do I always have to do everything?"

"Hey, girl," she says. Copying the drawl. "That
don't butter any parsnips with me."

"What does that even mean?" Jimmy asks from his
seat on the couch.

"How do I know? My mom used to say it to me."

"Hey, listen to this. Directions for making head-cheese. 'Have the butcher clean the head, taking out snout, tongue, and brains. Remove root and skin from tongue and cut into pieces the size of large wal-nuts. . . .' "

"Yeuucch!" Julie covers her ears. "That's gross. Jame, don't read any more!"

"Couldn't we just have a regular conversation?" she asks.

Silence. They look at her in amazement. As if she has suggested they hang by their heels from the ceiling.

Harry speaks for them. "About what?"

After dinner she cleans up the kitchen, looks over Julie's list of spelling words, runs Harry up to Block-buster Video. All with this ache in her heart that refuses to go away.

When she was living alone in her apartment, she used to go out for long walks; walking and thinking of him, of their coming life together, made her feel strong. Looking up at the sky with its bowl of stars, thinking about the world trundling along on its axis. Drinking in the smells, falling under the spell of the night.

She doesn't do this anymore; there's no comfort out there now. Instead, something looming in the darkness, ready to cause her harm. And he doesn't feel it, doesn't sense its approach. Or he won't admit it. This, then, is the real source of their separation.

Tom Chase said something to her the other day. Something about men who are in love with loss. They think they're in a Russian novel, he said. They can't let go of tragedy. It's the only part of the game they understand.

I promise you, you'll be very sorry. Agonizing over it, feeling guilty about it, almost as if she's the criminal. But she's not, is she? "She accused me of wrecking her life. . . ." And he had said, "Her life was wrecked long before you came into it." True. Lucia's life isn't the only one thrown into chaos by all of this.

Annie comes in at ten, tosses her coat on a chair. Jess fills her in on the phone call.

"I don't want to go to Mom's for dinner," she says.

"Maybe we could have them over here."

"I don't think I want to sit at any tables with Dad for a while." Her back is to Jess as she picks through the leftovers from the refrigerator. "God, I'm tired. I never thought working could be this hard."

All the time she was growing up, Jess could always crawl into her sister's bed at night, tell her darkest secrets. This was the way her sins were forgiven. Annie was the finder of solutions; she, the producer of clues. But Annie has other preoccupations now.

Jess wants to talk to her about all of this, wants to ask if Annie thinks she is, in fact, this heartless woman who cares only about her own happiness. Last week she sat here with Ryan while they again watched *Mrs. Soffel.* Except, this time, she was amazed to discover the minister's wife hadn't died, after all; she'd been rescued from her romantic liaison, pronounced insane, locked away in an asylum.

28

"Here's a story," says Rex, "about a guy who gets killed in a traffic accident and they take him to the morgue. He's there for two days and all of a sudden they hear weird noises. So they open up the box and guess what? He's still alive." He pops a Dorito into his mouth. He's lying on his back in the middle of the floor, a can of Coke balanced on his forehead.

"Bullyatz," Harry says.

"Uh-uh. Really happened. His girlfriend wouldn't have anything to do with him after that because she thought he was a zombie." The can stays in place as he chews. "Or how about we make an earthquake movie? That cop flyin' off the freeway, that'd be a great scene."

Jimmy yawns. All of Rex's ideas come from the *Weekly World News.* Last week it was Bat Boy who grew up in a cave. "How about one about a guy who's been in bed since 1932? That'd be interesting."

Rex sits up. "You gonna help us, Pulie? You be lookout, maybe we'll let you in on it."

"Whoopee. Anyway, you guys are gonna get

caught. You'll end up in Juvie. Who's gonna keep this camera after you lift it?"

"What d'you care?" Harry asks, rolling to his stomach. "All right," he demands. "Who cut it? Was that you, Beers?"

"Smells like somebody's dead body. That means you."

Harry gives a fiendish laugh. "You ever notice Grandpa's farts?" He looks at Jimmy. "Sheesh! Megabombs!"

Rex points to Jimmy's hand. "What's that?"

It is where he has drawn the diamond symbol with wings, in blue ink on the back of his wrist. He hides it under his back. "Nothin'. Power symbol."

"What kinda power?"

"He copied it out of a book," Harry says.

"Stay outta my desk, Nose-ass."

"That book's two months overdue. How come you can lift something from the library but not from Best Buy? Oh, right, the library's not gonna send you to Juvie."

"What kinda power?" asks Rex.

"*Secrets of the Druids . . .*" Harry intones.

"Shut up." And to Rex: "It's a way to find things out."

"What things?"

"Anything. Whatever you want to know."

"Let me see it."

He shows Rex the symbol again. "It means containment of the universe."

"It's some kinda religion, isn't it? Like Baptist? No, thanks."

"It's way before Baptists."

Harry snickers. "They believe in square dancing. Hey, Beers, let's go over to Linklers and shoot hoops."

"They believe in human sacrifice," he says, "and necromancy."

"Sex with dead people?"

"Not sex. You talk to them. To find out things you want to know about life, about the future."

Harry twirls his finger beside his ear. He ignores this, holds his hands, inches apart, in front of him. "They're this far away from us all the time. Only you don't see them because of the veils."

"What veils?"

"Between the worlds. They screen the stuff out so you won't go crazy."

"Too late," Harry says.

". . . Because if you knew everything that was out there . . ."

"How about puttin' that design on me?" Rex asks.

"You can't just put it on somebody."

"Why not? It's a club, isn't it? We'll join."

"How many members you got?" Harry asks.

"Nobody gets in without being initiated." He gets up, removes his shirt to reveal the upside-down blue triangle connecting his nipples to his navel, the lines outlining his ribs.

"I suppose you're the head guy," Harry says, with a smirk.

"I'm Lug. God of medicine."

"Who'm I?" Rex asks.

"You can be Mabon. The white bull. Your job is to keep out the unbelievers."

Upstairs in their bedroom, he reaches into the back of his drawer for the blue Magic Markers.

"Copy this design on your chest. Leave it on for three days. After that you can wash it off, but it'll still be there, just invisible to the naked eye."

"This is so lame," Harry says, but he's taking off his shirt.

"So when do we find out about the human sacrifice?" Rex asks.

He reaches into the desk drawer for his cloth bag, lifting out the pressed oak leaves. He gives one to each. "Druid means Oak Man. It's the sacred tree. Keep these someplace where nobody can find 'em. They're like a passport."

Rex is circling his nipples with wide loops, drawing the outline of his ribs.

"Looks like a raccoon with whiskers," Harry says. "Man, this stuff better come off. . . ."

"It will. You gotta scrub hard."

With the Magic Marker he traces half circles under his eyes. On both cheeks he draws the sign of the universe. Outside the light is disappearing.

"Okay," he says. "When you're done put on your coats and go outside. Use the front door. I'll meet you behind the garage."

"This better be good," says Rex. "We better be contacting some dead people pretty soon."

Julie looks up from her book. "What's that all over your face?"

"Tell Mom I had to go to Rudimans' for a while. I'll be back. Harry's coming with." A dumb lie; why would Harry be going over to Rudimans', to help him feed a couple of cats? He rummages in the closet for matches and charcoal lighter, a ball of string, stuffs it all into the bag. "We'll be back by six-thirty."

Julie is staring at him. "Ugh, that looks so bogus."

He slams the door, hurrying to where Harry and Rex are waiting behind the garage.

"So far this whole thing seems Mickey Mouse," Harry grumbles. "Where we goin'?"

"Down by the park."

The Christmas tree is still here, where he has hidden it behind a pile of cardboard. He lifts it upright. "We gotta take this with us."

"What the hell for?"

"Part of the ritual. They've been doing this for thousands of years. You have to promise not to tell."

"Tell what? I haven't heard anything yet."

Cold air slides up underneath his jacket as they walk, and it's dark by the time they get there. He

turns on his flashlight, leads them back to the baseball diamond.

Rex laughs, his breath blue in the chilled air. "This
is gettin' kinda cheesy, Puker."

"You're Tanarus," he says to Harry. "God of fire.
You get to anoint the sacred tree. First tie this up on
top." He hands him the mistletoe he stole from
Grandma Lewis's doorway at Christmas. They tie the
tree between the bleachers, fastening it to each of
the railings. Stepping back and closing his eyes, he
repeats the lines he has memorized:

> *"No wee aku labadura*
> *No wee aku minoru*
> *Scribiato atol. . . ."*

"The first fire was started by lightning. But that's
all right. Now we take off our jackets."

Harry groans. "Are you kidding? It's frickin'
freezing!"

But he has already stripped, and they follow suit.
The blue lines on his chest look eerie in the beam
from the flashlight. He reaches into the bag, hands
Harry the matches and lighter fluid. "Soak it good."

Harry takes the can of lighter fluid. Carefully he
wets down the tree, squirting extra fluid onto the
lower branches.

"Now, before we light it we say a prayer." Aiming
the flashlight at his chest. "This fire, made to

symbolize the sacred lightning that gives us wisdom, is lit to summon those beyond. Believe and you will soon know all. Tanarus will now light the tree." He motions Harry forward, and Harry strikes the match, hurls it at the branches.

With a sound like a giant intake of breath, the air swooshes upward; a cloud of yellowish-white light. The tree explodes, crackling, spitting sparks, and they spiral to the sky, whipped by a mysterious wind. Incandescent orange diamonds, forming patterns. He can see a horse galloping, a huge cone of light. A thin sliver of moon floats above the line of trees.

Harry has reeled backward and is leaning against the bottom step of the bleachers, a hand to his eyes. The string that holds the tree upright burns through; it falls backward to the ground. He stares into the glowing branches, mesmerized. Harry picks up a handful of snow, rubs it over his face. The tree is smoking now, hissing. Sparks fly from it. A large branch splits away.

"What's the matter?" Rex is looking at Harry.

"Nothin'. Just got some dirt in my eyes. We'd better get goin'. Somebody'll be out here checkin' up . . ." Bending over, he picks up his jacket. Rex steps to throw snow on the burning skeleton; puffs of steam billow into the air. He stomps at the ashes with his boot.

They take the back way, through the alley. He

leans into the wind, jacket open, feeling the heat from the moon, like an invisible shield. Beside him Harry walks silently, carrying the can of fluid.

"I'll see you guys tomorrow," Rex says when they reach the house. He climbs on his bike, riding off into the darkness.

"D'you think they'll notice anything?" Harry is touching his forehead gingerly.

"Why?"

"I might've got burned a little. . . ."

He looks. "I don't see anything."

"That was all pretty much bullshit, Jame."

"Maybe. Maybe not." He shrugs, wanting to talk to Harry about what he thinks happened out there. How to begin? He wants to tell him about a book he once read. About lake storms. Those huge waves, capable of taking a merchant ship the size of the *Edmund Fitzgerald* to the bottom of the lake bed, are called Christmas trees. *Calm down, it's nothing to be afraid of.*

"Let's leave the stuff outside. We'll head upstairs."

They enter through the sliding glass door. Harry pushes the curtain aside. His mother and his aunt are in the kitchen, getting dinner. She glances up as they pass. "Oh, my God, Harry! What did you do?"

Their aunt turns to look. "Your eyebrows . . . !"

"Nothin'. We just burned up the Christmas tree."

"What's that smell?" Julie asks. "Like gasoline or something. Eek, your hair! It's all burned in front!"

"It was just in a pile of junk out behind the garage. So we decided to get rid of it. . . ." He runs a palm over his forehead; crinkled black hairs come off in his hand. "I gotta go take a shower."

"James Andrew," says his mother, "what is this all about? Whose idea was this?"

"They were with Rex," Julie says, and Harry turns on her.

"Stay out of this! You don't know shit!"

An odd tingling in his fingertips. The tops of his ears are burning hot. He can feel her eyes on him. Suddenly he is exhausted, empty of everything.

"Mom, we didn't . . . it was an accident. . . ."

"What do you mean an accident? Did you set it? How can that be an accident?"

Harry is disappearing up the stairs, and he wants to go with him, go to his room and lie down, take a long rest. He doesn't want to think about this. Not yet.

His aunt is looking at his mother. "He's a follower, huh?"

Let this power pass from me. He sits across the dinner table from Harry, avoiding the naked face slightly tinged with blue, the frizzled hair. Harry's eyelashes and eyebrows are gone. He looks haunted, like some wild-eyed stranger.

After dinner he goes to his room, takes out his math homework. He likes to test himself; his record for doing an assignment is six minutes, forty-two seconds. Harry comes in to get undressed. His chest is still red from the scrubbing he gave it in the shower; yet the blue lines remain.

"You still want to join the club?" he asks.

"What club? There's no club." Harry pulls his pajama top over his head.

He leans back in his chair. "Why d'you always have to act like such a cool guy?"

"Why d'you have to be so fuckin' weird?"

He doesn't want things to go this way, wants to explain that it feels as if he's sitting on top of a mountain, looking down at a road where he can see everything. The people are cut off from each other, aware of only the small section of path ahead; they can't see around the next turn. He's seen around the turn, can't unsee it now. *Let this power pass from me.*

"You're an asshole, you know it?" he mumbles. Not what he means to say at all.

"Just quit reading stupid books, okay?" Harry says coldly. "Nothing's gonna get fixed from you reading stupid books. And if I see you take another ten from Mom's purse, I'm gonna tell her."

"I never took anything from Mom's purse!" Cheeks burning, he sits up straight in the chair. "Quit talkin' to me, asshole. You and your asshole friends who borrow other people's money and say they're gonna pay it back. You know damn well they're not gonna pay it back!"

"What did you give it to him for? Nobody made you."

"Who told him I even had it? And who knew my bike wasn't locked?"

An ominous silence. "What're you saying? You saying I had something to do with that?" Harry's voice, edgy with warning, brings him down; he's gone too far, he knows it, would like to take it back, but he won't.

"Anyway, I don't want you in it. For sure I don't want any of those dicks I play hockey with. And it doesn't matter whether you believe in it or not. It works either way."

Late that night he awakes with a start, raises up on his elbows in answer to some unknown dread. Looking at the clock, he sees that it's twelve-thirty. He can hear the murmur of voices coming from the living room. The two of them up late again, talking into the night. It used to be a comfort to him. Not anymore.

He glances across to Harry in the other bed, head buried beneath the pillow. At hockey practice the other day he heard Kevin Galtier say something to Jamie Mack about a sleepover. He wasn't invited. Who cares? He doesn't need anything from those jerks. Dumb Jamie'll be sorry, he'll give him a stick in the ankle that'll make him sorry. He hates them all.

Climbing out of bed, he goes out to the landing, where a chill breeze is blowing up the stairway. His mother's voice, barely audible, has that scary, flat tone; he wonders if Mr. Sharpe told her about the scene in the lunchroom with Gordy Bando when he tipped over a table on him. She never said a word. Probably saving it up, like she does with Harry. How did Harry guess about the money, anyway? He can't believe he ever saw it. Everybody's a liar.

He hears his aunt's voice in answer to something: "Annie, you know they're good kids. . . ."

"I don't know anything. What I see is that they're mean-tempered and sneaky and they treat each other like enemies," says his mother.

His aunt sighs. "Then maybe you should talk to them. If you really feel like that."

"Talk to them? That's the last thing I want to do!"

Good. The last thing he wants, also. He doesn't wait to hear more, turns around and tiptoes back to his room, climbs into bed, pulling the covers tight around his ears. Sleep it off. Don't think about it, don't think about anything. This is what he gets for communing with the gods.

29

In the world of human relations, certain laws prevail; that being in the worst possible shape, you will have the most encounters with Bad Energy.

Today at the grocery store the clerk singles her out: she bought twenty dollars' worth of groceries and wrote a check for fifty, wasn't she aware the limit is fifteen dollars over purchase, blah, blah, blah, while the people in line behind her rearrange the food in their baskets, trying not to listen. She concedes that she forgot. The clerk studies her printout: "But, ma'am, you cashed one here for seventy just yesterday."

So, not only is she trying to beat the system, now she is branded a liar. Handing her her change with thinly disguised contempt, the clerk goes on to the next customer and Annie slinks out with her ill-gotten gains, wondering how on earth she managed to spend seventy dollars since yesterday. She's broke, that's why she wrote that check today—to pay the paperboy, buy a pair of hose to wear to work, give the kids their weekly lunch money. She reaches the car and it dawns on her: she wrote a check for seventy dollars and bought sixty dollars' worth of groceries! That's where the money went—back into the damned store!

For a moment she's on the verge of going back, just to tell the clerk how it feels—as a longtime cus-tomer, and in front of her fellow citizens—to be treated like this—! She opens the car door, acciden-tally brushing the side of the car next to hers. From inside it comes a growl: "You always ram into people's vehicles like that without looking?"

She barely touched it; not a scratch, not even a scraping of the layer of dirt. Yet these encounters, back-to-back, are more than she can stand. These Bad Energy People—BEPs, Keith used to call them—roaming the city, seeking out the weak, the desperate. Just dying to pounce on you and put you in the wrong! Dangerous to leave the house whenever they're on patrol.

"Why is it every time I come here the weather turns lousy? Or is it just because Detroit only has lousy weather?"

"We're having a bad winter," she concedes.

They are on their way downtown, to the symphony. Rich's car crawls through the snow in heavy traffic toward Ford Auditorium.

"You look great," he says, glancing over at her. "Is that a new haircut?"

A giver of compliments. She remembers this about him. She didn't want to go out of the house tonight, but he was insistent. "Listen, these are great tickets, sixth row, center. It's a terrific concert, you're going to love it. . . ."

She finds it hard to talk to people these days, losing the thread of conversations, becoming impatient, anxious for them to get on with it, finish up. Not with Rich, though. Never a need to fake it. After all, he was Keith's best friend. They have always understood each other, even if she did think he was a bit of a phony. Even if he used to call her Miss Goody Two-shoes. She relaxes against the seat, feeling as if she could fall asleep here in this cradle of buttery leather, the heater pouring warmth over her legs.

"Guess who I ran into the other day?" he asks. "Ben Hawthorne. Remember him? Red hair, freckles, always wore dress shirts with his Levi's. Now he's a divorce lawyer in Chicago. Very successful." He laughs. "He oughta be. Done it enough himself. On his fourth. Said to say hello. Said he was sorry to hear about Keith." He looks over at her, checking her reaction. What is there to say? People are constantly testing the waters, wanting reassurance.

She ignores the invitation, saying, "Why am I not surprised that you remember about the dress shirts? You're such a clotheshorse. You always were."

"I am not a clotheshorse! I have a few nice ties!"

He pulls into the underground lot below the auditorium. Despite the weather, it is nearly full.

"Last time I was at a concert," he says, "I sat behind a guy who bitched all the way through it. Then at the end he got up and booed. Said he was a music professor and he was exercising his right of disapproval like people used to in the old days. Little guy with a mustache like a toothbrush. At intermission I went up to him and told him if he did that in the second half, I'd deck him."

"So did he?" she asks.

"What? Boo? No. But you should've seen people streaking up the aisles, trying to get away when I told him. You'd've thought the place was on fire."

He laughs, and she echoes him as they follow the crowd up the narrow stairway and into the auditorium. Rich helps her out of her coat, arranges it over the back of her chair. She opens the program: Beethoven's Symphony no. 8 in F Major. *The*

Seasons, Alexander Glazunov. *Metaboles,* Henri Dutilleux. Carefully she reads through the program notes:

Alexander Glazunov
b. August 10, 1865, St. Petersburg;
d. March 21, 1936, Paris.

Seventy-one years. A ripe, old age, as they say; a proper age to die. People don't wonder about it, don't ask you what went wrong.

The orchestra comes on stage, then the concert-master; at last the conductor arrives, looking crisp and confident, acknowledging the applause. Then a hushed silence. She relaxes against the seat, lets the music flow over her.

The second piece is lively and dramatic; even the musicians are having a good time, bobbing in their seats. A theme emerges, something she recognizes. An old radio show. She finally gets it—*Sergeant Preston of the Yukon*! "On, King! On, you huskies!" Preston and his dog team, trekking across the wilderness, chasing the bad guys in the snow. Thinking of it makes her laugh.

The Dutilleux she hates. Noisy, chaotic, without a plan that she can either predict or interpret. The way her life would sound if it were put to music. It makes her uneasy, and she can feel pain spreading slowly across the middle of her back. A tinny, shattering climax that goes on forever. She glances over at Rich; he's listening intently. When it's over, he rises to applaud.

"Great, wasn't it?" he asks, leading her up the aisle.

"Wonderful," she lies, feeling cowardly and ignorant.

"Want to stop for a drink?"

"I don't think so. The snow . . . and it's almost eleven. . . ."

"Right. Just like in college. 'Sorry, can't have fun, gotta go study.' "

"You're saying that's me?"

"Oh, yeah." He grins at her. "And every time I'd get drunk at a party, there you'd be, peering at me over the top of your glasses with that 'Poor Richard' look."

"I never did that!"

"Remember that party we went to . . . it was in an apartment up over the post office? At Paul Moran's place."

"We went to a lot of parties."

"Yeah, but this one was special. Where Miss Goody Two-shoes left early because everybody was drunk, including the host. He was in the bedroom banging somebody's date."

"I remember," she says. "He was banging her on my raincoat."

"I think maybe it was my date," he says. Reaching into his pocket, he pulls out a strip of paper. "Hey, look what I got in my fortune cookie at lunch." He reads it aloud to her: " 'You will attend a party where strange customs prevail.' "

"Sounds scary," she says.

"Yeah, I can't wait."

On the drive home he keeps her entertained with stories: of the sailboat that he is planning to build, his trip to Barbados, his search for a good cleaning lady. They're harder to find than wives, he says.

"How would you know?" Annie asks.

"Hey, you think I haven't been looking? I almost found one a few years back. When I was in the navy. We were ready to set the date and then the church burned down. I took that as an evil omen." He looks over at her, grinning. "Uh-oh. That look again."

"You say it like it's some sportcoat you were thinking of buying," she says. "What kind of look does that deserve?" She shakes her head. "Evil omen."

"Okay, okay." He reaches over to squeeze her hand. "Anyway, I guess I've been lucky. Not finding the perfect mate. At least I'm not in despair over having lost her."

He stops then. Knows he's made a mistake. Good. She's glad; she's weary of having these little talks with people. It doesn't change anything. She keeps her eyes firmly on the road. Don't be angry, she thinks. Not his fault. Not his fault, either, that he's a successful lawyer with plenty of money, that he's healthy.

After a time she says, "Tell me about the case you're working on."

He makes a face. "Too idiotic and dull."

"Okay. Then tell me about your apartment in Chicago."

"My apartment. Okay, it's on the North Shore. A strange, little building with strange, little tenants."

"Like . . . ?"

"Like the guy above me who plays the hammered dulcimer at five o'clock every morning. And the woman across the hall who runs around trying to get herself impressed."

She laughs. "Is that anything like undressed?"

"A lot like it." He glances over at her. "How's your job coming? Things any better there?"

"No, it's worse. She just gets more hostile and loony as the days go by. No matter what I do, I can't seem to please her."

"Quit trying," he advises. "Do something different."

"Like what?"

"Start being a troublemaker. Talk back, misplace things. You know, take charge of your own bad behavior."

"And then she fires me."

"So what? You're not planning on working there forever, are you?"

Again she looks away, out of the window. "I don't know what I'm planning."

"What does that mean?" When she doesn't answer, he says, "You know, back in school I used to think of you as the Gloria Steinem/Diane Keaton type. Cute, slightly crazy career woman. Somehow I never saw you as a mother. But it worked out okay, right?"

"Ask me some other week."

"I never talked to Keith about it," he says. "Were all of your kids planned?"

"I wasn't pregnant when we got married, if that's what you're asking."

"You were the smartest woman I knew." He eyes her meditatively. "English honors. Straight A's all through school. I was surprised when you dropped out. Little did I know you were secretly planning a life in the 'burbs with a bunch of kids."

Little does he know that less than a mile from here is the corner where, a few short months ago, she booted her eldest from the car. She's sick of motherhood, hates the word, even: Mother. *Motherrrr!* Dumb, blaming word, like some crime that she's committed. Suddenly she feels very tired. Tired of talking, tired of being with Rich. She'd rather be home in bed with the comforter pulled up, eyes closed, heading for oblivion. She stares out the window at the street signs: Oak, Maple, Sycamore. Soon they'll be nearing her street, turning into her driveway.

Rich clears his throat. "I think what you need, Annie," he says, "is to go back to school."

"Right now what I need is money. Money and benefits. So if anyone else gets sick or dies, I can afford it."

"No one else is going to die here. Listen. . . ."

"No, you listen. Just lay off the words to the wise. It always feels like bullying to me."

They drive in silence for the rest of the trip. Rich's eyes are fixed on the road. When he reaches her driveway, he turns in, shuts off the ignition, and sits back against the seat with his hands braced on the wheel.

"Okay," he says. "About people giving advice. It's just a way of getting noticed. Like, 'Hey, are you glad you met me, or what?' " When she doesn't reply, he says, "It's what friends do for each other, Annie."

She shrugs her shoulders. "You make me out to be some kind of a flake."

"I never said you were a flake!"

"It's in your tone."

"Ah. Then I'll have to watch my tone, won't I?" Said lightly, without an edge; he reaches across the seat to touch her hand. "C'mon. Tell me what's going on."

"What d'you mean?"

"I mean, what are you feeling? Every time I try to find out, you duck away. You're like some rock that sits below the surface of the water. Easy to read as long as things are calm. Then the slightest wind comes up and you disappear."

"Poetic."

"Yeah, I'm poetic." He turns to her. "So, are we friends?"

"Of course." But she looks away. Takes a deep

breath. "Okay, then. I'm faking it. I go to work, to the store, to concerts. Have dinner with my folks, talk to my sister, fight with my kids. I act like I'm alive. But I feel terrible. I feel terrible all the time."

A silence. Then: "I'm sorry."

"I guess I'm . . . rethinking why I'm here. Wondering if there's any point to it."

"What do you mean, any point . . . ?"

"I'm giving myself a time limit," she says. "If I don't feel better by a year from now . . ."

"What? Lord, Annie, what are you saying?"

"You asked me how I'm feeling," she says. "I'm telling you."

He's still holding on to her hand. There's a good reason why she doesn't do this with people. The curtains part and for a moment things are clear; too clear. She's at the edge of the abyss. She can feel it calling to her. If she doesn't watch out, she'll go crashing over. And would that be so bad? My kids would be pissed, she says to herself. But would they? They'd have her parents, and Jess; people who truly care about them, about their future. People who know what they're doing in this world. What good is she to them now?

She used to view people as either crazy or not crazy—nothing in between. A line drawn down the middle; step over it, and you're there forever. Now it feels as if the line has moved, and she's crossed it, on the way to some new identity. She was a strong person, capable, a problem solver. Now she has no idea who she is. Someone who's going through the motions, living another person's life. "You will attend a party where strange customs prevail." Maybe that's it.

Rich leans his head back against the seat. "Things happen randomly," he says. "I've always known that. Ever since those guys died on the railroad track. Remember? When we were in school. They knew the train schedules. There'd never been a train on Saturday. So one Friday night they decide to sleep on the tracks. Sure, it was stupid. But they were good guys, wild-ass guys. And they were our *friends*. They didn't deserve that kind of punishment for one stupid mistake." He closes his eyes. "Nature is morally blind. And let's face it, the odds of people dying in this world are impressive, to say the least."

She opens the door. "It's late," she says. "I've got to go in."

Outside the car she breathes in the fresh, cold air as he takes her arm, steers her around a patch of ice in the driveway. They walk in silence to the door. When they get there, he turns her around to face him.

"Maybe what has to happen here is that we learn to accept the permanence of grief. That it's never going to go away. I mean, why the hell should it? He was a great guy, and you two had a great life together."

"Maybe," she says.

"I'll call you the next time I'm in town. Take care." He leans down, kisses her gently on the cheek. "I hope I didn't say anything wrong. If I did, forgive me."

"You didn't," she says. "Thank you for the nice evening."

He smiles. "You don't have to say that."

And then he's gone, and she's staring at the red taillights of his car as they disappear around the corner. She lets herself into the house, turns off the light on the hall table, walks slowly up the stairs. Maybe it's not just her. Maybe everyone's crazy. Or lost. Or else lying. Faking it. *Accept the permanence of grief.* Well, she's done that. She's done it, and it hasn't helped. What is there left to do?

30

"Things were worse in Yucatán," Ryan says. He's standing in the doorway of the place they've rented for the weekend. "The Mayans had the same word for love and pain."

"Is that how we're going to talk about this now?"

Moving to the window, Jess stands with her back to him, arms resting on the sill.

"I'm sorry. I'm sorry you're upset. Look, it's a small delay. A few months at the most."

"We're living in these months, Ryan. They're going by. They're adding up."

"I know that."

It is still early evening; they came here straight

from work. The woman who runs the place has opened windows to air out the little cabin, checked to make sure the ice trays are filled. There's a refrigerator and gas stove at one end of the living room; a wooden table forms the divider between it and the kitchen. She stares out at the dogwood trees, at their tight pink buds ready to burst into bloom.

"It's only until the lawyers resolve this issue about Cheryl. . . ."

She turns to face him. "Why do I get the feeling that nothing's going to change? That, years from now, you'll still be talking to lawyers, figuring out what to do about some new issue?"

"You know that's not going to happen." He comes up, puts his hands on her shoulders. "Look, I worry all the time about what goes on when I'm not around. About her having bad days and taking them out on Cheryl. Hell, I worry about what she might be doing right now, while I'm up here with you! I know I can't save her, I gave that up long ago. For eleven years I let myself be talked into things, manipulated into things. I did everything, lost every shred of pride I ever had just to keep the goddamn fucking peace . . . and that was my problem, I know that now. But I'm drawing the line at my daughter. Because if I don't take a stand here, I'll get to see her on holidays and every other weekend. And meanwhile Lucia will do her damnedest to invade that kid's life and make sure it conforms to her own weird fantasies. . . ." He drops his hands. "Should I have waited until after the weekend to tell you about it? That would've been fucking dishonest, wouldn't it?"

"Oh, heaven forbid."

A silence. He rubs his hands over his eyes. "Jess, let's not do this, okay? Let's not spend what little time we have together . . ."

"That's just it," she says. "Our time. My time. It's whatever's left over, Ryan. Whatever hasn't been used up by your other life." She's had two glasses of wine since they got here, and it's given her a headache. She moves away from him to sit down at the table. "I'm not angry. It's worse than that. I feel as if I'm bleeding from about ten different places."

"Jess, what will satisfy you here? I don't know what you want me to do."

A long silence while she contemplates this. She doesn't know either. "I was in the parking lot at Farmer Jack's the other day," she says, "and there was a car parked down near the end with the motor running. A couple sat in it, necking. And right away I thought, 'They're having an affair.' Why else would anyone be doing that in a supermarket parking lot? And my next thought was, 'They're no different from us.' Ryan, how are they any different?"

He looks at her. "If you're seriously asking that question, then I don't know what the hell to say."

"I'm seriously asking," she says. When he doesn't answer, she shrugs. "Well. What do I expect? She told me I'd be sorry. And here I am."

At this he comes to her, puts his arms around her

shoulders. "I love you, Jess. I refuse to say there's something wrong with what we're doing. I can't help it if there's no time . . . there's no damn time for anything! I work, I grocery-shop, I go home, I do laundry and take care of two sick people! And once in a while I get to do what I want to do! I feel like I'm on some kind of damn treadmill. . . ."

"Except for sex. There's always time for that, right?"

He sighs. "The fact that we have great sex," he says, "doesn't mean that I don't love you."

"Don't joke about it!"

"Jesus, I'm not!"

She stands and leaves the table then, going into the bedroom and closing the curtain between them. She knows what it is, that he's preoccupied with sex, uses it like a drug—to avoid work, divorce, misery; to keep from thinking.

Of course, she can take it or leave it. Going into the bathroom, she turns on the light. *To see what an adulteress looks like.* The window is open. Insects bump and scratch against the screen.

"Go away," she says. She splashes water on her face, trying to cool herself off. What we are tampering with here, she thinks, is trust. A belief in the cosmic justice of things.

When she comes out, he's waiting for her.

"What do you want, Jess? Just tell me. I'll do whatever it is that you want."

She looks toward the window, where, outside, darkness is falling. An early moon rising behind the tamaracks, their ghostly trunks covered with lichens. Beyond them is the river, rushing its way across the landscape. Suddenly she is itchy with desire, for his tongue in her mouth, his tongue everywhere, licking salt from her skin—oh, Lord, this is a drug. She can smell his sex on her already, this good Catholic boy, as he pulls her down on the bed, thighs pressed against hers, burning her flesh. Holding her face between his hands, he kisses her hair, her eyes, her mouth. The bedroom is spinning. She drank too much, she loves him too much. But how can it be wrong? How can anything that feels this good ever be wrong?

He bends over, staring into the river. "Damn. How did that happen?"

"What?"

"I thought I had those Cokes wedged in between the rocks. They must've floated away somehow."

She comes to stand beside him. They've taken a walk down by the river on this first Saturday in April; bright and warm, but the ground is still cold; the sun has yet to bite into the rocks, soften them up. Bending, she strips off socks and shoes, rolls up the cuffs of her jeans.

"They can't be far. I'll look for them."

"Wait, let's think about this a minute. . . ."

"What's to think about?"

"You could lose your footing. Those rocks look slippery."

"So? I can swim." The water is clear. On the bottom are ripples of sand, sculpted by the current of the river. She takes a step, and it's deeper than she thought. Clarity distorting perspective. She sees the six-pack, adrift downstream and lodged behind a rock. She wades over to it. Water slides up over her sleeve as she reaches for it, sending shivers up her back.

"That was brilliant. Now you're soaked."

"The proper response would be 'thank you.' "

She wades back, taking his outstretched hand. Across the river, swallows are winging, disappearing into holes in the sandbank. The sun seeks out every curve, flooding the bank with warmth. A damp green-house smell, rich and fecund.

"Want to go back and change?"

She shakes her head. Her back is to the sun, and he opens a Coke, hands it to her over her shoulder.

"Looks like Ireland over there. At least what I think Ireland would look like. We should go there sometime, huh?"

He sits beside her, traces the line of her collarbone, underneath her shirt. This morning, in bed, they worked the Isaac Asimov quiz from the paper:

"Only sculpture to be signed by Michelangelo."

"David."

"Nope. The *Pietà*. Patron saint of lost causes and desperate situations."

"St. Thomas."

"Close. St. Jude." He laughed. "I know all these answers. One of the perks of being Catholic. Can you imagine spending your entire childhood on your knees in front of a damned statue? 'Get down and pray to the Blessed Virgin, Ryan, ask her to forgive your sins.' I can't believe I actually did that."

But she can. Don't underestimate this guy, her friend Sharon told her. He's a hardball player. She thought it meant being serious about what you wanted. Maybe not. Maybe it means you don't count the pain inflicted. Or you count it as your due. Punishment for services rendered. And what about herself? How much pain is she willing to endure? Is that what she's after, then, too?

"I want to ask you something," she says.

"What's that?"

"Why you think it happened. The accident."

He rests his head on his folded arms. "You mean, in the cosmic sense?"

"No. Not that."

"What, then? They hit an abutment . . . I don't understand. What is it you want to know?"

She looks at him. "I think she did it on purpose."

No answer. He doesn't raise his head.

"I don't believe it was an accident. I believe she meant to do it."

A silence. "That can't be, Jess."

"Why can't it? You tell me you worry about her mental state, about what might happen to her on a bad day. . . ."

"That's different. She's not . . . she wouldn't do something . . ." He raises his head to stare angrily across the river.

"Not even to get back at you? Or to make me sorry?"

"No. Jesus, you're talking about full-fledged craziness. You're talking mental illness. . . ."

"Yes. Mental illness. And if you suspect it, you ought to be suing for full custody. Either that or staying behind, to stand guard."

"She'd never do that, she wouldn't risk something happening to Cheryl . . . it was raining and the roads were slippery. And there was an accident. That's what happened."

Silence. She moves her body forward.

After a moment he looks across the water. "I have to say, I don't like hearing this from you."

"I don't much like it myself," she says. But this is a lie. It gives her a measure of relief at last to say it. She feels more alive than she has in weeks. The wind shifts suddenly, moves in from the north, and she rubs her hands up and down her arms.

"Almost every night," he says, "she has nightmares. She wakes up crying, and I go in there to her. But she doesn't want me, she wants her mother."

"What does that prove?"

"Nothing." His voice is hard. "But if she did it just to get back at me . . . no, I can't accept that. Then it would be my fault, don't you see? How could I ever live with myself?"

The drive back to the city is silent. They stop for dinner at a small café on the highway. It's filled with religious knickknacks—all of them for sale— wooden plaques inscribed with the Lord's Prayer, dioramas of the manger scene, wall clocks with cherubs and flower-entwined crosses. The waitress takes their order, disappears through a doorway, above which is mounted: THE LORD IS MY SHEPHERD.

She glances out the window at the faint streaks of light in the evening sky—red, pink, and gold. The flat, open fields along I-75, not yet plowed or planted.

"I want to be married to you," he says. "I want to be working on our house, painting the bedrooms, putting up the storms. I want to drive home from work and know we'll be having dinner. I want to be fighting over whose turn it is to run the damned errands."

"I know. But life's more complicated."

"It doesn't have to be, Jess."

Even here and now, in this restaurant full of religious kitsch, she has the urge to lean forward, kiss that part of his thumb; the inside pad, whitish and plump, resting in sex on her knee, her shoulder, the bones of her neck. She looks away, and he asks, "What are you thinking about now?"

"Psychology of the Deviant Individual," she murmurs. "Psych 142. I took it in college. I've been trying to remember the name of it for weeks. . . ."

He smiles. "And I remind you of it?"

A picture of rocks comes to her mind, slippery with moss. Lying in water at the lake, submerged dolphins below the surface. One year Annie decided they were a swimming hazard, and she and Jess would remove them. They positioned themselves around the smallest and, at a signal, heaved and shoved until they collapsed, laughing, into the water. There wasn't a chance of budging them, not even one inch.

Behind the two of them, in a booth, is a plump, pale family—mother and daughter, father and son. She noticed them when they first came in; the boy, no more than four, sucking his thumb and waving a balloon in the air; the girl whining, "I don't see why we always have to eat here!" Now the mother says in a loud voice, "Bang your father on the head with a balloon for a while, see how he likes it."

She glances at Ryan, to see if he's heard; his eyes are down, his hand smothering laughter. No point in taking life too seriously. No point in watching it through a telescope, either, from millions of miles away. It works out, or it doesn't; nothing to decide tonight.

She buys homemade oatmeal cookies on the way out. On the wall behind the cash register, an oil painting of Jesus hangs from the ceiling on a long cord. He raises a hand in blessing as the cashier takes their money.

31

Saturday, 8:00 P.M.

Today is April Fools Day and I short-sheeted everyone's bed. Mom's, too, but she probly won't even laugh. Every year she use to sew up our pjs, but she never does stuff like that anymore, all she does is sleep and work. Aunt Jess and Ryan went away for the weekend, to a cabin somewhere. They said they were going fishing.

It is twelve days to my birthday. I am not having a party because they never turn out right. My worst one was on Good Friday when I had an egg-dying party and Bobby Coffleman hit me in the head with a base-ball bat. Everybody said I had the biggest egg. Ha! It was an accident but he never even said he was sorry.

Pinky asked if I was getting a new kitten and I said no because all they do is get hit by cars. I didn't write in here about Mrs. Bennett getting killed and now I don't really want to. We buried her in the back yard. I wrapped her up in the blanket from my doll cradle. Pinky says there will be another death because they always come in threes. I said no one else is sick but she says it doesn't matter. Aunt Jess said that was just an old wives tale. I thought it was cathlick. She said she didn't think so but she is going to ask Ryan.

Sunday, 3:00 P.M.

Rex Beers came over today. He said Melony Raymond wears a padded bra and Harry told him to shut up so I know for sure Harry has a girlfriend. Plus they talk on the telephone every night.

I have a boyfriend too. His name is Graham Fuller. He is in fifth grade and he says hi to me every day in the hall. I wish Mom named us names like Melony and Graham instead of boring Julie and Jimmy and Harry. When I grow up I am changing mine.

Pinky came over when Rex was here. She was pulling on his ear ring and he kept making up stupid words, like for a snack he wanted a vardoo float. He told me my tibbin was open and I knew he meant my fly so I said it's not a tibbin and it's not open.

When I told Pinky that Ryan was cathlick she said Aunt Jess was living in sin having a boyfriend whose cathlick and not being married. She says cathlicks can't marry noncathlicks unless they turn. If they do get married Aunt Jess will have to raise all their kids cathlick. Then she laid down on the floor in front of Rex and Harry with her shirt unbuttoned and her butt up in the air. I told her to go home if all she wanted to do was show off around stupid boys all the time.

Tuesday, 10:00 P.M.

It is nine days to my birthday. Aunt Jess came home from the cabin but she said they didn't catch any fish. The snow is almost gone but it still feels like winter. I can't wait until the lilacs bloom and you can pull off the tiny flowers and suck out the honey!

Last night I dreamed Mrs. Posen had an operation and had a bunch of kittens taken out of her stomak. I like her better because she is nice to me and always asks if I'm having a good day.

I forgot to tell about the fire. Harry and Jimmy burned up the Christmas tree and Harry burned off all his eyebrows and eyelashes. He looks like a geek! Well, I have to go take a bath and wash my hair. Then I'm going to watch Prince of Foxes on the disney channel.

Saturday, 3:15 P.M.

Here is why I don't like Pinky Corelli anymore. She had a sleepover last night at Joanne's and when I called them Joanne said she wasn't there but I could still hear her laughing. I know why she likes Joanne. Because she has three brothers in 5th 6th and 7th grades. I don't care!!! When she sleeps over here she never washed her neck or brushed her teeth. Now she says she's changing her name too just because I said I was! She wants to change it to Pinky Coral. I told her Coral or Corelli you still got a dirty neck.

I heard Aunt Jess talking on the phone to Ryan and

she was crying. She said something about taking care of herself. Maybe she is sick or something. I hope they don't get in a fight because I like him a lot. I remember when Mom and Dad would get in a fight Jimmy would always say Mom Dad don't get divorced! until they started laughing and everything would be all right. But you can't do that when people aren't even married. She said she forgot to ask Ryan about death coming in threes. I don't really think it's true anyway but if it is I hope it isn't somebody I like.

Saturday, 9:30 P.M.

It is five days to my birthday. I wish Dad was here. I guess that is dumb to say but he always gave the best presents. He bought me a night light that looks like a lighthouse and a polisher for my petoskey stones. He will always be my favorite person in the whole world.

I like Aunt Jess too, because she always does nice things for us, for instance on St. Patrick's Day she made us green pancakes in the shape of snakes because St. Patrick drove the snakes out of Ireland. I wore my green sweater that day and Pinky wore hers only with red tights so she looked like a Christmas tree! I will never ask her over here again as long as I live.

Monday, 8:30 P.M.

Today I rode my bike around the block and saw tiny handprints on the sidewalk that looked like an animal. Mrs. Bennett had little pads on the bottom of her feet and she use to clean herself all over with her tongue. It was rough as sandpaper! I'm glad Dad doesn't know what happened to her.

I rode by the house where a boy I knew use to live. When I was in kindergarden I had to give him a nickel every time I went by his house or else he wouldn't let me. I never told Mom or Dad. I had to walk three extra blocks just to get by him until finally he moved away! His name was David Rice. He had four sisters all older than him. They called him baby all the time. I wish I could be the oldest in this family. I get tired of always being the baby.

Thursday, 10:00 P.M.

Today is my birthday. I am ten. Aunt Jess took us out for dinner to Castaways because Mom had to work. It looked like a big ship and all the waiters dressed like pirates. I had french fries and a vanilla malt. Jimmy had spaghetti. So did Harry. Aunt Jess had a ruben sandwich.

Then Grandpa and Grandma came over and brought a chocolate cake and rocky road ice cream. They gave me a white sweater with roses on the collar. Mom gave me six different color socks and a new wallet. Aunt Jess gave me underpants with lace on them. Harry gave me glowworm nail polish and Jimmy gave me a card that said know what I wish for on your birthday? and you open it up and it says I wish I'd win the lottery. Ha! Fat chance. First you have to buy a ticket and he is such a tightwad! When I blew out my candles I wished we were up north and it was last summer.

I thought Ryan was coming over too but Aunt Jess said someone was sick, I think his little girl. She has been sick for a long time! The last time I saw him he said I would get something special for my birthday. I guess he forgot. Mom says he has a lot on his mind.

Emily gave me peach flavored lipstick and an autograph book. On the first page she wrote

> U R
> 2 good
> 2 be
> _____
> 4 gotten

I am going to ask her to be my best friend. The only problem is her mom is so STRICT! They can only watch one TV show a day and they have to choose. And everything is always a TREAT. For instance if we come in from school and have peanut butter on crackers its a treat so if we want something else, no, you already had your treat. At least Mom doesn't do that.

Well it is after ten P.M. and I still have to do a worksheet on electro-magnets and study for the spelling test. I am going to always write in my notebook because it helps me keep track of things. I am Julia

Margaret Eleanor Browner and I have blond hair blue eyes a tiny birthmark on my elbow in the shape of Africa and no freckles. I have two brothers and no sisters. Two mothers and no father. I am ten years twenty-two hours and thirty-five minutes old as of this minute. Goodby for now.

32

A week of warm weather, with white, fluffy clouds overhead and water running in the streets. Taking the back roads on their bikes, Harry and Rex fly into puddles, reckless, veering to splash each other. A bus from the grade school passes, and they give it the finger. The boys in the backseat pound on the windows.

"See that? Guy called me a dickhead!" Rex yells over his shoulder. "Puny fourth grader calling somebody a dickhead!" His head tilts up and he bawls at the tree branches:

> *"Oh, the moon shines tonight*
> *on Mrs. Cartwright. . . .*
> *She couldn't fart right . . .*
> *her ass was airtight . . . !"*

They lean their bikes into the curb, rounding the corner of Rex's street.

"Saw your girlfriend after gym today. With Robbie

Taft. They were walkin' down the hall holding hands." Rex grins at him. "Think I'm lying, don't you?"

"I know you are. She wasn't in school today."

"Maybe it was yesterday, then. Yep, it was old Melanie, comely slut that she is. I heard she did the nasty with Mr. Edmonds once. During study hall."

Rex's house sits at a cocky angle, not quite in line with the rest of the street. A pile of tires in the side yard. The porch roof sags; the storm door scrapes along a well-worn groove in the ceiling. A red truck is parked in the driveway.

Rex spins to a stop at the front steps. "Fuck. I thought she'd be at work by now." He pulls open the door and Harry follows him inside.

"Take off your boots!" From the living room the command is issued. He remembers what it is that he hates about this place—the smell of stale food. The draperies in the living room are closed tight, the TV blaring.

Rex heads down the hall toward the kitchen. Dishes are piled in the sink, awash in scummy gray water. An open loaf of bread on the counter. The floor feels sticky as he walks across it. What is that smell? They don't even eat dinner here, Rex's mother and sister both work nights. He takes it all in, vaguely ashamed of his discomfort. His own house never approaches this level of disorder; his mother wouldn't stand for it.

Rex pulls a bottle of Coke from the refrigerator.

Above his head a door slams and footsteps click back and forth across the bare floor: Rex's sister, Geneva, getting ready for work. The owner of the red truck is her boyfriend. He has huge beefy hands, a thick neck with the hair shaved up the back. He wears sweaters without shirts, so his chest hair pokes up through the V. Geneva doesn't own a car. The boyfriend's job is to drive her to work. According to Rex, it's his only job. That, and banging Geneva.

"Mr. Hart's up in front of the class," Rex is saying, "and his fly's wide open, geez! So Kayla Prete says, 'Mr. Hart?' real polite, and he says, 'Yes, Kayla?' And then she says, 'Your hogan's hanging out.' " He laughs, tipping backward in the chair, taking a long swig of the Coke. Not offering any of it to him. "Listen, I say we lift the camcorder this Saturday." Reaching into his pocket, he pulls out a sheet of paper covered with X's and lines. "Here's the map. They only got one guy watching the camera aisle, I checked it out. There'll be a zillion people up there, everybody carrying stuff around. We just pretend to look it over and then we mosey out the door. If anybody chases us we can just melt into the crowd."

"Just like Velveeta, huh?"

"Don't be a chickenshit. Yes or no?"

Geneva clatters down the stairs and comes into the kitchen. She's wearing her nurse's uniform—slacks and white blouse, white clunky shoes. She walks right by him as if he isn't there.

"Rex, do some laundry. Mom will have a catfit if it

doesn't get done today. Here's three bucks for dinner."

She is beautiful, with creamy skin and huge blue eyes; her hair is thick, copper-colored, in a loose pile on top of her head. She pulls on her coat as she sails out the door. "Ben, I'm gonna be late!"

The door bangs behind her as the boyfriend comes into the kitchen. He glances at Rex. "Clean this place up while you're at it."

"Screw off," says Rex, taking another swig from his Coke. "Just because you're boffing her don't mean I work for you."

It happens so fast he's barely aware of it—three fierce blows, *punch, punch, punch*—and the blur of the Coke bottle spinning upward into the air—and Rex is on the floor, arms over his head. The boyfriend steps lightly away, zipping his jacket. "You got quite the attitude problem." He's out the door, closing it behind him.

Blood streams from Rex's nose; his upper lip has turned inside out. He gets slowly to his feet, heading for the sink, veering off to sit in a chair. Harry stoops to pick up the Coke bottle.

"You okay?"

"Shit, yeah! What d'you think?" He wipes his nose on the sleeve of his shirt.

Harry doesn't answer, looks to the floor, spattered with blood. From the TV in the living room comes the familiar tune:

". . . mysterious and spooky . . .
. . . they're altogether ookey . . .
. . . THE AD-DAMS FA . . . MILL . . . EE . . . !"

"Asshole," Rex mutters. "I'm gonna kill him someday. The day he moves in here, Man, I'm gone. . . ." Getting up from the chair to go to the sink; splashing water on his face, wiping it with a dish towel. He heads for the living room and Harry follows him, where he drops into the fat chair covered in yellow-and-orange flowers that sits in front of the TV. Taking out a handkerchief, he holds it to his face. "Listen," he says, "we gonna do this thing Saturday or not?"

Harry doesn't sit. "I don't know, I might have to do something else."

"Like what?"

"Something I promised my aunt . . ."

"Bullshit. You're gonna weasel out, aren't you? Babyass. Don't even have the balls."

He looks at the drab, stuffy room, reeking of cigarette smoke. Why did he come here today? Keeps seeing Rex's body, like a rag doll flung against the dark linoleum, the starry coins of blood.

"I better go home."

"Why? It's only four o'clock."

"Yeah, I got some stuff to do."

Rex looks at him. "Okay, fine. Go ahead."

He lets himself out the front door, keeps his eyes

focused on the ground. Nothing but dead grass and sodden leaves everywhere. He picks up his bike and rides off down the street, keeping his eyes on the road, watching for potholes. After a block, he veers off onto the sidewalk. Head down, legs pumping hard, he pushes at the pedals, feeling blood pounding in his ears. A terrible emptiness wells up, and he closes his eyes against it; no reason to go home, he's free to come and go as he pleases, answering to no one. Not responsible for anybody's pain, either, *goddammit*.

He passes the old farmhouse that was part of the Underground Railroad; a historic landmark. Each year they read about it in social studies. A retired doctor lives there with his ancient black Lab, chained to a post in the backyard. The dog snaps and snarls at people as they go by. The doctor drives an old green Buick Riviera. Whenever he goes out in the car, the dog goes with him, sitting up in the front seat. The doctor isn't friendly, either; his porch light is always off on Halloween, even though everybody knows he's in there. What would it be like, he wonders, to live in a beat-up old house with nobody but your dog for company? He'd like to try it.

He turns the corner onto Vinsetta Boulevard, noticing shadows of deep, translucent blue on the lawns; the street looks dirty, vaguely menacing. How did he get here? He's been avoiding this street for months, taking the long way around. It is the street that the church is on.

Extinct Is Forever. He read it on a bumper sticker. That day in the church. Rooms full of ugly paintings, the smell of flowers. Afterward, vanilla cake heavy with white frosting. Groups of people he didn't know, all of them talking at him, saying, "Now you're the Man of the Family. . . ."

What does that mean? It's all up to him? How can it be? He's exactly the wrong person for this job, only knows how to get into trouble, not how to fix anything. *I can't do it.*

There is one person to whom he could explain all of this, one person who would have understood. He pedals faster as the ground unrolls before him, taking deep breaths to outrun it, closing his heart against this thrill of howling, aching loneliness. It is nothing that can be fixed.

33

"You have shingles," the doctor says. "You're lucky you came in when you did." Sitting across his desk from her, he writes out a prescription. "If it isn't treated in time you can end up with chronic pain. Acyclovir should take care of it."

"Is it contagious?"

"Only to people who haven't had chicken pox. The virus usually stays dormant until something triggers it—another illness, or some kind of stress."

The kids have all had chicken pox; so has Jess. She brought it home from school and gave it to her older sister. She remembers the humiliation of it—a baby disease at thirteen!

"Keep taking the aspirin. The pain can get pretty bad. I've had patients who've had it in the chest area and thought they were having a heart attack."

The doctor is blond, young, very studious looking. She got his name from Terry. She won't go back to Dr. Evans, doesn't ever want to see him again.

"What you need is rest and lots of fluids. No undue excitement, no problems." He grins across the desk at her. "Can we manage this?"

"I'll try."

An hour later, back at her own desk, surrounded by unanswered letters and orders, she cautiously rubs at her burning left side. The blisters have come out. She always feels worse when she's at work.

Below her, the hum of activity goes on—people buying fertilizer, grass seed, shovels, rakes, mops, and brooms for spring, the season of renewal. She should get busy so that she, too, can hurry out, go home. *And do what?* A new season. Yet it seems far away to her, as far away as oblivion.

Why did she take this job? It won't save her. As if it were yesterday she can hear her mother saying, "Annie, if you drop out of school now you'll be sorry the rest of your life." So it seems. These days she's sorry about everything. Should have finished school, shouldn't have had kids so soon, shouldn't have allowed her life to become unmanageable. Should have died with him.

A wave of panic at the thought; she presses her hands to her cheeks. Lord, she's too sick to be at work, too angry. She's been angry since last August. Now she knows it. And she hates this job. She's going to be fired, anyway, by the time Denise is finished with her. She knows it's coming. Why not get it over with?

George Rice looks up as she enters. "Do you have a few minutes?" she asks.

"Sure. Sit down."

She explains about her visit to the doctor, and his brows knit in sympathy.

"Hey, this is nothing to fool with. I've had it myself. You need to go straight home and rest. We'll take care of what's out there for now."

She presses her hands together in her lap. "I don't know how long it will be," she says. "Maybe three weeks or more. I think the best thing to do is just quit."

He looks startled. "Now, why would you want to do that?"

She doesn't have a ready reply, casts about for a place to rest her eyes, settling on a crude clay figurine at the corner of his desk—green-and-purple-spotted dragon. One of his kids must have made it for him.

He gets up to close the door. When he comes back, he puts a hand on her shoulder. "I know Denise is a difficult person," he says. "She's having a hard time. With the divorce and all. But I'd like you to stay on, if you would."

She stares up at him. Denise getting a divorce? How can this be? She feels the panic rising again; this is not the way the conversation was supposed to go.

"I see how this trouble is carrying over into her work," he says. "It's too bad. But she's been with me a long time, ever since the store opened. And she'll pull out of this, I'm sure. She's tough. Like you."

She takes the cup of coffee he offers her, holding it with two hands. If she isn't careful, she will break down and cry in front of this man. How will that help anything?

"I've been meaning to talk to you, anyway," George Rice says. He reaches for a framed photograph on his desk, turns it around to face her. "This is my son, Tony. He's a senior at Albion." She's seen it before, a picture of a handsome redhead, the image of his father. The same freckles and blue eyes and strong chin. "The Rice chin," his relatives probably say, as they would say "the Lewis nose." "The Lewis walk."

"When your application came in, I recognized the name right away. Tony was in your husband's English-lit. class. I knew you were Keith Browner's wife." He does not say "widow," and she notices, feels relieved. The world divides into those who use the word and those who do not.

"He was always a good student," George Rice says. "He was into athletics and had lots of friends. Then all of a sudden in his junior year, things fell apart. I guess at first we didn't notice. Or we didn't want to. I was busy with the store, my wife with our girls . . . and then one day I got a call from school. Your husband was concerned and wanted to talk to me. I was annoyed, more than anything, didn't want to believe it. But he just kept calling. And then Tony had an accident and totaled the car. And I got the picture." He walks to the window, looks out. "I was scared shitless. He was depressed, drinking, having thoughts about suicide. Through it all, your husband was great. He talked to him, got him to see a therapist, went out of his way. That whole senior year he was there for him, he was a friend." He turns to look at her. "He'd never have made it if it wasn't for Keith Browner. When I read the obituary in the paper, I called Tony at school and we both just cried."

Silence. She doesn't know what to say to this, remembers listening for his car in the driveway each day, his step at the back door. Remembering how he would sit at the kitchen table, watching her while she cooked dinner, and tell her about his day. The name Tony Rice doesn't register. But there were so many of them.

"I knew you could do the job when I read your application," George Rice is saying. "I don't want you to think it was any kind of gift. But I saw it as a chance to pay him back. So, you can see why I'd rather you didn't quit, can't you? Take some time off. Come back when you're ready."

She gets up from the chair. "I'll have to think about it. . . ."

"Fine. Listen, I know this job isn't all that challenging for you. But it could be. We're opening up two new branches and I'm looking for some good people. It might mean relocating to either Grand Rapids or Lansing. How does that sound?"

"I don't know." Dizzy with shock, she doesn't argue, doesn't try to explain that she is a person on the way down, not the way up. How could he have done this to her? What does it mean? Is she supposed to be grateful, then? Is this proposed as some kind of substitute for all she has lost? She can't think about it now, stops at her desk to pick up her purse, leaves without speaking to anyone.

"How are you feeling?" Jess asks that night.

"All right. Fine." She isn't, but doesn't want to talk, not with her back on fire, itching despite the calamine, despite the aspirin the doctor said would take care of the pain.

"What did Mr. Boxer want?"

"I don't know."

When she got home there was a message to call Mr. Boxer at the school. She dialed and got their machine: "You have reached the switchboard of Clara Barton Junior High. No one is here to take your call. . . ." Fine with her, she didn't want to talk to anyone anyway. Now, glancing at her bedside clock, she sees it is too late to call him at home: ten-fifteen. Do you know where your children are?

The last she saw of Jim and Harry they were outside playing kick-the-can in the street with the neighbor kids; Julie is in bed, asleep. She'd like to be, too, wishes Jess would go away and leave her in peace. She'd like to sleep the entire next week away. Close your eyes, wake up a different person. That isn't going to happen.

"Annie," Jess says, "we need to talk." She sits down on the bed. "I think Harry's in trouble. I don't know exactly what it is, but something's going on. . . ."

She steels herself for what she knows is coming. The moment you allow yourself to be vulnerable, people take it as an invitation. If Jess says another word about the kids, she will ask her to move out. It's not her job to sit in judgment.

"It feels as if he's crying out for some kind of direction. . . ."

"He's fourteen years old. He'd better have some direction of his own by now."

Jess sighs. "But you're the person with the power here. If you'd talk to him . . ."

"I drive them places, I feed them, I see to their needs. That's all I can do right now."

"And it's a lot," Jess soothes, "but if there were—"

"If there were half as many people wanting to help," she says, "as there are second-guessing. What a wonderful world it would be."

Silence. "I want to help, Annie. What can I do to help?"

For some reason this infuriates her. "Stop advising

me on how I should get my shit together," she snaps. "You think this looks easy? Wait until you have kids. Wait until you and Ryan have real problems, then you can trot out the lecture and recite it to yourself." Meanness, pure and simple; she can't help herself. In fury she stares out the window at black limbs of trees, at the leaves barely beginning to unfold. She could learn to hate this season.

"That's not going to happen," Jess says. "Because Ryan and I are through. I broke it off last week."

"What?" She turns to look at her. "I can't believe that. He's solid, Jess. Like a rock. You can depend on him."

"Yes, he's dependable. He's a good person. And he loves me." Biting her thumb and looking away. "It's everything I ever wanted. Except that it's not continuous. Not for me. After this crisis, there'll be another. . . ."

"What crisis? What are you talking about?"

"Lucia changed her mind about joint custody. The court won't award it unless both parents want it, and she says she'll sue for sole custody if he goes ahead with the divorce. The lawyer said because of the accident and her present situation, if they push for it now, all of the sympathy will be with her."

"So, what does this mean? That you have to wait? So you wait. Sooner or later, when the divorce goes through . . ."

"I've stopped calling it 'the divorce.' That's what made it seem real. As if it were actually happening.

But it's not. I don't know that it ever will." She rubs the back of her neck. "Let's just say I'm no longer convinced of his intentions. Or his dilemma."

"I don't understand," Annie says. "You say that he loves you. . . ."

"Do you believe love is the only reason people are together? Because I don't."

"So everything isn't perfect, so what? Did you really expect that you two would get to have it so good?" The sarcasm of it shocks her. But Jess doesn't seem to hear.

"I didn't expect to be married to them both. And I will be if I don't get out now."

Annie shakes her head. "Why are you doing this, Jess? It's a mistake."

"Maybe." She turns away. "But if you can't be on my side in this, Annie, then please stay out of it."

"So you're just going to let that crazy woman win?"

"It's not about Lucia. When I think of her, it gives me hope. It's when I think about myself that I've stopped hoping. You were right. He married her. He's the one who keeps on living with her."

"Have you told Mother and Dad yet?"

"Yes. The other night."

"But not me."

"I wanted to talk to you," she says. "When did we ever have the time? You haven't been exactly . . . look, I don't want to get into an argument. I'm telling you now. . . ."

"Fine, and what about the kids? What do I tell them?"

"I'm sure they already know." Amazingly, now it is Jess who's angry. "They're not stupid. About anything that goes on here."

"Meaning?"

"Meaning there's a lot happening. Meaning, you're not the only person with problems. Look around, why don't you? Pay some attention."

She leans back against the headboard. "You and Paula and Nell and Rich," she says. "You all know so much, don't you? Get your shit together, Annie. It's been all of eight months, what are you waiting for? Eight whole months, my God, and she's still in a state. She ought to be taking up a hobby, she ought to be dating, she should get some decent clothes, a new hairdo, a good job. . . ."

"Nobody's saying any of that. . . ."

"Nobody gives a damn about how I feel!"

"I do. I give a damn!"

"The doctors screwed up, do you know how that feels? Knowing he'd still be alive if it weren't for a stupid mistake? He'd be alive and maybe even getting better. . . ."

"Oh, Annie," Jess says. "He wouldn't. He was so sick. He knew it better than any of us. That weekend when we went up north and he talked to Ryan about not taking the chemo . . ."

"When did they talk about that?"

"On the beach. He told Ryan he wouldn't drag you

through this, because he knew it wouldn't save him, wouldn't do any good. . . ."

Silence. "I don't believe you," she says at last. "He would never have said that. And he wouldn't have talked to Ryan about something that important, that personal . . . not without telling me. He never said a word to me."

Jess is looking at her, stunned. And in this look she reads the truth. But he couldn't have, would never betray her like this. . . .

"Listen," Jess says. "It doesn't mean anything. He was dying, he didn't know how long he had or how bad it would be."

"I want you to start looking for a place," she says. "I don't want you here anymore."

"Fine, then. I'll start first thing." Jess moves to the door. "You're a stubborn person, you know it?" A hint of tears; she hardens her heart against it. "You're not the only one who's suffering here." And then the doorway is empty.

She reaches up to turn off the light, lies, with her arms over her head, eyes closed. Honesty. A game they used to play when they were kids. You tell me the worst thing you know about me and I'll do the same for you. It always ended in tears and remorse. Not tonight. From now on she'll be more careful. This is what she knows: that, of mind and body, nothing is permanent. Not love or trust, nor anything that is human. As for this God that she is supposed to put her faith in, this God who cares only about scarring people for life, she is through pleading. What good has it done her? *Can't You see how I've suffered, how unbearable all of this is? Yet I've done what I'm supposed to do, what's expected of me. So when will the punishment stop? When is he coming back?*

34

She has been driving northward for several hours; passing cars, obeying the lights. Her left side a map of weeping sores. She glances at her watch: it is nearly one o'clock in the afternoon. The trip passes beneath her wheels without leaving a memory.

She reaches out to turn on the radio, quickly scans the stations: ". . . and in the middle of the mitten, folks, the temperature is sixty-two degrees . . . now we know there's been a big change here, in the world of soft drinks—" She snaps it off again. Beside her on the seat are her pills. She should stop for gas, take her medications.

When she was a little girl she once read a fairy story about a maiden who saved the birds and beasts by hiding them in a cave until the wicked ogres had battled themselves to the death over who ran the world. She believed she'd been born to some important task like that. For years she had waited to discover it, wondering how and when it would present itself.

In high school she was vaguely uncomfortable with teachers who offered her advice on how to improve her chances. What could they possibly know? Those backwater citizens whose dreams had dried up years ago or they wouldn't be stuck teaching in this dull suburb. Her own dreams were full of magical challenges, opportunities they wouldn't have the courage to consider. And what has she done with all of that? From the rearview mirror her own eyes stare coldly back at her.

She woke up this morning with a plan; over breakfast she presented it to Jess. They both needed some time off. She would take the kids to Mother and Dad's tonight; they would have the weekend over there, and next week they could go to school from their house. But Jess had a plan of her own.

"I think you need to be by yourself. I can watch the kids for a while, they'll be fine. You just take off."

All the things left unsaid: you're no good to them anymore, they need a break from you, don't come back until you know what you're doing.

"I think you should go," her sister urged. Not angrily, but what has passed between them is large enough to leave a space. They were both being careful with each other. She went upstairs to put on some clothes and, in doing so, made her decision. She was packed and in the car before the kids had left for school. Jess brushed her cheek with her lips as she went out the door. Judas kiss.

"I'll call and let you know where I am," she said. Having no idea where she was going. On her way out she noticed an unopened letter on the hall table; from her mother-in-law, postmarked from Florida. She picked it up and took it with her.

She stops for gas in Standish. The first thing she sees is the FourSquare Gospel Church, at the corner of Tenth and Main. Close to the road, with its red brick darker at the foundation. From groundwater seepage, no doubt. *Church's one foundation is Jesus Christ her Lord* . . . a tune from her early childhood. She can still remember all of the words.

She picks up the letter, lying loose on the seat beside her:

April 18
Anne,

I've decided to stay on down here as William won't be using the place this year. I am playing bridge every day and walking the beach. It has done wonders.

I hope things are going well. Give the children my love. How was Julia's birthday? Did she get my card and check?

Best,
Nell

Bridge and the beach. Good for her. No "Dear Anne." And no "Love, Nell." Give the children my love. Not you, though. What does she expect? This is an even exchange.

All these months of blaming the wrong people.

Not the doctors' fault, not Nell's or William's either. He knew he was leaving, knew it all along. The week before he died, when he told her he was no longer afraid of anything. She took it to mean he was looking forward to September, to the task of getting better. She'd been so relieved! But he was lying; clearly he'd meant the opposite.

She pays for her gas, drives out onto the street, then on impulse makes a left turn off Main Street. Looking for houses, some evidence of a town with people. All she's ever seen are gas stations and bars, a Dairy Queen, the Buick dealership, a huge Kmart. She drives aimlessly—left on Oak, left again on Patterson, right on Linden to the school yard, left on the winding lane to Willow Street. All of the houses are small and closely set, bungalows of frame and stucco.

God, she is so angry at him! Angry Annie, he would tease, don't ever think about it, just be mad. His making fun of her temperament, her way of coping if things didn't go her way. Once he told her that her insistence on knowing everything was like trying to be God. But shouldn't one be allowed to know *something*? She feels dumb and blind to the ways of the world, to its meaning. Yet she has been trying to keep going without it. Keep going, keep moving, don't stop. When you stop is when terror floods in.

The road to Wurtsmith is empty of cars. The air base has been closed since 1993. It was a part of the economy of the town of Oscoda for some fifty years. During the Gulf War they flew transport planes to Kuwait. Now it's gone. Nothing but flat fields of concrete, weeds growing up between the cracks, fat black crows strutting along on the apron.

She turns onto a trail leading off into the woods, her car bouncing over roots and hard-packed sand. Another hundred yards or so and the trail opens onto a field where the discards begin—chairs and couches, mattresses, carpeting, ancient sinks and stoves, old cars without wheels or windows, the paint on them long since rusted away. Everything riddled with bullet holes. An obscene dump site in the middle of the woods, the ground littered with empty shotgun shells; yellow plastic with rusted metal ends. *Zapper .22. Remington Long Rifle.* Even here in the woods you will find death. If that's what you are looking for.

She turns the car around, heading back down the trail. A sharp turn to the right, a short distance along the Cyclone fence still proclaiming every twenty yards or so:

WARNING
U.S. AIR FORCE INSTALLATION
UNLAWFUL TO ENTER WITHOUT
PERMISSION OF BASE COMMANDER

Bissonette Road follows the north side of the river, weaving its way west to Glennie. Years ago it was high-crowned, gravel, with berry bushes thick along its shoulders. They would come out here after dark with the kids, hunting for deer. Now the berries have dried up, the deer have gone deeper into the swamp. A sudden drop through fields of cattails and yellow swamp candles and she comes upon the river. Ancient deadheads lift their branches from the water in a salute. Around the next curve is the dam. Waiting for her at the top of the hill.

She parks and takes the wooden staircase down to the river. Behind her is the redbrick building full of humming machinery with its narrow windows looking onto the concrete spillway. Foote Dam, the last of seven on this sinuous river, as it loops and turns, finds its way to Lake Huron. She leans across the guardrail, staring into the dark water. Along its lower banks, fishermen snag for salmon with their ugly treble hooks, even though it's illegal. They toss the huge green-and-silver fish into the bushes at the edge of the shore. Below her is a sign:

DANGER: WATER RISES RAPIDLY

AFTER SIREN SOUNDS

She's never been here when the dam was opened. What would it be like? A wall of water the color of root beer, or dark tea, gushing in torrents over the spillway, carrying all before it. She has watched the fly fishermen with their rods, working the bank. Jimmy would go down to talk to them: "Guy had two really nice trout." No fishermen here today, no traffic. What would it matter if she had run the car off the road into the river? When would they find her? Who would care?

Water glides smoothly over the mossy ramp. So easy. As easy as he'd done it, just left her. Disappearing into the watery night. She was asleep, lost somewhere in the dream, feeling slowly and urgently drawn up. His hand on her hip, pulling her toward his shadow in the darkness, dark as time.

Waking, she'd seen the shifting pattern of tree branches against the window, curtains blown inward; she could feel his hand on her leg, pressing, insistent. Heavy breathing, a flicker of panic. Seated at the edge of her consciousness, he was leaning in toward her, willing her to wake. Suddenly he was lying across her lap. And in that same flicker he was gone. She couldn't call him back.

Call everyone else; call the doctor, the sheriff's department, call Jess. An ambulance bumping eerily down the road, lights flashing, making no sound. Too late, too late! Herself flying down the stairway to open the door to them. Magicians, saviors. They would know what to do. And the medical examiner saying, "Ma'am, you might want to have the kids go into another bedroom. . . ." Why? So they won't notice he's gone?

That whole morning going by in a blur; Jess arriving, helping with the kids. Driving her over to the funeral home in Lincoln to sign the forms: certificate of death . . . funeral contract . . . forwarding of the remains . . . embalming and other preparations . . . application for burial . . . viewing and ceremony . . . caskets . . . cemetery plot. All the time her mind was back in the bedroom, still trying to make sense of it. That was where he was waiting for her. Did he know what was happening? What was he coming upstairs to tell her? A confession of sorts? *Forgive me. Forgive me for not telling you.* She can feel the tears starting; again, there is nothing she can do, not a goddamn thing. Angry Annie, with all the answers. Here's one, then: apart from kindness, or pity or protectiveness, he had lied. One of his final acts on earth; one of the things he left to her.

Years ago, when they were first married, they'd gone to see the Tutankhamen exhibit in Toronto. Standing before the body suit made for a princess— tiny rectangles of jade held together with golden chains—he'd said, "I wonder if she's still in there." And later that day, running to catch the subway to the hotel, she'd caught her heel in a crack on the platform. He was ahead of her; the subway doors were closing. In that instant he'd reached back to snatch her to him. *Why won't you do that now?*

She can't stay for these thoughts, hurries up the steps to her car. Back on Rea Road, she imagines herself charging along, driving with tremendous speed, bumping and jerking with everything out of control. And suddenly she is doing it—foot to the floor, watching the needle arc its way across, hovering at eighty, eighty-five. The sound outside the window is deafening, taking over the noise in her head. *Oh, God let me get to the end of this, let me be sixty years old, my children grown and married and living far away.* No comfort here, no help. Something pushing, forcing itself upon her awareness. *No, not here, not now . . . what will I do?* And then the huge wave that washes out everything, every underpinning. Nothing left, nothing to hold on to, nothing to save her. While, outside and above, looking down, indifferent, is the cold and wordless moon.

She passes a highway grocery store with a sign in the window: STORE LOOKS DIM BUT WE'RE OPEN TILL TEN. No need for that here in this parking lot of the Springport Inn. It's well lit, sitting back from the highway, a pink-and-green Victorian confection on a slight rise leading to the lake. She can hear it now, crashing in the darkness.

She goes up to the door and rings the bell. In a moment it's answered by a pretty, dark-haired woman wearing jeans, a red T-shirt, dangling ear-rings. She follows the woman up the steps, grateful for her cheerfulness, her unconditional goodwill.

"Have you ever been to Harrisville before?"

She shakes her head. No need to say she knows this town, its shops and restaurants, gas stations and grocery stores, knows the post office and the marina, even the old train depot at the end of Dock Street.

Knows it for the traitor it is: the place where he would rest and get well.

"We've been here nearly ten years," the woman says. "We fell in love with it when we came up on vacation." She laughs. "The first owner of this place was a merchant shipper on the Great Lakes. He's still around, too. Old Van Buskirk. He usually hangs out in the attic. Don't worry, though, he's a friendly ghost." She smoothes the lavender-and-white-figured quilt on the bed, picks a fluff of dust from the porcelain sink. "This room's my favorite. There's extra towels and blankets in the dresser, and the bath-room's right down at the end of the hall."

Annie stares down at carpet the color of the forest floor. She feels an overwhelming need to close her eyes and go to sleep. Already she has forgotten the woman's name.

"You saw the fireplace downstairs. You're more than welcome to use it. Wood's in the kindling box on the side porch."

At last she leaves and Annie closes the door, turns to unpack. From out of her suitcase she takes the blue nightgown her kids gave her for Christmas. Beneath it are her jeans and sweaters; then, the box. Why has she brought it along? A mistake. She has no desire to open it, hasn't touched it since she put it at the back of the closet last August. She sets it on the dresser; doesn't want anything from him, not now. Not while she's still so angry.

Going to the narrow east window she stands, staring down at the railroad track and beyond it, the dark bowl that is the lake. Again, without warning, a sweeping wave of pain. On the other side of the road is the cemetery, with its ancient Santa Claus guarding the steel drawers of the crypt. Nearer town is St. Anne's, the Catholic cemetery. The fall after Julie was born, they came up here for a weekend and sat across the street from it, in the State Park Café, staring out at the row of fiery maple trees. He was in love that day. "I never knew how much I wanted a daughter. She's so fragile, Annie, I just want to take care of her forever." It was her hope that they wouldn't have to do that. "Yeah. But what do I do when she's seventeen and going with some punk who smokes and has an earring and drives like a maniac?" They had laughed over this, secure in the knowledge that it would never happen, not to their perfect daughter. Odd, now, to think it wasn't the babies who were fragile, after all.

She sits down on the bed, resting her head on her arms against the iron railing, left temple against right wrist, her watch pressing a hard, sharp oval into her cheek. They were so young, then, believing they had discovered some secret, thinking it would last forever. The world is a more dangerous place than either of them imagined. Better to sit in your house, never moving, never breathing. Even then, you cannot keep people safe.

35

He lies in his bed, listening to the silence of the house. Jimmy is up and gone already. Seven-thirty. Did the alarm go off? He didn't hear it. He'd better not miss the damn bus again. Sitting up, he swings his legs over the side, sees his schoolbooks on the desk, where he left them. They haven't been touched. Because today is Saturday.

He lies back down, staring at the red leaves of the tree outside his window. Soon they will turn that dark jungle green. What's the name? Swedlar maple. Stupid facts, cluttering up his brain. He doesn't care about this stuff, why remember it? He rolls to his face, head buried in the pillow, trying not to think who taught him the names of all the trees in the yard, the names of the warblers who come each year on their way to Canada. Warbler Weekend coming up. The second weekend in May. Then Memorial Day, then his birthday, then Fourth of July. Everything going on, just as before.

Saturday. The day for errands and chores. Run the vacuum, pick up your room. Go to the cleaners, the hardware, the grocery store. Eat lunch, watch TV, rake the yard, go for a bike ride. Eat dinner, watch more TV, go to bed.

He reaches out to turn on the radio:

. . . trout fishing excellent off Point Lookout . . .
good perch catches . . . at the mouth of the Au Gres
. . . in the bay at thirty-five feet on Hot-N-Tots . . .

Maybe he'll go fishing. He won't ask Rex, hasn't
seen him in two weeks. That is, he's seen him, in the
halls at school, walking Nina Stratton to class. Nina
of the purple lipstick and nail polish, the blue, accor-
dion-pleated hair. They haven't spoken since that
weird afternoon at his house. Mainly it's been a
relief. Being around Rex all the time is exhausting.
Listening to his half-baked ideas; distracting him
from imagined insults, keeping him from getting into
brawls with people he doesn't even know.

Last night, a dream about his mother that made
him feel the same way; he woke up sweating, his
heart beating hard. Something bad was happening to
her—he can't remember what, but somehow it was
all his fault. He got out of bed and walked around the
house, watching the moon as it poured eerie light
down on the rooftops of the houses across the street.
He knew he couldn't go back to bed, played solitaire
on the computer until four o'clock in the morning.

. . . brown trout are biting on brown magflies at
Mio in the Au Sable . . . on the Black River they're
catching steelhead near the Lake Shore bridge . . .

What was it she said to him when she left? *Don't
think these grades don't matter.* She was sure Mr.

Boxer was calling to say he'd been goofing off again.
But he wasn't. She's not interested in hearing anything good about him. Jumping up, he pulls his
sweatshirt over his head, puts on his jeans and tennis
shoes, reaches out to snap off the radio. Fine, then.
That's the way it will be between them. Don't let
your mind wander, leaking into places that cause
pain. But there seems to be nothing for his mind to fix
on that doesn't harbor these hidden traps.

Jimmy is on the couch, watching Bugs Bunny and
Tweetie. He doesn't look up when Harry enters the
kitchen. Going to the refrigerator, he takes out the
carton of milk, pours Cheerios into a bowl. He eats
quickly, then gets up to go through the cupboards for
potato chips, a dark chocolate Milky Way. That will
take care of lunch.
    "You gonna be around for a while?"
    Jimmy looks up. "Why?"
    "I'm going fishing. Tell Aunt Jess, will you?"
    No answer.
    "You want to come?"
    Jimmy shakes his head no. "Where you going?"
    "Drummer's Point, probably."
    "Don't take anything of mine."
    He ignores this, finishes his breakfast, goes to the
basement. In a moment Jimmy follows him.
    "Tell Rex if he wants to go, to get his own gear."
    "I'm not going with Rex."
    "Who, then?"

"Nobody."

Another silence. "So you ask me."

Harry sighs. Does he expect an answer to this? He goes to the corner by the furnace, where his aunt's stuff is piled. There is the Peg-Board, where his father would hang the rods, by size and type; the narrow shelf below, where he kept the reels. Nothing there now. The Peg-Board is empty except for two old rods that used to belong to his grandfather.

"The stuff's over by the workbench," Jimmy says. "That's where I put it."

He digs out his green tackle box, sees the rods and reels, landing net, rubber waders tossed into a pile. Opening the box, he digs through it for the lures he wants.

"Maybe I'll go," Jimmy says. "What about Aunt Jess, though?"

"What about her?"

"It's chore day."

"Fine. Stay home and do chores."

He pockets two spinners, some jigs, and small snap swivels. Underneath the lures is the Swiss army knife he thought he'd lost. It's been missing since last summer. He slips it into his pocket, reaches for the graphite rod with its spinning reel.

"That's Dad's."

"So?" He stands up. "You coming or not?"

They ride parallel on the bike path. Then Jimmy moves ahead of him, on his old bike that he took back

from Julie, his rod stashed neatly in the holder he
made from a length of plumber's pipe. The Great
Inventor. Still, Harry wishes he'd thought of something like that. The rod is hard to hold, making it
awkward to steer. He's aware of a faint ssshhhing
sound—his back tire rubbing against the fender. He
should stop and twist it out, but Jimmy is already disappearing along the river path, beyond the tunnel of
alder and sumac.

He passes the drinking fountain—strange landmark on this rural path. He's not sure who owns this
field, but it's neatly mowed and tended. He wouldn't
mind that job—boss of the bike path, tooling around
on a riding mower all day. He shifts the rod to his left
hand, taking a firmer grip on his handlebars. This is
the rod that his father bought the summer he taught
them both how to cast.

High above his head in a cedar tree he hears the
call of an ovenbird: *teacher, teacher, teacher!* He can
see the river now. ". . . it's got triple ball bearings . . .
a lot of touch, like your grandpa's old fly rod. The fish
just has to breathe and you can feel it. Someday when
you guys get older, I'll buy you both a rod like
this. . . ." He lowers his head, riding faster, into the
wind, listening hard to the rushing water beside him
that drowns out everything.

"What're you using?"
"Mepps Three with a bucktail."
Frowning, Jimmy gives a shake of his head.

Meaning he doesn't like the choice, or he hasn't got one himself, Harry isn't sure; he doesn't ask. Already he's sorry he invited him. He's trashed the fishing spot (nobody ever catches anything this far up), the weight of the line (four pounds too heavy), the place where Harry dropped in.

"In the eddies is where they like it. You keep hitting there, you're gonna get hung up."

The trouble is he hasn't had a strike yet. Getting pissier by the minute. He thought if he came up here to cast, he wouldn't have to listen to him. But Jimmy's voice carries:

"This place is for shit, I'm going over by the bridge."

Go, then. The air is warm today, heavy with the scent of sweetfern. Across the river he notices a slight movement beneath the shadow of leaves playing on the water. A speckled trout, it must be. Moving in and out of the light. He casts again to the far bank, feels the line settle, then jerk suddenly. *No way, not this quick!* He reels in against the pull, and Jimmy's voice follows him:

"Don't yank . . . keep it steady!"

He comes running with his orders as Harry steadies the rod in toward the curve, coaxing the sliding shadow of fish. A huge shadow; it hugs the opposite bank. All because of Dad's lucky lure. He used to call it the Holy Fooler.

"He's comin' up! Watch it!"

A quiver, and another sharp jerk; then the line goes dead.

"Ah, you lost him. You flipped him off." Scorn in his voice. "What was it, did you see?"

"Speck."

"Couldn't be. Had to be a rainbow. Specks don't swim up this far." Jimmy starts back down the bank. "Might as well move downstream. He won't be back."

Ignoring this, Harry casts again toward the pool. As if on its own power, the line lifts suddenly, settling in a branch of a tree above the opposite bank. *Damn!* He tugs at it, pointing the rod on a plane with the line, the way he was taught. *". . . What you want to do is put firm, steady pressure on the line . . . make it separate. . . . "* The voice in his head as he pulls at the rod, arcing it from side to side. Nothing. He gives the reel a crank as the line bumps and drags through the leaves.

"Give it some slack," Jimmy advises.

Instead he cranks the reel tighter, jerking hard, and the tip bends, making the rod tremble in his hands. Now is when he should let up, he knows; jiggle, zigzag, look for the weak spot, tighten up slowly. But something about the way this day is going makes him feel desperate; he won't lose this lure. Shouldn't have put it on in the first place. He gives the rod another fierce jerk.

"You're pullin' too hard!"

"Shut up!"

Suddenly the line is free, hurtling up toward the sky. A strange whistling sound; he looks into the sun, sees only the blur of an arrow spinning through space, feels the soft pull of its landing. Then Jimmy lets out a cry. Still he keeps on staring for precious seconds, then stumbles through the brush.

He slowly makes his way down the incline to where Jimmy is kneeling, head bent at an odd angle. Playing Wounded Man on the Run, the way they do when they watch *N.Y.P.D. Blue*. No. Changing his lure, that's what he's doing. But Jimmy's rod is halfway down the grassy bank, the tip bent backward against a rock. He should be careful; it could snap off.

He's lying on his side, knees drawn up, head on his outstretched arm as if he's asleep. Or dead. A favorite trick: pretending injury after a fall, pretending not to breathe. His T-shirt is halfway up his back and there's a smear of mud across his face. Harry sees it all in exquisite detail: candy wrappers, empty potato-chip bag, red-and-white teardrop spinner floating on his cheek, the bucktail near his eye. The two hooks face outward, gleaming like miniature tusks. Where is the other hook?

Heart beating in his throat, Harry puts one hand to the ground to steady himself as Jimmy rolls to his back.

"It's okay . . . doesn't hurt . . . it's not in deep." The voice high and firm, daring him to disagree.

And now he can see the third hook, buried in Jimmy's closed eyelid, the narrow slit of open eye below it. He feels himself go light-headed; the world is spinning. He hears his own voice, as if from a long distance: "Not bad, I don't think . . . no blood . . ." Bending for a closer look. He will take back those seconds, take back that arrow twisting overhead in a bowl of blue. It didn't happen, can't be happening. There is a way out of this. If only he can find it.

"I gotta get my rod." He scrambles up the rise.

Behind him Jimmy pleads, "Don't go. . . ." as he picks up the rod, following the line back through the brush. *Careful, don't snag it on anything. Hurry, hurry.* Feeling for the knife in his pocket as he runs.

"I gotta cut this line loose, Jim."

"Okay. Just . . . don't touch it."

"I won't."

His hand trembles as he pulls at the blade; it slides smoothly from the handle. *Good knife.* Then it slips from his fingers and falls to the ground. Frantically he fishes for it through dead leaves and pine needles.

Jimmy's hands are at his sides. "After this, let's just go home, Har. . . ." The voice slurred, sleepy-sounding. "Better not tell Mom. . . ."

He grabs up the knife. Holding the line taut, he draws a quick stroke, snaps it free from the rod. Then he leans down, staring at a spot below his breastbone so as not to see the hook.

"Okay, Jim. Let's go."

"I think I need to sleep for a while. . . ."

"No. We gotta go now."

He pulls him to his feet and together they stumble up the bank. Jimmy leans heavily on his arm.

"Sorta dizzy . . ." he says. "Where are we . . . ?" Swaying away from Harry, he turns to slump down in the grass, rolls to his side.

Harry stares dumbly at him, then up the bank to where the bikes are parked; it feels like miles away. Blinding sunlight beams down on them.

"Jim, listen, we gotta get going."

No answer. One arm has moved to shield his face, and Harry stands a moment, looking down at him; then he sprints to the bikes, grabbing his up by the handlebars, calling over his shoulder: "I'll be right back. I'm gonna go get Aunt Jess. You hear me? Wait right here."

He pushes off, pedaling hard, staring down at the strip of black asphalt amid a sea of green. *Don't think, keep your eyes on the path.* The drinking fountain; the sumac bushes, their limbs dragging in the mud. His eyes are watering and his throat feels dry. A column of pain pierces his chest. He reaches the highway, and beside him the Saturday traffic is fiercely humming.

At the first intersection he swerves around a car pulling into the gas station and the driver bangs on his horn, jabs an angry finger toward the stop sign. *Doesn't matter. Never mind.*

Thinking, now, which is the fastest route: behind

Arby's and over the bridge. *Please let him be okay. I won't call him pussy, won't touch his stuff, won't tell on him ever . . . !* He makes the turn onto the dirt path, and a bunch of little kids are playing up near the bridge; they scramble to get out of his way. One of them yells after him: "Big turdface!"

He pumps his legs, staring down at the hard-packed dirt, thinking about distance, about the moments ahead. He knows every inch of this track, anticipates each obstacle. Around the next curve is where the path narrows and winds, a series of hairpin turns gradually widening to the back entrance of the subdivision. Three minutes; four at most and he will be in his own driveway. Aunt Jess will be there. She will know what to do. He rides onward, the sun a fiery, punishing weight upon his head.

36

In the kitchen Jess looks across the driveway to the neighbors' backyard. Saturday morning and she's watching the couple who moved in have breakfast at the picnic table with their kids. The little girl is a blonde, the boy a brunette, both under five, she'd guess. The boy looks like a French doll—thick, dark curls and pink cheeks, velvety-soft eyes. He's the one they dote on. The little girl tries to get her father's attention by throwing crusts of bread up in the air; they land in the butter dish, in the centerpiece of violets and lily of the valley. Sunlight pours down on them from above. The perfect family. Things seem so simple for some people.

Last night they watched TV; a cop show with a handsome white hero, a handsomer black one, both looking like fashion models as they ripped through a series of adventures and, in the end, engineered the bizarre and bloody death of the villain. She was shocked at the pleasure she got from it. Most of the time her heart just hurts, as if tiny knives are cutting away at it.

She leans her body against the sink. Nothing new in the world these days; everything makes her tired. Watching the kids, running errands, cooking. Working at a job that is beneath her. (At least Annie was right about that.)

The phone rings and she knows it is her mother. Asking them all over for dinner tonight, wanting to help out. The cost is more than she can pay. "You said he was an alcoholic, but he stopped drinking? Well, alcoholics want credit for intentions, I know that much. A nice guy, I'll admit, but he would never have left her. You know, it's not the bums and rotters of the world who'll break your heart, Jessie. It's nice guys, like him. You're better off."

Better off. She remembers at Keith's funeral someone saying words like that. People think they are giving you comfort. It's clear they don't have a clue. They're relieved it didn't happen to them, and they think it has something to do with . . . what?

Intelligence? Being solid citizens, obeying all the rules. Ridiculous. She knows better, it's nothing but luck. Bad luck Keith got cancer. Bad luck she didn't meet Ryan first.

She picks up the receiver.

"Jess. It's me."

Not her mother, after all. Her heart leaps. His voice over the telephone sounds young, almost boyish. She never will get over this, never. Not as long as she lives.

"I'm . . . it's a beautiful day, and I thought I'd take Cheryl out for a drive, maybe up to Franklin, to the cider mill. Just sit in the park and enjoy the fresh air. It'd be good for her. . . ." His voice trails off. "I just . . . I wanted to hear your voice." He clears his throat. "What are you doing?"

"Getting dinner."

"At ten o'clock in the morning?"

"Thinking about it." She was about to get out the corned beef and put it on the stove, turn the burner to low. Listen to the comforting *plop plop* of boiling water over meat, smell the scent of cloves in the air. "I wish you wouldn't call me like this," she says.

"I can't help it. I'm dialing the number thinking, 'Better not, better not. . . .' "

"Next time listen."

"Jess, I can't accept this. There's got to be some other way. If we talk to the lawyers, if . . ."

She stops listening. More of the same. No plan, no forecast, just that strange stubborn optimism that, when she turns it around, looks more like fantasy than anything else. Yet her heart will leap.

"Do what you have to do," she says. "I don't want to hear about it. I'm going to hang up now." Does it this time. Strange to think that she can have what she wants. It's a matter of paying the price, of deciding. While her sister doesn't get to decide; for her the choice was made. She shouldn't have told her about the chemo. Stupid. Just like the people at the funeral. No wonder she blew up.

Julie comes downstairs. Like a cat she rubs up against Jess's shoulder. "Where is everybody?"

"Don't know. They were gone by the time I got up."

"I don't see why Mom couldn't rest and get better here."

The second time she's said that since Annie left. Jess turns to give her a hug, again looking out the window. The family is gathering the remains of breakfast, preparing to go inside. She stares at the woman's face, so smugly content. The father is giving orders to the kids: "Carry it with both hands, now, that's the way. . . ." Remember to make good choices, too. That's important.

"When's she coming home?"

"Soon, honey."

She's uneasy with this answer. Or else, picking up on some other uneasiness. "Aunt Jess, are you and Mom having a fight?"

She wants to deny it, but Julie's lips fold in as she

waits. Wearing her hand-painted flamingo earrings that her grandmother sent to her from Florida. The look on her face makes Jess want to weep.

"Did you hear us the other night?"

"Some of it. Are you really going to leave?"

"Oh, honey." She pulls her in close, strokes the golden hair. "You know I wouldn't go far."

"I don't want you to go," she says. "I don't want you two to be mad. . . ."

Someone is pounding up the back steps. Harry enters the kitchen, out of breath: "Aunt Jess! You gotta come! Jim, he's . . . he got hurt!"

"Oh, Jesus, please, not on Eleven Mile . . ."

He shakes his head. "We were fishing . . . c'mon, we gotta hurry!"

His face is waxy looking, wet with sweat. A scrape on the inside of his arm, red dots in a brushlike pattern.

"Are you all right?"

"I just . . . I fell off my bike when I came in. . . ." He draws a ragged breath. "Down by Drummer's Point . . . we need to take the car!"

She grabs up her keys from the counter, tells Julie to wait for them there.

"Should I call Mom?" she asks.

"No!" And they are out the door.

He directs her down the highway and to an exit, then down a curving road past a freshly plowed field. At the edge of the woods he says curtly, "Park here!"

The second she stops, he is out the door and running. She follows him up the path as it veers inward, toward the river; soon the water is rushing along beside them. She reaches out to swat the horseflies zooming in toward her. Her side aches; yellow circles swirl in front of her face. At last he slows, and she sees a large oak tree up ahead, bordering the path.

"That's where the rapids start. He's up here."

"Was anyone else with you?"

He shakes his head, starts running again, and a wave of panic rips through her. It must have taken him at least a half hour to ride back from here. How badly is Jimmy hurt? *God, please . . . !*

They come to a place where the path is overgrown, the bushes thicker. Here the trail cuts even closer to the river. Ahead of her Harry is calling: "Jimmy . . . Jimmy!"

"Do you know where you left him?"

He doesn't answer, starts down the bank, and she follows him. Over her own gasps for air she can hear the sighing of the wind in the trees.

"Aunt Jess! Here!"

Harry is bent over Jimmy's body beside the path. She sees the smudged T-shirt, a paste of dried mud on his cheek. Then she's staring down at the evil-looking hook, barely visible through the swollen curve of his eyelid. He's lying very still, his head resting on a small mound of grass. Harry looks up at her, his own face streaked with sweat, eyes pleading.

It's not that bad, right? She kneels beside her nephew, keeping her voice calm.

"Can you hear me, Jimmy? It's Aunt Jess."

Eyes closed, he turns his head toward the sound. "It's okay . . . doesn't hurt . . . I can't feel it. . . ." The words slurred, as if he's talking in his sleep.

She feels a wave of panic, pushes it away. *Not now, not now. Think what to do.*

"Honey, we have to walk out of the woods. Do you think you can walk with me?"

"Where's Harry?" The voice light, without strength, like a six-year-old's. How will she ever get him up? She sits beside him, trying to stay calm. Harry is scrambling in the weeds down by the river, and she calls to him sharply; in a moment he comes running.

"We need to walk, hon," she says to Jimmy again. "Can you do that?"

Kneeling beside his head, Harry slides his hands under Jimmy's shoulders while she straddles him, lifting him by the waist; together they manage to get him on his feet. Once there, he leans heavily against her, nearly topples her over. Please, don't let him fall down, don't let him faint. We have to get out of here. She holds him firmly by the arms. His bones feel fragile, as if they could break.

"My fishing rod . . ."

"I got it," Harry says. And, miraculously, he does, reaching down in the grass to sweep the rods up while he slips his other arm under Jimmy's shoulders.

Between them they steer him down the path. *Must not panic, must not lose her footing, must just hurry them along the path.* She can't look at his face, at the pillowy, puffed eye; looks instead at the sandy trail and the tunnel of leaves ahead. Jimmy makes no sound, doesn't cry out, but she can hear Harry's harsh breathing, sees his pale face staring grimly forward.

"Only a little further . . ."

"Where we going?" Jimmy murmurs.

"To the hospital."

"Do we have to? Aunt Jess, it doesn't hurt. . . ."

"It's all right," she says. "But we need to just see the doctor. . . ."

"Stop a second," Harry says. He shifts his weight, lifting Jimmy's arm higher across his shoulders. They continue on toward the car.

"Don't tell Mom," Jimmy says. "Okay, Aunt Jess? Please. Don't tell her. . . ."

It's cold inside the room, all full of sterile metal and the underhum of machinery. Jimmy lies, naked to the waist, on the high table. She wants to cover his bare chest and arms with her sweater.

She stands, with Harry, next to the wall while the nurse checks Jimmy's heart and lungs, takes his blood pressure, loosens the belt on his jeans. His hand moves at once to his fly; a soft, moaning sound issues from his throat.

The doctor is suddenly there, but she didn't see

him come in. He leans over the table, talking firmly to Jimmy's upturned face:

"Jim. Can you hear me? I'm Dr. Garrett. I'm going to help you. Can you hear me, Jim?"

"Yeah . . ." The voice so soft she can barely recognize it.

"Good. How old are you, Jim?"

A longer pause. "Twelve and a half . . ."

"What school do you go to?"

"Clara Barton . . ."

"Ever been in a hospital before?"

The moments drag by. "Just . . . when I was born . . ."

In spite of her fear, she has to smile; Harry takes her hand, squeezes it hard.

"Okay, this will hurt a bit, Jim," the doctor says. "Just try to relax. . . ." The nurse hands him something that looks like an eyedropper, then moves to the end of the table, where she rests her hands at each side of Jimmy's head. The doctor's back is to Jess, blocking her view. Jimmy cries out—a low, guttural sound—and her heart knocks against her rib cage. The bones of her knees are melting away. She braces herself against the wall.

"Sorry, that's the worst of it. Okay." And a moment later: "Pain gone yet?"

"Yeah . . ."

"Good."

He moves away and she can see Jimmy's face, pale

against the green of the hospital sheets. The hook is still there. She lets out a long breath. Beside her, Harry leans his head back, closing his eyes.

". . . laceration of the eyelid . . ." the doctor is saying. "Looks like the cornea may be punctured . . . could be internal bleeding . . ." He looks up. "Call Dr. Mischke, will you? And get some Fluorescein. And the slit lamp."

A pain just below her heart; she presses it with both hands. *God. Please. Let us be one of the lucky ones. This time. Please.*

The doctor is walking toward her now. "We need you to wait outside, Mother. . . ."

"I'm his aunt," she says. "His mother's not here. She's out of town. . . ."

She can see the nurse bandaging Jimmy's head. *Why? What are they doing now?* She wants to ask if she can stay; at the same time she's terrified of being in the same room with the horrible hook, with him lying there on the table so still.

The doctor walks them both toward the set of double doors that is the entrance to the emergency room.

"Do you know when he had his last tetanus shot?"

"A year ago January," Harry says. "He got hit by a hockey skate at practice."

"He's all right, isn't he?" she asks. "He'll be all right . . . ?"

"There could be some damage to the cornea. I can't be sure. I want the ophthalmologist to have a look." He leaves them at the door. "It won't be long. Just have a seat out there."

The waiting room, with its gray walls and hard blue chairs, has a menacing look. Suddenly she's dizzy, feels as if she could fall down. Trying to steady herself, she grips Harry's arm; they move toward a bank of chairs against the wall. It can't be bad; there wasn't any blood. A smear of it on his shirt, that's all. It can't be too bad. But the bandage! It must mean that they were trying to keep the thing in place, keep it from doing further damage. What did that long hike on an uneven dirt path do? ". . . laceration . . . cornea . . ." What does that mean? Why didn't she think of that while they were walking!

She'd better call Julie. At least let her know where they are. And then she must call Annie. Again, her heart lurches. Annie has to be told. Right away. Or should she wait until they know something? To make that three-hour drive without knowing . . .

Beside her, Harry is seated with his head bowed, elbows on his knees.

"Why didn't they just take it out, Aunt Jess?"

"I don't know. . . ."

The doors open and two orderlies come out wheeling a stretcher. But it can't be Jimmy. An IV on a stand; plastic tubes snaking from under the sheet. It must be someone else. The stretcher disappears around the corner. Dr. Garrett comes toward her then, and she stands up to meet him.

"The hook went through the cornea. We're going to have to operate. He'll need a general anesthetic. . . ."

"But he'll be all right . . . ?"

"Can't tell yet," he says. "Chances are good, though. Dr. Mischke's the best, he's done this a thousand of times, believe it or not. It'll take a little time to get him prepped for surgery. The nurse has some papers for you to sign."

"How long will he be in there?" She can't think of another thing to ask him.

"Not long. You can wait upstairs."

And then he is gone. And there is nothing left to do but fill out the forms, sign permission papers, get directions to Ophthalmology. Wait for the elevator. Wait for word to come to an identical waiting room on the third floor. Wait.

She calls Julie from a pay phone in the hall. It's answered on the first ring.

"Is he okay?" Julie asks. "What happened, Aunt Jess?"

"He got a fishhook in his eye."

"Oh, yeaucchh! Did they get it out?"

"Not yet," she says. "Will you be all right there by yourself?"

"I will if you come pretty soon. Are you gonna bring him home, then?"

"I don't know. Julie, I need the number of the place where your mom is staying. Do you see it there, on the bulletin board? A five-one-seven area code."

"Yes, it's right here." She reads the number to her and Jess takes it down, hangs up the phone. Harry is standing beside her.

"Mom's going to be really upset."

"She'll be upset, hon. But she'll know it was an accident. . . ."

He turns away from her. "I just yanked it out of the tree when I should've gone across and gotten it. I could've done that. Or else cut the line and just let it go. It was so stupid. . . ."

Before she can answer he goes to sit stiffly, fists on his knees. Shoulders anchored to the chair, he leans back, closes his eyes, his expression bruised, helpless. What can she say to him? To have some relief, that's all. A long spill of normal and uneventful days, where nothing bad happens. To escape the feeling that you are fixed in the eye of some cruel and dangerous force. That is what she would wish for them all. She looks down at the paper in her hand and, with a sigh, dials the number.

37

The room is cool; everything dark. He feels calm and unburdened. Nothing to do but lie here. On the inside of his eyelids, a greenish-white landscape; it looks like the print on a dollar bill. A breeze blowing through trees, making a rushing sound. Or is this inside his head? He isn't sure. He puts a hand up to his eye, feels the rough bandages.

"You awake?" someone asks. It is a woman's voice. "How are you feeling?"

"Where are we?"

"In the eye room."

He can't get over the fact that there's actually a place here called The Eye Room. "Is it all over?"

"All over. That didn't take long, did it?"

How would he know? He can't remember anything after they wheeled him in here. She's helping him to sit up now, with her arm about his shoulders. He feels dizzy, his stomach slightly queasy.

"You're going home," she says. "As soon as we can get a wheelchair up here."

And then a new voice; one that he doesn't recognize. "I hear you're quite the fisherman, Jim. What were you after?"

"Bass." He clears his throat; it feels scratchy, and he's suddenly very thirsty. "Bass and specks."

"Specks?"

"Speckled trout."

"Ah. And how were they biting?"

He thinks about this. "They don't bite," he says. "They strike. Can I have a glass of water?"

"Better to wait a few minutes. Sometimes the anesthetic makes you feel nauseous." He moves around the table. "I'm Dr. Mischke. I'm the ophthalmologist. What kind of lure was that you were you using?"

"Jitterbug. But the one in my eye was my brother's. A Mepps spinner with a bucktail."

"Mind if I keep it? We've got a mannequin here, decorated with every fishhook known to man. People get these things caught in some weird places."

He should tell him to ask Harry. But he's too tired. For some reason he suddenly feels like crying, but he's not about to do that here. Not now that it's over and they are helping him down off the table. The doctor is talking to someone else and he tries to listen:

"The pupil looks good . . . iris is clear, too . . . there's no gross damage. Just what we hoped."

"There wasn't much blood. . . ." It is his aunt's voice.

"No, it's not a vascular area."

"So he'll be all right?" He catches the faint odor of her perfume as she drops a hand gently to his shoulder.

"There's some danger of infection, so we'll need to see him tomorrow. Be sure to have him drink plenty of liquids. In the meantime he stays in bed with his head slightly elevated, no activity whatever. Got that, my man?"

The doctor's hand is on his other shoulder. He has no desire for activity of any kind, would promise anything in any case, just to be home safe in his own bed.

". . . On Tuesday you can bring him back again and we'll take out the stitches."

"And the bandages?"

"They can come off Monday. It's best to cover both eyes, just so he isn't tempted to move them. But the hook came out fine, once we got rid of the barb. Here's a prescription for the pain. It'll be plenty sore for a while. . . ."

"Where's Harry?"

"I'm right here, Jim."

He's surprised at this; didn't sense his presence. The wheelchair has arrived, and they help him down off the table and into it. Then the nurse is wheeling him down the hall. Outside the doors he feels the warmth of the sun on his head.

"Feeling okay?" she asks, and he nods. He's not going to answer this question every two minutes.

They stop, then, and he hears his aunt opening the car door; a blast of heat from its interior. He stands up and Harry's hand guides him into the front seat.

"Where's my rod?"

"It's in the trunk."

The minute his head hits the back of the seat, he falls asleep. In his dream he wanders the docks with Harry, watching as the fishing boats gas up—*Wavewalker, Bittersweet, HelRay-Zer, E Z Lovin, Dobber II.* Smelling the fresh, fish odor of the docks. Hearing scrappy cries of blue jays in the trees. Walking around town, aimlessly, stopping by the tennis courts, then on to the Mill Pond. He reads the bronze raised letters of the sign:

HARRISVILLE FOUNDED 1872 BY THE
HARRIS BROTHERS, FISHERMEN AND SHIPPERS

His heart beating in a calm, slow rhythm. Yet he knows what day this is. And suddenly there is pain—circling, touching bone. His eyelid is a roll of puffed skin. He can sense the weight of the hook in his eye, the stiff shank of the lure. An odor of pine needles next to his face. His heart pounding out a rhythm in time to the pulsing wound. But he is Lug, god of medicine. He can fix this, can't he?

Harry, who thinks he is such a hot banana, makes a map of the woods behind the school. Then they walk it using his map, and soon they are lost. Harry keeps heading left, and he knows this was wrong, they will never find their way back that way. The cage of trees goes on and on until finally he decides to take charge, declaring that he will go his own way and Harry can either follow him or not. He gets them back, but hours late, after his father has already driven the streets on a search and his mother has been waiting for hours in the driveway. Is this part of the dream? Maybe all of it is. Wonderful, miraculous thought. All of it—the death, the funeral, Mrs. Bennett, the accident—just one bad dream and he will awaken to find everything back to the way it used to be.

On the day his father died, he and Harry walked the streets of Harrisville, waiting to be summoned. He was crying and Harry, with tears streaming down his own face, kept telling him to quit it, quit being such a damned baby.

•   •   •

"I brought you some lemonade."

She puts the glass in his hand and he raises it to his mouth. Tart; icy cold on his tongue. He can feel the liquid all the way down in his chest.

"Did you call Mom?"

"Yes." She smooths his pillow. "She'll be home in a couple of hours." He is careful to keep his head forward of her hand. He knows he will cry if she so much as touches him.

"How's your eye? Do you need another pain pill?"

"No," he says. "I just don't want her to feel bad about this. . . ."

"Don't worry. Everything will be fine."

But something else is on his mind; he needs to talk to her. "I decided what I want to be, Aunt Jess. I'm going to be a doctor."

"Good. You'll be a good one."

"Maybe even an eye doctor." He reaches a hand up to the bandage. "It was Dad's idea. Sort of . . ." What is with all of this baby stuff? He can feel hot liquid seeping out from under his lids. Clearing his throat, he says: "I talked to him today. While I was waiting for you guys to come."

A silence, then.

"D'you believe me?"

"Yes," she says. "I believe you."

"It's not the first time, either." He lies back on the pillow, and her hand reaches out to hold his.

"Did you see him, Jim?"

"No. It's different than that."

"More like a phone call?"

"No. That'd be great, though. If he'd call me up when he wanted to talk. Wouldn't it? No, he just . . . said not to be afraid. That I shouldn't worry. Stuff like that . . ."

"He always was pretty calm," she says. "That time you fell out of the tree. And your mouth and eyes were so full of dirt you couldn't even scream. That was about the scariest thing you've ever done. That is, until today."

"I wanted to tell somebody," he says. "But I thought it'd be too weird. D'you think it's weird, Aunt Jess?"

"No," she says. "I knew he was around. Maybe I'll get to talk to him one of these days, too."

"I tried to tell Harry about it once, but he just got mad."

"I think it's a little scary to some people."

"Not to me." He yawns, then, feeling suddenly very tired. "What's scary to me is thinking of not talking to him."

Harry comes in later, pulls up the desk chair to sit beside the bed. He starts to sit up, amazed to discover that his arms won't work; they feel weak, watery, like when he butted heads with Jamie Mack at hockey practice.

"You're not supposed to move," Harry warns.

"Yeah, I know." Lying back against the pillow, he

turns his head toward Harry's voice. "You got my rod, didn't you?"

"That's the third time you asked."

"How about my lures and stuff?"

"I got everything. Don't worry."

"Listen," he says. "I didn't mean what I said to you before, about my bike. I know you didn't have anything to do with that."

"Oh, man," Harry says. "You still thinking about that? Anyway, it wasn't Perez, I'm sure. Or any of those guys. They're jerks, but they wouldn't do that."

"I know. It was my own stupid fault. I just wanted to be mad at somebody."

"It wasn't," Harry says. "You left it for two lousy minutes and some mean fucker ripped it off. That doesn't make it your fault." The chair scrapes back. In an odd, husky voice Harry says, "I wish it was this morning again. I'd like to start the whole damn day over."

"Why?"

"I dunno . . . I woke up thinking everything was shitty and it couldn't get worse. And then all of a sudden it got a lot worse."

"Nothing's worse," he says. "It all worked out okay."

"Why was I even fishing there? What an asshole . . ."

"That's a dumb thing to say." Remembering it was he who'd told him that. "It's just like when the Christmas tree burned up. Whose fault was that?"

A pause. Then Harry says: "Yours."

They both laugh, and he slides his shoulders back and forth against the pillow, scratching his back.

"I read in the paper," Harry says, "about some guy who hooked himself in the ear with a Zara Spook."

"Yeah? What happened?"

"They had to amputate."

"Bullyatz!"

Again they laugh, and he says, "I kept hearing voices out there while I was waiting for you guys."

"Jim, don't start. . . ."

"No, I mean I thought it was you. Coming back across the river. I heard somebody talking, and it seemed like they were right over on that other bank. Only, they never came."

"Maybe it was the damned Druids."

"Mom home yet?" he asks.

"No. Not yet."

Why did he say this? They both fall silent before it. At last Harry gets up.

"I'm gonna go take a shower. You want anything? Some chips or candy?"

"No, thanks."

"That doctor who did the operation was a dude," Harry says. "I liked him, though. He seemed like he really knew what he was doing."

"He was okay, I guess." He yawns, lying back against the cool pillowcase. "He didn't know jack about fishing."

38

It's raining when she wakes up. She can hear the sizzle of truck wheels on the highway. Can't see anything through the cracked windowpane except sky.

She pulls herself upright, reaching for her robe at the foot of the bed. A strange dream of going to the airport, trying to explain to the clerk behind the counter exactly where it is she wishes to go. The clerk won't listen, shakes her head: "No, that's not allowed, not allowed." She reaches out, grabs the front of her dress, clutches at her throat, her fingers digging into her windpipe: "You're ungood! You're ungood!" All the while twisting her hands in the soft flesh of the woman's neck. What did it mean?

She gets up and goes to the window, watching the rain stream down the pane. A truck goes by on the highway, its silver body bearing the name HARRY'S OIL COMPANY. Ever since he learned to read he has called them his trucks.

The room feels cool. She walks to the dresser for the box she put there last night. Going back to the bed, she opens it on her lap, lifts out the Penworthy notebook he bought last summer, to keep track of his medications. Beneath it is the clipping from the *News/Free Press:*

Keith Robert Browner, 38, of Royal Oak died August 4 in Harrisville. A teacher of English and Language Arts at Redding Senior High in Birmingham, he had been on indefinite leave of absence since June. Survived by his wife, Anne, and three children— Harry, James, and Julia, his mother, Eleanor, and a brother, William, of Seattle. Services August 7 from Dixon-Burns Funeral Home in Royal Oak; interment at White Chapel.

She must have cut it out, put it here for safe-keeping. She doesn't remember doing it. Beneath that, a copy of the death certificate. Then his last letter to her, written on a sheet of notebook paper. Dated August 1. She found it in a drawer when she was packing his clothes to take them home. She takes it out, reads it again:

To my best friend,

I miss you already. I wish you were coming with me. I would like to have lived another year so that I could have known you at least as long as I didn't know you. I love you so much.

Be kind to yourself. Make peace with what is. Don't be afraid of confusion. Don't put anyone out of your heart, there's room for all. Above all, don't worry about your decisions. We only get about thirty seconds to make them anyway.

Oh, shit, what am I doing? This was supposed to be a love letter. I can never resist giving advice. Trying to figure it all out and then tell it to you. I should know better. You will find it all out for yourself. You are the smartest person. Any secrets I have, you already know. Any secrets you have, you can tell me later.

Love, love, love,
Keith

She can see the chapel, with its narrow dome; the twelve angels set in mosaic tile; an inscription in gold leaf at their feet:

UNTIL * THE * DAY * BREAK *
AND * THE * SHADOWS * FLEE * AWAY

Above it, the flowing robes of the seated figures: FAITH. HOPE. CHARITY. LOVE. Her mother-in-law's voice, then: ". . . I know that he's watching me, looking down on me in my loneliness. . . ." Had she meant God? Keith? Her long-dead husband? She never thought to ask.

All around her, the women in their dresses—gauzy and sleeveless, light-colored—making her think of spring. Only it wasn't. The dead end of summer and hot, so hot the men carried their jackets to the graveside; the Queen Anne's lace and field asters were wilting on the casket.

Jimmy and Julie next to her; Harry standing with her father and mother. Jimmy's pants were new and too long, bunched around his ankles. Her father's hand was on Harry's shoulder, patting, patting, until she wanted to reach out, make him stop.

Afterward, people standing around in her house, talking, eating, and drinking. Pondering life's mysteries. Waiting for the widow to confirm their belief that it was "all for the best." A man came up and told her he went to Michigan, taught with Keith when he was in Clawson. She had no idea who he was, never saw him before in her life. She couldn't think; she was in a dream.

Coming in through the back door, she had seen his khaki fishing hat hanging there on its hook; the sight of it stunned her so that she sagged against the kitchen table, gripping it with both hands. He was home, then! Returned from wherever it was he'd been these nightmarish hours. The funeral, the arrangements, the people—all a dream, a mistake. It was then that it hit her: he was truly gone. He wasn't coming back. But how could this be? If anything could bring him back, it would be his hat, hanging there on its hook.

Moments later she and William parted company forever. He came out to the kitchen to talk to her about his mother's financial affairs.

"Everything's in order," she assured him. "I've kept up the payments. The car insurance isn't due until September. . . ."

Keith had always taken care of everything, along with all of her heavy chores: cleaning gutters, raking and shoveling, putting up storms and screens. In one dismissive gesture William waved it all away. His mother could afford to hire someone for all of that.

As for the business end, no point in him doing it long-distance; he would find someone here to take it on.

"I can't imagine why he didn't do that. I guess he had his reasons. At least this way, you know it's being done right."

For a moment she blanked. And then blood poured into her brain, filling her with rage. He, the reaper of his mother's silly adoration, which he did nothing to earn, who looked so much like his brother people couldn't help remarking on it; in fact, her own children couldn't resist it, so desperate were they for comfort. He, the busy man, much too valuable at his workplace to take time out to visit his dying brother, here he stood before her, healthy, and still alive!

"You are such an ass," she said. "It isn't possible to hide it, even for three days, is it?"

And then Jess was moving toward her, arms out, while down the hallway Nell told everyone who would listen:

". . . his company is involved with the government . . . he goes to the Pentagon at least once a month. . . ."

Don't put anyone out of your heart. Hers is pounding right now, her mind clattering along at full speed. His sons growing up without him. His daughter's children never knowing who he was. Someday they'll be looking at snapshots, asking, "Why's he holding up that big balloon? What's he laughing at? Is that a newspaper he's reading? Why is it upside down?" And those left behind will say: "Because. That was just who he was." But it won't be true; he'll have slipped away for good by then. Nobody will even remember when and where the pictures were taken.

The Cove is closed, so she goes to Mooney's for an ice-cream cone. Ten o'clock in the morning, but they are open. The cement-block building is painted blue; a black ceiling fan twirls overhead, the air heavy with sugary perfume. She orders a single-dip butter-cream sugar cone.

The boy behind the counter looks younger than Harry. He's scraping ice cream from one of the five-gallon bins. She's seen other kids working in Harrisville who look underage; maybe the rules are different up here. Maybe they just look younger, because of the fresh air, the moist wind coming off the lake. She knows her ideas about growing up here are romantic.

He gives her a friendly smile. "Still raining out?"

She nods her head. The last time they were in Mooney's, he ordered Superman ice cream. Julie scolded him: "You should never eat anything blue, Daddy."

The town is quiet in the lightly falling rain. She parks in front of the old blacksmith's shop, its wide double doors fastened by a heavy padlock. Next to the storefront lawyer's office: THOMAS COOK,

ATTORNEY in gold letters across the window. Riebow's Hardware, Century 21 Realty, ALCO Theater,
the Laundromat. On the corner is the IGA, where
people meet to exchange news and lend comfort. She
walks past it, past the bank and Daisy's Fudge and
Antiques, down Main Street to the marina, where she
and Keith would sit, look out at the lake, watch the
boats coming in and out of the harbor.

Any secrets I have, you already know. Not true,
not true. Why didn't he tell her? Was he afraid she'd
try to change his mind? Back then, when she was
about to lose him, she wouldn't have believed it.
She looks out at the water, ebbing and flowing. Here
and gone. Glancing up into the tall cedars, their
trunks like huge columns, she knows she is waiting
for some kind of signal. At any moment she herself
could disappear.

A freighter crawls by on the horizon. Flat and rust-
colored, it has those squat white smokestacks at the
front and rear. Pushing a ruffle of water before it. The
lake beats softly, like someone breathing beside her.
Above her head the seagulls are circling, screaming.
She needs to walk, has walked up and down in lots of
places, searching for what? Her lost self. If she walks
long enough, waits long enough, perhaps she will see
herself coming.

She walks rapidly on the beach, hands in her
pockets. From out of the brush comes a skinny black

dog, looking more like a rat than any breed she can recognize. He sidles up to her.

"Go," she whispers. "Go on."

At last she stops, opens his notebook, holds it so as to shield it from the mist with her hand. The first few pages are drawings of the side porch, the beach in front of the cottage, the lake, the marina. Rough sketches, done with a pencil. She leafs past them to the dated entries, beginning with the week they arrived. She turns the pages slowly:

June 15,

When I start to wonder what the hell I'm doing here, the answer comes up: looking for the soul. Does that sound pretentious? Maybe just dumb.

On an envelope that came today: damaged in processing by high-speed canceling equipment. Please accept our apologies. U.S. Postal Service. Damaged in processing seems as good an answer as any to the question Why me? Focal seizures. Paralysis. These are words that scare the shit out of me, but they are part of my life now. You don't get to choose. If you decide to open yourself up to LIFE, then you must be there for all of it. How can I argue with my own existence?

June 20,

So much of what goes on in life we try not to experience. You can get so good at denying that you lose track of any deeper levels of living. Mother doesn't want to believe this is happening. I understand this, but what happens to those levels if you ignore them?

Maybe it's the only way she and William can function. It's not such a bad thing. I used it myself, back in November, when we first found out. But it's a relief not to have to fake it. All we have left now is love.

June 25,

Thinking about my sons today. Harry, the daredevil; Jimmy, the dreamer. Both of them smart, but Harry is reckless. We were always within an inch of losing him. Jimmy as a newborn. So small! Tiny, little skull with its bones not knit together. Fontanel. Beautiful word for such a scary thing.

They are so different. Will they ever be friends? I think, when they learn to value what they now despise in each other.

June 29,

My daughter, who carries the burden of both grandmothers' names, yet not like either; her own person. There's so much she could teach her brothers, but they won't listen. After all, she's the baby of the family. What could she possibly know?

I remember when she was four years old, watching me put out drinks:

—What doing, Daddy?

—Little party, Toots. Cocktails.

—What are cowtails?

—Pop for grown-ups.

—I know it's pop, but what else?

—Liquor.

—Licorice?

July 7,

Ah, the terrors of parenting, the endless influence! Harry at three, pointing at something: "Dad, what da hell is dat?" My words and tone; he had it down pat. The awful shaping going on, even when you don't want it! Don't swear, don't think an unkind thought. Don't ever fail to listen. Humbling, trying to live up to yourself as this perfect human being.

July 10,

Headline in the paper this morning: THOSE WHO CAN'T EXPRESS ANGER ARE GREATER CANCER RISKS. I don't know how I got this disease, but it seems enough, dealing with dying, without assigning blame for past behaviors, past mistakes.

I haven't even mentioned the weather. It's been perfect, warm, not a cloud in the sky. Help me, please. I want to do this right. But it's hard. I never died before.

July 15,

Letting go this dream of existence: as husband, father, brother, son. As teacher, Little League coach, lover of jazz, bridge, poetry. Snow shoveler.

Gardener. Carpenter. Sailor. The trick is to learn to release these illusions without fear or regret. To live each day as a gift.

July 23,

> *Riddle of destiny, who can show*
> *What thy short visit meant, or know*
> *What thy errand here below?*
>   Charles Lamb

I read this quote today. It seemed so right. This is one hell of a riddle. Suppose, before we are born, we choose this life. Suppose it is a working out of our own acceptance. Our understanding that caring and suffering cannot be separated. All separation is an illusion. It is connectedness that makes us whole. Does that make any sense? More on this later.

There was no more. She closes the notebook, holds it with her two hands pressed to her chest.

Oh, my dear, what are we to do about this death of yours, this death of yours and mine? How to begin? Is it about giving up all illusion, then? The illusion that you are in control. Surrender to the fact that life is neither ordered nor disordered; it simply is.

All we have left here is love. But we don't, it's gone, disappeared somewhere in the punishing months that followed. "Mom, you can be so mean,"

Jimmy said to her. Punishing them, too, for all that she's been feeling, all that she was afraid to feel.

Any secrets you have, you can tell me later. What is her secret? That she's been too afraid? She's no good to her kids anymore, poison to them, can't help them, can't keep them from suffering. . . .

She sits down on the wet sand, stares out at the lake. All of her energy going to that impossible end. And all this time he was here with her. She was the one who wouldn't let him in. Keeping him shut out with her anger. Yet he's here now; she can feel it: his presence in the air around her, in the breathing of the lake. And she is all eyes, all ears, seeing, hearing, remembering everything.

The year they took the kids to Cedar Point. Those whirling rides set in exotic places—*Mysterious Orient, South Sea Islands, Mountains of Europe.* Waves of harsh, tinny music, and gnomelike figures, dressed in costumes. A young man sitting on a high stool, microphone in hand:

Exit to the right, folks, watch your step, and thank ya fer ridin' the Bluestreak!

Harry the daredevil in the front seat, arms raised, eyes wide with excitement. Jimmy standing in the line with them, pretending until the last minute that he was going, then ducking under the gate: "I'll just wait here." He knew his limitations, Keith said.

The little dog is still with her, standing at her side, looking alert, ears pointed forward. A man is approaching with his own dog in tow. He calls out: "Is it a 'he' or a 'she' ?"

"I think a 'he.' "

"No, I meant you!"

And she laughs. He means this as a joke, doesn't stop, instead walks on, moving away, up the beach.

Make peace with what is, he told her. Last November, even before they truly believed in it. Whatever happens, it will be okay. You will still have yourself. And that he has said to her right here. In this very place. That first week of June, when they arrived here.

Farther down the beach, she can see a sign. She tries to focus her eyes, can only make out part of it:

POSITIVELY

XX XXX XXXXXXXX XXXX XXX XXXXX
XXX XXXX XXXXXXXXXXXXXXX XX

ON THIS BEACH

A good way to be, then. Positively. On this beach. For now, maybe nothing more has to be known.

She parks in front of the inn, entering by the side door. There's a fire in the fireplace, and she takes off her raincoat, staring into the flames. Fire patterns fascinate her: blue flowing air currents and orange coals; fingers curling over the backs of logs, yellow and white at the base, like fossil bones or dinosaur teeth. A faint chattering sound, as of birds singing inside the chimney.

She sees the woman—Becky is her name, she remembers it now—hurrying down the stairs in her direction and moves toward her, smiling.

39

He needs something to do with his hands while he's waiting, goes down into the basement. Unwinding the old line from the reels, he removes them from the rods, takes them apart. The task they used to do together each fall, before school started, he and Dad.

He puts the tiny screws on a piece of cloth, making sure they won't get lost in the collection of junk on the workbench. They're so tiny—like the ones jewelers use to fix eyeglasses.

With a small brush he cleans each reel, getting rid of the dirt and junk from the water. He sprays them with reel oil—not too heavy, not too thin—and carefully reassembles them. He wipes down the rods, replaces them in the rack. Then he cleans out his tackle box, sorting the various lures into their compartments.

He wanted to ask for the Mepps spinner back, but he didn't. Maybe when they go back tomorrow. He picks up the Little Cleo; the one he was using last summer at the Mill Pond. And then he is inside the shade-darkened bedroom, holding up the stringer with the fat trout, its pale belly gleaming. The rest of the picture is dark. Like the beam of a flashlight, illuminating only what's in its path.

That awful morning. Awakening to a bloodred sun, the sound of his aunt's voice in the hallway. The drop of some heavy weight upon his head. Because he knew. In that very instant he understood all of it; how his life had been changed forever. No need to wait for the funeral, people coming up to hug him, telling him he was such a brave boy. *Now you are the man of the family.*

Confined by others' grief, and smothered by their attention. They expected something of him; every five minutes someone asked him how he was doing. He was doing fine, now that it was over. He had known for months it was coming, and then it came. It seemed to him then that knowing was the worst; the finality of it was a relief. Now he knows better.

Once when he was eight years old he bought a mouse at a garage sale. Twenty-five cents, and it came with a little shoe box—a tiny pink-and-white creature with miniature claws; the body perfect and complete, with blue veins pulsing in the triangular skull. He fed it all that day—bits of lettuce and rice, milk from an eyedropper. That evening, when he wanted to bring it inside, she had said no, it didn't belong in the house. So he placed it tenderly, wrapped in a clean washcloth, in the basket of his bike. In the morning when he went to check on it, the mouse was dead.

He was horrified. Wordlessly he carried the stiff corpse into the house, held it out to her. She hugged him as he cried. These things happen, she said. It was a baby, too young to live on its own; it would have died anyway. Not his fault. But he knew better. He could have freed it so it could have saved itself, found its own food and a place to keep warm. Instead he wanted to own it, kept it a prisoner in a shoe box. It was the last time he remembers crying in front of her.

Everything wrong, for a long time. Even before his father died. That summer he and Jimmy helped him work on the deck, and he had to sit down every few minutes to lean back against the wall of the house, his face a mask of pain. Eyes that never looked directly at you anymore. He had pretended not to notice. Now it haunts him. He's drowning in it, unable to find a single rescuing thought. Now you are the man of the family. Terrible, terrifying joke.

A wave of dizzying, unbearable pain makes him drop his head into his hands. Upstairs a telephone is ringing. He rises to his feet automatically, goes to answer it. His feet are made of lead, fastened to stumps of legs.

"Hey, Harry."

It is Ryan.

"How's Jimmy feeling?"

"Okay. How'd you know . . . ?"

"Your aunt called and left a message. She around?"

"She's at the store."

"Is your mother home yet?"

"Not yet," he says. "You coming over?"

"Not just now." A pause. "That was good thinking. You going for help like that."

"I couldn't get him up on the bike." He turns to look through the window into the backyard.

"Hey," Ryan says. "You okay about this, Har?"

No answer. He can feel his throat closing. He'd like to keep him on the phone, doesn't know what else to say about this. Pinching the bridge of his nose with his free hand, he swallows the pain down.

"If he gets an infection . . ." he says.

"He won't," says Ryan. "He's tough, he'll fight it off." Then, after a moment: "Just tell your aunt I called, will you? Take it easy now."

He hangs up, leans for a moment against the wall, eyes closed. When he opens them, his aunt is coming up the back steps with a bag of groceries in her arms. He pushes the screen door open, goes out on the porch to meet her.

"Ryan called."

"Thanks." She blows a piece of hair back from her face. "Your brother okay?"

He nods.

"Where's your sister?"

"Upstairs in her room. You going to call him back?"

"In a while." She starts to put away the groceries and he moves to the table to help her.

He sits on the front porch, watching for her car to turn the corner. When he sees it, he stands up. She pulls into the driveway, gets out and slams the door, starts across the lawn toward him. It rained an hour or so ago, and her shoes leave wet footprints on the grass.

"Mom, he's okay. . . ." he calls to her. His hands in the pockets of his pants are curled into fists. She has on her old green sweater and jeans, with her hair pulled back from her face. He stares hard into her eyes, trying to read his sentence there. Behind him the front door opens and his aunt comes out on the porch.

"He's home, Annie. He's here, he's upstairs. . . ."

"Thank God, I thought I ought to come here first."

"I tried to call you back, but you'd already left."

"I packed up in ten minutes." Across the strip of lawn that separates them, his mother draws a ragged breath. "What did they say?"

"It went through the cornea, but that's all. They want to see him tomorrow. They said they'd know for sure in thirty-six hours, but if there's no infection . . ." His aunt comes down the steps. Without a word his mother reaches out to her, and the two of them embrace.

"Annie, I'm so sorry. . . ."

"Sshhh . . . sshhh . . ." His mother holds her tightly. They are both crying.

And then, to his horror, so is he, the tears streaming down his cheeks. He turns to make his escape, stumbling blindly up the steps.

"Harry . . . !"

But he can't wait, hears himself bursting into loud, coughing sobs. Why can't he find the handle of the door? And then his mother's arms are around his waist. "Harry, Harry . . ." Her hand on his back, gently rubbing at the pain between his shoulders. His chest hurts so that he can barely breathe. Sobbing, he stands still, lets her turn him around to face her. His head falls against her chest.

"I didn't mean to . . . it was an accident! I jerked too hard on the line. . . ."

"I know . . . sshhh. . . ."

She holds him in her arms, sits with him on the steps, rocking him gently. Her warmth is like a blessed curtain between him and the terror; he can feel it moving away, receding into darkness. He can breathe once again. Pulling one arm free, he encircles her neck.

"I'm sorry, Mom . . . sorry for everything. . . ."

"Not your fault . . . it's all right." She kisses him. "You're a good boy," she whispers. "You're always my good boy. . . ."

He lifts his head. "Mom, I don't want to keep

missing him like this. . . ." He is weeping again. "It hurts so much. . . ."

"I know. . . ."

Now she is crying softly, too, wiping her eyes with the edge of his T-shirt.

"What are we gonna do?"

"I don't know," she says. "I don't know . . . I love you, Harry."

"I love you!"

She lets go then, and he wipes his eyes.

"It's all right," she croons against his hair. "All right . . . all right . . ."

He awakes with a start. Moonlight streams through the window, leaving a snowy rectangle on the bedroom floor. He sits up, sees the outline of his brother's body on the other bed, the stark white of the bandages. Jimmy's arms are at his side, hands open, palms upward on the sheet.

This life, their life together in this house, is so mysterious; he will never understand it. Maybe that's the way it's meant to be. He thinks back to a time up north when they took the raft out and poled it beyond their depth. The wind came up, started to blow them out into the lake, and they screamed toward shore, where Dad was washing the Sunfish. In seconds he pushed off, snapped the sail up, skimmed out over the green water to rescue them.

"I wasn't scared," Jimmy said. "I knew it would be

okay. Remember, don't worry about what might happen, just worry about what does." He was still talking like a baby, then; said "wuwwy." And his mother had cried, scolding their father: "You were supposed to be watching them!"

Who is watching them now? A world so fraught with dangerous moments; yet, if you don't close your eyes to them, you'd never do a damned thing.

A thought slides into his mind, and he bolts out of bed. Jimmy's bike. It is still out in the woods. Stupid! He never brought it home! Out there for someone to steal. And someone will do it, without doubt. Hidden under some alder brush, but that doesn't mean it won't be found.

He grabs his jeans and shirt, lying on the floor; pulls them on. Searching in the darkness for his shoes. In the hallway, he stops to listen: his aunt's door is closed, but his mother's is open; he can see the corner of her bed, the white embroidered quilt, feels a sudden surge of such helpless love that it makes him turn away.

He tiptoes down the stairs, stops to get his bearings. Not yet starting to get light. The kitchen clock is ticking, but he can't read the time. Four o'clock, maybe even earlier.

He hears a sudden noise, turns to see Julie standing behind him, the pale nightgown a bloom of pink in the darkness.

"Where you going?" she whispers.

"Nowhere. Go back to bed. . . ."

"I heard you get up. What're you going to do?"

"Shh! Don't talk so loud. I gotta go get something. . . ."

"What? The bike? I already got it. It's out in the garage."

"You did not."

"Go look if you don't believe me." She yawns, giving him a look. Don't you wish you were as smart as me?

"How'd you know where it was?"

"In the bushes, right where you always put it. Remember when you took me out there? You said I could fish, but then you made me just sit on the bank and watch you!"

He knows she is telling him the truth, but goes outside to check, anyway. When he comes back she's moving around at the stove. She laughs at him, but he is too relieved to care.

"When did you go and get it?"

"Yesterday. While you guys were at the hospital."

"You and Emily?"

She shakes her head. "Rex rode me over on his bike." She waves the wooden spoon at him. "You want some cocoa?"

"Sure." He sits down at the table. Outside, a ribbon of pink silk is slowly lifting across the sky. He watches as she measures the ingredients into the pan. She talks to herself the same way his mother and his aunt do when they're cooking.

"Salt and a little sugar ... now some water, to make it smooth ... now the milk ..."

"Why'd you ask Rex, anyway?"

"Because." She licks sugar from her fingers. "I like him." Again, the sly look; he thinks about Rex Beers, whom he has pushed away, discarded out of fear of his strangeness. He even moved his seat in math class; yet each day at lunch he feels the pull of the blue eyes, staring into him. His guilt at having done this. Talking to Melanie about it. "You don't need to like everything about a person in order to be friends with him. . . ." But it's not about liking.

Staring at his sister now; really looking at her. Maybe for the first time in his life. She is someone that he scarcely recognizes—blond hair curved against her cheek in a sexy pose; trim little legs beneath the shapeless nightgown. Startled, he lays his palm upward on the table; she turns to slap it smartly, grinning at him.

"I got to take a pee," he says.

"Oh, thanks so much for telling me!"

He goes to the lavatory off the kitchen and, in the pale light of morning, looks at himself in the mirror. Eyebrows starting to grow in; hair not so wispy in front. His face creased from sleep. His eyes are the same clear blue as his father's. He focuses for a moment on this stranger, also, staring back at him in the glass. In three weeks he will turn fourteen. He has lived through the hardest year of his life. There will never be a harder one, he knows this, just as he knows that his brother's eye will be all right, that he has nothing, nothing at all to be afraid of. At least, not on this beautiful summer day that lies ahead; for soon it will be morning, and the start of his future. Not that he'd ever dream of saying anything so corny to anybody.

ABOUT THE AUTHOR

JUDITH GUEST is the author of *Ordinary People* and *Second Heaven*. She lives in Edina, Minnesota, and Harrisville, Michigan.

(continued)

Grimes, Martha, *Rainbow's End*
Grimes, Martha, *Hotel Paradise*
Hepburn, Katharine, *Me*
James, P. D., *Original Sin*
Koontz, Dean, *Dark Rivers of the Heart*
Koontz, Dean, *Intensity*
Krantz, Judith, *Lovers*
Krantz, Judith, *Spring Collection*
Landers, Ann, *Wake Up and Smell the Coffee!*
Lindbergh, Anne Morrow, *Gift from the Sea*
Mayle, Peter, *Anything Considered*
McCarthy, Cormac, *The Crossing*
Michener, James A., *Mexico*
Michener, James A., *Miracle in Seville*
Michener, James A., *Recessional*
Mother Teresa, *A Simple Path*
Patterson, Richard North, *Eyes of a Child*
Patterson, Richard North, *The Final Judgment*
Phillips, Louis, editor, *The Random House Large Print Treasury of Best-Loved Poems*
Pope John Paul II, *Crossing the Threshold of Hope*
Pope John Paul II, *The Gospel of Life*
Powell, Colin with Joseph E. Persico, *My American Journey*
Rendell, Ruth, *Simisola*
Rooney, Andy, *My War*
Shaara, Jeff, *Gods and Generals*
Truman, Margaret, *Murder at the National Gallery*
Tyler, Anne, *Ladder of Years*
Tyler, Anne, *Saint Maybe*